£2.95

The Making of Minty Malone

Isabel Wolff was born in Warwickshire and read English at Cambridge. Her first novel was the bestselling romantic comedy, *The Trials of Tiffany Trott*. Her freelance articles have appeared in many national newspapers, she presents radio documentaries on the BBC World Service and reviews the papers for *Breakfast News* on BBC1. She lives in London.

BY THE SAME AUTHOR

The Trials of Tiffany Trott

ISABEL WOLFF

THE MAKING OF MINTY MALONE

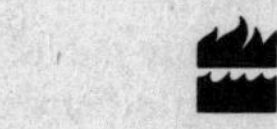

HarperCollins*Publishers*

This novel is a work of fiction. The names, characters and incidents portrayed in the story are products of the author's imagination, other than the names of the actors and actresses who appear in fictionalised incidents in the story. Any resemblance to actual persons, living or dead, events or localities is entirely coincidental.

HarperCollins*Publishers*
77–85 Fulham Palace Road,
Hammersmith, London W6 8JB

The HarperCollins website address is:
www.**fire**and**water**.com

A Paperback Original 1999
1 3 5 7 9 8 6 4 2

A catalogue record for this book is available from the British Library

ISBN 0 00 651340 9

Set in Meridien

Author photograph © Eric Roberts, Sygma

Typeset by Rowland Phototypesetting Ltd,
Bury St Edmunds, Suffolk

Printed in Great Britain by
Clays Ltd, St Ives plc

For Jonathan and Catharine
Anja and Paul-Mattias

Acknowledgements

I am indebted, as ever, to my brilliant agent, Clare Conville, and to my wonderful editor, Rachel Hore. Every author should be so lucky. I have many other people to thank as well, notably Peter Welch and Peter Parkinson for information about the world of insurance; Natasha Grüneberg and Julia Fleming for their insights into radio stations; Sam North and Williamson Howe for the lowdown on life in Hollywood, and Robin Chandler and Jo-Ellen Grzyb for inviting me back to the Nice Factor. I am also grateful to Melissa-Jo and co. at the Candy Bar, to Roger Harrison at Eurostar, to Gerry Pitt at the Four Seasons in Beverly Hills, and to Jerry Seinfeld for being such a good sport. My thanks too to Chris 'Kipper' Dodds of Kip's Flowers; to Tito and Sandra at Paul Nath Hair; to Darryl von Däniken for being such an entertaining walker, and to Harold and Deanna Pender – and their pet parrot, Rob – for expert psittacine advice. For translations from Neapolitan and Spanish I'd like to thank Maura Romano and Karina Fane. I'm also indebted to my parents, Paul and Ursula, and to Louise Clairmonte, for reading the manuscript and giving me invaluable feedback – and ideas – along the way. At HarperCollins I'm grateful to Anne O'Brien for her hawk-eyed honing, to Amanda McKelvie for another lovely cover; and to Fiona McIntosh, Cecilia McCullough, Jenny Parr, Yvette Cowles and Alex Young. At A.P. Watt I owe a huge debt of gratitude to Linda Shaughnessy, Barbara Taylor, Daniela Petracco, Yvonne Negron and, as always, Marian McCarthy.

July

Where is it where is it where is it please please please where IS it? Where. Is. My. Bloody. Tiara? Oh God oh God where did I put it? I *had* it two minutes ago. I had it here, right here. I took it out of the box and then I put it down while I did my nails. I had it I had it I HAD it and now it's gone and I can't find it anywhere but it must be somewhere it just must be and oh no, I'm SO behind with everything and oh God what a nightmare I'm going to be so *late*! They'll be slow hand-clapping by the time I get there, that is if they haven't walked out or gone to the pub. Well, they'll just have to bloody well wait because nothing's going to happen without me. It's my day. Not theirs. Mine. That's what everyone's been saying to me, ever since I got engaged. 'It's *your* day, Minty! You must have *exactly* what you want!' In fact, Mum said it again, just ten minutes ago, as she headed out of the front door.

'Remember, it's your day, darling!' she called serenely from the garden gate. 'You must have *exactly* what you want!'

'Yes, but what I want is your *help*, Mum. My dress has got thirty-five loop fastenings.'

'Yes, I know that, darling, but I've got to get down to the church.'

'And aren't you supposed to brush my hair or something?'

'I haven't got time, Minty – it's bad form for the bride's mother to arrive late.'

'And it's bad form for the bride to arrive without her frock on, which is what's going to happen if I don't get some help round here.'

'Now, keep calm, Minty,' said Mum blithely. 'Helen will be back soon, and *she'll* help you. That's what bridesmaids are for. See you later, darling – byee!' She blew me a customary kiss and was gone. Damn.

And then the phone rang. It was Helen, ringing on her mobile from the church, where she was still fiddling with the flowers.

'Bit of a crisis, Mint – the peonies are wilting. They've gone all floppy in the heat.'

'Oh dear.'

'But don't worry,' she said soothingly, 'I'm just sticking fuse wire up their backsides and then I'll be on my way.'

'Well, please don't do that to me if you see me begin to wilt.'

'I'll be there in half an hour,' she said calmly. 'And that will leave us with a good – ooh, ten minutes to finish getting ready. OK?'

'OK. What? No! It isn't OK. What do you *mean*, ten minutes?''

'Now look, Minty, it's going to be fine, so please don't panic – it's much too hot.' Helen's right. It is. Much too hot. In fact it's boiling. Thirty degrees already. And I'm afraid I *am* starting to panic because I haven't got enough time and I'm not going to turn up all red in the face and crying with my make-up sliming off. I'm not I'm not I'm NOT, and oh *God* the car's going to be here in forty-five minutes and I'm still in my knickers and bra and I haven't done my face and there are going to be two hundred and eighty people staring at every square inch of me and I don't know WHERE my tiara is OR my veil and my nails STILL aren't dry so I can't put my dress on and I'm completely out of control here and – AAAARRRRRGGGGHHHH!!!! Oh God – the phone again! Just what I need.

'YES!' I said.

'Minty!' It was Amber. My cousin. Beautiful. Very beautiful, but bossy. 'Now keep calm!' she barked. 'Keep calm there!'

'I can't,' I replied. 'I've lost my tiara and I haven't got my dress on and I don't know *where* my veil is and it's *much* too hot, and Mum's gone off to the church and I haven't got anyone to help and I'm totally out of CONTROL!'

'Right, deep breathing time,' she said. 'Sit down, Minty. Sit down and b-r-e-a-t-h-e d-e-e-p-l-y. That's it. In . . . Out . . . In . . . Out . . . *And* relax. Right. Feeling better?'

'Yes,' I said. And I was. 'Much better. Pheeeewwwwww. How's Charlie's speech going?' I said as I blew on my nails.

'Well, it's all right *now,*' she replied. 'But of course I had to completely re-write it for him.'

'Why?'

'Because it was useless, that's why. And he said, "Look, darling, it's my speech. I'd rather it was in my own words." So I said, "Don't be so bloody ridiculous, Charlie, I'm the writer round here."' This is true. She's a novelist.

'Anyway, at least he *looks* smart,' she went on. 'Can't have the best man looking a mess. Anyway, must dash. Now, don't worry, Minty. And remember,' she added, 'it's *your* day – you must have *exactly* what you want!'

Well, I am getting exactly what I want. Or rather exactly *who* I want. And that's Dominic. My beloved. *He's* exactly what I want. Why? Well, he just is. And that's all there is to it. Right. Quick glance at the kitchen clock: forty minutes to go. I've been trying to keep panic at bay by consulting my marriage handbook, *Nearly Wed,* but it's not much use. Where's Dad? Oh, there he is – standing by the clematis, having what he calls a 'nutritious cigarette'. At least he's ready. That's something. But then it's so easy for men, isn't it? I mean, all Dominic's got to do today is put on his penguin suit and stand there and say 'I do.'

OK, nails are dry. On with the slap. Not too much. Just a touch. Don't want to overdo it. Some brides look awful – ten tons of make-up and hair sprayed to the texture of a Brillo Pad. All I'm going to have is a quick flick of eyeliner . . . mascara – waterproof, of course, in case I blub, which I'm sure I will . . . lip-liner . . . a smidgen of lipstick and . . . a little powder on nose and chin. *Voilà*! Quickly check in mirror and – ah! *There* it is. Silly me. My tiara. On my head. OK – dress. Damn. Bloody loop fastenings. Can't do them up. Hands shaking. With nerves. And exhaustion. Hardly surprising after organising this nuptial jamboree entirely by myself. But then, to be fair, Dad's still working full-time and Mum's been very busy recently, what with the badger sanctuary and the campaign to save the Venezuelan swamp hog. She loves fund-raising. In fact, she's addicted to it – has been as long as I can remember. And naturally I'd never have asked Dominic to help. He's much too busy with his work. He's doing terribly well at the moment. Making a mint! – no irony intended. Minty Lane. That's what I'll be in approximately an hour and a half from now. Araminta Lane. Or rather, Mrs Dominic Lane. That sounds OK. Could certainly be a lot worse – Mrs Dominic Sourbutts, for example, or Mrs Dominic Frogg. Not that it would have made the slightest difference – I'd still have loved him to bits, and I'd still be marrying him today. Right. Shoes. One. Two. Satin. Very pretty but a bit tight.

At least my horoscope was OK. Highly satisfactory. Extremely auspicious, even. 'Libra,' wrote Sheryl von Strumpfhosen, 'your love life takes an upward turn this weekend, when romantic Venus enters Leo.' Not that I take astrology *seriously*. A load of bollocks really, isn't it? Having said which, I think she's clearly spot-on with her prediction that 'Saturday will be emotional and rather revealing as important foundations are laid.' Oh God, these bloody buttons!

'Minty –' it was Dad, calling from the garden – 'need any help?'

'Well . . .' I could hardly ask my father to do up my wedding dress. On the other hand, it was only the top ones, and I was desperate.

'Now, where's your mother?' he enquired as he did them up. 'Has she gone to rattle a bucket somewhere?' he went on wearily. 'It's Saturday so it must be the Elderly Distressed Dolphins Association, or is it the Foundation for Drug-Addicted Spanish Donkeys?'

'No, she's gone down to the church. Thanks, Dad.'

Dad jokes about Mum's charitable activities, but the truth is he finds it very difficult. He hardly ever sees her. Says she's always at some fund-raising do or other. Or some committee meeting. He says he can't compete with Mum's myriad good causes. He says she's a charity junkie. But she won't scale it down. Though I think she probably will when he retires in a couple of months. But for now she's obsessed with being what they call a 'tireless campaigner', though her methods are a bit unorthodox. I mean, I thought her buffet in aid of the Belgravia Bulimics' Association was not in very good taste, and nor was the drinks party she organised for Alcoholics Anonymous. The invitations said, 'Sponsored by Johnny Walker'. But then she always says gaily that 'the means justify the ends.' That's her answer to everything. And of course she does raise loads of money. Thousands, sometimes. Which is why they turn a blind eye. Anyway, because of her charity commitments she left the wedding entirely to me. And Dad has kindly picked up the bill, which is incredibly nice of him, because it's enormous. It's twenty-eight thousand pounds. In fact – look, don't think I'm bragging or anything – that's more than twice the cost of the average London wedding.

'Well, you look lovely, Minty,' said Dad, standing back to admire me. 'And it's going to be an unforgettable day.'

He's right, I thought. People will talk about it for years. Well, weeks maybe. But the Malones are pushing that boat right out. That's what Dominic wanted, you see. A 'smart' London wedding. Something a bit overstated. For example, the reception's at the Waldorf. A sit-down lunch for two hundred and eighty people. That's a lot, isn't it? Quite a few of them are Dominic's clients, actually. I've never met them, but if I can help him in his career by inviting ninety-three total strangers to my big day then I really don't mind at all. Because I love Dom to bits.

Take this dress, for instance. Very chic and all that, but it wasn't my first choice. When we first got engaged I said I'd like an antique lace dress, Vic-Wardian style, with lots of sequins and beading and a long, floaty train. But Dom pulled such a face that I somehow lost enthusiasm for the idea. He said that modern wedding dresses were best, and explained that Neil Cunningham's ones are 'the business', and he pointed out that that's where Ffion Jenkins and Darcey Bussell got theirs. He'd read that in Nigel Dempster. Or was it *Tatler*? Anyway, to cut a long story short, Neil Cunningham it is. And never mind that people kept saying, 'It's your day, Minty, you must have *exactly* what you want!' because even though it wasn't exactly what I wanted, it didn't take me long to realise that Dom was absolutely right – this dress *does* look great! And I only *thought* I preferred the other one. He's got very good taste, you see. Much better than mine. And he loves this dress. He absolutely loves it and, yes, I *know* what you're thinking. You're thinking that it's bad luck for the groom to see his bride's wedding dress before the big day. But he didn't. He just asked if he could see a *picture* of it. And naturally I agreed, because I wouldn't want to wear anything that he didn't think looked right. Because the only thing I want, the thing I want '*exactly*', is for Dominic to be happy.

Here's what we're having for lunch: a tricolore salad of vine-ripened tomatoes, followed by pan-seared swordfish, with a Riesling gateau and strawberry coulis for pudding and a lake of Laurent-Perrier. Now, that little lot works out at eighteen grand alone; and then my dress cost two and a half thousand, and Helen's bridesmaid dress was another grand, and what with the engagement announcements, wedding stationery, car hire, the church, the organist's fee, the going-away outfits, the ring, the honeymoon and the photographer (stills and video), the grand total comes to twenty-eight thousand six hundred and thirty-two pounds and seventy-two pence, including VAT. That's how it all breaks down.

Ah – here's my veil. On top of the cupboard. Mmmm . . . looks nice. Petticoat's a bit scratchy, though. Yes, it's going to be a really big bash with a string trio and everything. Mum wanted to run a tombola during the reception for the Hedgehog Foundation, but I told her I didn't think it would be appropriate. Anyway, as I say, it's a big wedding, though I'd have been happy with something much smaller – no more than a hundred. In fact, fifty would have been fine. Or even forty. Or thirty. Or twenty. And I can quite understand why some people opt for a beach-side ceremony in Bali or a skinflint register office job. But Dominic felt we should do it properly and have something really upmarket. So we are. He thought we might even be able to get it written up in 'Jennifer's Diary', so I rang *Harpers & Queen*, and they were very polite, and said it certainly sounded like a splendid occasion, but somehow I don't think they'll be showing up today. But at least Dom will know I tried.

I'm quite laid back in lots of ways. Unlike Dominic. He's much more ambitious than me. For example, he persuaded me to invite lots of people from work in case it helps my career.

'Professional schmoozing is *important*, Minty,' he said, when we were having dinner at Le Caprice one evening.

'I'm not so sure,' I said, fiddling with my fork.

'It *is*,' he said. 'It helps to oil the wheels.'

'No, I think the best thing is to break your bottom and deliver the goods.'

'Oh, darling,' said Dominic with an indulgent smile, 'if you carry on with *that* silly attitude you'll *never* get to be a radio presenter.'

'Won't I?'

'No. You'll simply carry on being a reporter. Honestly, Minty, you are a bit of a twit – you should be wining and dining the bosses whenever you get the chance.'

'Should I?'

'Yes,' he said, firmly. 'You *should*.'

Dom's quite ambitious for me, you see. Which is nice. He's very keen for me to do well at London FM. He thinks it's about time I was promoted, because I've been working there for over three years. And I try and explain that it's not like that. That there's no smooth career progression from reporter to presenter. You have to be incredibly lucky for that to happen. Or incredibly well-connected, like our 'star' presenter, Melinda. Dom says I should be more pushy. And although I don't really agree with him – and to be honest, I'm pretty happy as I am – I do like the fact that he's so interested in my career. You see, I don't really get that at home. I mean, don't get me wrong: my parents are great. But they're not that interested in what I do. Never have been, really. Mum's priority has always been her charities, and Dad's always been so involved at work. He works incredibly long hours because he's got his own firm of chartered accountants. And then my brother Robert's been living in Australia for the past four years. So no one in the family takes much interest in what I do. But Dominic does. He takes a close interest. And that's nice. He makes me feel very *secure*, I suppose. Not just because he's successful – though he is – but because he's very good at organising everything. He likes to set the agenda. He's definitely the one in charge. I don't mind any more. I've got used to it. And most of the time I find myself going along with whatever he wants to do. I suppose I've got set in his ways. Dom has a *very* nice lifestyle; we eat out quite a bit, for example. He likes to go to expensive places, like the Ivy or the Bluebird Café. Which is lovely, and well, why not? He's got the cash, and it's fun. And he's always springing surprises on me – like that lovely three-day cricket match at the Oval, and a super golfing weekend at Gleneagles. Not that I play myself. And fishing, of course. We go fishing a lot. Well, he fishes, I sit on the bank and read. Which I quite enjoy. There are so many nice surprises like that with Dominic. He always knows what he wants, too. He's very clear about that. And what he seemed to want right from the very start was me. I was a bit taken aback by that, because he's a very attractive and successful guy. I mean, he could have had anybody. But he chose *me*, and of course I found that really, really flattering.

Another good thing about Dom – he's very practical. And that makes me feel sort of safe with him. For example, he suggested we take out wedding insurance, just in case anything goes wrong. So he sold Dad a policy with Paramutual, which will cover potential disasters such as my dress not being ready in time, or the Waldorf burning down, or flash floods in the

Strand. He felt it was important for us to have 'total peace of mind' on our big day. And he's right. Do you know there are even policies to protect newlyweds in case their marital home is burgled while they're on honeymoon? We didn't think that was necessary as we won't be away for very long because Dominic's so busy at the moment. Between you and me, I'd have loved two weeks in the Caribbean, on Nevis, say, or Necker. Or ten days in Venice – that would have been wonderful. But we can't do that because Dom won't fly anywhere. He thinks it's too risky with our overcrowded skies, and, because of his work – insurance, or 'Risk-Biz', as he likes to call it – he is in fact *au fait* with the crash and fatality records of all the major airlines. So we're going to Paris, on Eurostar, for four days. Which will be fab. And I don't mind the fact that I've been to Paris eleven times before, because a) it's a *lovely* city, and b) I'm sensitive to Dominic's fear of flying. He can't help it. You see, he tends to anticipate things that can go wrong. And he's right. So many unexpected disasters *can* happen in life, so it's always best to be prepared. Which is why he persuaded me to fill in a comprehensive prenuptial agreement when we got engaged. I don't blame him. He's got a lot to lose. And, of course, we've taken out travel insurance for Paris. Just in case.

Actually, that's my secret nickname for him: 'Justin Case'. But I haven't told him that. I'm not sure he'd find it funny. I did try teasing him once or twice, in the beginning, but it was obvious that he didn't really like it, so I soon learned not to do it again! But he's a complete whizz when it comes to business. He's got a magic touch. That's how we met. He rang up one day, totally out of the blue, and said he was a friend of a friend of a friend of a friend (I still can't remember for the life of me exactly which friend it was), and he said there was something '*very* important' he wanted to discuss with me. He wouldn't say over the phone what it was, but it certainly sounded intriguing, and he had *such* a lovely voice, and he was so friendly, and before I knew what had happened, I'd agreed to meet him. Largely out of curiosity. So he offered to come up to my flat in Primrose Hill. And the bell rang, and there on the doorstep was this incredibly attractive man. He was so good-looking I nearly fainted! He was tall, with blond hair – not that wimpy white-blond hair, but a deep, burnished sandy colour, as though he'd just trekked across the Sahara. And his eyes were this startling blue. Like the blue of Sri Lankan sapphires. And he stood there, holding out his hand, and smiling at me – very good teeth, too, incidentally. So I invited him in, and made him a cup of coffee while he asked me questions about my date of birth, my general health and whether or not I smoked or had AIDS, and he made some *very* flattering comments about my interior décor – even though he confessed not long afterwards that he hadn't liked it at all! Then he whipped out his laptop computer and a pile of graphs and charts, and looked at me in a very serious and meaningful way which thrilled me to my core.

'Now, Minty, here you are. Here. In 1970,' he said pointing to the left-hand side of the graph, 'and you've just been born. OK?' I nodded. I was indeed born in 1970. Then he pointed to the extreme right-hand side of the chart. 'And here you are again, Minty. In the year 2050. And you're dead.'

'Oh. Um, yes. Suppose I am.'

'Now, Minty,' he went on, fixing me with a penetrating look, 'what are you going to do about it?'

'Do about it? Well, there's not much I *can* do really.'

'Oh *yes* there is, Minty,' he said with a zealous gleam in his eye. 'There's a *lot* you can do about it. You can protect yourself – and your loved ones – against it.'

And suddenly, the penny dropped. I don't know why it had taken so long, I suppose I was distracted by his genial manner and his good looks.

'You're an insurance salesman,' I said, and I couldn't help laughing.

But he didn't laugh. In fact, he bristled.

'I'm an IFA, actually,' he pointed out. 'An Independent Financial Adviser. And it's not insurance, Minty. It's *ass*urance.'

'Oh, sorry,' I said.

'Now, Minty, I *do* think you could benefit from my help here,' he went on with a benevolent smile. And I don't know what it was, his compelling personality, the way he kept using my Christian name, the heady scent of his aftershave, or his irresistible charm, but before I knew what had happened I had signed on several dotted lines, thereby embarking on a life-long commitment to the Dreddful Accident Insurance Company, the Colossal Pension Fund, as well as purchasing accidental death coverage with Irish Widows. And now here I am, a mere eighteen months later, making a life-long commitment to him too. And I really couldn't be happier. I mean, Dominic and I just clicked after that first encounter. We *really* clicked.

As I say, I find him terribly attractive. You see, I've always had this secret thing about blond men. Some women don't go for them at all, but I've always liked them. They're unusual, for a start, and then they're so different to me. I look vaguely Mediterranean, with long, wavy, dark hair and eyes the colour of espresso. But Dominic's the opposite. He's so fair. So English. I'll tell you who he looks like: Ashley in *Gone with the Wind*. Gorgeous. Physical attraction is so important, isn't it?

And of course we're very compatible. Well, we are now. In the beginning we weren't. I'd be the first to admit that. As I say, he liked fishing – I hated it. He played a lot of cricket. It bored me to bits. He loved shopping – especially for clothes – and, frankly, I'm not that bothered. He wasn't a bit interested in going to art galleries and the theatre, whereas I *adore* seeing exhibitions and plays. And films. I love films. In fact, I'm quite well-watched. I'd travelled an awful lot too, whereas Dom was terrified of flying and had hardly set foot outside the British Isles. So, to tell you the truth, it didn't look good at first. But now, the situation's changed completely. We're terribly compatible. Because I've made myself like all the things he likes! So I go and watch him fly-fishing; I watch him play cricket; and I'll happily sit and watch Eurosports with him. Unless it's snooker. Or darts. And if there's some fascinating documentary or first-rate period drama, well, I can always watch it upstairs on his tiny black-and-white. But that's how we get on. And I *know* we're compatible, because we filled in a compatibility questionnaire – and we passed! And I haven't just given up all my previous interests. I mean, I still get to go to the theatre sometimes, and the Tate, but I go with my girlfriends, because of course I'd never make Dominic do anything he didn't want to do.

But I know what you're thinking. You're thinking I shouldn't give way so much. And I do know what you mean. But these are minor things to me, and in any relationship there's bound to be a lot of give and take. And I'm keeping my eye on the wider picture here, which is that I really love Dom. So these are small sacrifices to make. And in any case, I absolutely hate making a fuss about anything. I'm very 'nice'. That's what everyone says about me – that I'm terribly 'nice'. They've always said that. And I simply *loathe* confrontations of any kind. I just can't handle them at all. So, if it's a small matter, I'm more than happy to give in because, to my mind, it's simply not worth making a fuss. And as far as Dominic's refusal to travel goes, well, I'm philosophical about that because I've already seen lots of places. Anyway, I quite like holidays in England or Wales. I mean, it's all very well gadding about in Malaysia or Mauritius, the Med or Martinique, Venezuela or Venice, the Caymans, Kenya or Hong Kong – but just think of what you're missing on your own doorstep! Dominic and I have had some lovely weekends in Norfolk. And Scotland. And the Lake District. Been there twice. In any case, one should try and be satisfied. And I am. I'm very happy with my lot, thank you very much. And you've got to decide who it is you want. Who you want to be with. And, for better or for worse, I want to be with Dominic. Because I adore him. Absolutely. He's The One. Nothing makes me happier than being round at his place, cooking something for him. Although I'd be the first to agree with him that I'm a pretty rotten cook. I mean, you don't so much carve my roast chickens, as shake them! But I'm going to do a course and learn how to do it properly, because I'm really mad about Dominic.

Mind you, now we're on the subject, it wouldn't be true to say that I like *everything* about him – that would be impossible. No one likes everything about their partner, do they? Between you and me, I really don't like the way he tries to sell people policies at parties. I do find it a bit embarrassing. Not that I'd mention it to him, of course. And I don't think he should automatically call people by their Christian names. And I'm not too keen on the way he wears his sunglasses all the time, even when it's overcast. And the funny thing is that when it's hot and bright, he wears them on top of his head! And I'm not that crazy about his low-slung, red, Japanese convertible – it's really not my kind of car at all. I feel a bit idiotic in it, to be honest, and it certainly isn't eco-friendly on the fuel front, which drives Mum mad as she's a fund-raiser for Pals of the Planet. And I'm not mad about the way he snaps his fingers at waiters, and does a little scribble in the air when he wants the bill. And it does depress me when he goes on and on about his great days at Uppingham. It's so unnecessary and, I mean, it's not exactly a big deal, is it? And one of these days someone will say, 'Oh, really? I was there too, you know. Which house were you in?' and then he'll be sunk. He's been very lucky so far. And naturally I always keep quiet and change the subject as soon as I can. Personally, I can't see what's wrong with saying he went to Sutton Coldfield Secondary Modern. But for some reason he seems rather ashamed of it.

Another thing: he rarely mentions his father. In fact, he isn't even invited to the wedding, which is awful. Though what can I do? Dominic insists that it would upset his mother if he were there. I think the *real* reason is that his father's a mechanic. And there's nothing wrong with that. Being a mechanic is fine. But Dom doesn't seem to think so. Whenever I ask him about his dad, or suggest we go and see him, he just changes the subject, and I think that's a terrible shame. Dom's much closer to his mother, Madge. In fact, he adores her. It's 'Mummy' this, and 'Mummy' that, which is rather sweet. In a way. Anyway, I do think it's *great* to be marrying a man who has such a strong relationship with his mother. She thinks the world of him too. She's terribly proud of what he's achieved, and he's been *very* good to her. Bought her a house in Solihull after her divorce. He's devoted. And she'd never let on that his real name isn't Dominic at all. It's Neil. I discovered this by accident a few weeks ago when I happened to see his driving licence. I was quite surprised, and so I asked him about it. And he confessed that the reason was that when he came down to London fifteen years ago he felt that Neil wasn't quite the right kind of name for him. To be honest, I think Neil's a pretty awful name too, so I don't blame him for changing it. And I mean, *I* can't talk, because Minty isn't *my* real name either. Or at least, it's only my middle name. I was actually christened Irene Araminta, after my two grandmothers, but from day one I've always been known as Minty. But Dominic just wanted to be Dominic because he thought it had the right sort of ring.

So, as you can see, he's got his little tender spots, his problem areas and his peccadilloes. And I'm not blind to them. I can see them all. As clear as day. But they don't affect how I feel about him. Because a) I love him, and b) I understand him. I'm no psychiatrist, but I've got him sussed. And when you know where someone's coming from, then you can overlook their little foibles, because to understand is to forgive.

Because the fact is, despite his confident exterior, Dominic's pretty insecure. About his background, mostly. Wants to feel he's transcended his unpromising beginnings, although I'd rather he was open about it and proud of having come so far from, well, a sort of council estate, really. But it seems to bother him, though I really don't know why. I thought *everyone* wanted to be working class these days. But his mother says he's always been very 'aspiring'. That's the word she used. Keen to 'improve himself', as they say. That's why designer labels are so important to him, and being seen in the 'right' places, and saying the 'right' things. And that's why he's very keen on books about etiquette, etc. For example, in his downstairs loo, you'll find *The Sloane Ranger Handbook*, Jilly Cooper's *Class*, *The Done Thing*, and *Miss Manners*, because he's very keen to cut the mustard in smart circles now. He does make quite a lot of money, actually. Commission, most of it. He's done terribly well out of pensions. And he gets invited to lots of corporate do's by the insurance companies whose products he sells – they ask him to Ascot and Henley and all that, and so he really wants to pass the test. And that's only natural, isn't it? And the point is that I love Dominic. I do, really. I love him for who he is, and for what he's achieved, and for the fact that he's worked so hard and come so far. I admire him all the more precisely because he wasn't born with a silver spoon in his mouth and didn't have the benefit of granny's money, like I did, which is how I was able to buy my flat. Dominic had to do it all by himself. And he did. And I *do* respect that. But I just wish he could have a little more self-confidence. I hope that's something that marriage will give him.

So I encourage him as much as I can, and I'd never, ever criticise him – even if I wanted to, which I don't – because a) he's always promptly dropped girlfriends who did criticise him in any way whatsoever, and b) I'm certainly not perfect myself. Far from it, in fact, as he often likes to point out. Because here I am letting you in on Dominic's little foibles, when, let's face it, I've got plenty of my own. For instance, Dom thinks I talk too much. He's always said that – right from the start. I thought that was a bit odd, to be honest, because no one else has ever said that to me, but I guess I must have been doing it without realising. Dom doesn't like it if I try and have conversations which he thinks are too 'serious', because he thinks that's boring and not the Done Thing. He read somewhere that smart people don't talk about serious issues. They mostly like to talk about things that are 'amusing'. Not politics, for a start. Or *King Lear*. Or Camille Paglia. So I often have to bite my tongue to make sure I don't say anything interesting and annoy him. Because he does get quite annoyed. Well, very annoyed, actually.

My taste in clothes is not that great either, but luckily Dominic's really improved it for me. Because he's always impeccably turned out. Which I like, because, let's face it, so many men don't bother much these days. Anyway, no one had ever pointed out to me that I could do with a bit of advice on that front. He said I looked like a 'superannuated student'. And he was right. I did. I probably picked it up from Mum. She favours the Bloomsbury look – her things are long and floaty and a bit 'arty' – all from charity shops, of course. Dom said he'd never let *me* go round looking like that. Now, he likes clothes that are well cut, expensive-looking and 'smart' – Gucci, for example. Which is a bit hard when you're on a small salary like I am, though at least I don't have a mortgage. And so when I first started going out with him I found there were lots of things I couldn't wear. He called them my 'nightmares'. And that surprised me too, because none of my previous boyfriends felt like that at all. Anyway, Dom told me to throw them all out, but I objected to that, so I put them in boxes under my bed.

He's always buying me things. Clothes, mostly. He loves shopping for clothes for me. I felt a bit awkward about that to begin with. In fact, it made me feel quite uncomfortable. And I wasn't at all sure it was right. But Madge said I should let him do it, because he wants to, and he can afford to. So I go along with it. Even if I'm not crazy about spending most of Saturday in Harvey Nichols, and even if I'm not crazy about his choice. I mean, he bought me a Hermès bag recently. I know – *so* expensive! He said he wanted me to have one. And of course I threw my arms round him and said how *thrilled* I was, and how generous he was – which he *is*, don't get me wrong. He's *very* generous. But, to be frank, I don't actually like it – though I would never have said so in a million years. And naturally I use it all the time. Now, whenever *I* give him something that *he* doesn't like, I'm afraid it has to go back to the shop. I've sort of got used to it now, I suppose. But I really like to please Dominic because, well, it makes life so much easier, doesn't it?

I've always been like that. I've always liked to smooth things over, for there to be no arguments or conflict, and for everything to be . . . nice. That's what everyone says about me –

'Minty's *so nice*!' And that's nice, isn't it? That they all think I'm so nice. And because I do like to be nice, I always indulge Dominic, because I know him so well, and you have to accept everyone as they are. That's what Dominic says. And you can't change people, can you? Especially when they're thirty-five like he is and –

Oh God, here I am droning on, as Dominic would say, boring you to bits, and look at the time: 10.15! God, God, God. Maybe I should pray. I do feel quite scared, to be honest. 'Till death us do part,' and all that. 'As long as ye both shall live.' The awesome commitment we're about to make to each other. The fact that I'm about to become Mrs Dominic Lane and – oh, thank goodness, thank goodness, Helen's back.

We set off for church within fifteen minutes. Helen checked that my thirty-five loops were all fastened, and that my make-up and hair looked good, then I did up her dress, we shouted for Dad and jumped in the Bentley, which had been waiting for half an hour. We all sat in the back; I had Helen's bouquet of white anemones and pink roses lying on my lap. It wasn't one of those stiff, wired bouquets that I always think look equally at home on top of coffins; it was a simple posy, loosely tied, as though she had plucked the flowers from the garden minutes before. In fact, they'd been hot-housed in Holland, flown in overnight, and she'd bought them from New Covent Garden at three o'clock that morning. Helen's a genius with flowers. It's as though she's just stuck them in – like that – with absolutely no thought or planning. But hers is the art that conceals art, and her arrangements have the informal, tumbling beauty of Dutch flower paintings.

Anyway, Helen and Dad and I were chatting away nervously as we left Primrose Hill in the leaden heat of a mid morning in late July. The twenty-eighth, actually, a date I knew I would remember all my life, as I remember the date of my birth. And I was so glad to have Helen with me. I've known her for twelve years – since Edinburgh – and we've remained in pretty close touch ever since. She read economics and then went to work for Metrobank, where she did terribly well. But three years ago there was one of these mega-mergers and she was made redundant, so she used her pay-off to fund her pipe-dream: it's called Floribunda, and it's in Covent Garden, where she lives. It's so tiny – Lilliputian, in fact – that you hardly dare turn round for fear of sending tubs of phlox and foxglove flying. But she's really in demand – she got a call from Jerry Hall the other day. And what's so nice about Helen is that she's totally unspoilt by her success. Her bridesmaid's dress looked lovely: ice blue, also by Neil Cunningham, and designed to harmonise with mine. She'd tied her hair – a hank of pale apricot silk – into a neat, simple twist, and dressed it with two pink rosebuds. And although she looked gorgeous, I'd have liked little bridesmaids too, a Montessori school of tiny girls nose-picking and stumbling their way up the aisle. But I don't know any of the right age. I'm sure someone could make a bomb hiring them out. Anyway, I wanted to have someone to support me – after all, Dominic had Charlie – so I asked Helen to be my maid of honour.

As we made our way through Camden, past Euston Station, and Russell Square, I felt like the Queen. The car shone with a treacly blackness and the two white ribbons fluttered stiffly on the bonnet as we drove through the hot, crowded streets. People looked, and grinned, and one or two even waved. And then we went down Kingsway and passed the great arched entrance to Bush House, and turned left past St Clement Danes into Fleet Street. And there were the Law Courts, and the old *Daily Express* building, and Prêt à Manger, and I thought happily, I'm Prêt à Marrier!

I could hear the bells tolling – I mean, *ringing*. And then suddenly there was the tall steeple of St Bride's, with its five tiers, like a wedding cake, and I thought, clever Christopher Wren. And one or two late-comers were hurrying into the church and by now my stomach was lurching and churning like a tumble-dryer and – Oh God, Melinda! London FM's star presenter with her boring husband, Roger. Trust her not to turn up on time. And what a terrible dress! All that money, I thought, and so little taste. I mean, I know she's five months pregnant and everything, so I don't want to be unfair, but it really was *awful*. Chintz. Pink. Very Sanderson. She looked as though she'd been badly upholstered. And to top it all, she'd got this kind of Scud missile wobbling on her head.

I stepped out of the car, smiling for the video man and the official photographer who were waiting on the pavement. Then Helen smoothed the front of my dress, I took Dad's arm, and we all walked into the cool of the porch. I spotted Robert – he was ushering – though I couldn't see Dom. And I suddenly panicked! So I got Dad to go in and have a peep, and he just smiled, and said that, yes, Dominic was safely there, at the altar, with Charlie. And I could hear the hum of muted voices as the organist played the Saint-Saëns. Then the music drew to an end and a hush descended and Robert gave us the nod.

'OK, Minty, we're off,' whispered Daddy with a smile, and we stepped forward as the first chords of the Mendelssohn rang out and everyone rose to their feet. And suddenly, in that instant, I was so, *so* thrilled I'd chosen St Bride's. It's not that I'm particularly religious – I'm not really, and nor is Dom. In fact, he said very little during our sessions with the vicar. But of all the churches in Central London, St Bride's was the one that felt right. It's the journalists' church – the Cathedral of Fleet Street – and that was another reason for choosing it. And you see, I've always had this thing about churches that were bombed in the War. Coventry Cathedral, for example, or St Paul's. And St Bride's was bombed too; in December 1940, a single V2 left it a smouldering shell. But it arose, like a phoenix, from its ashes. And the vicar explained that the destruction had a silver lining, because it laid bare the Roman crypts. And no one had known they were there, and this enabled them to add a thousand years to the history of the church. Which proves how good can sometimes come out of the most terrible events because without that devastation St Bride's would never have revealed its hidden depths. And I was thinking of that again as I walked up the aisle, adren-aline-pumped and overwrought and nervous, and tearful, and happy. As the sunlight flooded in through the plain glass windows in wide, striated rays, I lifted my eyes to the vaulted ceiling painted in white and gold, and then dropped my gaze to the black and white marble tiles which were polished to a watery sheen. And the air was heavy with the sweet smell of beeswax and the voluptuous scent of Helen's flowers. Her two arrangements took my breath away. They were magnificent. As big as telephone kiosks – a tumbling mass of scabious, stocks and pink peonies, freesia and sweet peas; and she'd tied a little posy of white anemones to the end of every pew.

And there was Dominic, with his back to me, his blond head lit by the sun. And I thought, he looks like the Angel Gabriel himself in the *Annunciation* by Fra Angelico. Charlie was standing next to him, looking typically serious and kind, and he turned and gave me such a nice, encouraging little smile. Because the box pews face sideways in St Bride's, I could see everyone as we passed, their Order of Service sheets fluttering in their hands like big white moths. First I spotted Jack, my editor, smiling at me in his usual amused and sardonic way, and next to him was his wife Jane and her sulky-looking teenage daughters, both dressed in post-Punk black and pink; and there was Amber looking wonderfully cool and elegant in lime green. In the pew behind was Wesley from work, with Deirdre, of course – oh, she *did* look dreary, but then she always does, poor thing; between you and me, I think weddings are a sore point with her. And there was my mother in her flowing Bohemian dress, and her extraordinary, flower-smothered hat. On the groom's side I spotted Dom's mother, Madge, and lots of people I didn't recognise who must have been his clients. And everyone was looking at me, and smiling, and I knew that I was, as the expression goes, 'the cynosure of every eye'. Then Helen lifted my veil and took my bouquet, and tucked herself into a pew next to Mum. The wedding had begun.

And it was going well. Really smoothly. It was all so . . . lovely. Dominic looked a bit anxious, so I gently squeezed his hand. And we sang 'He Who Would Valiant Be', he and I singing it quite quietly, and he looked a little agitated, but that was because there was this wasp buzzing about, and it was hovering close to him, and he had to flap it away once or twice. Then Amber stepped forward and read the 'Desiderata', beautifully, because she's got a fantastic voice. Then we sang 'Jerusalem' and then came The Marriage. And the Rector, John Oakes, said why marriage was important, and why it should not be undertaken lightly, wantonly or unadvisedly; and then he called on the congregation to state whether they knew of any impediment why Dominic and I should not be joined together in Holy Matrimony. And that was a heart-stopping moment. In fact I hated it – even though I knew that no one was likely to come crashing in at the back raising loud objections or waving marriage certificates about. But still it made me very anxious, and so I was relieved when that bit was over and we went forward to the next part. But the wasp kept buzzing about, and it simply wouldn't leave Dom alone, and he was getting a bit rattled and red in the face, so I gently swotted at it with my Order of Service. And the vicar said:

'Dominic, wilt thou have this woman to thy wedded wife, to live together according to God's law in the Holy estate of matrimony? Wilt thou love her, comfort her, honour and keep her in sickness and in health; and forsaking all others, keep thee only unto her, so long as ye both shall live?'

There was a pause. An unscheduled pause. What we radio people call 'dead air'. And the pause went on for quite a bit, greatly to my surprise. But then, eventually, Dominic spoke.

'We-ll,' he began, and he swallowed, as though he might otherwise choke. 'We-ll,' he said again, then stopped. Then he heaved this enormous sigh. And then he just stared at the painting of Christ, crucified, over the altar. And in the ensuing silence, which felt like an eternity, but was probably no more than five seconds, I felt as though I'd been plunged into a bath of ice-water, despite the oppressive heat of the day.

'Wilt thou?' repeated the vicar helpfully. There was another silence, which seemed to hum and throb. I watched a bead of sweat trickle down Dominic's face, from his temple to his chin.

'Wilt thou? Mm?' The vicar's face was red too, by now. And his brow was gleaming and moist. He stared at Dominic, willing him to speak. And at last, Dominic did.

'Well . . .' he stuttered. Then he cleared his throat. 'Well . . .' he tried again.

'*Wilt* thou?'

'No, John,' said Dom quietly, 'I'm afraid I won't.'

I was staring at the vicar, and the vicar was staring at Dominic. And then I looked at Dominic too, and was suddenly very sorry that I'd chosen St Bride's because my by now reddening face was fully visible to every single person in that church.

'Come along, Dominic,' said the vicar, *sotto voce* with a tight little smile. 'Let's try it again. Wilt thou love Irene Araminta and honour her etcetera, etcetera, *etcetera* – so long as ye both shall live?'

'No,' said Dominic, more forcefully this time, ''fraid not.' And now, as I stared at him, I was conscious of the sound of wood gently creaking, as people shifted in their pews.

'Dominic!' It was Charlie. 'Come on, old chap. Let's press on with it, shall we?'

'I can't,' Dominic said, with a slow, regretful shake of his head. He looked terrible. He looked distraught. 'I just *can't,*' he said again. And at that point, somehow, I managed to speak.

'Are you ill, Dom?' I whispered. 'Do you feel unwell?' He looked at me, and moaned.

'No. No, I'm not ill. I'm well. There's nothing wrong with me.'

'Then what's the matter?' I croaked. My mouth felt dry as dust and I was aware of disconcerted susurrations from behind.

'The matter is . . .' he said. 'The matter is . . . that these are such *serious* vows, Minty. Vows I may not be able to keep. And it wouldn't be so bad if it wasn't for the fact that we're in *church.*'

'Yes,' I said weakly, 'I know.'

'And in church you just can't lie and hope to get away with it,' he went on. 'And I've been thinking about God a lot recently, because actually, Minty, although you may not have realised this, I'm a deeply religious person.'

'Dom, whatever are you talking about?' I murmured. 'You *never* go to church.'

'Yes, but you don't have to go to church to be religious, and now that I'm standing here, before the altar, in the sight of God, I know I just can't go through with it. Because I'd have to promise to love you and comfort you and keep myself only unto you and all the rest of it, Minty, and that's pretty serious stuff, you know.'

'Yes. Yes, I do know that, actually.'

'And it's only now that I'm standing here, that I realise how *huge* these vows are. It's only now,' he went on, 'that I'm beginning to comprehend the enormity of what I'm being asked to do.'

'Not "enormity", Dom,' I whispered, 'that means something bad. I think you mean enormous*ness*.'

'Please don't correct me, Minty. I mean the magnitude of it. Of what I'm being asked to give up.'

'Yes, but, you knew that *before*,' I breathed, aware of a lemon-sized lump in my throat.

'Yes. But I didn't *understand* it before. What it truly means. But now I'm here, in church, I do. These huge promises. And I'm just not prepared to make them because, frankly, Minty, as you well know, there are lots of things about you that really . . . *annoy* me.' At this a sudden murmur arose from the pews, like the uprush of small birds from a field. I could hear nervous, interrogative titters, and the sound of breath being sharply inhaled.

'They say it's the little things that get to you in the end,' he said, 'and it's the little things that have got to me about you. I mean, you're so untidy,' he went on, getting into his stride now. His tenor voice was rising to an almost girlish timbre, which is what happens when he gets worked up. 'You talk such rubbish half the time,' he went on, 'and you never know when to shut up.'

'What do you expect?' I said, my heart now banging in my

chest. 'As you know, I'm a) half Irish, and b) a professional broadcaster.'

'You really get me down,' he whined. 'I've been trying to put all my doubts about you to the back of my mind, but I can't any longer, I simply can't, because I think we'd . . . we'd . . . we'd be *bound* to come unstuck! I'm sorry, Minty, but I just can't go through with this.' My jaw dropped. It dropped wide open. I must have looked a picture of cretinous idiocy as I absorbed what he had just said. I glanced at Dad, but his mouth was agape too. And Mum and Helen seemed frozen, in a state close to catatonia. Then Charlie intervened again.

'Look, do us all a favour, old man. Cut the crap, will you – sorry, Vicar – and just say "I do", there's a good chap.'

This seemed to be the last straw, and then that bally wasp came buzzing back.

'No. No, I won't,' said Dom, swatting it away from his perspiration-beaded face. 'I won't say that, simply to please you and everyone else. I'm not a puppet, you know. This is a free country. You can't make me go through with this. And I won't. I'm determined to think of myself – at *last*!' He turned ninety degrees and faced the gawping crowd. And I could see the fear in his face as he realised how exposed he now was to their contempt. 'Look, I'm . . . sorry about this everyone,' he said, nervously running a finger round his wing collar. 'I . . . er . . . know some of you have come from quite a long way. A very long way away in some cases, like my Aunt Beth, for example, who's come down from Aberdeen. But, well, the fact is, I *can't* do this. I hope you all understand. And once again, I'm . . . well . . . I'm sorry.' Then something of the old Dominic returned, as he felt himself take command of the situation once more. 'However,' he went on smoothly, 'I would like to point out that there is a comprehensive insurance policy in place, which should take care of everything.' He swallowed, and breathed deeply. And then he looked at me.

'Look, Minty. It just wasn't going to work out. I think if you were honest, you'd admit that yourself.' And then he began to walk away from me, down the aisle, with a very determined air. And as he picked up speed he almost skidded on the highly polished floor, and I actually shouted after him, 'Careful, Dom! Don't slip!' But he didn't. He carried on walking until he reached the door, his shoes snapping smartly, almost brightly, across the gleaming tiles.

I don't really remember what happened in the minutes immediately after that. I think it's been erased from my mind, as one erases unwanted footage from an old video. I do remember trying to recall some comforting or possibly even useful phrases from *Nearly Wed*, but couldn't think of a single one, except for the chapter heading: 'How to Survive the Happiest Day of Your Life'. Apart from that, I think I simply stood there, immobile, clutching my Order of Service. I didn't have a clue what to do. I just hoped that the camcorder had been switched off. Charlie had run after Dominic, but had come back, three minutes later, alone.

'He got on a bus,' he whispered to me, and to Dad and Helen, who had now stepped forward in a protective pincer movement around me. And I found this piece of news very odd, because Dominic loathes public transport.

'Couldn't you have chased after him?' suggested Dad.

'No, it was a number 11, it was going pretty fast.'

'I see,' said Dad seriously. We looked vainly at the vicar but he didn't seem to know what to do.

'This has never, *ever* happened during my ministry,' he said, a piece of information which did little to cheer me up.

By now, people were whispering loudly in their pews, and many looked distraught. Amber was opening and closing her mouth like an outraged carp.

'What the *hell*'s that plonker *playing* at?' she demanded in her over-bearing, Cheltenham Ladies way. 'What a bastard!' she added, as she clambered out of her pew. 'What a sh—'

'Shhhh! Madam,' said the vicar, 'this is a house of God.'

'I don't care if it's the house of bloody Bernarda Alba!' she flung back. 'That man's just jilted my cousin!'

Jilted! It cut through me like a knife. *Jilted*. That was it:

I'd been jilted. Amber was right. And it wasn't a moment's aberration, because the minutes were now ticking by, and Dominic still hadn't reappeared. And I could hear another wedding party gathering outside, so I didn't see how Dom and I were going to have time to make our vows even if he did come back, which by now I very much doubted. And anyway, if there's one thing I know about Dominic, more than anything else, one constant, immutable characteristic, it's the fact that once he's made up his mind to do something, he will never, *ever* go back.

Dad sat down, and put his head in his hands. Mum and Helen looked equally distraught. And then I looked down the pews, scanning the faces of those who had witnessed my shame. There was Jack, not knowing where to look, and his step-daughters, who were stifling giggles; next to them was Melinda, her podgy hand clapped to her mouth in a melodramatic tableau of shock; and Wesley was tut-tutting away to Deirdre and shaking his head, and Auntie Flo was crying, and no one knew what to say or where to look. But they were all trying hard not to look at me, in the way that nice people avert their eyes when passing the scene of some dreadful crash. And that's what I felt like. A corpse, lying on the road. Hit and run. I hadn't been cut. I didn't have a scratch, but my blood had been spilled for all to see.

By now Charlie and the vicar were conferring agitatedly. Someone would have to decide what to do, I realised vaguely. Charlie took charge. He came up to me, and laid his hand on my arm in a reassuring way.

'Shall we go to the Waldorf, Minty? Do you want to go?'

'What?'

'We can't stay here.'

'What? Oh . . . no.'

'You see, I don't think Dom's coming back and the next party's starting to arrive. I suggest we all go to the Waldorf, try and calm down, and at least have a little lunch and plan what to do. Do you agree, Minty? Is that OK? Remember, it's your day. We'll all do *exactly* what *you* want!'

'Well . . . yes, why not?' I said, with a reasonableness that astounded me. I think I even tried to smile.

'She's in shock,' Amber announced loudly. She put her arm round me. 'You're in shock, Minty. Don't worry, it's only to be expected.'

'I'm sure everything's going to be OK, Minty,' said Helen, taking one of my hands in both hers. 'I'm sure he's just been possessed by some temporary . . . you know . . . insanity.'

'I don't think so,' I said calmly. 'Please could someone tell the photographer and the video chap to go home?'

'What a bastard!' said Amber, again.

'Please, madam,' repeated the vicar.

'Come on, Minty,' said Mum. 'We're going to the hotel!' And she and Dad led me out of the church, one on each arm, as though I were an invalid. Indeed, the waiting Bentley might as well have been an ambulance – I half expected to see a blue flashing light revolving on its roof. And the shocked voices of the congregation were drowned out by the voices clamouring in my head. They said, Why? Why? Why? Why? WHY?

'Um . . . this is a somewhat *unusual* situation,' announced Charlie, as we all sat down to our vine-ripened tomatoes in the Waldorf's Adelphi Suite half an hour later. He nervously fiddled with his buttonhole as he faced the assembled guests. 'Now, I don't want to speculate as to why Dominic seems to have got cold feet –'

'Cold?' interjected Amber acidly. 'They were deep frozen.'

'Thank you, Amber. As I say, I refuse to speculate about Dominic's behaviour this morning,' Charlie went on, 'except to say that he has been working rather hard recently. Very hard, in fact. And he has seemed rather preoccupied lately, so, er, I suspect that er, professional pressure is largely to blame. And I think the best thing is if we just try to enjoy our lunch, and, er, try to, er, well . . .' his voice trailed away '. . . enjoy our lunch.'

And the waiters came round with the Laurent Perrier – in the circumstances we'd decided not to have a reception line –

and people drank it, and chatted in low, respectful voices. They sat huddled round their tables like spies, as they swapped theories about Dom's dramatic exit.

'– another woman?' I heard someone ask.

'– dunno.'

'– already married?'

'– nervous breakdown?'

'– always a bit flaky.'

'– totally humiliating.'

'– what about the presents?'

I was on the top table, of course, but instead of sitting there with my new husband, I was next to my bridesmaid and the best man, and my parents, brother and cousin. And Madge, unfortunately. She'd come along to the Waldorf, too.

'Well, at least I got to wear my new Windsmoor,' she said with a satisfied shrug. 'It cost an absolute bomb.'

'Windsmoor? *I say,*' said Amber incredulously. She seemed more outraged than me.

'Do you have any notion as to why your son has done this?' Dad enquired with stiff civility.

'Well, I suppose he felt that it wasn't *right,* and that he just couldn't go through with it,' she offered. 'He's got such integrity like that.'

'Integrity!' Amber spat.

'Amber, Amber, please,' said Charlie. 'It doesn't help.'

'Nice tiara, by the way, Minty,' said Madge.

'Thanks.'

'And you can keep the griddle pan.' I was too shocked to take in this happy news.

'Never mind, Minty, darling,' said Mum, putting a solicitous arm round my shoulder. 'I always thought the man was a first-class shyster and rotter, I can't deny it, and – oooh, sorry, Madge!' Mum blushed. 'An appalling waste of twenty-eight grand, though,' she added regretfully.

'Is that *all* you can think of, Dympna?' Dad asked wearily, as a waiter flicked a large napkin on to her lap.

'Well, just think of all the homeless bats and battered wives you could save with that lot!' she retorted. 'What about the insurance policy?' she asked.

'Charlie phoned the helpline on his mobile,' Dad replied. 'I'm afraid it doesn't appear to cover stage-fright.'

So we sat there eating our lunch, amid the curiously merry clatter of cutlery on china, and the pan-seared swordfish arrived and everyone said it was very good, though obviously I couldn't eat a thing; and the string trio were playing 'Solitaire', which I thought was extremely insensitive, and I was just making a mental decision not to tip them when Charlie's mobile phone went off. He flicked it on, and stood up.

'Yes? Yes?' I heard him say. Then he said, 'Look, Dom, don't tell me this, tell Minty. You've got to talk to her, old chap – I'm going to put her on to you right now.'

I grabbed the outstretched phone as though it were a lifeline and I a drowning man. 'Dom, Dom it's me. Listen . . . Yes . . . Yes, OK . . . Thanks . . . No, Dominic, don't hang up. Don't. Please, Dom, don't! . . . Thanks, Dom. No, don't go, Dominic! Don't, Dominic . . . Dom –'

He'd gone. And then, at last, I burst into tears.

'What did he say?' asked Charlie, after a minute.

'He said . . . he said, I can keep the engagement ring.'

'Ah, that's nice of him,' said Madge with a benevolent smile. 'He was always *very* generous like that.'

'And the honeymoon.'

'Heart of gold, really.'

Mum shot her a poisonous look.

'But how can I go on my honeymoon on my *own*?' I wailed.

'I'll come with you, Minty,' Helen said.

And so at ten to five Helen and I left the Waldorf in a cab – she'd already dashed home to get her passport and a weekend bag. And we were waved off by everyone, which felt rather strange; I decided, in the circumstances, not to throw my bouquet. I left it with all my wedding gear, which Dad said he'd take back to Primrose Hill. And as I crossed the Thames in the taxi with my bridesmaid instead of my bridegroom, I kept thinking, 'Where's Dominic? Where is he? *Where*?' Was he still on the bus? Unlikely. Was he back in Clapham? When had he decided on his course of action? Was it pure *coup de théâtre*, or a genuine *éclaircissement* – and why was I thinking in French?

'I don't think he'll be back,' Madge had announced, as she sipped her coffee.

'What makes you so sure?' Charlie enquired testily. Tempers were frayed by now.

'Well, once he makes up his mind about something he *never* changes it,' she said, patting her perm. 'Like I say, he's got *such* integrity like that.'

'Oh, why don't you shut up about Dominic's blasted "integrity"?' said Amber, with a ferocity which struck me as rude. 'Look what he's done to Minty!'

'Well, it *is* unfortunate,' agreed Madge, with an air of regret. 'But much better to pull out now than later on.'

'No!' I said in a voice I barely recognised as my own. 'I'd rather he'd gone through with it, just gone *through* with it, and divorced me tomorrow, if that's how he felt.'

'But he's got such a lot to lose,' she said.

'Well, I've lost all my dignity!' I replied. 'It's so humiliating,' I wailed, as I tried to avoid the pitying looks of the catering staff. 'And in front of every single person I know.' And it was then that I suddenly regretted having let Dominic persuade me to invite half the staff of London FM. How could I work there again, after this? I looked at my napkin – it was smeared with mascara, which annoyed me because I'd paid £24 for it and had been assured by the woman in the shop that it was completely waterproof. I looked at my watch. It was ten to four, and the train to Paris was at five fifteen.

'I think you should go,' said Dad again.

'Why don't *you* go,' I said, 'with Mum?'

'I can't,' she said. 'It's the Anorexia Association Ball on Tuesday. I've got to look after Lord Eatmore, he's the sponsor.'

'Go with Helen, Minty,' said Dad. 'That way, if Dominic wants to ring you, he'll know where you are.'

Oh yes. Dominic would know that all right. The George V.

The Honeymoon Suite. That's what he'd asked me to book and, very obediently, I had. So that's where he could ring me. He could ring me there and explain. Perhaps he'd even come over and talk to me in person. But deep down, I knew he wouldn't – because I knew that Madge was right.

In *The Scarlet Letter* by Nathaniel Hawthorne the heroine, Hester, is made to wear the letter 'A' on her dress. 'A' for Adultery. 'A' to indicate her public shame. As Helen and I swished through the Kent countryside on Eurostar, I thought, maybe I should wear 'J', for jilted. This would save people constantly coming up to me in the coming weeks and asking me why I looked so strained, and why I hardly ate, and why I had this mad, staring expression in my eyes. It would be the emotional equivalent of a black armband, easily read from afar, and leaving nothing to be said – except perhaps for the occasional, and entirely voluntary, sympathetic gesture.

And I thought too, as I gazed at the sunlit fields, of how incredibly unlucky I'd been. I'd had more chance of being blown up by a terrorist bomb, or hit by a flying cow, than being deserted, in church, mid marriage. And I thought of Sheryl von Strumpfhosen and of how she'd got my horoscope so horribly wrong: 'Your love life takes an upward turn this weekend,' she'd written. *Upward turn*? And then I remembered my marriage manual, *Nearly Wed*, and a grim smile spread across my lips. I thought as well of all the kind things people had said as I left the hotel. 'Chin up, Minty!' 'Probably all for the best . . .' 'Expect he'll come running back!' 'Thought you looked lovely, by the way.' They had crawled and cringed with embarrassment, brows corrugated with confusion and concern. I'd felt almost sorrier for them than for myself. I mean, what *do* you say? And then, I realised, with a heart like lead, that it wasn't just the people who were in church. It was the hundreds of others who'd read that I was engaged.

Because it was in the papers, of course. In the engagement columns of both the *Telegraph*, and *The Times*. That had been the first cog to turn, setting in motion the invincible wedding machine. And then I regretted putting it in on a Saturday, when it would have been spotted by everyone I know. And so for months to come I would have to explain again and again that, 'No, I'm still Minty Malone, actually,' and 'No, I didn't get married, after all,' and 'No – no particular reason, ha ha ha! It just didn't, you know, work out.' 'These things happen,' I'd have to say, brightly. 'All for the best and all that.' Oh *God*. I was interrupted from Bride's Dread Revisited by the distant clink of a trolley.

'Please eat something,' said Helen. 'The steward's just coming –' She reddened.

'Up the aisle?' I enquired bleakly.

'Please, Minty,' she said, as he approached. 'You didn't eat anything at lunch.'

Eat? I was still so shocked I could hardly breathe.

'Champagne, madam?'

Champagne? I never wanted to see another glass of *that* as long as I lived.

'No, thank you,' I said. 'You have it, Helen.'

'Lamb or duck, madam?'

'Neither, thanks.'

'Nothing at all for madam?' enquired the steward with an air of concern.

'No. Nothing for madam. And, actually, it isn't madam, it's still miss.'

The steward retreated with a wounded air. Helen picked up her knife and fork.

'I'm sure Dominic will be back,' she said, trying to comfort me, yet again.

Helen's like that. She's very kind-hearted. She's very optimistic too, like her name, Spero – 'I hope.' In fact, her family motto is *Dum Spiro, Spero* – 'While I breathe, I hope.' Yes, I thought, Helen's always hopeful. But today she was quite, quite wrong.

'He won't come back,' I said. 'He never, ever changes his mind about anything. It's over, Helen. Over and out.'

She shook her head, and murmured, for the umpteenth time, 'Incredible.' And then, determined to cheer me up, she began to regale me with other nuptial nightmares she'd read about in women's magazines. The groom who discovered he'd married a transsexual; the best man who didn't show; the bride who ran off with a woman she'd met at her hen night; the collapsing or flying marquees. Helen was an expert. Helen knew them all.

'Did you hear the one about the coronation chicken?' she asked, as she sipped her Bordeaux.

'No.'

'It claimed five lives at a reception in Reigate.'

'How dreadful.'

'Then there was this awful punch-up at a marriage in Maidstone.'

'Really?'

'The bride spent her wedding night in jail.'

'Oh dear.'

'And there was a woman in Kent who was married and widowed on the same day!'

'No!'

'The groom said, "I do," then dropped stone-dead. Heart attack, apparently, brought on by all the stress.'

'Oh God.'

'And I know someone else whose granny croaked at the reception.'

'Really?'

'She went face down in the trifle during the speeches.'

'Terrible,' I murmured. And though Helen meant well, this litany of wedding-day disasters was beginning to get me down. I was glad when we pulled into Paris.

'Well, perhaps it's for the best,' she said, as we got off the train. 'And I'm sure you'll meet someone else – I mean, *if* Dominic doesn't come back,' she added quickly.

And I thought, yes, maybe I'll meet someone else. Maybe,

like Nancy Mitford's heroine, Linda, in *The Pursuit of Love*, I'll encounter some charming French aristocrat right here at the Gare du Nord. That would be wonderfully convenient. But there were no aristocrats in sight, just an interminable queue for the cabs.

'*Le George V, s'il vous plaît,*' Helen said to the driver, and soon we were speeding through the streets, the windows wide open, inhaling the pungent Parisian aroma of petrol fumes, tobacco and *pissoirs*. At the bottom of Rue La Fayette stood the Opera House, as ornate and fanciful as a wedding cake, I reflected bitterly. Then we crossed the Place de la Concorde and entered the bustling Champs Elysées.

'Elysian Fields,' I said acidly. The sight of a shop window full of bridal gowns dealt me a knife-blow. A wedding car festooned with white ribbons pulled past and I thought I was going to be sick. Ahead of us was the Arc de Triomphe, massive and emphatic. It seemed to mock me after my decidedly unheroic disaster in St Bride's. I was glad when the driver turned left into Avenue George V, and we couldn't see it any more.

'Congratulations, Madame Lane!' The concierge beamed at me. 'The Four Seasons George V Hotel would like to extend to you and your 'usband, our warmest *félicitations*! Er, is Monsieur Lane just coming, madame?'

'No,' I said, 'he isn't. And it's still "mademoiselle", by the way.' The concierge reddened as he called a bellboy to take care of our bags.

'Ah. I see,' he said, as he slid the registration form across the counter for me to sign. '*Alors*, never mind, as you English like to say.'

'I do mind,' I pointed out. 'I mind very much, actually. But I was persuaded not to waste the trip, so I've come with my bridesmaid, instead.' Helen gave the concierge an awkward smile.

'*Eh bien*, why not?' he said. 'The Honeymoon Suite is on the eighth floor, mademoiselles. The lifts are just there on your right. I 'ope you will enjoy your stay.'

'I think that's rather unlikely,' I said. 'In the circumstances.'

'Please remember, madame –'

'–oiselle.'

'– that we are entirely at your disposal,' he went on. 'At the George V no request is too big, too small, or too unusual.'

'OK. Then can you get my fiancé back?'

'Our staff are on hand night and day.'

'He ran off, you see, in church.'

'If you need help, unpacking your shopping . . .'

'In front of everyone I know . . .'

'Or you'd like something laundered or ironed . . .'

'It was so humiliating . . .'

'Then we will be pleased to do it for you.'

'It was awful.'

'At any time.'

'Just awful.'

'We are here for you round ze clock.'

'It was terrible,' I whispered. *'Terrible.'*

'Oui, mademoiselle.'

The marble reception desk had begun to blur and I was aware of Helen's hand pressing gently on my arm.

'Come on, Minty,' she said. 'Why don't we go and find the room.'

To call it a 'room' was like calling St Paul's a church. The bedroom was about thirty feet long, with an enormous walk-in wardrobe. There was also a private sitting room, a huge bathroom, a separate shower room, and a terrace. The walls were painted a soft yellow, and there were antiques everywhere. A crystal chandelier hung from the ceiling; its lustre drops looked like tears.

'It's lovely,' I said, sinking into the boat-sized bed. I looked at the huge bouquet of congratulatory pink roses and the bottle of chilling champagne. 'It's lovely,' I said again. 'It's just so . . .' A hot tear splashed on to my hand.

'Oh, Minty,' Helen said, and she was almost crying too.

'Incredible,' she repeated, putting her arm round me. 'Just unbelievable.'

'Yes,' I wept, 'but it's true. He *did it*. And it's only now that it's beginning to sink in.'

'But *why* did he do it?' she said, shaking her head.

'I don't know,' I sobbed. 'I don't *know*.'

'Oh, Minty – you're well out of it,' she said, furiously blinking away her tears. 'You don't want a man capable of such a cowardly, despicable act. You're *well* out of it,' she reiterated, crossly.

And I thought, I'm going to keep on hearing that – again and again. That's what people will say: 'You're well out of it, Minty. *Well* out.' And though it won't help, they'll be right. It's bad enough when a man breaks off his engagement, but doing a runner in the *church*? Outrageous! 'You're well shot of him!' everyone will tell me confidently. 'What a cad!' they'll add. Oh God.

Helen stood up and opened the French windows. I followed her out on to the terrace. Pretty pots of tumbling geraniums stood in each corner, and a white satin ribbon had been threaded through the wrought-iron balcony. The table had been laid, for two, with a white damask cloth, sparkling silver cutlery, gleaming porcelain, candles and flowers. The perfect setting for a romantic sunset dinner *à deux*. I just couldn't bear it.

'I'll ask them to clear it away,' I said, bleakly. Then I sat down and took in the view. Ahead of us, to the right, was the Eiffel Tower, its cast-iron fretwork now illuminated like electric lace. To our left was the spire of the American Cathedral, and, further off, the gilded dome of Les Invalides. And then my eye caught the Pont de l'Alma, and the eternal flame by the tunnel in which Princess Diana had died. Worse things happen, I thought to myself, with a jolt. This is dreadful. *Dreadful*. But no one's dead.

'You will come through this, Minty,' Helen said quietly.

'You won't believe that now. But you will. And I know you'll be happy again one day.' And as she said that her gold crest ring glinted in the evening sun.

'Dum Spiro, Spero,' I said to myself. Yes. While I have breath, I hope.

'Audrey Hepburn stayed here,' said Helen excitedly in the hotel dining room the following morning. 'And Greta Garbo. And Sophia Loren. And Jerry Hall.'

'And Minty Malone,' I added bitterly, 'the world-famous jiltee – and winner of the Miss Havisham Memorial Prize.'

Lack of sleep had left me in an edgy, sardonic mood. It wasn't that Helen's presence in the bed had disturbed me – it was so big I'd hardly noticed. It was simply that I'd been far too stressed to sleep. So at two a.m. I'd got up and wandered around the suite in my nightie, wringing my hands like Lady Macbeth. Then I'd rung reception.

'Oui, madame?' It was the same concierge, still on duty.

'You did say "round the clock", didn't you?' I whispered.

'Oui, madame.'

'Could you get me something then?'

'Of course, madame. At the George V no request is too big, too small, or too unusual.'

'In that case, can you get me a copy of *Great Expectations* by Charles Dickens. In English, please,' I added.

'And you would like this when, madame?'

'Now.'

'Eh, bien sur . . . we do have a small *bibliothèque*. I will 'ave a look.'

'Thank you.'

Five minutes later there was a knock on the door and a bellboy appeared, clutching a leather-bound copy of the book. I gave him twenty francs. Then I sat down in the sitting room and turned the thin pages until I found what I was looking for.

> [Miss Havisham] was dressed in rich materials – satins, and lace, and silks – all of white. Her shoes were white. And she had a long white veil dependent from her hair, and she had bridal flowers in her hair, but her hair was white . . . But I saw that everything within my view which ought to be white, had been white long ago, and had lost its lustre, and was faded and yellow. I saw that the bride within the bridal dress had withered like the dress, and like the flowers, and had no brightness left but the brightness of her sunken eyes. I saw that the dress had been put upon the rounded figure of a young woman, and that the figure upon which it now hung loose, had shrunk to skin and bone . . .

'How are you feeling, Minty?' I heard Helen say.

'How do I feel? Well, just a bit pissed off.' My new, ironic levity surprised me. 'I'm going to design a new range of bridal wear,' I added.

'Really?'

'Yes. I'm going to call it "Anti-Nuptia".'

'Oh, Minty.'

I looked round the dining room and felt sick. It was full of infatuated couples. Just what you need when you've been abandoned by your husband-to-be. They all looked sated with sex as they locked eyeballs, and tenderly rubbed ankles under the tables.

'Why don't you eat something?' Helen said.

'I can't.'

'Go on, try,' she said, pushing a basket of croissants towards me.

'Impossible,' I said. And it was. I've never dieted. I've never really had to. But now it was as though someone had turned off the tap in my brain marked 'Eat'. The *petit pains* might as well have been made of plastic for all the interest they aroused in me. All I could manage was a few sips of sugary tea.

'What shall we do today?' I said.

'I don't know,' said Helen. 'I haven't been to Paris since I was twelve.'

'I know it pretty well,' I said. 'In fact, I've been here eleven times.'

'Minty,' said Helen slowly, while she delicately chomped on a *pain au chocolat*. 'Why did you choose Paris for your honeymoon when you'd already been here so often?'

'I didn't choose it,' I replied. 'Dominic did. I would have preferred Venice,' I went on with a shrug, 'but Dom said the train journey would take too long, and so Paris it was.'

'I see,' she said, archly. 'That was nice of you.'

'And of course Paris is a *lovely* city.'

'Minty . . .' said Helen, carefully. She was fiddling with her teaspoon.

'Yes?' Why on earth was she looking at me like that?

'Minty,' she began again, 'I hope you don't mind my saying this, but you often seemed to do what Dominic wanted.'

I thought about this for a few seconds.

'Yes,' I conceded. 'I suppose I did.'

'Why?'

'Why?' *Why*? God, why did she have to ask me that? 'Because I loved him,' I replied, 'that's why. And because . . .' I felt my throat constrict '. . . I just wanted him to be happy.'

She nodded. 'Well, what *shall* we do today?' she said, briskly changing the subject.

'We can do whatever you like,' I said, bleakly. 'We'll be tourists.'

And we were. That first morning we walked along the Seine then crossed the Jardin des Tuileries into the Rue de Rivoli. People strolled under the colonnaded passageways or sat outside, smoking in the warm sunlight. We crossed the Place du Carrousel and walked towards the Louvre. Helen gasped when she saw the glass pyramid, its triangular panes glinting and flashing in the midday sun.

'It's incredible!' she said. 'It's like a gigantic diamond.'

'Yes,' I replied flatly. I fiddled with my engagement ring – a solitaire – which I still wore, on my right hand.

'Let's find the *Mona Lisa,*' said Helen as we made our way inside. We walked up the wide balustraded stairway on to the first floor of the Denon Wing. We paused before paintings by Botticelli, Bellini and Caravaggio, and altarpieces by Giotto and Cimabue. In one gallery was a painting by Veronese, so vast it filled one wall.

'It's the *Wedding at Cana,*' said Helen, looking at the guide. 'That was Christ's first miracle, wasn't it, when the wine ran out?'

I found myself wishing He could have performed a similar stunt for me when my husband-to-be ran out. We passed through a long, window-lined corridor, which glowed with rich paintings. Mantegna's martyred St Sebastian, pierced with sharp arrows, couldn't have been in more pain than I. My shards were psychological, but no less sharp for that.

We followed the signs and found the *Mona Lisa* behind bulletproof glass in Room 6. A bank of people stood in front of her, discussing her elusive smile.

'– Oh, she's so *cute!*'

'– *Che bella ragazza.*'

'– *Sie ist so schone.*'

'– That's real *art,* Art.'

'– *Elle est si mystérieuse, si triste.*'

'– her child had just died, you know.'

'God, how awful,' said Helen. Then she read from the entry in the guide:

'"When Leonardo began this portrait, the young woman was in mourning for her baby daughter; this is why she wears a black veil over her head. To lift her spirits, Leonardo brought musicians and clowns into his studio. Their antics brought a smile to her lips, a smile of indefinable sadness and great gentleness which made the portrait famous." So she was feeling terrible,' Helen added. 'And yet she managed to smile.'

That's what I'll do, I thought. I'll erect my own bulletproof glass, and shield myself behind that. And I'll wear a smile, so that no one will detect my pain. I decided to practise. I straightened my shoulders and raised my drooping head. I opened my eyes wider, and turned up the corners of my mouth. And it began to work, because as I looked up I caught the eye of a young man and, to my surprise, he smiled back. It reminded me of the lovely smile that Charlie had given me in church. And I suddenly remembered wishing that it had been Dominic who'd smiled. And now I knew why he hadn't.

'You're *well* out of it,' said Helen again, as we wandered downstairs. I was too weary to reply. In any case, I didn't have the energy for anger – I was still anaesthetised by shock.

'I mean, why go that far – *that* far – and then say "no"?'

'He's in the risk-business,' I said bleakly. 'He was unhappy with the small print so he decided not to close the deal. He exercised the ultimate get-out clause.'

'Yes, but *why* was he unhappy?' she asked.

'I don't know,' I replied. 'I don't know.'

'What a *cad,*' said Helen. 'You should sue him for breach of promise.'

'It doesn't exist in British law.'

'Well, make him pay for the wedding, then.'

'No – too undignified.'

'If it were me, I'd be instructing solicitors,' she said. 'And fancy letting himself down like that in front of all his clients. I hope they all leave him,' she exclaimed.

'They won't,' I said. 'And even if they did, he'd soon pick up new ones. He's very persuasive.' Dominic's powers of persuasion were indeed legendary. He had once famously sold a Pet Protect policy to a woman who had no animals. Oh yes, Dominic would survive all right. The question was, would I?

The next two days passed in a blur as we wandered slowly around the city. We visited the Musée d'Orsay, the Bois de Boulogne and the cemetery at Père Lachaise. And I'd thought Père Lachaise would be too sad, but it wasn't, it was a surprisingly happy place, like a friendly little citadel of the celebrated dead. We found Colette's grave, and Balzac's and Chopin's and Oscar Wilde's. And Jim Morrison's, of course, which was strewn with red roses, candles and cigarette butts, and empty whisky bottles.

The next day, our last, we walked to the Eiffel Tower. We queued for an hour at the Pillier Ouest, while hawkers tried to sell us souvenirs. 'To help you remember your stay in Paris,' one of them pleaded.

'I could *never* forget it,' I said. We bought our tickets then went clanking skywards in the lift. Up and up it went, the vast wheels turning and grinding like the wheels of a Victorian mine-shaft. We passed the first landing stage, then the second, our ears popping as we floated up through the elaborate iron fretwork to the top. We were nearly a thousand feet above ground as we stepped out on to the viewing platform, the wind snatching spitefully at our hair and clothes. Up here, a slightly hysterical atmosphere prevailed. People grinned and gasped as they took in the view. Their eyes popped in disbelief. A young couple laughed and hugged each other as they peered out through the suicide-inhibiting mesh. Below us, to the left, was a football pitch which looked as though it had been cut from green felt. The players scurried across it like ants, and we could hear the whistles and shouts of the fans. In front of us was the Palais de Chaillot, and the broad brown band of the Seine. Along its banks, barges rocked gently on their moorings, and the reflected ripples of the river dappled the windows nearby. Away to our right was Montmartre, and the slender white domes of Sacré-Coeur and, ahead of us, further off, the brutalist towers of La Defense. The whole city lay spread beneath our feet, topped by a pale miasma of carbon monoxide. We could hear nothing but the whistling wind, and the dull roar of a million cars.

'Look how *far* we can see!' Helen exclaimed. 'It must be fifty miles or more!'

Indeed, the distance to the horizon made me feel strangely elated, intoxicated almost, and a poem by Emily Dickinson sprang into my mind: 'As if the Sea should part/And show a further Sea/And that – a further . . .' And I thought, that's what I'll do. I'll go right to the horizon, to the circumference, far, far away from what happened to me in church. I refuse to let Dominic's desertion become the defining event of my life. I refuse to let one man destroy my dignity and sense of self. I resolved in that instant to be the exact opposite of that sad old relic, Miss Havisham. She entombed herself in her house, and her silk wedding dress became her shroud. But *my* bridal gown would be a cocoon, from which I would emerge, reborn. I will *recover* from this, I vowed, as the wind whipped my face and made my eyes sting with tears. I'll start again. I shall be reborn. Made new. New Mint. I shall turn my catastrophe into a catalyst for change. I shall . . . I shall . . .

All at once I felt dizzy. It might have been the height, or the strange perspective, or maybe it was lack of food. I clutched the rail, and shut my eyes. Then the squeak and shriek of the pulley announced the return of the lift. The doors drew back with a throaty click, and a new batch of tourists was disgorged. Helen and I stepped in and began our long descent to the ground.

'Where now?' she said, as we walked away, slightly unsteadily, through the milling crowd.

'Latin Quarter?'

'OK.'

'A little stroll in the Jardins du Luxembourg?'

'Fine. How do we get there?'

'Let's take the Metro,' I said.

As we walked down the steps into the station at Champs de Mars, we were hit by the dank, oily aroma of the underground, and the sound of a violin. Its tone was rich and sweet, and as we entered the tunnel it grew louder. I found myself wanting to follow the sound as though it were Ariadne's thread. Halfway down the main walkway we found its source. An old man in a shabby black coat was playing a honey-coloured violin. His hair was sparse and white. His hands were papery and thin, and the veins on them stood out like pale blue wires. He must have been in his late seventies, maybe more. He'd rigged up a portable cassette player to provide ad hoc accompaniment, and he was playing Schubert's *Ave Maria*.

We automatically slowed our steps. He drew to the end of the piece, lifted off the bow, paused for a second, then began to play an old, familiar song. And as we stopped to listen, the words ran through my mind.

I see trees of green, red roses too . . .

'How lovely,' said Helen.

I see them bloom, for me and you . . .

'Lovely,' she repeated.

And I think to myself, what a wonderful world.

His violin case was open at his feet. A few coins shone brightly against the worn black felt.

I see skies of blue, and clouds of white . . .

I put my hands in my jacket pocket, and drew out a 50-centime piece. Not enough. Not nearly.

The bright blessed day, the dark sacred night . . .

I opened my bag for a note.

And I think to myself, what a wonderful world.

Twenty francs? That would do. Or perhaps fifty. Or a hundred? It was only a tenner, after all.

I see friends shakin' hands, sayin', 'How do you do?' They're really sayin', 'I love you.'

That's what Dominic said to me, when he proposed. But it wasn't true. I knew that now. I looked at my diamond ring, sparkling on my right hand. Its facets flashed like frost.

I hear babies cry, I watch them grow,

They'll learn much more than I'll ever know . . .

I hesitated for a second, then pulled it off, and placed it amongst the coins.

And I think to myself, what a wonderful world.

'Merci, madame,' I heard our busker say. *'Merci, madame. Merci.'* He looked uncertain, so I smiled. Then we turned and walked away.

'Are you sure?' Helen said, handing me a tissue.

'Yes,' I said quietly. 'I'm sure.'

And I think to myself . . . what a wonderful world.

*

'What a wonderful place,' said Helen half an hour later as we strolled through the Jardins du Luxembourg in the late afternoon sun. Middle-aged men played chess under the plane trees; people walked their dogs across the lawns, and children spun their yo-yos back and forth, flinging them out with theatrical flourish, then reeling them in again, fast. Lining the paths were flowerbeds filled with roses, and, in the distance, we could hear the soft 'thwock!' of tennis balls. Helen consulted the guide.

'Isadora Duncan danced here,' she said. 'And Ernest Hemingway used to come and shoot the pigeons.'

'That's nice.'

We passed the octagonal pond in front of the Palais, and walked down an avenue of chestnut trees. Joggers ran past us, working off their *foie gras*; sunbathers and bookworms lounged in park chairs. We could hear the yapping of small dogs, and the chattering of birds. This unhurried existence was a million miles from the fume-filled avenues of the centre. There was childish laughter from a playground. We stopped for a second and watched a group of children rise and fall on their swings.

'Do you want kids?' I asked Helen.

She shrugged. 'Maybe . . . Oh, I don't know,' she sighed. 'Only if I meet the right chap. But even then I wouldn't want them for at least – ooh, three or four years. I'm much too busy,' she added happily, as we turned out of the gardens. 'And do you know, Mint, I really *like* being single.'

'I wish *I* did,' I said. Then I glanced at my watch. It was almost seven. We decided to get something to eat.

'Chez Marc', announced the bar in a narrow cobbled street off the Rue de Tournon. The tables outside were all taken, so we went inside. Waiters with white aprons whizzed round with trays on fingertips as though on invisible skates. A cirrus of cigarette smoke hung over the bar, and we could hear the chink of heavy crockery, and staccato bursts of male laughter. We could also hear the crack of plastic on cork. By the window a game of table football was in progress. Four young men were hunched over the rods, their knuckles white, as the ball banged and skittered around the pitch.

'I used to love playing that,' I said, as we sipped our beer. 'On holiday, when we were little. I used to be quite good.' The players were shouting encouragement, expostulating at penalties and screaming their heads off at every goal.

'– *hors-jeu*!'

'– *c'est nul*!'

'– *veux-tu*?!'

'French men are so good-looking, aren't they?' said Helen.

'Aah! *Putain*!'

'*Espèce de con*!'

'Especially that one, there.'

'That was a banana!' he shouted, in a very un-Gallic way. 'Bananas are not allowed. You've got to throw the ball in *straight*. Got that? !'

'*Bof*!' said his opponent. '*Alors* . . .'

'And only five seconds to size up a shot! OK? *Cinq secondes*!'

'*D'accord, d'accord*! Oh, le "Fair Play",' muttered his opponent crossly.

A free kick was awarded. A quick flick of the wrist, and the ball shot into the net.

'Goal!' Helen clapped. She couldn't help it. They all turned and smiled. I didn't have the energy to smile back. Then the waiter appeared with our pasta. I had eaten what I could when two of the players put on their jackets, shook hands with their opponents and left. The Englishman remained at the table. I looked at him discreetly. Helen was right. He *was* rather nice-looking, in an unshowy sort of way. His hair was dark, and a bit too long. His face looked open and kind. He was wearing jeans and Timberlands, and a rather faded green polo shirt. To my surprise he turned and looked at us.

'*Vous voulez jouer*?'

'Sorry?' I said.

'Would you like to play?'

'Oh, no thanks,' I said with a bitter little smile. 'I've had enough penalty kicks recently.'

'Go on,' he said. 'It's fun.'

'No, thank you,' I said.

'Oh, but my friend and I need partners,' he urged.

I shook my head. 'I'm sorry, but I really don't want to.' I looked at Helen. She had a funny expression on her face.

'You play with them,' I said to her.

'Not without you.'

'Go on. I'll watch.'

'No, no – we'll both play.'

'No, we won't,' I said, 'because I don't want to.'

'Well, *I* do, but I don't want to play without you. Come on, Minty.'

'What?' Why on earth was she insisting?

'Come on,' she said again. And now she was on her feet. 'We *would* like to play, actually,' she announced to the waiting men.

Oh God. And in any case I couldn't even get out. I was jammed in behind the table. Suddenly the English boy came over to me and stretched out his hand.

'Come and play,' he said. I looked at him. Then, very reluctantly, I held out my hand.

'I'm Joe,' he said, as he pulled me to my feet. 'Who are you?'

'Minty. That's Minty *Malone*, by the way,' I added. 'Not Lane.' And, again, my sardonic tone took me aback. I think it took Joe aback, too, because he gave me a slightly puzzled look. Helen was already at the table, partnering the French boy, whose name was Pierre.

'Do you want to be forward?' Joe enquired.

'What?'

'Centre forward?'

'Oh. No, I prefer to defend.'

'Right. No spinning, OK?' I looked blank. 'No spinning the rods,' he cautioned. 'It's cheating.' I nodded. 'And no bananas.'

'I don't even know what they are.'

'It means putting the new ball in with a spin so that it goes towards your own side. Not done.' I looked at the figurines.

Twenty-two plastic men dressed in red or yellow jumpers stared vacantly on their metal rods. They looked as empty and lifeless as I felt.

We grasped the rods. Pierre put the money in, and the ball appeared. He placed it between the two centre forwards, whistled, and the game began. The ball reeled and ricocheted around the pitch as Pierre and Joe competed for possession, then it came to my half-back. I stopped it dead, then kicked it forward to Joe. The tension was unbearable as he hooked the player's feet round the back of the ball, lifted the rod, and then – bang! He'd shot it straight into the goal.

'Great team work, Minty,' he said. 'Fantastic!'

I smiled and blushed with pride, and despite myself I could feel my spirits begin to lift. Two minutes later, Pierre equalised. It was my fault. It was perfectly saveable, but I didn't move my goalie fast enough. I felt like David Seaman when England lost the penalty shoot-out to Argentina in the World Cup.

'Sorry about that,' I groaned.

'Forget it,' he said with a laugh. 'We'll still win.'

Now my heart was pounding as Joe and Pierre wrestled for the ball again. The excitement was high as it skidded around the pitch, and it was hard to concentrate, because Joe talked all the time.

'What do you do, Minty?'

'Oh, er . . . I'm a radio journalist,' I said, amazed that he could simultaneously concentrate on the game and converse. 'What about you?' I enquired, though I was only being polite.

'I'm a writer,' he replied. 'And where do you work?'

'London FM. On a magazine programme called *Capitalise*.'

'Oh, I know it. Current affairs and features.' Suddenly, Helen's half-back kicked the ball so hard that it bounced right off the pitch. Play stopped for a few seconds as she went chasing after it.

'I like *Capitalise*,' said Joe. 'I listen to it quite a bit.'

'Do you live in London, then?' I asked him.

'On and off,' he replied. 'I'm teaching a creative writing

course here for the summer, but I'll be back in London in mid October. Where are you staying?'

Why all the questions? I wondered. And then Helen reappeared with the ball.

'OK – le throw-in!' said Pierre.

'So where are you staying?' Joe asked again, as the ball bounced on to the pitch.

'Umm, the George V, actually.' I didn't want to explain why. He gave a long, low whistle, then he passed the ball back to me.

'Le George V. Wow!'

'Only for four days,' I said, as I moved my goalie across to counter the threat from Pierre's centre half.

'Good save, Minty!' Joe exclaimed. 'And when do you go back?'

'Tomorrow. Tomorrow morning.'

Why was he so inquisitive? I didn't even know the man. He fired at the goal. And in it went.

'Thank you! That's two–one,' he yelled. 'Can I give you a ring?' he said suddenly, as Helen put a new ball down.

'What?' I said, as play resumed.

'Can I call you?' he repeated. 'Can I call you when I'm back in London?'

'Well, I don't know,' I replied, surprised.

'We could play table football,' he said. 'We could play at Café Kick.'

'Oh.' How forward. And how very *depressing*, I thought. He was trying to pick me up. He obviously did this all the time. With women he hardly knew. I didn't need this, I thought crossly. I'd just been jilted, for Christ's sake. I didn't want a man ringing me *ever* again. Humiliating me *ever* again. Hurting me *ever* again.

'Penalty!' shouted Pierre.

'Would it be all right if I took your number, Minty?' Joe asked me again, as he passed the ball back.

'No.'

'What?'

'No, it *wouldn't,*' I repeated tersely. I struck the ball, hard, and a shout went up.

'Own goal, Minty!' everyone cried.

August

''Ad a nice time, luv?' enquired the driver of the cab I flagged down outside Waterloo. Helen had gone to Holland Park to see her parents.

'Sort of. Well, not really.'

'What was it, 'oliday?'

'No,' I said. 'Honeymoon.'

'Where's your 'usband then?'

'I haven't got one.'

'You ain't got one?'

'No. He ran away.'

''E did a *runner*?' said the driver incredulously. He turned round to face me and almost crashed the cab.

'Yes,' I confirmed. 'During the service. So I went with my bridesmaid instead.'

''E did a runner!'

He was chortling and shaking his head.

'Bleedin' 'ell. I 'ope you never catch him.'

'I shan't even try,' I said.

My spirits drooped like dead flowers as we drove through the dusty streets. My brief holiday was over; reality was rolling in. I could have wept as we passed the Waldorf. And the sight of a church made me feel sick. I thought, sinkingly, of work and dreaded having to return. How would I face my colleagues, and what on earth would they say? I would be an object of pity and derision, I decided as we bounced north. I would be suffocated by their sympathy, choked by their concern.

We drew up outside my flat and I saw the 'For Sale' sign.

It would have to come down, I realised; I wouldn't be going anywhere now. And for the first time I felt a flutter of something like relief, because Clapham Common isn't really my scene. And I knew that the one thing I wouldn't miss about seeing Dom was that twice-weekly fifteen-stop trip down the Northern Line. Then I realised, with a stab of dismay, that I'd have to retrieve my stuff from his flat. There wasn't much; very little, in fact, considering that we'd been engaged. Just my toothbrush, an old jacket and some books. Dom said he didn't want me to leave too much there in case Madge thought we were 'living in sin'. And I was just wondering how I'd get my things back, and thinking how agonising this would be, when I noticed two bulging Safeway bags leaning against the front door. Stapled to one was an envelope marked 'Minty' in a familiar backward-sloping hand. I turned the key in the lock, picked them up, and went into the silence of my flat. I grabbed a knife from a kitchen drawer and opened the envelope with a pounding heart.

I thought this would make it easier for you, Minty. Sorry, but I just knew it wasn't right. No hard feelings?
Best wishes, Dom.

Best wishes! Best wishes? The man who just four days ago I was set to marry; the man whose children I was going to have; the man whose boxer shorts I had washed – and ironed – was now politely sending me *best wishes*? And actually, if you don't mind my saying so, I *do* have hard feelings, Dom! In fact, they're as hard as granite or flint. No hard feelings? They're as hard as an unripe pear. And look how quickly he'd returned my things! Hardly am I back from my honeymoon before I'm bundled out of his life in two plastic bags. Outrageous! After what he did. *Outrageous*! For all he knew, I might have thrown myself in the Seine.

Fired up by a Vesuvius of suppressed anger, I tore off my jacket, threw open the windows, and put on my rubber gloves. Others may drink or take drugs to relieve stress. Personally, I clean. So I hoovered and dusted and tidied. I mopped, and polished and washed. In a frenzy of fastidiousness, I even scraped the gunge out of the oven, and wiped the grime from the window panes. Only then, when I'd spent three hours in a state of hysterical hygienicity, did I feel my blood pressure drop.

Now I felt sufficiently calm to confront the wedding presents. Dad had left me a note saying he'd put these in the sitting room. I'd deliberately avoided looking in there, but now I opened the door. Attractively wrapped packages were stacked in vertiginous piles on the sofa and chairs and almost covered the floor. It was like Christmas, without the joy. They were encased in shining silver or pearly white, and topped with tassels and bows. Tiny envelopes fluttered on the ends of curled ribbons and bore the legend, 'Minty and Dom'. I looked again at the note from Dad. 'Everyone said you can keep the presents,' he wrote. 'They're for you to do with as you want.' I had already decided what I would do. I opened each gift, carefully noting down what it was, and who it was from. An Alessi toaster. Dominic had asked for that. It was from one of his clients. Right. Oxfam. An oil drizzler from Auntie Clare. That could go to Age Concern. Some library steps from Cousin Peter – *very* nice: Barnado's. A CD rack from Pat and Jo: the British Heart Foundation shop. His'n'Hers bathrobes from Dominic's old flatmate: Relate, I thought with a grim little smile. An embroidered laundry bag from Wesley: Sue Ryder. Two pairs of candlesticks: Scope. I plodded through the vast pile, mentally distributing the items amongst the charity shops of North London, as bandits distribute their loot. But the most expensive things I kept for Mum, to be auctioned at her next charity ball. The painting that her brother, Brian, had given us, for example. He's an Academician, so that would fetch quite a bit. A set of solid silver teaspoons from my godfather, worth three hundred at least. Six crystal whisky tumblers bought from Thomas Goode, and the Wedgwood tea service, of course. Mum was more than welcome to that – she'd paid for it, after all, and there was no way I could keep it now.

In fact, I wasn't going to keep anything. Not a thing. Miss Havisham might have turned herself into a living shrine to her day of shame, but I would do the reverse. There would be no reminders of my wedding: no yellowing gown, no mouldering cake – not so much as a crumb. I would divest myself of everything associated with that dreadful, dreadful day. I would remove every trace, as criminals attempt to eradicate the evidence of their crimes. I went and looked at my wedding dress again. The dress I hadn't even liked. The dress I had bought to please Dom. It was hanging, heavily, in its thick, plastic cover on the back of my bedroom door. And on the chair were my satin slippers, wrapped in tissue, and placed side by side in their box. And the bouquet was laid out on the windowsill, where it was already drying in the warm summer air, and the sequins on my veil sparkled and winked in the rays of the late evening sun.

On the bedside table were some Order of Service sheets. I picked one up, sat down on the bed, and turned it over in my hands. 'St Bride's Church, Fleet Street, London,' it announced in deeply engraved black letters; 'Saturday, July 28th'. And beneath, on the left, 'Araminta', and then 'Dominic' to the right. There were also two boxes of confetti. Unopened. At these, I almost cried. But I didn't. Instead I found myself thinking about Charlie, and about how well he'd tried to cope, and how awful it had been for him too, and how decent and good he is. And I thought how lucky Amber is to have him. He would never have done what Dom did. It'll be their turn next, I reflected, enviously, as I wrapped tissue paper round my veil. But their wedding will be joyful, I thought, unlike my cruel and shambolic day.

In my study were three boxes of embossed 'thank you' cards, engraved with my new married name. So on each one I Tippexed out Lane, and wrote 'Malone' instead. *Alone*, I realised bitterly. I thought it best, in the circumstances, to keep the messages brief, though in certain cases, I did mention Paris and how delightful I'd found the George V and how nice it was of Helen to come with me and how we'd sort of enjoyed ourselves, in a funny sort of way. But I avoided saying how 'useful' I was going to find their spice racks, or their milk frothers, or their hurricane lanterns, because it wouldn't have been true. They were all destined for other hands. And I must have been sitting there for about two hours I suppose, writing card after card after card, when it happened. The tears came, and I couldn't see to write any more. I was just so angry. *So* angry. It possessed me like a physical pain. How *could* he? How could he have hurt and humiliated me so much? And then just casually dropping off my things like that and suggesting there'd be no hard feelings?! *No hard feelings*?

I did what I had resolved not to do – I picked up the phone. I'd speak to him. I'd bloody well let rip with a few hard feelings. He'd be dodging my hard feelings like stones. My heart was banging in my chest as I started to dial. 01 . . . I'd tell him what I thought of him . . . 81 . . . I'd been so good to him . . . 9 . . . even inviting his . . . 2 . . . bloody clients to my . . . 4 . . . bloody wedding – people I'd never even *met*. And Dad picking up the bill for all this . . . 5 . . . without so much as a word . . . 2 . . . 3 . . . And then Dom just running out of church as though he were leaving some boring play. By now I burned with an incandescent fury that would have illuminated a small town. I'd *never* take him back after what he'd done to me. I was white hot. I was spitting fire I . . . I . . . Christ! Who was that?

The doorbell had rung, and was ringing again, hard. I slammed down the phone. Dominic! It was Dominic! He'd come to say that it was all a terrible mistake and to beg my forgiveness and to tell me that he would wear sackcloth and ashes for a year – no, two – if only I would take him back. I wiped my eyes and hurtled downstairs. Dominic! Dominic! Yes, of course I'll have you back! Let's wipe that slate clean, Dominic! We can work it out. I flung open the door.

'Domin– Oh! Amber!'

'Oh, Minty!' she wailed. She staggered inside and flung her arms round me. 'Oh, Minty,' she wept. 'It was so *awful*!'

'Well, yes it was,' I said. 'It was terrible.'

She was sobbing on to my shoulder. 'I don't know how he could *do* that.'

'I know.'

'It was such a *shock*.'

'You're telling me!'

'Such a *dreadful* thing to do.'

'Yes. Yes, it was. Dreadful.'

'*Woof*!'

Oh God, she'd brought Pedro, I realised. Her parrot. And then I thought, *why* has she brought Pedro? And why he is she here at ten p.m. with Pedro and a weekend bag?

'Amber, what's going on?'

'It's . . . it's – Charlie,' she sobbed.

'What's happened to him?'

'Nothing's happened to *him*,' she howled. 'It's what's happened to *me*. Oh, Minty, Minty – I've been *dumped*!'

There's nothing like someone else's misery to make you forget your own. I don't really like to admit this, but Amber's anguish instantly cheered me up. Even though I'm terribly fond of her, and have known her all my life. She staggered inside with her stuff, and sat sobbing in the kitchen. Pedro was squawking in the sitting room – I'd decided to install him in there because he's an incredibly noisy bird and our nerves were on edge.

Great fat tears coursed down Amber's cheeks as she told me what had occurred. It was all because of me, apparently. Or rather, it was because of what had happened to me in church. I suppose you might call it the Domino Effect – or perhaps the Domin*ic* Effect.

'When Charlie heard Dom say those things to you, about not being able to make those promises, it really affected him,' she explained between teary gasps. 'He said he knew then that he could never make those promises to *me*.'

'But you've always seemed so happy.'

'Well I thought so too,' she wept, throwing up her hands in a *pietà* of grief. 'I mean, *I* was happy.'

'I know.'

'But Charlie was so shocked by what Dom did to you that the next day he blurted out that we'd have to break up too.'

'I don't understand.'

'Because he said he knew he could never do such an awful thing to me. So he said it had to come to an end, now, before it went too far, because . . . because . . . He says we just don't have a *future*.' Her large green eyes brimmed with tears, then overflowed again.

'Why does he say that?' I asked, intrigued.

'Because of the *children*,' she howled.

'What children?'

'The children I don't *want*!'

Ah. That. The baby issue. It's the big issue for Amber. Or rather, there isn't going to be any issue, because Amber has never wanted kids.

'But he knew how you felt about having children, didn't he?'

'Oh yes,' she said, pressing a tear-sodden tissue to her blood-shot eyes. 'He's always known, but he was hoping I'd change my mind. But I'm not going to. And he should respect that, because it's my choice. But he can't see that,' she wailed. 'Because he's so selfish! He says he wants to have a family. Bastard!'

'Er, that is quite an important . . .' I said tentatively. 'I mean, I always assumed he knew your views and didn't mind.'

'Well, he does mind. He's *always* minded; and we've been together two years. And he said if I still don't want kids, then we've got to break up, because he'd like to find someone who does.'

'Hmmm, I don't entirely . . .'

'And so we had a huge row about it,' she went on. 'And I pointed out that I'm not a bloody breeding machine and he should want me for myself!'

'I see . . .'

'But he won't accept that.'

'Ah . . .'

'So I told him that in that case he'd have to move out,' she went on. 'And he said, "But it's my flat."'

'Oh yes. So it is.'

'So I came straight round here, Minty. Because I need somewhere to stay. Is that OK? Just for a bit.'

'Er . . . of course.'

'Thanks, Mint.' Her tears subsided. 'Gosh, it looks clean in here.'

I always thought Amber should have bought her own place. She should have done it years ago. It's not as though she didn't have the cash. She did. We both did. Granny was loaded, you see. Her books had made her rich. And when she died, we were each left eighty grand. Robert used his to emigrate to Australia; I put mine towards this flat. But Amber invested hers very cleverly so that she could live off the interest, leaving herself free to give up the day-job and write. She's a novelist too, like Granny. She bangs one out every year. And although she's only thirty-three, she's already written eight. But where Granny wrote good romantic fiction, Amber's are harder to define. For example, her latest book, *A Public Convenience*, is a sort of political mystery. It was published six weeks ago, but I don't think it's done very well. She's already halfway through her ninth novel, which will be published next June. Apparently this one's an 'unusual' love story, set in an abattoir. Anyway, Amber had always rented before she moved in with Charlie, and that's why she needed somewhere now.

I have the space – my flat's quite big. And in any case, I'd never have refused. We're first cousins but we feel more like sisters, probably because our mothers are twins. But to look at us you'd never guess that Amber and I were related. She has a shining helmet of honey-blonde hair and enormous, pale green eyes. She's absolutely gorgeous, in a foxy sort of way, with high cheekbones that taper to a pointed chin. She's slim, like me, though taller. Much taller. In fact, she's six foot one. But she likes her height. She's proud of it. No slouching or stooping there. She's rather uninhibited. And she's very clever.

Well, in some ways she is. She's also extremely well read. You can tell that from the way she talks. It's Thackeray this, and Dr Johnson that and William Hazlitt the other, and, 'As Balzac used to say . . .' She reviews books too, occasionally. It doesn't pay much, but it keeps her 'in' with the publishing crowd. Or what Dominic liked to call 'Lit-Biz'.

Anyway, I gave her the spare room, which isn't huge, but it's fine as a temporary measure, and she installed her things in there. And of course she had to bring Pedro – I understood that. They're inseparable. And although he's rather annoying, I'm fond of him too, in a way. He reminds me of Granny. And that's not just because Granny had him for so long, but because he sounds exactly like her.

'Oh, *super*, darling!' he likes to say. And 'No! *Really?*' in a scandalised tone of voice. 'I *say*!' he squawks sometimes, like an avian Terry Thomas. Or, 'What a funny thing!' – Granny used to say that all the time. He's got her cackling laugh too. Down to a tee. It's shattering, and so authentic that I find myself saying, 'What's so funny, Granny?' although she's been dead for six years. Whenever the phone rings he says, 'Oh, *hello*' – like that. And then, 'How *are* you?' And, 'Yes . . . yes . . . yes . . .' in a desultory sort of way. When he's not having one-sided telephone conversations, he whistles, and screeches and – this is really annoying – he barks. Whenever he hears the doorbell, he emits a volley of soprano yaps because that's what Granny's Yorkshire terrier, Audrey, used to do.

Pedro's a Festive Amazon, just over a foot long, with pea-green plumage, a blue and red cap, and a vivid, scarlet waistcoat which is only visible when he spreads his wings. Granny bought him in Colombia in 1955, when she was doing the research for *An Amazon Affair*. She'd stopped at a little town called Leticia, on the border with Brazil and Peru, and in the market was a man selling young parrots which were crammed into crates. Granny was so appalled she bought Pedro, and brought him home on the plane. He spoke very good Spanish in those days – he'd picked it up in the market. He could say, '*Loros*! *Hermosos loros*! *Comprenme a mi*!' – Parrots! Lovely parrots! Get your parrots here! And '*Page uno, lleve dos*!' – Buy one, get one free! He also used to shout, '*Cuidado que pica*!' – Watch your fingers! and '*Cuanto me dijo? Tan caro*!' – *How* much? You must be fucking joking! He's forgotten most of his Spanish now, though I think it might come back if we practised it with him. He loves really authoritative female voices – Mrs Thatcher's, for example. He used to shriek with excitement and bob up and down whenever he heard her speak. These days Esther Rantzen tends to have the same effect. Anyway, he and Granny were inseparable for almost forty years. And when she died, we didn't know how he'd cope. But in her will she left him to Amber – 'An Amazon for an Amazon,' she wrote wryly – and luckily, though parrots are loyal to one person, Pedro adapted well. In fact, they adore each other. He likes to ride around on her shoulder, and nibble her blonde hair, or listen to her reading out bits of her latest book.

Anyway, Amber and I have always been very close, so the next morning she offered to drive me round London while I disposed of the wedding gifts. She said she didn't mind, and that she'd welcome any distraction from her distress. She'd looked awful at breakfast, obviously hadn't slept, and she kept trying to put the sugar in the fridge.

'Are you sure you can concentrate enough to drive?' I asked.

She nodded. 'I'll be fine.'

'Woof! Woof!'

We'd already had the post – who on earth could that be? I opened the door to find a man standing there with a huge bouquet.

'Miss Amber Dane?' he enquired, as I stared at the profusion of pink roses.

'No,' I replied. 'But she's here.' I signed the proffered delivery sheet and carried the bouquet into the flat. The cellophane said 'Floribunda'. How *odd*. Why on earth would Helen send Amber flowers?

'They're from Charlie!' Amber screamed, grabbing the tiny white envelope. 'It's his handwriting, and he wants me back. It's only been a few hours, but he's already realised he's made a *dreadful* mistake.' She ripped open the envelope and removed the small, rectangular card. She read it in a flash, then I saw the light fade in her eyes.

'He should have sent a wreath,' she said bitterly, handing the card to me.

'I'm really very sorry it had to be like this,' Charlie had written. *'I do hope you're all right, Amber, and that you'll wish to be friends one day.'*

And I thought, Dominic didn't send me flowers. Dominic didn't offer me the hand of friendship. Dominic offered me nothing but a few of my possessions stuffed into two plastic bags.

'I can't bear to look at them,' said Amber, as she picked up her car keys and bag. 'I'll give them to the hospital.' So we went first to the Royal Free, where she left the bouquet at the reception, then we got on with the task in hand. We had to make a total of five trips because there were so many wedding presents and Amber's car is very small. Her black Mini hovered like a fly on the double yellow lines while I dived in with the gifts. I felt like Lady Bountiful with a horn of plenty as I distributed my brand-new luxury goods. Cut glass and kettles and picnic rugs flowed forth from my outstretched arms.

'Don't you want this?' said the woman in the Red Cross shop as I handed her an exquisite Waterford bowl.

'No,' I said firmly. 'I don't.'

Amber was a bit aggrieved about the Antonio Carluccio truffle-grater and the *River Café Cookbook,* but I wouldn't relent – it all had to go. Every item. Every atom. And as we drove round Camden and Hampstead her mood began to lift. And she went on and on about what a bastard Dominic was and how she'd like to kill him for what he did to me. And then she went on about what a bastard Charlie is, too, which isn't true at all. And I don't blame him for dumping Amber, though I'd never dare say that to her. So I tentatively asked her if she was sure she wasn't making a mistake with Charlie and that she wouldn't one day change her mind.

'Of course I'm sure,' she snapped. 'Do you really think I'd

want to go through *that*? It's barbaric!' And then she went on and on, again, about the awful things that happen when you're pregnant. The nausea and cramps, the swollen ankles and the varicose veins. 'The heartburn and the thousand natural shocks,' as she likes to put it, not to mention the haemorrhoids and hair-loss.

'Basically, Minty, a foetus is a parasite,' she declared as we pulled away from the kerb. 'It will suck the calcium out of your teeth, the iron out of your blood, and the vitamins from your food. It's like a fast-growing tumour, taking over your body.' And then she went on about the horrors of childbirth itself. The pain of parturition: the screaming, the stitches and the blood. But worse than any of these, she says, is the loss of mental power.

'It is a well-known fact that a woman's brain shrinks during pregnancy,' she said, with spurious authority, as I got into the car again.

'Well, yes, but not by the 70 per cent *you* claim,' I replied, as we set off. 'I think that statistic may be, you know, not quite right.'

'I'm sure it *is* right,' she said, pursing her lips and shaking her head. 'I have a number of *extremely* intellectual friends who, the *minute* they got pregnant, took out subscriptions to *Hello*!'

And then she started talking about Dominic again and what a 'total shyster' he was and how, if it hadn't been for him jilting me, Charlie would never have dumped her. I didn't agree with this analysis, but obviously I didn't say so. I never argue with Amber. I've never really argued with anyone, though I'm beginning to think I should. And then she went on and on about how she's going to put Dominic in her next book. And I said, 'Please, Amber, please, please *don't*.'

'Oh, don't worry,' she said with a sly smile as we hurtled home. 'I'll do it very subtly.'

Subtly? Amber has all the subtlety of a commando raid.

'No, really, Minty, I'll disguise him *totally*,' she went on in that pseudo-soothing way of hers. 'I'll call him Dominic Lane, thirty-five, a blond insurance salesman from Clapham Common, so no one will know who he is!' And she laughed maniacally at this as she jumped another red light.

That's just the kind of thing she *would* do, though. Because the truth is, she doesn't disguise people at all. It's appalling. I don't know how she gets away with it. For example, I featured in one of her books, *Fat Chance*, as 'Mindy', a frustrated radio reporter with ambitions to be a presenter. She'd even given 'Mindy' my long curly dark hair and the same address in Primrose Hill. Mum was in the next one, *The Hideaway*, which was a sort of Aga-saga set in London W9. And of course everyone knew it was Mum. In fact, Amber made it so obvious I don't know why she didn't just call the character Dympna Malone and be done with it. And when Mum and I eventually said that we'd really rather not be in any more of her books, thanks, because, well, we'd just rather not, she went into her usual spiel about how she was only creating 'composites' and how no one could *possibly* think it was us. And we'd heard that convenient, self-serving lie so many times before.

'Why don't you try using a little, you know, *imagination*, dear?' Mum suggested sweetly. 'Next time, why don't you just try and make the characters up?'

Amber gave Mum this funny, and not particularly friendly look, while I stared at the floor.

'Auntie Dympna,' she said seriously, 'I'm a *novelist*. It's my job to "hold the mirror up to nature," as the Prince of Denmark himself once put it.'

'Yes, but it's a *metaphorical* mirror, dear,' Mum pointed out without malice.

At this, Amber picked up one of her books and opened it at the second page. '"This novel . . ."' she announced, reading aloud, '"is entirely a work of fiction. Any resemblance to actual persons living or dead, events or localities, is entirely co-incidental." *Entirely*,' she added, pointedly.

So that was that. At least we haven't come off *too* badly in Amber's books, though I don't think Mum enjoyed being portrayed as an eccentrically dressed, late middle-aged woman, indiscriminately raising money by highly dubious and quite possibly criminal methods for any charitable cause she could lay her hands on. But it's worse for Amber's exes. She's terribly hard on them. In they all go. Unfavourably, of course, as paedophiles, axe-murderers, benefit cheats, adulterers, gangsters, drug-dealers, hairdressers and petty crooks. Totally defamatory. I'm amazed they don't sue. Too embarrassed, I suppose, to admit it might be them. I guess this is what Amber banks on, but one day her luck will run out.

Still, even though there are certain, well, tensions, there, I like having her around. At the moment we help staunch each other's wounds. Hand each other hankies. Try and make each other eat – I've lost six pounds since Saturday, and my hips are starting to show.

Amber's making Charlie pay to have all her stuff sent over in a van. She said that as he'd dumped her, he'd have to pay to get her out. So on Friday a white transit van pulled up in Princess Road and out came box after box. Loads of books, of course, and her computer; three pictures, and a couple of lamps; a bedside table and an easy chair, and several suitcases of clothes. And there was kitchen equipment too. I felt sorry for her as she took the things in, with tears streaming down her face. I was a bit concerned, to be honest, about where it would all go. Well, she'll only be here for a while, I told myself. And I've a big half-landing, and a shed.

'Hello!' squawked Pedro. The phone. Dominic! I picked it up. Dom –!

'Minty . . .' My heart sank. It was Jack.

'Hello, Jack,' I said warily.

'Minty, look . . .'

'What is it?' I said, though I knew exactly why he'd called.

'I won't beat about the bush, Minty. When are you coming back?'

I sank on to the hall chair.

'I'm not ready yet,' I pleaded. 'It's barely a week. Please, please give me more time.'

'Well . . .'

'Compassionate leave?'

'You don't qualify – you're not bereaved.'

'I am bereaved!' I moaned. 'In a way . . .' I just couldn't face them all yet. 'I'm . . . *bereft,*' I added quietly, swallowing hard.

'I need you here, Minty,' Jack said. 'And I think it will be good for you to come back to work. Get it over with. As you know, we're all very . . . sorry.'

'That's what makes it so much *worse,*' I wailed. 'I don't *want* your sympathy.' I was crying now. I couldn't help it. 'Dominic took all my dignity,' I sobbed. 'Every shred of it. Every last bit. I'd rather he'd have shot me!'

'I'd rather you'd have shot *him*!' said Jack. 'A hundred years ago someone would have done it for you. Would you like me to get up a posse?' he added. 'I'm sure I could round up a few willing volunteers to avenge your wounded honour.'

All at once, I had visions of Dominic being pursued round London by lasso-wielding cowboys, led by Jack, with a shining sheriff's badge. And at that, I laughed. I laughed and laughed. And I suddenly realised it was the first time I had laughed since Saturday. Then I laughed again, madly, and couldn't stop. I was hysterical. I was *literally* hysterical, I think.

'Nine o'clock on Monday, then?' said Jack brightly, after a pause. I sighed, deeply. Then sighed again.

'Make it nine-thirty,' I said.

The next day, Saturday, my 'weekiversary', I dealt with my wedding dress and shoes. These I took to Wedding Belles, an upmarket second-hand bridal dress agency just behind Earl's Court. I looked at the ranks of white and ivory gowns rustling on their rails, and wondered what tales they might tell.

'It's lovely,' breathed the proprietor, as she inspected it for ice-cream stains and drops of champagne. 'I should be able to charge £800 at least,' she went on enthusiastically, 'so that's £400 for you.' Or rather, for Cancer Research. 'You must have looked *fantastic,*' she added as she pinned a label on to the dress. 'Did it go well?'

'It was sensational,' I replied. 'It went without a hitch.'

'And did you cry?' she asked as she hung it up.

'Oh yes,' I said. 'I cried.'

And that was it. Nothing left. Or almost nothing. Dad had already taken Granny's tiara back to the bank. All that remained now was *Nearly Wed*, my bouquet and my veil. So on Sunday evening, at about nine, Amber drove me down to the Embankment, and we walked up the steps on to Waterloo Bridge. Gulls circled, screeching, over the water, and the windows from the office buildings flashed red and gold in the setting sun. A river cruiser passed underneath, and up floated music, voices and laughter. I watched the wake stream out, spreading and widening to touch both banks. Then I opened my bag, took out *Nearly Wed* and dropped it into the water. Amber and I didn't exchange a word as I removed my veil, and a pair of sewing shears. She helped me hold it over the rail as I cut into the voile, slicing the fabric into fragments which the stiff breeze snatched away. One by one they flew up, then fluttered down like confetti. Some pieces seemed to go on for miles, dancing up and down over the water like big white butterflies. All that remained now was the bouquet. I looked at it one last time, remembering how happy I had felt as it had lain across my lap in the beribboned Bentley just a week before. The petals were no longer plump and fresh, but hung limp and translucent on their stems. I recalled how much I had been looking forward to throwing it on my wedding day. I would throw it now, instead.

'Go on,' Amber urged.

I grasped the posy firmly, pulled back my arm, and hurled it with a force which lifted me on to the balls of my feet. It shot out of my hand and flew down. I heard the faintest splash, then saw it quickly borne away, spinning gently in the whorls and eddies which studded the surface of the river. In a few hours, I reflected, it would reach the open sea.

'Your turn now,' I said.

'Right,' declared Amber with a fierce little laugh, 'I'm going to change *my* life too!' She opened her bag, and removed from it a well-thumbed copy of *The Rules*. She smiled sweetly, ripped it clean in half, then tossed both bits over the side. 'I'm not *interested* in "capturing the heart of Mr Right"!' she yelled. 'I'm not going to give a damn about being single either!' she added. At this she took out *Bridget Jones' Diary*, and flung it as far as it would go. 'Bye bye, Bridget Bollocks!' she called out gaily as it hit the Thames. Then she took out *What Men Want*. Up that went too, high into the air, then down, down, down. 'I don't *care* what men bloody well want!' she yelled, to the amusement of a couple passing by. 'It's what *I* want. And I *don't* want babies. I don't even want marriage. But I *do* want my books to win prizes!'

Ah. That was a tricky one. I tried to think of something tactful.

'Maybe you'll get the Romantic Novelists' Prize,' I said, with genuine enthusiasm. But Amber gave me a dirty look and I knew that I had blundered.

'It's the *Booker* I was thinking of, actually,' she said tartly. 'And the Whitbread, not to mention the Orange Prize for Fiction. Of course, I wouldn't expect to win all *three*,' she added quickly.

'Of course not, no,' I replied. 'Still, there's a first time for *everything*,' I said, with hypocritical encouragement as we walked down the steps to the car.

'You must understand that my books are *literary*, Minty,' she explained to me yet again, as she opened the door. 'The Romantic Novelists' Prize is for' – she winced – '*commercial* books.'

'I see,' I said, though I didn't. Because I've never really understood this literary/commercial divide. I mean, to me, either a book is well written, and diverting, or it isn't. Either it compels your attention, or it doesn't. Either the public will buy it, or they won't. And the public don't seem to buy very many of Amber's. I wanted to drop the subject because, to be frank, it's a minefield, but Amber just wouldn't let it go.

'I have a very select, discerning readership,' she acknowledged, 'because I'm not writing "popular fiction".' This was absolutely true. 'So I accept that I'm never going to be a bestseller,' she enunciated disdainfully, 'because I'm not in that kind of market.'

'But . . .' I could hear the ice begin to crack and groan beneath my feet.

'But what?' she pressed, as we drove up Eversholt Street.

'But, well, writers like, say, Julian Barnes and William Boyd, Ian McEwan and Carol Shields . . .' I ventured.

'Yes?'

'. . . Helen Dunmore, Kate Atkinson and E. Annie Proulx.'

'What about them?' she said testily, as she changed up a gear.

'Well, they're literary writers, aren't they?'

'Ye-es,' she conceded.

'And *their* books are often bestsellers.'

Amber looked as though she had suddenly noticed an unpleasant smell.

'Clearly, Minty,' she said, as the speedometer touched fifty-five, 'you know *nothing* about contemporary fiction. No, I'm really going to go for it,' she vowed as we hurtled through our third red light. 'I'm simply determined to break through.'

As for me, I'd decided I was simply determined to survive.

'Erectile problems? Try – NIAGRA!' said the cheery pseudo-American voice-over artist as I pushed on the revolving door.

I entered the building, flashed a smile and my ID at Tom, then walked slowly up the stairs. London FM's output poured forth from every speaker; it's a bit like pollution – hard to avoid. It's in the reception area, the corridors and the lifts. It's in the boardroom and the basement canteen. It's in every single office, and the stationary cupboard. It even seeps into the loos.

'So remember – NIAGRA! Get out £9.99 and get it UP!'

Delightful, I thought, as I studied my pale reflection in the Ladies on the third floor. And then I thought, oh dear. You see, whenever London FM is going through a bad patch, the ads get worse and worse. In fact, they act as an unofficial barometer for the station's health, which is not very good right now.

'Unsightly fat on your upper arms?' enquired a solicitous female voice. No, I thought as I lifted them up to brush my long, dark hair. *'Ugly dimples on hips and thighs?'* I gazed at my shrunken middle. Nope. *'Introducing the new Bum and Tum Slim – THE fast, effective way to lose inches.'* I don't want to lose any more inches, I thought – I'd lost half a stone in a week.

I glanced at my watch, and a sharp surge of adrenaline began to make my heart race. Nine thirty. No putting it off. I'd have to go in and face them all now. At least then it'd be over with, I thought wearily, as I picked up my bag. The staring. The stifled titters. The sudden silences when I walked by; the giggles by the coffee machine, the furtive conversations by the fax.

Breathing deeply, I walked through the newsroom, passed the sales department and went into the *Capitalise* office. Mayhem met my eyes. Once again, the cleaners had failed to show. Books and papers spilled across desks; wastepaper bins overflowed. A spaghetti of editing tape lay on the floor, while an upturned cup dripped tea on to the carpet. In one corner a printer spewed out sheets of script which no one bothered to collect. Where was everyone? I wondered. What on earth was going on? Then, from the adjacent boardroom came a shrill, familiar voice, and I realised that the planning meeting had started early. I opened the door and crept in. Good. They were too busy arguing to notice me.

'CWAP!' screeched Melinda Mitten, our 'star' presenter, and I marvelled yet again at how a woman with a serious speech impediment could have become a professional broadcaster. Actually, there's a simple explanation for this: a) her uncle owns the station and b) her uncle owns the station. He's Sir Percy Mitten, the hosiery king. Very big in tights. And his stockings were always said by those who knew to be the *'denier cri'*. But two years ago he sold Pretty Penny for, well, a pretty penny, and decided to buy London FM. Like many a business baron he wanted to move into the media, and owning a radio station had become *de rigueur*. Once derided as brown-paper-and-Sellotape outfits struggling to survive, commercial radio stations had acquired a certain *cachet*. In fact, they were the ultimate accessory for the successful industrialist with his eye on a seat in the Lords. And so we turned up for work one day to find we'd been the target of a takeover. Our owners had sold us, like a used car, to the Mitten Group. No one had had a clue. Not even Jack. It was a *fait accompli*. He'd been informed about it on his mobile phone as he made his way into work. For a while, chaos reigned. No one knew what to expect. Words like 'rationalisation' and 'belt-tightening' were bandied about like balls. Anyone over thirty-five was told to expect their cards. Bob Harper, 'the voice of London FM', was summoned and summarily sacked and, the next day, Melinda arrived in a Porsche and a cloud of Poison.

'Hello, evewyone,' she'd said amiably. 'I'm the new pwesenter.'

In the event, apart from Melinda's arrival, life remained remarkably unchanged. There was gossip about us in *Broadcast*, of course, and there were also dark mutterings about Jack. Some claimed he had lost his authority and should have fallen on his sword. But he was forty, a dangerous age in an industry driven by youth. I was very relieved that he stayed. It was Jack who'd given me my first break. I didn't know anything about radio – I'd been teaching for five years – but all of a sudden I got the broadcasting bug, and so I pestered Jack. I wrote to him, and got a rejection letter. I wrote again, and got another. Then I went round to London FM, just behind the Angel, and asked his assistant, Monica, if he'd see me. She told me he was too busy. So I went back again the next day, and this time, he agreed. Monica showed me into his office. Jack was sitting staring at his computer. He was in his late thirties, and he was very attractive.

'Look, I don't mind seeing you,' he said, after a minute. 'But, as I told you, I don't have any vacancies. In any case, I only employ trained people.'

'Can't you train me?' I asked.

'No,' he said firmly, 'I don't have the money.'

'Well, how much does it cost?'

'That's not the point,' he said, slightly irritably. 'It's not even as though you've been a journalist.' This was true. I wasn't exactly an enticing prospect. 'Whenever I appoint someone,' he explained, 'I have to justify that choice to Management. And I'm afraid I just don't have the budget to run a kindergarten for beginners.' He handed me back my CV. 'I'm very sorry. I admire your persistence, but I'm afraid I really can't help.'

'But I want to be a radio journalist,' I said, as if that were all the explanation that was required. 'I really think I'd be good.'

'You haven't got any experience,' he countered wearily. 'So I simply can't agree.'

But I'd stayed in there, trying to make him change his mind. Looking back, I'm astonished at my boldness. In the end, he'd nearly lost his temper. He had shown me the Himalayan pile of CVs lying on his desk. He'd made me listen to the show-reels of three of his top reporters. He'd told me to try my luck making coffee at the Beeb. But, like Velcro, I had stuck.

'I'll work for nothing,' I said.

'We're not allowed to do that,' he replied. He leaned towards me across his huge, paper-strewn desk, hands clasped together as if in prayer. When he spoke again, he was almost whispering. 'You can't edit tape; you've never interviewed anyone; you've no idea how to make a feature, and you wouldn't know a microphone from a baseball bat. I need competent, talented, experienced people, Minty, and I'm afraid that's all there is to it.'

'OK, I know I'm not experienced, but I *am* very enthusiastic and I'd learn very quickly if you'd just give me a chance, and you see, I've been reading this book about radio production, so I already know quite a lot.'

'A book?' he said, wryly. 'Very impressive. Right,' he said, with a penetrating stare, 'what are "cans"?

'Headphones.'

'What does "dubbing" mean?'

'Copying.'

'"De-umming"?'

'Taking out all the glitches – the ums and ah's.'

'What about "wild-track"?' He had picked up a piece of yellow leader tape and was twisting it in his hands.

'Er . . . background noise, like birdsong, or traffic.'

'More or less. What's "popping"?'

'Distortion on the microphone.'

'OK. What are "bands"?' He had swivelled round in his chair and was tapping something out on his computer keyboard.

'Edited speech inserts,' I said.

'What's a "pot-cut"?' He went over to the printer, which started up with a high-pitched whine.

'An early coming-out point on an insert, when a live programme is running short of time.'

This quiz was starting to get me down. He tapped something out on his computer.

'What does "i.p.s." mean?'

'Inches per second.'

'Very good. What's a "simulrec"?' And now he was printing something out.

'I really haven't the faintest.' This was ridiculous.

'The same interview recorded in two different places and edited together later.' He was scanning the page with his eyes.

'What's a segue?' he asked.

'Oh, I don't know.' I didn't like this. I was on my feet.

'Music or speech which follows on from something else without an intervening explanatory link.' He folded the printout in two. 'What's a "Lyrec"?'

'I haven't a clue,' I said. 'And I don't really care any more.'

'It's a portable reel-to-reel tape-recorder, rather old-fashioned but still used for OB's. What's an "OB"?'

'An Outside Bloody Broadcast,' I said, sweeping up my bag from the floor. 'These are just boring technical terms,' I said. 'I don't have to know them. I want to be a reporter, not a sound engineer. I'm sorry to have bothered you. I think I'll try somewhere else.' I reached for the door handle, but Jack was holding that piece of folded paper out to me. I took it and opened it up.

'Right,' he said. He was behind his desk, staring at me with his dark brown eyes. 'That's a news despatch about the environmental protest in Lambeth. There are plans for a hyper-market there, with a new link road, and the eco-warriors are creating.'

'I know,' I said. 'In fact, my Moth–' I bit my lip. I decided to keep Mum out of it. 'It's been in the papers,' I said.

Jack clasped his hands behind his head, and leaned back in his chair.

'I want you to go down there and collect some material. I want some wild-track of the bulldozers, and a few vox-pops from the protesters – no more than six – which will accompany an interview we're running tomorrow. My assistant Monica will get you a tape-recorder,' he said, as he turned back to his computer. 'Make sure you hold the lead still so that it doesn't crackle, and keep the mike no more than a hand-span away from your subject's mouth. When you get back I'll find a spare producer to help you cut it down.' He looked at me, seriously. 'I expect you to mess this up a bit, because you've never done it before. But if you screw it up completely, I don't want to see you again.'

That's how I got started. And because Mum was there, collecting for the pressure group Eco-Logical, she knew all the campaigners and helped me get some really good quotes. Jack was happy with what I'd done, so he gave me a freelance reporting shift. Then, a week later, he gave me another. And then another. Soon, I began to compile longer pieces, quite complex ones – they took me ages to begin with. Sometimes – though I'd *never* tell anyone this – they took all night to do. Then, a few months later, it happened: one of the staff reporters was poached by Channel 4 News and there I was, on the spot. That was three years ago. My life seemed complete. I had fallen in love with radio; and then I fell in love with Dominic too.

'That weely is *cwap*!' Melinda screeched again, as I sat down in the boardroom on my first day back.

'I thought Wesley's idea was rather good,' Jack said.

'Oh, thanks, Jack,' simpered Wesley. 'Do you really think so?' And then Wesley noticed me, and smiled.

'Oh, hel-lo, Minty,' he said. Then his features folded into an expression of sympathetic concern. 'Minty, look, I'd just like to say –'

'Wesley!' Jack cut in. 'Kindly tell us all who you would invite into the studio for this item on astrology.'

'Well,' he began. 'Well . . .' Wesley *never* has any ideas. His mind was clearly as empty as the Outback as he pursed his lips, then stared at the floor.

'How about an astrologer?' Jack prompted crisply.

'Yeah!' said Wesley. 'Fab! Brilliant idea. There's that woman from the *Weekly Star* . . .'

'Sheryl von Strumpfhosen?' I offered.

'Yeah. Thanks, Minty.'

'She's no good,' I added bitterly.

'Minty, look,' said Wesley, 'I'd really just like to say –'

I felt my face redden, and my heartbeat rise, but Jack deflected him again.

'What other ideas do you have, Wesley?'

'Well . . .' Wesley began. 'Well . . .' He ran a limp hand over his balding head, then fiddled with the top button of his polyester shirt. He cast his watery blue eyes to the ceiling, and made funny little sucking noises with his teeth, but inspiration clearly eluded him.

'Anyone else?' said Jack tersely. Silence. As usual, none of the producers had a clue. They always leave it to Sophie, our new researcher. She's just out of Oxford, ferociously ambitious, and as sharp as broken glass.

'Sophie, are you prepared to help your clueless colleagues?' said Jack.

She consulted her clipboard, tucked her hair behind one ear and pushed her wire-rimmed glasses up her nose.

'There's a report out today on drug-taking in schools,' she

began crisply, 'and there's another appeal being launched to save Bart's. I see from the publishing catalogues that a new biography of Boris Yeltsin is published this week, so I've put in a bid for the author, and of course the shortlist for the Turner Prize is being announced in three days.'

'Excellent,' said Jack. 'Anything else?'

'Yes, I've spoken to Peter Greenaway's publicist and I've set up an exclusive interview pegged to his new film. We've also got another special report coming down the line from the Edinburgh Festival.'

'Good,' said Jack. But Sophie hadn't finished.

'There's been yet another resignation at the Royal Opera House; and I'd like to draw everyone's attention to a very interesting new survey on the declining popularity of marriage,' she went on enthusiastically. 'The statistics show that marriages have fallen to an all-time low, so I thought we could get Minty to compile a report on "the myth of wedded bliss" – it's an absolutely fascinating subject, you know –'

Jack opened his mouth to intervene, but Melinda got there first:

'How can we *possibly* ask Minty to do *that?'* she enquired indignantly. 'The poor girl's just been JILTED!'

My face reddened and my bowels shrank. Bloody Melinda. Stupid cow. Then, to my horror, Melinda stood up, and placed two fat, richly bejewelled hands across her vast stomach.

'I'd like to say that I think we should all be vewy *kind* to Minty,' she announced, 'because she's just been thwough something *tewwible*. Something weally, weally, *humiliating*. And I just want to say, Minty, that I think you're VEWY BWAVE!' She had finished. She sat down and beamed at everyone, as though expecting a round of applause.

In the embarrassed silence they all looked at the floor, while I tried to remember when Melinda's maternity leave was due to start. It wasn't that long now. Two or three months? I couldn't wait. And then I looked at her again and I thought, Amber's *right*. She's right about the horrors of pregnancy, and here was the living proof. Melinda's fat, bare legs were veined like *dolcelatte*; she needed iron girders in her bra; short and plump to begin with, she looked as though she'd swallowed a tractor tyre. Particularly in those defiantly tight maternity clothes she sometimes wears. Today a skimpy T-shirt was stretched over her epic bulge. 'Let Me Out!' it read. No, let *me* out, I thought. And she's a really terrible broadcaster. She can't say her 'R's, for a start. And she makes *so* many fluffs – it's appalling. You could stuff cushions with them. I mean, she's always mis-reading her script. Spoonerisms, in particular, abound. Here are a few she's slipped up on recently: 'Warring bankers in the City'; 'The shining wits of New Labour'; and *twice* now she has managed to mispronounce the 'Cunning Stunts' theatre company, despite extensive practice beforehand. We all cringe – and the letters of complaint that we get! But it's all water off a duck's back to Melinda. She thinks she's marvellous. The *cwème de la cwème*. Well, she's certainly rich and thick. I mean, who but Melinda would have welcomed David Blunkett into the studio with the cheery salutation, 'Hello, David! Long time no see!' But if there's the slightest whiff of criticism of her, she goes bleating to Uncle Percy. In the end, that's why everyone tolerates her. We simply have no choice.

'*Vewy bwave*,' she muttered again, then gave me an earnest sort of smile.

You see, the fact is, she likes me. That's the awful part. Probably because she relies on me to write her cues. She's useless, you see. Especially when it comes to current affairs. For example, she thinks Bosnia Herzegovina's the Wonderbra model. Nor is she much better on cultural things. In May she astonished Ian McEwan – and all of us – by describing him as 'one of Bwitain's finest Shakespearwean actors'. Anyway, because she's so hopeless, she's forever asking me for help. And though I don't like her, I've always obliged. Why? Because I'm nice. That's what everyone says about me. 'Minty's really nice.' 'Why don't you ask Minty?' I hear them say. 'She'll help you,' and, 'Oh, just take it to Minty.' 'Oh, no, Minty doesn't mind,' they add. But actually, Minty *does* mind. Minty minds rather a lot. That's what nobody realises. And though I smile and nod, inside I'm in a *rage* because, recently, I've started to realise that I'm fed up with being nice. The fact is my colleagues exploit me. They really do. And it's beginning to get me down. Wesley's the worst. He never edits his interviews down in time, and then he rings me from the studio half an hour before he goes on air and says he's way over and please would I come and cut six minutes out of this feature, or five and a half out of that, and so I stand there, with my heart banging like a drum, slashing tape against the clock. I could really do without the extra stress, but somehow I can never say 'no'.

'*Vewy* bwave,' muttered Melinda again. And then her eyebrows drooped theatrically, and she flashed me this compassionate smile.

But I was determined to salvage my pride. I was determined to keep my vow. I was determined not to cave in. I was determined, *determined* to come through.

'I'm *perfectly* happy to compile that piece about attitudes to marriage,' I said stiffly. 'Why on *earth* would *anyone* think I'd *mind*?' They all shifted uncomfortably in their seats.

'OK, then,' said Jack, 'do it, and we'll run it tomorrow. But don't forget Citronella Pratt.' Damn! Citronella Pratt! I'd forgotten. *Quelle horreur* – and on my first day back.

'Do I have to?' I said, backtracking. 'I'd rather chew tinfoil.'

'I'm afraid you do,' said Jack. 'You know how it is.'

Yes, I do. You see there's *one* thing I don't like about working in commercial radio and that's the constant concessions we have to make to our sponsors and advertisers. For example, Mazota cars advertise regularly on London FM and, believe it or not, this affects our news priorities. Balkan massacres, Middle Eastern airstrikes and catastrophic earthquakes are wiped off the bulletins if there's anything about road pricing, or taxation on company cars. It's sickening, and I suppose it's corrupt; but we just have to live with it and remember that old adage about the piper and the tune. And Citronella Pratt, a right-wing housewife with a column in the *Sunday Semaphore*, falls into this category too. We often interview her for our programmes. Not because we admire her brain, which is mediocre, or her views, which are venomous, but because her husband is the chairman of Happy Bot, the nappy manufacturer which sponsors our weather reports. So to keep Mr Happy Bot happy, we have to interview his wife. And she would know if we used anyone else, because she listens to us all the time.

'Sorry about that, Minty,' said Jack, as the meeting broke up. 'Just a quick Citronella soundbite will do.'

I went over to my desk, which had been borrowed during my absence and left in a terrible mess. I began to clear up, then realised that someone was standing over me. It was Wesley and he looked distraught.

'Minty, I'd just like to say –'

'What?' I said, as I took my portable tape-recorder out of the top drawer.

'I don't know how he could do that,' he went on miserably, shaking his balding head. 'How could anyone do that to you?'

'How could anyone do that to *anyone*?' I said quietly, as I slotted in a clean cassette.

Wesley stood a little closer. 'You're so wonderful Minty,' he whispered.

Oh God, *no*. No, not this.

'You're so attractive . . .'

Please. *No*. I'd forgotten that my newly single status meant that I'd be fighting off boring old Wesley again. When I was with Dominic he'd at least had the decency to stop.

'I know you rejected me before,' he went on, with a martyred air, 'but I just want you to know that I'm still here for you.'

'Thanks, Wesley,' I said disinterestedly, as I plugged in the microphone. 'Testing, one, two, three, four, five. Hey, who's been using my tape-recorder? The batteries are almost flat!'

Wesley had now perched on the edge of my desk as I did my best to ignore him.

'Dominic wasn't right for you, Minty,' I heard him say as I

put in four new Ever-Readys. 'And look how he's let you down.'

'I'm not discussing it,' I said, rather sharply. 'Anyway, I've got far more pressing things on my mind, like this feature, which I have a day to prepare.' I got out my contacts book and turned to 'M' for marriage. Wesley glanced round the office to make sure he couldn't be heard.

'I'd do anything for you, Minty,' he murmured, 'you know that.'

'Then please let me get on with my work,' I replied. But he didn't seem to hear.

'I'd even leave Deirdre for you.' Oh no. Not *that* again.

'I don't think you should,' I said with uncharacteristic firmness as I picked up the phone. 'In fact, Wesley, I strongly advise you against *any* such course of action!' Wesley looked a bit shocked at my spiky tone of voice, and, to be honest, it surprised me too. I wouldn't normally have been so sharp, I realised, as I began to dial.

'Deirdre's just not very . . . exciting,' I heard Wesley say. This was true. They were a perfect match. 'But you're wonderful, Minty,' he droned. 'You're so clever, you're such fun –'

'Leave me alone please, Wesley.'

'You've always been the girl of my dreams, Minty,' he whined, with a wounded air. '*Why* won't you give me a chance?'

'Because – Oh, hello, is Citronella Pratt there? – because I'll never give *anyone* a chance, ever again.'

In the long run I was grateful to Jack for making me come back to work. I had very little time to think about Dominic as I rushed round London that first day, collecting material for my feature. I interviewed two couples who preferred to cohabit; a divorcée who refused to remarry; a woman who was happily single, and a spokesperson from the marriage charity, It Takes Two.

Then, with a sinking heart, I went to interview Citronella Pratt. I'd left her until the end, so that I could truthfully say

I was short of time. I always sit there, like a prisoner, an expression of polite interest Grip-fixed to my face, while she drones on about the success of Mr Happy Bot, or the new car they're buying, or the wonderful villa they're doing up in Provence, or the prodigious progress of the infant Sienna.

A pretty girl, who I knew to be the nanny, opened the door of the Pratt homestead in Hampstead, a rambling Victorian house in a road leading up to the Heath. 'Leave us, please, Françoise!' said Citronella, as though the girl were a lady's maid. And this surprised me, because Citronella often fills up her column with guff about her 'miracle nanny, Françoise', and how she's better than anyone else's nanny, and about the lavish gifts she bestows on her as an inducement to stay. Last week she bragged that she'd given Françoise a top-of-the-range BMW – there was no sign of this, however, in the drive.

We went through the toy-strewn hallway to the 'study', which resembled the childcare section of my local Waterstones. Books on child psychology, baby care and pregnancy lined the walls from floor to ceiling. This, they seemed to declare, with territorial emphasis, was Citronella's field of expertise. I glanced at her as I unravelled my microphone lead, and wondered yet again at the gap between her photo-byline and the reality confronting me now. The girlish image in the photo, chin resting beguilingly on steepled hands, bore little resemblance to the pneumatic, late thirty-something woman with grey-blonde hair and beaky nose who sat before me now. I also found myself reflecting on the power of patronage. Citronella had never been a journalist, and had nothing very edifying to say; but her views on women chimed with those of her reactionary editor, Tim Lawton. They had met at a dinner party six months before, and so impressed was he with her poisonous opinions about her own sex, that he had taken out his cheque book and signed her up on the spot. And so Citronella had become Goebbels to his Hitler in the war he was waging against women. Her pieces should have been headlined 'Fifth Column', I always thought, as week after week she set out to demoralise successful, single females. She wrote of boats leaving port, and of women left 'on the shelf'. She wrote of the 'impossibility of having it all'. Men, she had once notoriously opined, do not want to marry career women in their thirties. In fact, she went on, they do not want to marry women in their thirties at all. For thirty-something women, she explained, are no longer attractive, and so men – and who can *blame* them? – naturally want women in their twenties. In her piece the following week she had bragged that the twelve sacks of hate-mail she had received were simply 'proof positive' that she was right.

When not using her column to persecute single professional women, Citronella likes to boast of her own domestic 'bliss'. 'In our large house in Hampstead . . .' her pieces often begin. Or, 'In our corner of Gloucestershire . . .' where the Pratts have a country house. Or she will rhapsodise about the joys of motherhood as though no woman had ever given birth before. I adjusted the microphone and pressed 'record' with a heavy heart.

'I *do* think it's so *sad* that marriage is going out of fashion,' she said, sweetly, as she smoothed down her sack-like dress. 'When I think how happy my own marriage is –' *Here we go,* I thought – 'to my wonderful and, well . . .' she smiled coyly, 'very *brilliant* husband . . .'

'Of course,' I said, as I surreptitiously pressed the 'pause' button, and remembered the hen-pecked little man who had carried her bag at our Christmas party.

'. . . then I *grieve* for the women today who will never know such happiness. Now, I have many single women friends,' she went on. I did my best not to look surprised. 'And of course they're very *brave* about it all. But I know that their cheerfulness masks *tremendous* unhappiness. It's so sad. Are *you* married?' she asked.

This took me aback. My heart skipped several beats. 'No,' I managed to say. 'I'm single.'

'But don't you *want* to marry?' she enquired. She had cocked her head to one side.

'Not any more,' I said casually. 'I did once.'

'Why? Did something *awful* happen to you?' she enquired. Her tone of voice was soft and solicitous. But her eyes were bright with spite. A sudden fear gripped my heart. Did she know what Dominic had done to me? Perhaps she'd somehow heard, on the grapevine. It was sensational, after all. Everyone would know. My skin prickled with embarrassment and I felt sick to think that I would now be the subject of a kind of awe-struck gossip:

'– *Did you hear what happened to Minty Malone?*'

'– *What?*'

'– *Jilted.*'

'– *Good God!*'

'– *On her wedding day.*'

'– *No!*'

'– *And in the church!!*'

It was all too easy to imagine. I fiddled with the tape-recorder while I struggled to control myself. I mentally counted to three, to let the lump in my throat subside, and then I managed to speak. 'Nothing happened,' I said with nonchalant discretion. 'I just don't want to marry, that's all. Lots of women don't these days. That's why I've been asked to do this piece.'

Citronella composed her features into a mask of saccharine concern, then smiled, revealing large, square teeth the colour of Cheddar.

'But don't you think you're missing out on one of life's richest treasures?' she pressed on, softly, as her quivering antennae probed for my tender spots. I darted behind my bullet-proof glass.

'My opinions in this are irrelevant,' I pointed out with as much cheery bonhomie as I could muster. 'I'm just the reporter,' I added, with a smile. 'I'd like to know what *you* think.' I pressed the 'record' button again and held the microphone under her double chin.

'Well, I do feel very sad,' she went on with a regretful sigh – 'sad' seemed to be her favourite word – 'when I look at women of my own generation who have had, yes, admittedly successful careers, but who now know that they will never marry or have children. Whereas my life is just, well, magical.'

'But people marry so much later these days,' I said.

'I don't think that's true,' she said.

'It is true,' I said, with a toughness which, again, felt unfamiliar. 'According to my research,' I continued smoothly, 'the average age at which men and women marry has gone up by six years since 1992. And the fastest-growing group of new mothers is the over thirty-fives.' This piece of information seemed to irritate her, but I pressed straight on.

'However, the fact remains that the number of weddings has dropped by 20 per cent. I'd like to ask you *why* you think there's this new reluctance' – I thought of Dominic – 'to marry.'

'The problem *is*,' she began confidently, 'that there's such a chronic shortage of single men.'

'I'm afraid that's not right,' I corrected her confidently. Though despite my new boldness, my heart was beating like a drum. 'There are actually *more* single men than single women.'

'Oh. Oh . . . Well, let me put it another way,' she said. 'There are so few single men *worth* marrying. *That's* the problem. It's awfully *sad*. In my own case, well, I was *very* lucky. I met Andrew, and apparently, he was just bowled over.'

'I can imagine,' I said. I even smiled. She smiled back.

'And so, just seven years later, we were married, and we've been blissfully happy ever since,' she went on smugly. 'Terribly happy.'

This was getting me down. So I stood up.

'Well, thank you very much for your time,' I said with professional courtesy. 'I think I'd better be getting back now.'

'But are you sure you've got enough material?' she enquired.

'Oh, yes,' I replied. '*Plenty.*'

'Did you know that the Fred Behr Carpet Warehouse is having a half-price sale?'

'A half-price sale?'

'Yes – a half-price sale. Isn't that incredible?!'

'Incredible! Half-price, did you say?'

'Yes that's what I said – half-price. Imagine! That's 50 per cent off!!!'

'Did you say 50 per cent? I just can't BELIEVE it!!!'

'Nor can I – 50 per cent off!! I just CAN'T believe it EITHER!!!

'Nor can I!!! I just CAN'T believe it!!! I just can't BELIEVE it!!!'

Personally, I can't believe that our ads are now so bad. Lots of them are like that, presented as conversations between two increasingly amazed people. We used to have witty ads, ingeniously written mini-dramas brilliantly performed by famous actors. But now all our adverts are crap. The upmarket companies won't advertise with us any more because they know our audience share is falling. Worse, we're not even managing to sell all our advertising space, so our revenue's way down. When the figures are good, we all know about it because the sales team go round with deep tans from their incentive holidays in the Virgin Islands or the Seychelles. But at the moment their faces are as etiolated as chalk or Cheshire cheese. Not that we see much of them. We don't. They're on the phone all day, pitching desperately. Occasionally they come into the *Capitalise* office and give us grief if we've put an ad on air in an awkward place. We hate it when they do that, though I thought they were quite justified in blowing up Wesley for broadcasting an ad for the Providential Insurance Company – strapline: 'Because Life's So Uncertain' – during coverage of Princess Diana's funeral. He didn't mean to; as usual his timings were out and he was suddenly twenty-five seconds short. So he grabbed that ad because he knew it would fill the gap exactly. And it did. But the station got a lot of flak and Providential withdrew their account.

Wesley'd had lots of disasters like that, I reflected as I dubbed my interviews from cassette on to quarter-inch tape. The only reason he'd survived was because he'd been here so long he's unsackable. It would cost them far too much to get rid of him. They just don't have the cash. In fact, they don't have the cash for anything here, least of all the new digital editing equipment; at London FM we still use tape.

'Embarrassing nasal hair? Try the Norton Nostril Trimmer! –

Removes hairy excrescences from ears, and eyebrows too! Has removable head for easy cleaning by brushing or blowing! Just £5.95, or £9.95 for the deluxe model. All major credit cards accepted, please allow twenty-eight days for delivery!'

I glanced at the clock, it was five to seven.

'And now a quick look at the weather,' said Barry, the continuity announcer, with his usual drunken slur, 'brought to you by Happy Bot, the disposable nappy that baby's botty loves *best*.'

I turned down the speakers in the office. I couldn't work with that racket going on. I knew I'd be there all evening, editing, but for once I didn't mind. In fact, I was glad, because it gave me no time to think about Dominic. I was oblivious to everything as I sat there at my tape machine with my headphones on, my white editing pencil tucked behind one ear. My razor blade glinted in the strip lights as I slashed away, lengths of discarded tape falling like shiny brown streamers to the carpet-tiled floor. I love the physicality of chopping tape. It's so satisfying. Clicking a computer mouse on a little pair of digital scissors just isn't the same. But that's what we'll soon be doing.

As I wielded the blade, a tangled mess of cast-offs and cutouts fell on the floor at my feet. Citronella Pratt sounded like Minnie Mouse as I spooled through her at double speed: '*Very-happy – soawfulbeingsingle – terriblysad,pooryou – ohyesI'msohappilymarried – veryveryhappilymarried – Very*.' And I thought it odd that she needed to keep saying that, because I've always thought that happiness, like charm and like sensitivity, tends to proclaim itself. I salvaged one twenty-second soundbite from her fifteen minutes of boastful bile, then took my knife to the other interviews. Soon they were neatly banded up on a seven-inch spool, with spacers of yellow leader tape between, ready to be played out in the programme the following day. All I had to do now was to write my script. I looked at the clock. It was ten thirty. With luck I'd be home by one.

The office was deserted, everyone had gone home hours before. It had the melancholy atmosphere of an English seaside town in winter. I sat at the computer, and began to type. And I was just thinking how calm and peaceful it was and how the script wouldn't take that long to do, and I was congratulating myself too on not crying or cracking up on my first day back, despite the emotional stress I was under, when I heard the sound of a newspaper being rustled. It was coming from Jack's office. How *odd*. Who on earth was in there at this time? I opened the door. Sitting at his desk, at ten forty-five, quietly reading the *Guardian*, was Jack.

'Oh, hi, Minty,' he said.

'Er, hi. You're here late.'

'Am I? Oh well, I had some, er . . . stuff to do,' he said. Oh. That was odd. 'I hope your first day back wasn't too bad,' he added gently. 'Thanks for coming in. We need you.' And he gave me such a nice smile. So I smiled back. And there was a little pause. Just a beat. Then Jack lowered his paper and said, 'Are you all right, Minty?' And you know, how when you're really low, and someone you like and respect looks at you, and asks you if you're all right? Well, it's fatal. Before I knew what had happened my eyes had filled.

'It's OK,' I heard Jack say, as I struggled to compose myself. 'You can cry in front of me.' I sniffed, and nodded, and then a small sob escaped me, and suddenly my cheeks were wet.

'Come and sit down, Minty. It's all right.' I sat in the chair by his desk, and he opened his drawer and handed me a tissue.

'I guess you'll be doing this quite a bit.' I nodded. It was true. 'Can I give you a little advice?' he said softly. I nodded again. 'It's simply to try and remember that old expression: "And this too shall pass."'

No, I thought bitterly. This will *never* pass. A part of my life has been ruined. I'd been publicly deserted. I'd been ditched. I'd been dumped. I'd been discarded, dropped, dismissed. And it hit me that in the lexicon of rejection, all the words seem to start with 'D'. Dominic had disowned me. He had disavowed me. He had divested himself of me. He had disappeared. Through a door. Now he was distant. And I thought I'd *die*.

'Nothing stays the same, Minty,' I heard Jack say. 'And, for you, this won't stay the same.'

'It will. It *will,*' I sobbed. 'I'll never get over it. *Never.*'

'You will,' said Jack. 'And at least, here, you're among friends.' At that, he placed his hand, just for a moment, on mine. 'Now, how was the awful Mrs Happy Bot?' he asked, changing the subject.

'Well, she was . . . *awful*!' I said, dabbing at my eyes, and trying to smile. 'You know, the usual conceited guff. She's such a pain.'

'She certainly is,' he exclaimed. 'In fact,' he added, 'she's an absolute fucking pain in the *arse*!' And with that we both started laughing. And I suddenly wanted to throw my arms round Jack and thank him for being so nice. He has this cool, sarcastic exterior, but he's so, so kind. And he's so attractive, I found myself thinking, not for the first time. I'd had this secret little 'thing' about Jack when I first started at London FM. But nothing had ever happened because, well, he was my boss. And then he'd started seeing Jane and, not long after that, I'd met Dom. Still, Jack was lovely. A lovely man. But why on earth was he in the office so late?

'Aren't you worried about the time, Jack?'

'What?'

'It's eleven,' I said, glancing at the large clock on his wall.

'*Is* it?' he said, wonderingly. 'Oh yes, so it is.'

'Won't Jane be worried?' They'd only been married six months.

Jack didn't reply. In fact, he seemed to avoid my eyes as he reached for his jacket and put it on.

'You're right, Minty,' he said quietly. 'Guess I'd better be getting along.' Then he picked up his paper, and I saw that he'd almost finished the crossword.

'Yes,' he said, and he emitted a long, weary sigh. 'I guess it's time to go Home, Sweet Home.'

September

'What a funny thing!' screeched Pedro from his domed steel cage. Indeed, I thought, what a funny thing.

I was standing in the kitchen, where a strange sight had just met my eyes. All the cupboards, normally a refulgent white, had turned yellow overnight. They were plastered with primrose-hued Post-It notes. Every single one. They fluttered in the stiff breeze from the open window, like tiny Tibetan prayer flags, except that they tended to be deprecatory, rather than imprecatory, in tone. 'Snores!' said one, and then, in brackets, 'very loudly'. 'Could NEVER see my point of view', declared the next. 'Very poor judgement', accused its neighbour. 'Beginning to lose his hair', alleged a fourth. 'Just won't LISTEN!' snapped a fifth. 'Putting on weight', pointed out a sixth. '"Selfish"', announced the note on the freezer. 'Forgot my birthday', spat the one on the spice rack. 'Lousy taste in ties', trumpeted the one on the tumble dryer. 'Could be short-tempered', sneaked the one on the fridge. Everywhere I looked, every vertical surface, bore some unpleasant legend about Charlie. Amber must have used at least five packs.

'I *say,*' squawked Pedro. He emitted a long, low whistle. 'I *say,*' he said again. Then he clawed at the yellow Post-It on his cage ('Failed Ancient Greek O-level'), before shredding it with his razor-edged beak.

Poor Charlie, I thought as I peeled the one off the toaster ('Stubborn'), he didn't deserve all this. I put in two slices of wholemeal bread and turned it up to 'high'. There was a creak on the stairs, then Amber appeared, framed in the doorway in her velvet dressing gown, like some portrait by John Singer Sargent. What a pity, I thought. All that beauty, marred by bitterness.

'You've got to accentuate the negative,' she said, slightly sheepishly, as she removed a Post-It from the kettle ('Complete wimp') and filled it.

'You should do it too, you know, Minty,' she added as she unscrewed the jar of coffee ('Pathetic'). 'You'll find it really helps.'

'No, thanks,' I said wearily. 'It's just not my style.'

And then, out of curiosity, I tried to imagine what *my* yellow stickies might say. 'Jilted me, during my wedding, in front of every single person I know'; 'Extremely domineering'; 'Had a violent temper if crossed'; 'Constantly tried to sell insurance policies to my friends'; 'Very rude about my mother'; 'Dictated what I wore'; 'Criticised what I said'; 'Undermined me at every turn'. Oh, they would be far, far worse than anything Amber could come up with about Charlie. 'Shallow' was another obvious one for Dom, while 'Deeply neurotic' also sprang to mind.

Whereas Charlie's very stable. He really is. He's also honourable. In every way. He's the Honourable Charles Edworthy, you see, because his father's a life peer. And Amber told me that Charlie had been a bit surprised when Dominic had asked him to be his best man, because they hadn't known each other long, having only met through me. But I knew Dominic well enough to guess the reason at once – he'd thought it would look good in the 'Weddings' column of *The Times*. 'Best man was the Hon. Charles Edworthy,' it would say. But that announcement, like my marriage, had been unexpectedly cancelled.

In any case, I knew all the bad news about Dominic. I didn't need to write it down. It had been tucked into the back of my mind for the best part of two years. But the funny thing is that I'd accepted all those negative factors. It's not as though I wasn't aware of them – I was. They troubled me. And though, on the surface, I made out everything was fine, inside I was filled with dismay. So I did what I did at work. I edited the bad things out. I excised them, just as I remove the rubbish from my radio interviews. At work, I review all my recorded material, and then skilfully cut out the crap – all the bits that jar, or don't fit; the inarticulate, or plain boring parts, the hesitations and the repetitions – I remove them all, so that the end result is smooth and easy on the ear. And that's what I'd done with Dominic. But why? Why *did* I? People have begun to ask me that. Well, there's a complicated answer.

First of all, because I suppose I try to accentuate the positive. See the good things. And there were good things, too, about Dom. He was attractive, and generous, and successful. He was also very ambitious for me, which I liked. And of course he seemed to be very fond of me – though not, as it turned out, quite fond enough. But that's why I decided that I could live with all his faults. Because I thought he loved me. Because, out of all the women he could have had, he'd chosen me. And that was flattering. Then I'm not the sort of person to make a fuss, however unhappy I feel. As I say, I always like to keep things smooth and 'nice'. And that's the main reason why I kept quiet – because I hate confrontations of any kind and I really don't handle them well. Particularly when it comes to personal relationships. I'm terrified of giving offence. Because if I give offence, then I might be rejected. So I avoid giving offence, like the plague.

That's why I'm not going to say anything to Amber about the fact that she's making no attempt to find her own place. Nor am I going to complain about the way she leaves her washing up, despite being here all day. Nor do I intend to bring up the subject of the phone. She spends at least two hours every evening on it, droning away to anyone who'll listen about how 'bloody appallingly' she's been treated by Charlie. And I do wish she wouldn't do this, not least because I'd like to use the phone myself.

Amber, meanwhile, had opened Pedro's cage, and he was now perched on her shoulder, affectionately nibbling her hair.

They're very alike, I suddenly thought. Birds of a feather, in fact. They're strikingly good-looking, attention-grabbing, profoundly irritating and time-warped.

'*Super*, darling!' screeched Pedro, as she handed him a sunflower seed.

'I wish you'd learn how to say, "Charlie's a bastard,"' she said to him with a regretful air. This is extremely unlikely. a) Pedro was very fond of Charlie, and b) he hasn't added a single word to his vocabulary since 1962. He's like an old record in that way, and the needle is well and truly stuck.

'He's going in the next novel,' Amber said, with a smile.

'Who, Pedro?'

'No, Charlie, of course.'

'Oh dear. As what?'

'As an effete toff called Carl Elworthy who turns out to be a serial killer!'

'Poor chap,' I said.

'What do you mean, "Poor chap"?' she retorted, as she applied bitter orange marmalade to my toast. 'Poor *me*, you mean.' She bit into it with a loud 'crunch', then tore off a tiny piece for Pedro. He took it daintily, then his bulbous, black tongue ground it around his beak, like a pestle in a mortar.

'What a bastard,' she said again.

I wanted to tell Amber the truth – that I didn't blame Charlie at all. That I thought she was over the top. But I didn't because I'm a bit frightened of Amber, just like Charlie was.

'Scary, isn't she?' he'd once whispered to me, slightly tipsily, at a drinks party.

'Oh yes!' I said, surprised at his candour. 'I mean, well, you know, a bit!' And then we'd both blushed guiltily, like conspirators, and gone, 'Ha ha ha!'

'We're going to get *over* this, Minty,' Amber added, as Pedro waddled down her arm. 'We're going to forget men,' she said. 'We're not going to bother with the bastards at all. In fact, we're going to enjoy ourselves without them, we're going to . . .'

'Celibate?' I said wryly.

'No, *cerebrate,*' she announced happily. 'We're going to cultivate the life of the *mind*!' She stirred her coffee excitedly then buttered my second piece of toast. 'The key words for us, Mint, are Protect, Pamper and Improve – with the emphasis firmly on "Improve". And we're going to spend time with women, too, Minty. *Clever* women. I know,' she went on enthusiastically, 'let's start an all-women's book club! They're extremely fashionable – Ruby Wax is in one, and so are French and Saunders. We could call ours the BBBC.'

'What's that?'

'The Brilliant Broads Book Club!'

'I *say*!' Pedro squawked.

'We could have really *intellectual* evenings, with plenty of booze thrown in! We could hold them here!' she exclaimed. 'You don't mind, do you, Mint?'

'Oh! Well, no, all right, if you set it up,' I said as I picked up my bag. 'I haven't got time to organise it myself. And – Oh Christ, I'll be late for work!'

'Constipated? Then take Green Light for inner cleanliness . . .'

Oh God, not this one again, I thought, an hour later as I sat at my desk chewing the rubbery breakfast roll I'd bought in the canteen.

'Just one little Green Light and you'll be raring to GO! Only £3.95 from all good chemists. Or £5.95 for economy size.'

All of a sudden Jack appeared. He was tense. We knew this, because he was twisting a length of yellow leader tape in his hands.

'Meeting!' he barked. 'And you'd better have lots of ideas after our impressive performance in the ratings.'

We all knew about this – it was plastered over the front page of *Broadcast*. 'London FM Loses Grip! Audiences Right Down!' We'd slumped by a disastrous 10 per cent in the quarterly figures compiled by RAJAR. We trooped into the boardroom, where Jack was fiddling with the speakers, trying to eliminate the incessant sound of the output. It's like trying to cope with an unwanted guest, babbling away nonstop.

'Do YOU have athlete's foot? Then try Fungaway, the top-performance treatment for toe fungus of every kind. Fungaway works by –' Click. Jack had found the switch. Silence. Thank God for that.

Then Melinda's face lit up. 'I know!' she said. 'Celebwity diseases!'

'What?' we all said.

'Celebwity Diseases!' she announced. 'We could make it a wegular spot!' She then went on to explain that this Hollywood actor had herpes, and that director was said to have AIDS, and she'd heard that a well-known British soap star was known to have chronic piles, and why didn't we do a weekly feature in which the stars would discuss their ailments?

'Great idea, Melinda,' said Jack. 'We'll give it the thought it deserves.'

Melinda beamed, and shot me an excited smile.

'Anyone else?' said Jack.

This time, shaken by the declining audience figures, we had come fairly well prepared. Newspapers and magazines had been read, *Time Out* and *Premiere* studied, the *Celebrity Bulletin* had been scrutinised, and the Future Events List given more than a glance.

'– London Fashion Week.'

'– Tall Persons convention.'

'– New show by Theatre de Complicité.'

'– Alternative health exhibition.'

'– Royal Opera House – new crisis.'

Half an hour later we had come up with enough feature ideas and suggestions for studio guests to fill the next three editions of the programme. We'd bought ourselves some time.

'Minty's piece about marriage went down well with the listeners,' Jack went on. 'We've had lots of letters asking us to do more social affairs stories like that. So I'd like Minty to compile a series of in-depth features, and we could run one every week. Right. What are the big social trends of the moment?'

'Um . . . singleness?'

'– Divorce.'

'– Family breakdown?'

'– Child support.'

'– Nursery provision.'

'– Late motherhood.'

'– Fertility treatment,' added Sophie. 'The first test-tube baby, Louise Brown, is twenty-one this year,' she went on knowledgeably. 'We could use that as a peg to look at what reproductive science has achieved since then.'

'Minty could interview Deirdwe!' said Melinda happily.

'Why?' said Jack.

'Because evewyone knows that Wesley's been twying to get her pwegnant for *years*!'

'– er, anyone seen my stopwatch?'

'– good piece in the *Guardian* about Fergie.'

'– we really should do something about the cleaners.'

'– see *Prisoner Cell Block H* last night?'

'I know a *vewy* good fertility doctor, Wesley,' Melinda went on benignly. 'Not that I needed him myself!' she added with an asinine laugh as she tapped her bulging middle. 'I'll wite his name down for you,' she pressed on with tank-like persistence, as she groped in her bag for a pen. 'It's Pwofessor Godfwey Barnes.'

'It's quite all right, Melinda,' Wesley replied, curtly. 'I'm sure I'm quite capable of getting Deirdre pregnant in the conventional way.' It was a good retort, but I doubted it was true. I remembered Deirdre confiding in me at the London FM Christmas party that her lack of a baby was entirely Wesley's fault.

'It's certainly not my eggs,' she'd whispered, as we sipped cheap Frascati out of plastic beakers. 'I had my ovaries checked out and they're fine. Absolutely fine. My eggs aren't scrambled at all,' she went on with a tinkling laugh.

'Oh, well, good,' I said, feeling slightly embarrassed that she'd chosen to share this information with me.

'The doctor said it's all shipshape,' she continued. 'Even though I'm thirty-nine. He said it must be Wesley's sperm.'

'Oh dear.'

'It's lazy,' she giggled. 'A bit like him! But he refuses point-blank to come to the clinic.'

'Well, I hope he changes his mind,' I'd said. What else *could* I say? Poor Deirdre. She was laughing about it, but she was clearly very sad. I felt sorry for her. She was nice. And she'd lived with Wesley for eight years, with neither a wedding ring nor a child to show for it. And this must have been all the more galling for her, because she was the supervisor at their local Mothercare. No wonder she always looked so dowdy and downbeat.

'No, weally, Wesley, this doctor's jolly good . . .' Melinda was carrying on, impervious to our embarrassed coughs, while Wesley's face radiated a heat I could almost feel.

'Thank you very much, Melinda,' said Jack. 'Meeting over. Sophie, would you ring publicity, and tell them to make sure that all the radio critics know about Minty's series.'

Half an hour later, Jack and I had drawn up the plan for my Social Trends slot. It would be hard work, I reflected as I returned to my desk; but that was a good thing because then I'd have no time to think about Dominic. What's more, it was a good career move, and might take me closer to my professional goal.

'Post!' shouted Terry the delivery boy. I scooped my three letters out of the in-tray, and felt my heart sink. Oh God, not that creep again, I thought as I ripped into a carmine envelope, strewn with silver hearts. My stalker. We've all got them. Every single person who goes on air has their pet pest. Imogen who does the weather reports has an elderly man called Mike. He even turns up to see her at the station sometimes, but Tom never lets him in. Barry the announcer is stalked by a middle-aged woman called Fran. She knits him these hideous, neckless jumpers and interminable scarves. My pest is called Ron, and every few weeks he sends me a letter in which he mixes fanatical admiration with excoriating scorn – an unnerving combination. '*My dearest Minty,*' he began, as usual:

Just breaking off from my rocket science here to say how wondrous it was to hearken unto your dulcet tones again on the wireless last week. I could hardly drag my ears away from the set. I'd missed you, my darling. Where have you been? I was worried that you might have been 'doing it' with some other radio station and that I'd have to twiddle my dial to find you. Imagine my relief when I heard your phantasmagorical voice floating through the ether once more. You were talking about marriage, I believe, and may I say that my offer still stands. Your report was stupendous, Mint. Scrumptious. Your usual brilliant standard, in fact. But will you PLEASE LEARN HOW TO PRONOUNCE 'CONTROVERSY', YOU STUPID COW!!!! If you say 'CON-TROVERSY' one more time, I'm afraid I'll have to come round to London FM and SPANK YOU!!!

Your devoted and ever-loving Ron

Eeuuuugghhh. Into the bin it went. At least he doesn't send me things to eat, like some stalkers do. That's Rule Number One when it comes to Mad People Who Listen to the Radio and then Write to You: Never *ever* eat what they send – God knows what it might contain.

'What was that, Minty?' asked Melinda, suspiciously.

'Just another letter from my stalker,' I replied. 'Or perhaps I should call it a "sick note".'

Her face collapsed. 'Why haven't *I* got a stalker?' she whined.

'Why do you *want* one?' I said. 'They're sick and sad.'

'Because I'm the star pwesenter. *I* ought to have one too.'

'I wouldn't worry about it,' I said wearily. 'You're more than welcome to mine.'

'No,' she said firmly. 'I want my *own*. Evewyone else has got one. Why shouldn't *I*?' This was unfathomable. 'Min-teee . . . ?' She'd gone into wheedling mode. 'Would you give me a hand with my cues?'

'OK,' I said, wearily, as I went over to her desk. 'But then I've got to do my own work.'

'Now: Saddam Hussein,' she began, furrowing her brow,

'is it Iwan he's associated with, or Iwaq? I can never quite wemember.'

'It's Iwaq,' I said.

'This is going to be fun!' Amber called from the sitting room a few days later. She was 'busy' straightening the cushions in preparation for the first meeting of the BBBC, due to start in half an hour.

'It's going to be a real brain-fest,' she added enthusiastically, as I prepared supper in the kitchen. 'We should have a really stimulating literary debate, with so many brilliant women here.'

Amber had deliberately invited her four most intelligent friends: Joan, the astrophysicist, Frances the brilliant divorce lawyer, Jackie the geneticist and Cathy, the nuclear engineer. Amber loves the company of clever women. I'm happy in the company of nice ones, so I'd invited Helen, who I hadn't laid eyes on since our honeymoon. I'd rung her from work a couple of times, but she'd been uncharacteristically elusive. But finally I'd managed to get through to her, and she'd agreed to come.

Rather than spend the evening discussing just one book, we'd decided that for the first meeting, each of us would chat about a novel we admired. I was praying that Amber wouldn't be foolish or vain enough to –

'Let's do *A Public Convenience*!' she'd said. I had tried, as tactfully as I could, to talk her out of this. Apart from anything else, I couldn't bear to have to read it again.

'Well . . .' I began.

'Why not, Minty?'

'Er . . .'

'I hope your hesitation is not in any way connected with what that cow Polly Snodgrass said in the *Daily Post*,' she snarled. However, Polly Snodgrass's views, with which I was entirely in sympathy, were quite unconnected with my reluctance. The fact is, *A Public Convenience* is crap. The prose is not so much deathless, as lifeless, the characters so flat they might have been cut from the back of a cornflakes box.

'You know *why* Snotgrass did that, don't you?' Amber went on, as she opened a bottle of red wine. 'You know *why* she gave me such a beastly review?'

'Er . . . was it because you gave *her* book a very bad review last year?'

'No! That's not the reason!' she spat, as she sank into a chair. 'It's because the woman's *consumed* with jealousy.'

'Oh yes,' I said. Of course. I'd forgotten. It seemed to be Amber's answer to everything. 'Er, why is she jealous?' I asked. Amber rolled her eyes at the cosmic stupidity of my question.

'Because. My. Books. Are. *Good*,' she enunciated, as though giving directions to a cretinous foreigner. 'And. Her. Books. Are. *Crap*!'

I knew this to be untrue. Polly Snodgrass writes very well. She wrote a brilliant sequel to *Wuthering Heights*, as dark and as visceral as the Brontë.

'But to be, you know, quite impartial here for a second,' I ventured, 'I don't see why you would expect Polly Snodgrass to be nice about your novel when you had completely trashed hers.'

'Minty,' said Amber, with this slightly perplexed expression on her face, 'you don't normally argue with me about literary issues.'

This was true. I didn't. In fact, I didn't argue with Amber about *any* issues. Normally. But then I didn't feel quite so 'normal' any more.

'Well, why *should* she be nice about your book?' I persisted, disguising my new-found boldness with a nervous giggle.

'Because, Minty,' Amber began with the weary patience of an adult explaining something tricky to a slow-witted child, 'critics should be *objective*. They should put their personal jealousies to one side, otherwise they are palpably failing to serve the reader.'

'But in the *Evening Mail* you described her novel as having – correct me if I'm wrong – "all the appeal of an unflushed lavatory".'

'Yes,' she said, laughing snortily, 'I did! Thought it was

rather good, actually. But then you must bear in mind what she'd said the previous year about *The Hideaway.* She wrote, and I quote: "If this Dane were a dog, you'd put it down. As it was I struggled to pick it up."' Amber had an ability – of which she was perversely proud – to recite every bad review she'd ever received with word-for-word perfection.

'Oh,' I said, 'yes, that was a bit mean.'

'Mean?' Amber snorted. 'It was outrageous – and totally untrue! The literary world really is *beastly,* though,' she added as I whipped up eight egg whites for the chocolate mousse. 'It's full of talentless hacks who just use their reviews either to seek favours, or to settle scores. I'm going to bloody well *write* about it,' she announced, as she snapped a piece off the menier chocolate and bit into it. 'When I've finished *Animal Passion* I'll satirise all those bastards who've tried to belittle my books.'

'The literary world's already been done,' I pointed out.

'Has it?'

'Yes, in *Bestseller.*'

Amber ignored this. 'Can't we do my book?' she persisted. 'Go on, Mint. Please, please, *pleeease.*'

'Well, it's, er, not the done thing really,' I said carefully. 'To, er, discuss your own book. No reflection on *A Public Convenience,* of course, Amber – absolutely not. Splendid book. And I know you've sold, er, hundreds of copies.'

'So what's the problem?'

'Well, er, it's a bit like Elisabeth Schwarzkopf choosing eight of her own recordings on *Desert Island Discs,*' I replied. 'It just wouldn't go down very well.' I changed the subject by reeling off my short-list of suggested titles.

'*Captain Corelli*!' she said with a snort. 'You don't think that's any *good,* do you?'

'Well, yes – I do, actually. I'm not mad on the ending, but it's very vividly written.'

'And as for *The God of Small Things* – useless bloody book!'

'Well, she's sold 140,000 copies in hardback,' I pointed out. 'And over a million in paperback.'

'Yes, but she wouldn't have done that if she hadn't won the Booker, would she?' Amber spat triumphantly.

'Er, probably not, no,' I conceded.

'*Charlotte Gray*?' she groaned. 'Oh God. I can't *bear* Sebastian Faulks. It's just Mills and Boon with guns! I'll do *Enduring Love* by Ian McEwan,' she said. 'He's really quite good, you know. Shout if you need a hand,' she added, sinking into a chair.

'Oh no, no, no, don't worry, no,' I said as I frantically washed the salad.

'Why don't you make that really nice French dressing you do?' Amber suggested. 'But make sure you use Balsamic.' She sighed with frustration as she picked up her novel again. 'I just don't know why it isn't selling better,' she whined as I set the table. 'I blame the marketing people – they just didn't pull their finger out. I said I wanted a cinema campaign, and they wouldn't do it. Bloody ridiculous.'

Pedro squawked, then emitted a shrill peal of Granny's laughter.

'But that would cost millions,' I pointed out, as I passed a clean cloth over the wine glasses.

'I'm worth it, Minty,' she said. 'They should have pulled out all the stops.'

Amber was renowned throughout the publishing world for a number of things. She was notorious for comparing herself, in articles, to Dickens, Zola, and Tolstoy. She was famous for making dreadful scenes in bookshops if her novels were not prominently displayed. She was fabled for writing livid letters to critics who had rubbished her books; but she was best known for the inflated demands she made on her publishers, Hedder Hodline. 'How do they expect me to sell a *single* copy,' she added, 'when they didn't even give me posters in the Tube? I'll have to get them to put up the marketing budgets. Fifty grand at least.'

'But books sell largely by personal recommendation, don't they?' I pointed out as I chopped mushrooms for the home-made sauce. 'I mean, look at *Captain Corelli's Mandolin*: that had very little publicity, it just spread by word of mouth.'

'Clearly, Minty,' said Amber, shooting me a poisonous look, 'you haven't the *faintest* idea about publishing.'

'Well, I think your marketing people are rather good,' I said, thinking of the quotes they had managed to come up with on the back cover. For this they had doctored reviews of her previous books with the skill and nerve of a plastic surgeon, turning the scruffiest pigs' ears into the most lustrous of pearls. For example, Anthony Welch, writing in *The Times,* had famously described *Fat Chance* as 'quite stupendously awful – a stinker!' The Hedder Hodline publicity department had miraculously transformed this into 'Quite stupendous!' And Hedder Hodline had shown remarkable restraint too when it came to allowing Amber to include in her list of Acknowledgements a constellation of famous people, none of whom she had actually met. '*I am indebted to Tony Blair,*' she had written in the three pages of gushing gratitude which prefaced *A Public Convenience*. '*And I am profoundly grateful too, to my friend, Princess Michael of Kent. I would also like to express heartfelt thanks to Fay Weldon, for her tremendous encouragement and support.*' Now, Amber *had* met Fay Weldon, once. On a train. Fay Weldon had asked her if she'd mind awfully closing the window. In a paroxysm of appreciation, Amber went on to express her '*unending thankfulness to Gordon Brown, Twiggy, and, of course, my dear mentor, Sir Isaiah Berlin.*' I'd tried pointing out that Sir Isaiah Berlin had died a whole year before she'd actually put pen to paper. She'd assured me that no one would notice, let alone care.

'Publishers expect writers to name drop,' she'd said gaily. 'Just chuck in a few celebs – dead or alive!'

Amber picked up the book again and it fell open at the dedication page.

'If I'd known Charlie was going to dump me I would *never* have dedicated the book to him,' she said. 'I'll get it changed if there's a reprint. I'll dedicate it to Pedro instead. He loves me, don't you, darling? Now, Pedro, what do you think of this?' Amber picked up a page of her manuscript, and Pedro's golden eyes glazed over as she began to read aloud:

Cathy gazed lustfully at Tom over the mounds of gleaming viscera. Her gut instinct was to spill out her heart. To inform him how she felt. She watched his sweaty, shiny biceps flex as he stripped the hide from the steaming carcases. Brain was over-rated, she thought. What she really wanted was brawn.

'Tom' – she addressed his ripplingly muscled back. 'Tom, you know what, Tom, I've been thinking . . .'

'Woof woof!' Amber put down her manuscript and flew to open the door. Everyone had arrived at once. We sat down to supper, during which Amber held forth, yet again, about Charlie and about what a 'total shit' he was and how unceremoniously he had dumped her, and what a 'complete cad' he was. And everyone nodded sympathetically, though I was squirming and I noticed Helen blush and shift uncomfortably on her chair. Helen would never say so, but I don't think she likes Amber much. I think she finds her hard to take – a lot of people do. And I do too, sometimes, I don't mind telling you. But it's different for me, because she's family.

'I'm sorry I haven't called you,' Helen said quietly, as I made the coffee. 'I've been really . . .' she struggled to find the right word, 'rather overwhelmed lately. So many orders,' she added quickly. 'And I'm finding the early start for the flower market a bit hard going at the moment.'

'Don't worry,' I said. 'I really didn't notice and, in any case, I've been busy as well, thank God. No time to dwell on you-know-who.'

'Hasn't Dominic called you?' she asked.

'No,' I said, and a wave of rage – or something like it – swept over me at the mention of his name.

'Are you going to call him?'

'*No*! Yes. No. Perhaps. I don't know. No. No. Almost certainly not . . . Am I making sense?'

Helen nodded, and squeezed my arm. We rejoined the others in the sitting room, and everyone arranged themselves on the sofa and chairs. Then Amber kicked off with the Ian McEwan.

'Now, this is a clever book,' she began, 'with a satisfyingly ambiguous title. *Enduring Love* is about both the love that endures – the love between the protagonist, Joe Rose, and his girlfriend Clarissa – and a love that has to be endured, i.e. the unhealthy love felt for Joe by Jed Parry, a homosexual madman who becomes obsessed with him. Now –'

'*I* once had a man who was obsessed with me,' Joan the astrophysicist cut in. 'I hardly knew the guy,' she went on. 'I'd taught him for a term on quasars, but he was *convinced* I was interested in him and kept on ringing me up.'

'Please, Joan,' said Amber, 'I haven't finished.'

'Wouldn't take no for an answer.'

'As I was saying,' Amber persisted, 'Jed Parry develops an unexplained homo-erotic passion for Joe –'

'I had to change my number in the end.'

'– an obsession which threatens to destroy Joe's peace of mind –'

'It can work the other way too,' said Cathy, the nuclear engineer. 'A female colleague of mine was obsessed with a doctor,' she explained. 'She was mad about him – she told us all about it. She got herself taken on at his practice so that she'd have an excuse to see him. And apparently she kept turning up in his surgery, behaving like a complete Munchausen, inventing all these symptoms, including – get this – radiation sickness from her work on Sizewell B! But she admitted she just couldn't help it because he was so attractive and so nice and –'

'Look, can we stick to the book, please,' said Amber acidly.

'Anyway, he got married not long after, and that's what made her stop.'

Everyone tut-tutted at Cathy's story, except for Amber, who raised the book theatrically, and began to expound her thesis again.

'The opening chapter is described with heart-pounding tension. Five strangers are brought together as they struggle to hold down a hot-air balloon in which a little boy is trapped. Now the balloonist –'

'*I* once went out with a man who liked hot-air ballooning!' exclaimed Jackie the geneticist. 'We met at a DNAwayday. I went up with him quite a few times, but, to be honest, I didn't really like it. The noise from the burners is bloody frightening, it's like dragon's breath and – ooh, sorry Amber.'

'– as I was *saying,*' Amber carried on, 'the balloonist himself is saved, and the child comes safely down to ground a short while later. But in the meantime one of the rescuers, still holding on to the rope, has fallen 300 feet to his death. This catastrophe kick-starts Jed Parry's mania for Joe, a mania which places enormous stress on Joe and his partner, Clarissa. The book's really about a couple put under pressure by the intrusive presence of an outsider.'

'Well, that would be enough to break anyone up,' said Frances, the brilliant lawyer. 'When I was going out with Frank, my ex, something similar happened to us. You see, he had a colleague who he'd been quite friendly with, and when Frank and I got together this bloke just hung around all the time, and we could never get rid of him. Frank didn't want to hurt the guy's feelings because they'd been good friends, but when you start going out with someone you really want a little privacy, and this bloke, Adam, just didn't seem to understand that, so –'

By now everyone had stripped to their emotional underpants. No one was listening to Amber, and no one seemed to give a damn about the book. A discussion quickly developed about relationships, and how to conduct them without alienating your friends, and how you need your friends because at the end of the day the relationship may break up and then where would we all be if we'd neglected our pals?

'*Look,*' said Amber, furiously, after five minutes of this, 'the purpose of this reading group is to discuss *books*, not blokes!'

Everyone suddenly stopped talking, and stifled guilty giggles.

'Oh, OK, Amber,' said Joan good-naturedly. 'Well, my chosen book is *Armadillo* by William Boyd. Now, William Boyd is one of the –'

'– tastiest-looking blokes in the business!' said Jackie the geneticist with a drunken giggle. 'He is,' she went on. 'He's absolutely drop-dead gorgeous. I went to one of his readings once. I couldn't take my eyes off him.'

'Carry on, please, Joan,' said Amber, bossily.

'Anyway, *Armadillo* is a comedy, although it's darker than *A Good Man in Africa,* or *Stars and Bars.* Now, the hero of *Armadillo* works in insurance,' she went on. At this I thought of Dominic, with a dreadful pang. 'His name's Lorimer Black,' Joan continued. 'It's his job to sniff out fraudulent insurance claims, and to negotiate settlements by a mixture of persuasion, bribery and threat. He's a loss-adjuster.'

'*I* went out with a loss-adjuster once!' announced Frances. 'He was *terribly* nice. But he lived in Pinner and I'm in Kentish Town, and I just couldn't face the thought of having to go right to the end of the Metropolitan line to see him.'

'God, no, that *would* be a drag,' said Cathy. A heated debate then took hold with the speed of a forest fire, as they all expatiated upon the importance in London of living close to your lover.

'– No more than two postcodes away.'

'– or on the same Tube line, at least.'

'– you can end up spending a fortune on cabs.'

'– or sit fuming in traffic for hours.'

'Look, everyone,' said Amber, her temper fraying like an old Persian rug. 'What about William *Boyd*?'

To be honest, I didn't really mind about William Boyd, or Ian McEwan, or any of them. I was tired after working all day, then cooking supper, so I just let it all wash over me. It didn't bother me in the slightest that these clever women wanted to talk about men. Nor did I care if I didn't even get to talk about my chosen book. But Amber picked on me next.

'OK, Minty, your turn. And I think you want to talk about *Captain Corelli's Mandolin.*'

'Er, yes. OK.' I sat forward on the sofa. 'Well, you've probably all read it?' Everyone nodded. 'So I'll only be saying what you already know. Basically it's a war-time love story, set on the Greek island of Cephalonia. It's –'

'I went to Cephallonia four years ago,' said Frances, 'with Eric. He was the one I went out with before I went out with the one I went out with before Frank.'

'I see,' everyone said.

'We had a lovely time,' she went on. 'But we broke up not long after, because out of the blue he heard from an old girlfriend of his, and she told him that she was single again, and would love to see him and so, well, it was curtains for me!'

'What *happened*?' asked everyone, with the exception of Amber, who was rolling her eyes.

'They got married,' said Frances with a good-natured shrug. 'I guess it's one of those things. That's life. I'm just doing their divorce for them, actually.'

'Oh, nice,' we all crooned. Amber shot me a get-on-with-the-bloody-book look.

'Anyway, as I was saying,' I went on, '*Captain Corelli* is an unusual mix of carnage and high comedy. It's about occupation and takeover. The central relationship is the unconsummated affair between Antonio Corelli, the musical Italian captain, and the doctor's daughter Pelagia. The novel has a Latin American exuberance, and some of the language is very complex. I'm not sure about the way Louis de Bernières ends the book. There's a long coda which provides a sort of happy ending –'

'Well, we're all looking for a sort of happy ending,' said Joan. 'Whatever that means. But it doesn't necessarily mean wedding bells any more, does it?'

That was it – Louis de Bernières was drowned out by yet more animated gossip about men, and an impassioned discussion about the relative merits of marriage.

'I GIVE UP!' Amber shouted suddenly. 'A highbrow evening of intellectual stimulation seems to have degenerated into a HEN PARTY instead! Obviously, none of you wants to talk about books.'

There was a shocked silence, and then Helen spoke.

'Well, actually,' she said, '*I* do.' It was the first time she'd addressed the group all evening. 'I've brought a book with me,' she went on, as she opened her bag, 'and I think you all ought to know about it, because it's *brilliant*.' She held up one of these tall, slim paperbacks that suggest a serious sort of read. The title was *Pios*, and the author was Joseph Bridges. It was by Joe. Joe who we'd met in Paris.

'*Pios* is about the relationship between an autistic boy and his dog,' she said. 'It's set in Poland just after the war. It's really about the way animals have a unique ability to help heal the damage done to the human mind. The way they can open psychological doors. It's acutely observed,' she went on, 'it's also beautifully written, and I think you'd have to have a heart of stone not to find it very moving.' Everyone had gone completely quiet.

'It sounds *wonderful*,' said Cathy. 'Let me write the title down. *Pios*?'

'It's pronounced "Pea-yoss",' said Helen, as she handed Cathy the book. 'Apparently it just means "dog" in Polish.'

'Have you heard of him?' I asked Amber – just out of curiosity, of course.

'Oh yes, vaguely,' she replied, dismissively. 'I can't imagine it's any good.' Well, she would say that. I'm afraid she often gives debit where credit is due.

'It's superb,' Helen corrected her calmly, though I could see that her face had gone red. 'It says here that it was short-listed for two literary prizes.'

'Doesn't mean a thing,' said Amber crossly. 'It probably just means he was friends with one of the judges.'

'No, it's truly excellent,' Helen insisted, and then she looked at me. 'I think he's a writer worth getting to know.'

Ah. So *that* was it. *That* was why I hadn't heard from her. She was keen on Joe, but had been too shy to tell me. Or she didn't want to tell me that she'd fallen in love, and was happy, after what I'd just been through. But that would explain why she'd bought his book. It also explained why she'd been so keen for us to play table football in Paris. She'd fancied him. She'd said he was attractive, and that's why she'd insisted on playing. I cast my mind back to that day. I was still in such shock then that perhaps my memory wasn't that reliable. But I remember we'd all had a beer together after the game, and when I came back from the loo I did think that Helen and Joe looked rather ensconced. And why not? Just because I didn't want to give him my number didn't mean *she* couldn't. She obviously liked him. Well . . . fine. And that's why she'd been a bit elusive, because whenever Helen likes someone, she tends to go rather quiet and I don't hear from her for weeks.

'Have you seen Joe again then?' I asked her, casually, a little while later, as Amber showed the others out.

'He phoned a couple of times from Paris,' she said. 'And he's coming back to London next month. He's really nice, you know, Minty,' she added, pointedly. 'I'd lend this to you, but I haven't quite finished it.'

'That's OK. I'll buy a copy. It does look good. Anyway, give me a ring soon,' I said as she picked up her bag and made for the door.

'Yes, yes,' she said, with a slight hesitation. 'But I'm really a bit . . . involved at the moment.'

'Well . . . whenever you feel like it,' I said.

'Christ, that was a disaster!' said Amber, as I started to stack the dishwasher. 'A combined intellect the size of a small planet, and all they could talk about was blokes!'

'But that's what happens when women get together,' I said. 'However brilliant they are. I bet you if you were to put two Nobel prize-winning women physicists together, they'd probably end up talking about men.'

'It's pathetic!' said Amber, crossly. 'Honestly, Mint, it was a complete waste of an evening, not to mention a lot of hard *work*!' She stamped upstairs, while I finished clearing the kitchen. 'You know,' she called out, 'it was such a disaster I'm not going to damn well bother again!'

'I'm afraid I'm just not going to bother,' wrote Citronella Pratt in the *Sunday Semaphore*. 'I'm just *not* going to bother with my single women friends any more. I mean, yes, *of course* they have their good points,' she continued. 'They make *marvellous* godmothers, for example. Sienna's got six, and they all spoil her to bits. Constantly coming round with lovely presents. But then she's *such* an appealing child. I also think it's *wonderful* the way single women will always come to a dinner party at the very last minute; and they *never* complain when I have to sit them next to some rather *dreary* and unattractive man. So don't think I don't *appreciate* my single women friends. I do. However, I'm afraid they all commit one cardinal sin,' she went on mournfully, 'and it gets me down. They always end up complaining about the fact that they don't have *husbands*. It's really so boring and depressing. And although I'm *very* sorry for them and I think it's *very* sad, it's really *very* wearing having to listen to *that* all the time. They don't do it openly, of course. Not in so many words. But I can see through them. Because there they are, chatting away "happily" to me about their promotion, or their seat on the board, or their books, or their trips to Bhutan. And naturally I listen *very* politely, and only occasionally look at my watch. But I'm afraid I know the truth: underneath all that so-called "success" and "adventure" they're desperately miserable that they don't have what *I've* got. And they're all positively *drooling* over Andrew. But really, listening to all these desperate, sad, single women is a bore for us ecstatically happily married MOO's, or Mothers of One! (Sienna's just learned to say "convergence criteria", by the way.) So whenever my single women friends ring up now I'm inclined to reach straight for the "Please Leave A Message After The Tone" button. Because there are enough sad things in this world, without having to listen to one's unmarried women friends droning on about their *desperate*, unfulfilled lives. I'm sure you all agree.'

I was reading this mesmerising stuff in the office as I prepared for my piece on fertility treatment. I'd interviewed two women who were on the waiting list for IVF at the Lister Hospital. I'd also been to see a woman whose three children had all started life through egg donation. And I was going to interview the famous Professor Godfrey Barnes. But first, I had to get a quick quote from Citronella.

'Why can't she come down here?' I complained to Jack. 'It's a drag having to go up to Hampstead. If she wants to feature on our airwaves then she should get her saggy arse down to City Road.'

'Minty!' Jack exclaimed with an astonished expression. 'It's not like you to say something like that.'

I stopped, and thought to myself, no, it's not like me. It's not like me at *all* – whatever 'me' is these days.

'Mind you,' Jack added judiciously, 'I entirely agree. But unfortunately it's written into her contract that we go to her, and we just can't afford to alienate Mrs Happy Bot, especially not at the moment.'

So a couple of hours later I found myself standing on her doorstep again. The beautiful Françoise showed me in, and gave me what I thought looked like a conspiratorial smile.

'How's the BMW?' I said mischievously.

'Ze BMW? What BMW? I just have an old bike.'

'Oh. My mistake,' I said.

'Hello, Arabella,' said Citronella.

'Er, it's Araminta, actually.'

'Now, did you read my piece this week?'

'Er, no. Afraid I didn't,' I lied. 'Been rather busy.'

She was holding her handbag – it looked like a padlock – as she ushered me into the study.

'Tea, please, Françoise!' she called out, with a smart clap of her sausagey hands. As I got my tape-recorder ready we chatted in a general way about the statistics for infertility – one in six women trying for a baby are receiving treatment at any one time. We talked about the known causes – blocked fallopian tubes, abnormal sperm, ovary disorders and the effects of alcohol and cigarettes. But what I really needed from Citronella were some comments about the moral arguments surrounding fertility treatment. Is it right for doctors to play God, bringing about by science what might best be left to nature? And what about the ethics of egg and sperm donation, and the risks of multiple births? I unravelled my microphone lead and pressed 'record'.

'It is so *sad* that there are *so* many women who are unable to have children,' Citronella began, with a sympathetic smile. 'And of course for most women who seek treatment, only a *tiny* number will actually conceive.'

'Well, 15 per cent,' I said. 'I wouldn't call that tiny, compared with a natural conception rate of about 30 per cent.'

'Oh.' She looked displeased.

'And in fact some clinics, like Godfrey Barnes', have a success rate as high as 25 per cent.'

Citronella ignored this, apparently preferring, like Amber, to eliminate the positive.

'Now, I'm going to let the listeners in on a little secret,' she carried on. 'My own little Sienna didn't, well ... *happen* straight away.'

'Didn't she?' I asked politely, as I stifled an urge to yawn. I really couldn't have cared less.

'No,' she said. 'She didn't. And so I myself suffered, for a while, the *agony* of childlessness.' Her face had now assumed an expression of heroic forbearance.

'Oh dear.'

'But for me, the solution was not a test tube or a Petri dish,' she declared. 'It was not a syringe full of sinister, hi-tech drugs. No. For me, the solution was – THIS!' Suddenly Citronella had whipped out a red frilly corset with matching suspenders and was holding it aloft. It looked like something out of the Folies Bergères, painted by Toulouse-Lautrec after nine pints of absinthe. 'This is what we used to conceive Sienna,' she went on, laughing coyly. 'Let me describe it for the listeners ...'

'No, no, really, please, there's no need,' I said.

'It's a red satin basque, underwired –' I glanced at her flat chest – 'and cut enticingly low.' Anything less enticing than the image of Citronella dressed in this was hard to imagine. 'It has some very naughty details like these two flaps here –' she pointed to the chest. 'And the marabou trim along the straps. A friend of mine suggested it,' she went on, 'when I told her about our problem. So I bought it out of an Ann Summers catalogue, and, well . . .' She giggled. 'It did the trick. Within just three years, we had our daughter, so I can heartily recommend this approach to your audience.'

'What a nice story,' I said, whilst feeling sorry for Citronella that she'd had to put on sexy lingerie to get her husband to do the business. 'However,' I went on with as much tact as I could muster, 'I'd like to talk about the moral implications of reproductive medicine, rather than your own experiences.' I was desperate just to get the interview done, and get out. Eventually I'd managed to extract a couple of usable sentences out of her.

'I don't approve of fertility treatment,' she said. 'There are too many ethical issues involved. But those poor, *poor* women who are so desperate to conceive are hardly going to concern themselves with that.'

'I don't think women *should* concern themselves with the ethics of fertility treatment,' said Godfrey Barnes. 'I don't!' he added roundly. 'I don't give a monkey's about morals!'

We were sitting in his cluttered consultating room in his clinic near Camden Square, and I was delighted with his brilliantly uninhibited views. This would make great radio, I thought, as the cassette went round and round. He was forthright and robust – no mealy-mouthed circumlocution here. None of that mimsy, attention-killing, 'Well, on the one hand, this – but on the other hand, that. It depends . . .' sort of thing. Oh, no. He was almost reckless in what he said. He was also devastatingly attractive.

'My motto is, "Let There Be Life!"' he exclaimed, with a stentorian laugh. 'I'm here to bring babies into the world.'

This was fantastic. I was enjoying myself. I was actually *enjoying* myself, something I hadn't done for months – though, obviously, I wasn't actually flirting with him. It's very unprofessional to flirt with your subjects. And in any case I wasn't ready to start flirting with anyone yet. I was still so miserable about Dom. So, no, I definitely wasn't flirting. Absolutely not. Though I was glad that I'd bothered to put on scent, make-up, and my smartest little Phase Eight suit with the tiny slit up the side of the skirt. I flicked back my hair, then held the microphone a little closer.

'So you've got a lot of women pregnant then?' I said, with a kind of jokey provocation. He seemed to like this, because a broad smile lit up his handsome face.

'Oh yes,' he said, ruffling his right hand through his thick, auburn hair. 'I've made lots of women pregnant, hundreds and hundreds – as you can see!' He waved his right hand at the noticeboard, which was plastered with photos of babies. There were babies on their fronts, and babies on their backs; there were babies in high chairs, and babies in the bath. There were babies being pushed in their buggies, and babies being dandled on knees. There were babies in blue romper suits and babies in tiny pink dresses. There were twins and triplets. Boys and girls. He seemed to beam at them all with a kind of paternal pride.

'Do you see yourself as God?' I asked with a smile. 'That's how you're often described.'

He roared with laughter again, and I found myself laughing too. He really was an exceptionally charming and charismatic man. Thank God I remembered to put on some mascara, I thought, as I gazed into his twinkly green eyes.

'God is the creator,' he said. 'I'm simply creat*ive*. And don't forget, these women are paying – and fertility treatment doesn't come cheap.'

'Do you ever think it wrong that women should pay?' I asked. 'One of "your" babies – if I can put it that way – costs between five and ten thousand pounds.'

'Is it wrong for someone to pay to have a heart transplant?' he enquired. 'Or to pay to have their hip replaced? To me, an inability to conceive is simply a medical disorder, which reproductive science can cure.' He picked up a clean test tube and began rolling it between his hands. 'To me, being paid to treat an infertile woman is no more immoral than being paid to fit an elderly man with a pacemaker. In that instance, life is prolonged,' he added. 'In my own case, life is begun.'

'And finally, to what do you owe your exceptional success rate?' I asked. He laughed again, his handsome face creasing softly at eyes and mouth. Then, suddenly, his expression changed again, and he seemed hesitant, almost shy.

'I really don't know the answer to that,' he said. 'I just think I've been very lucky.' And he looked down, and then he looked up, and held my gaze in his. And somehow I didn't want to look away. In fact, my insides were melting. I wanted to sit there forever, and bathe in the light of his lovely, twinkly green eyes. What a remarkable man, I thought. I could have talked to him forever, but the interview had come to an end.

'That was *wonderful,*' I said truthfully as I stopped the tape. 'I don't know how I'll cut it down.'

'I'm sure you'll do it very well,' he said. 'You seem to be a capable young woman.'

'Goodbye, Professor Barnes,' I said, as I stepped out into the waiting room. 'It was very interesting meeting you.'

'Goodbye, Minty,' he replied. He shook my hand, and his eyes twinkled and sparkled again. 'Now,' he went on, clapping his hands together, 'my next appointment is with – Oh, there you are, Deirdre! That's it – come in, and let's get cracking!'

'It was rather embarrassing,' I said to Amber the following Saturday as we lounged by the koi carp pool in the Sanctuary spa. We were having one of our 'pampering' days. Amber had handed in her latest manuscript, and my piece on fertility treatment had gone down well. We had decided to reward ourselves with a day of sybaritic relaxation in an all-female environment.

'What did you do?' she asked, adjusting her thick white towelling robe. She reeked of geranium oil and patchouli from her recent aromatherapy.

'I just smiled at her, and said, "Hello, Deirdre!" What else could I do?'

'Did she seem embarrassed?' she asked above the gurgle of the fountain.

'Well, it's hard to tell. Actually, I think she probably was,' I said. 'Not just because I'd seen her in the clinic, but because she hasn't seen me since – ' I suddenly felt sick – 'the wedding.'

'Of course.' Amber grabbed my hand and squeezed it. 'Poor Mint.'

'So, Deirdre was probably just as embarrassed to see *me*. In fact, I'm sure she was,' I went on, 'because she wouldn't stop smiling. That's what people do when they're embarrassed: they smile to cover it up.'

'I bet it's the fertility drugs she's on,' said Amber with a grimace. 'All those hormones probably make you go mad.'

'Or maybe she's just happy that she's finally taking some action,' I suggested. 'I mean, she was grinning like an idiot as she went in to Professor Barnes' office. I don't know why Wesley wasn't with her,' I added. 'Perhaps he's already done his bit. Poor old Deirdre – I hope it works. She's so determined to have a baby.'

'And I'm really determined *not* to have one,' said Amber with a shudder. 'The thought of it makes me feel sick!' I looked at her lovely profile, and thought it a terrible shame. 'I always think Cyril Connolly put it very well,' she went on. 'He said that there is no more sombre enemy to great art than the pram standing in the hall.'

'Amber,' I said, fiddling with the frond of a neighbouring fern, 'can I ask you something?'

'Yes.'

'Something rather personal?'

'Feel free.'

'You don't have to answer if you don't want to.'

'It's OK. Go ahead.'

'No, really, because it's quite a difficult thing to ask someone, even if you know them very well.'

'What IS it?' she said.

'And I'd hate you to think I was being nosey.'

'Out with it.'

'Sure you don't mind?'

'Christ, I hope you don't conduct your interviews like this,' she groaned.

'OK. Right . . . Amber,' I said, 'if you're so keen not to have kids, then why, er, don't you get yourself sterilised?'

'Because, Minty,' she said, 'as you *well* know, I'm *terrified* of hospitals.'

Oh. I didn't know this, actually. I must have forgotten.

'I'm bored of all these books,' Amber added with an exasperated shrug. I looked at the pile of them stacked up on the wicker table by her side: *Stop Thinking Start Living; Happy No Matter What; The Power of Positive Thinking; Rainbows Through the Rain; Breaking Up Without Cracking Up; Pulling Your Own Strings; The Power is Within You; Be Happy – Now*!

'Don't they help?' I said.

'No,' she said. 'They don't. Bloody waste of ninety quid.'

After Dominic dumped me I'd found myself looking at self-help books like these, but none of them had appealed. I needed a book called, *How to Get Over It When You've Been Jilted in Front of Everyone You Know*, or *How to Maintain a Dignified Silence about a Dreadfully Embarrassing Incident in Your Past. How to Stop Having Homicidal Fantasies about Your Former Fiancé* would be a helpful one, too. Sadly for me, the shops didn't seem to have books with titles like these.

'God, Charlie was a bastard!' said Amber, yet again, as she put down *14,000 Things to Be Happy About*. And then she went on about him, non-stop, for half an hour. About how 'cruel' he was to dump her, and how 'callous', and how he'd 'wasted her time'. I mean, it's ridiculous. She's so self-deluding. Charlie wanted kids; she didn't. End of point. I didn't blame Charlie at all. He was a decent guy. He'd really tried to make it work. But he couldn't make it work because he and Amber were incompatible – or rather, their goals in life were. She keeps saying that what happened to her was 'shocking'. But it wasn't shocking. It was inevitable. And anyone could have seen it coming, because that relationship just wasn't working.

No, it was what happened to *me* that was shocking. A lightning rod. A bolt entirely out of the blue. I'd had no idea that Dominic could do that to me. I'd had absolutely no preparation for what happened. But do I sit here and bitch about Dominic and what a complete cad and utter bastard he was? No. I don't. And despite the awful thing that he did, and the fact that I still don't really understand it, I'm making steady progress. It's only been three months, but I'm moving on. Unlike Amber. I picked up a copy of *Elle* and idly flicked over the pages. And all of a sudden I found myself staring, mournfully, at one of the male models in a fashion feature. He reminded me a little bit of Dom. Something about the mouth. And his hair was a similar shade of blond. I let out an involuntary sigh.

'Maybe if,' I whispered.

'What?'

'Maybe if I'd put more effort into my relationship with Dominic.'

'Minty, what are you talking about?'

'Maybe if I'd put more effort into my relationship with Dominic, he wouldn't have dumped me,' I said quietly. Amber was staring at me. 'You see, I'm still trying to work out *why* it happened,' I explained. 'Maybe it was somehow my fault.'

'Minty,' said Amber, 'I have one thing to say to you: NO.'

'Maybe I could have done more.'

'No.'

'Maybe if I hadn't objected when *he* objected to the dress I wore for our engagement party.'

'No,' said Amber, again. 'Wrong!'

'Or maybe if I hadn't expressed regret about the fact that he wanted to go on honeymoon to Paris rather than Venice – having said which, I really didn't say very much about it. I didn't, you know, rub it in or anything.'

'Minty, nope.'

'Or maybe if I'd been a better cook.'

'I don't think so, Minty.'

'I mean, I'm not that brilliant at it.'

'You're a very *good* cook!' Amber retorted.

'Maybe if I hadn't talked too much when he was tired,' I sighed. 'He often was tired, you know. He didn't sleep at all well.'

'Minty, you're being boring.'

'Maybe if I'd shown more enthusiasm for fly-fishing. Maybe if –'

'Maybe if he'd been a decent, normal, *stable* man,' Amber cut in smartly. 'You must *stop* this, Minty. You're just deluding yourself. And worse, you're taking the blame. God, I'm getting bored of this place,' she added with a weary sigh. 'Pass me *Tatler* and *Harpers*, would you?'

I handed them across. I certainly didn't want to read them myself, because I knew I'd be unable to resist looking at the society wedding photos, and that would set me off. So I picked up *New Woman* instead, and was idly flicking through the fashion and the ads, when an article suddenly caught my eye.

'*ARE YOU TOO NICE*?' the headline demanded. '*Are you easily manipulated by others*?' it enquired. Yes, I thought to myself, I am. '*Do you constantly put other peoples' wishes before your own*?' Only if they want me to. '*Do you find it hard to say no*?' YES! '*Then you're a prime candidate for the Nice Factor.*' This, the piece explained, was a course for people who find it hard to say, or do, what they really want. I quickly scribbled down the phone number, then read on, with a thumping heart. '*Do you apologise when it's not your fault*?' Yes. But then it often *is*. '*Do you have a nice smile perpetually glued in place, while inside you're in a rage*?' Yes, yes, I thought, that's me. '*Do you constantly allow other people to set the agenda . . .* ?'

'Christ, I'm bored,' said Amber. 'I've had enough pampering, I think. Let's get out of here, Mint. Come on.'

'Oh.' I sighed inwardly. I wanted to stay a bit longer. We'd only been there two hours and we'd bought vouchers for the whole day. I was enjoying myself, it was so restful and calm.

'Come on, Mint,' said Amber, again. I reluctantly picked up my towel. We showered and changed, then walked down Long Acre towards the Tube. We looked in the windows of Paul Smith and Nicole Farhi, and then we came to Books Etc.

Amber drew to a halt. 'I just –' she began. Oh no. 'I just want to check how it's doing,' she said, as she went through the door.

I idly looked at the books as Amber searched the shelves. Then she went up to the till.

'*A Public Convenience*,' she said, 'where is it?'

'Sorry, what title was that?' the young man enquired politely.

'*A Public Convenience*!' she reiterated with theatrical puzzlement, as though she had said, *War and Peace*. But his face was as blank as a sheet of typing paper. We could hear no bells ringing there.

'Don't know that one,' he said, with a cheerful shrug. 'Never heard of it. I'll just look it up on the computer. Sorry, what was it called again?'

'*A. Pub. Lic. Con. Ve. Ni. Ence.*'

'Who's it by?'

'Amber Dane.'

'Nope,' he said as he tap-tapped away. 'Can't see it. Sorry, but we don't appear to stock that one.'

'Well, you should stock it,' said Amber, reddening with incipient rage. 'It's a *brilliant* book. It was number 63 in *The Times* top forty.'

'I can order it for you,' he went on helpfully. 'If you'd like to give me your name.'

Amber's quivering face suggested that an internal war was raging between ambition and embarrassment.

'Minty Malone,' she said suddenly, with a lop-sided little smile. 'My name's Minty Malone.'

I rolled my eyes and groaned.

'It'll take about a week.'

'Oh, now look here,' Amber went on. 'I'm sure you must have it. It's only been out since July.'

'Well, have you looked in the Contemporary Fiction section?'

'Yes. It's not there.'

'And have you checked in New Titles?'

'Yes. Ditto.'

'Then I'm afraid that means we don't have it.'

'Or,' she said, 'you *did* have it, and you've sold out.'

'Well . . .' he said carefully, 'I don't think that's the case, otherwise I'd recognise the name. What's the cover like?'

I wandered round the shop while Amber argued about her novel. Shiny book jackets featuring women in wedding dresses seemed to thrust themselves into my face. *Well Groomed*! punned one, *Altar Ego,* quipped a second; *Hitched,* said a third, and of course, *Lucy Sullivan is Getting Married.* Unlike Minty Malone, I thought bitterly. I spotted *A Sudden Change of Heart* by Barbara Taylor Bradford, and *What About Me*? by Alan Smith. Everywhere I looked there were fanged traps to catch my heart. I glanced at the Contemporary Fiction shelf. There was no sign of Amber's novel, but there were five copies of Joe's, and underneath was a tiny review, which had been hand-written by one of the staff:

This book is a gem. I loved it. In fact, it made me late for work. Although it's about a boy and his dog, it's told in an unsentimental way which makes it all the more powerful. This is a redemptive story which moved me to tears and laughter and lived with me long after I'd turned the final page.

Ruth

On a table nearby there were another eight to ten copies of *Pios* stacked up in a neat pile. A woman had picked one up and was turning it over in her hands. I watched her eyes scan the blurb, and then she took it over to the till. I decided to buy one too, just out of curiosity, of course, as we'd met. And I was standing in the queue, looking at Joe's photo on the inside back cover, and thinking that Helen was right, he really *was* quite good-looking in an unshowy, slightly scruffy sort of way, when Amber strode up to the counter, her face aflame.

'What the HELL do you think THIS is?' she demanded.

'Oh,' he said. 'Yes, I remember now. We did order one copy. I'm sorry about that. Where did you find it?'

'In the Humour section!' she exclaimed. '*God* knows what it was doing in *there*.'

'Please, madam, don't touch the display,' he added, imploringly. Amber ignored him as she reached into the window and placed her book in the centre, at the front.

'These people in bookshops are complete idiots,' she said furiously, as we left the shop shortly afterwards. 'They don't know their Archer from their Eliot, Minty. You really have to spell it out.'

'K-o-s,' I said, 'o-v-o –'

'So it's not double '"S"' then?' Melinda enquired.

'No, just the one,' I explained.

'It's *so* important to get the spelling *cowwect*, isn't it, Minty?'

'Well, it doesn't really matter,' I said.

'*Doesn't it*?' She looked confused.

'No,' I said. 'Not for radio.'

'Oh. Yes. *Wight*,' she said, as the penny clattered to the floor. She furrowed her brow as she pored over the thick file of cuttings. 'I think cuwwent affairs is borwing, don't you?' she said with an exasperated sigh.

'Er . . . not really.'

'Mind you,' she added, 'the Clinton thing was quite interwesting.'

'Mmm.'

'I'm weally glad he got off.'

'He certainly did.'

'And the weason Wichard Nixon *didn't* get off was because what he did was *so* sewious.'

'Really?'

'Oh yes, Minty. It was far worse. I mean – *buggerwy* in the White House!'

'Mmm.'

'Now, could you just give me a hand with the House of

Lords cue too,' she went on. 'I'm doing a live interview with Bawoness Jay.'

'Well . . . Wesley really ought to be briefing you, Melinda. He's the producer, after all.'

'He says he hasn't got time. He's still down in the studio, editing. Pleeeease, Minteeeeee,' she whined. 'Go on. I've only got two hours before I go on air.'

I sighed heavily. This was always happening, and I had my own work to do.

'OK.' I glanced at Melinda's fat form as I tapped away on her computer. Today she was wearing a bump-hugging bodysuit in electric purple, and enough designer jewellery to bring a weightlifter to his knees. Her brown hair had been hennaed, then coiffed into a mass of springy curls. Her nails had been skilfully varnished, with two contrasting tones of blue. She reached into her Louis Vuitton shopper and took out a bundle of knitting.

'It helps me concentwate,' she said, as the large grey needles click-clacked away.

'Something for the baby?' I said, as I rewrote her cue.

'No, it's a mohair pwegnancy dwess for me.'

'Melinda,' said Jack. 'How's it going?'

'I've done another twelve wows.'

'The script, Melinda. The script.'

'Oh, it's fine. It's going weally well. Don't wowwy – I'm all wight, Jack!' This witticism seemed to amuse her and her expansive frame wobbled with mirth.

'We're doing the House of Lords cue,' she explained. 'And I think it's *quite* wong that these people should have all these special wights and pwivileges just because of who they're welated to!'

'I couldn't agree more, Melinda,' said Jack tersely. 'I'll be back to read your script in an hour.'

'He's always so bad-tempered these days.'

'Well, a little bit.' It was true.

'In fact, he's a pain,' whispered Melinda as she lifted a loop of wool over the top of her needle.

'No, he isn't,' I said. 'He's wonderful.' She pulled a face.

'Oh, don't be such a cweep, Minty,' she said.

'Melinda,' I said sharply, 'do you want me to help you with this cue or *not*?' She looked taken aback by my tone. And I was pretty surprised myself. It felt new. It felt rather good. It felt nice, being a bit less . . . nice. 'Well, *do* you?' I said again.

'Oh. Oh, er, yes,' she said. 'Of course I want your help, Minty. You're so bwilliant at it.'

'Sophie!' we heard Jack call out as he returned to his office. 'Would you please empty the bloody fax tray. God knows what we've got lurking in there!'

Sophie was on the phone, huddled over the receiver in a furtive fashion, and giggling, so I went to empty the overflowing tray. There were press releases for fashion shows and private views, new plays and film festivals, publicity puffs for C-list celebs, and masses of publishers' hype. As I stood at the machine it emitted a high-pitched warble and began to extrude another sheet. 'Come to the Candy Bar this Sunday!' it announced. 'Girls only. Dress smart.' A women-only party. That sounded quite good fun, and in my present man-avoiding mood it seemed to appeal. Amber would probably come with me. I noted down the address then turned my attention back to Melinda's script.

'OK, that's done. I've also written down five suggested questions about the voting rights of hereditary peers.'

'Thanks, Minty,' she beamed. 'You're a bwick.'

I sat down at my desk with my cuttings on adoption, the subject of my next big feature. As I went through the articles, identifying useful contacts and people to interview, I found one that featured Helen, who's always been very open about the fact that she's adopted. I decided to ask her if she'd give me a quote for my piece. So I rang the shop and her assistant Anna picked up the phone.

'I'm sorry,' she said, 'you've just missed her.'

'I'll call her tomorrow, then,' I replied.

'Well, she won't be here tomorrow,' Anna explained. 'That's why she's gone home early. She's going away for the weekend.'

'How lovely,' I said.

'Yes. She's going to Paris.'

'Oh. Wow. Well, great.' I was *right*, I thought, as I put the phone down. My analysis about Helen and Joe was correct. But I didn't have long to ponder this because then Wesley called up from the studio, desperate.

'Would you come and help me?' he said. My heart sank so low it was practically underground. And then I thought to myself, no – no more helping other people. No more. That's it. Enough.

'I'm rather busy, Wesley.'

'But I've got problems with my timings.'

'Oh, well, I'm sure you can work it out.'

'I'm not sure I can,' he said. 'Without your help.' Oh God.

'Well, how much are you over by?' I asked.

'Not much.'

'How much?'

'Well . . . about an hour and a half.' An hour and a half? Christ! The programme was only forty-five minutes long.

'Look, I'm busy,' I said. 'I've *got* to start phone-bashing for my next piece.'

'Please, Minty,' he whined. 'I won't ask you again. Promise. Promise. Promise. And I don't want Jack to know. He's really stressed: he's been twisting bits of leader tape all day.'

'Oh God, I . . . look, Wesley, I've only just finished writing Melinda's script – and *you're* supposed to do that.'

'I know, Minty. But I'm really behind. Please, Minty . . .' he whined, 'you're so good at it.'

'But . . .'

'You're so fast at editing.'

'Look, I've got –'

'I just don't think I can do it without you.'

'Oh.' God. God. God. 'All *right* then,' I hissed. 'But this is the *last* time I do this, Wesley,' I said with new-found directness. 'Do you hear me? It's the LAST time!' Then I slammed down the phone. And when I looked up, everyone was staring at me as if I were a stranger.

'Oh, Minty, I *knew* you'd help,' said Wesley when I opened the door of Studio B five minutes later. His pale blue eye seemed to mist over with gratitude. 'You're *so* nice, Minty,' he added as I surveyed his pile of unedited tapes with a sinking heart. 'In fact, Minty, you really are the *nicest* person I know.'

October

'Yes, I suppose he was quite nice,' I heard Amber say, as I took off my coat yesterday evening. She was on the blower, as usual. Our phone bill is equivalent to the national debt of Vanuatu. 'I know,' she went on seriously. 'It's awfully sad.' Sad? What was she talking about? I don't normally eavesdrop, but I was gripped. So I went into the kitchen, and put on the kettle.

'Yes . . . yes . . . tragic, really,' she said. Tragic? What was tragic? What on earth was she talking about?

'Yes, that's right,' she said. 'Stone dead.' Who was dead? What was this? 'It was at the Newport Pagnell bypass,' she went on smoothly. 'Yes, that's right, by the Little Chef. He ran into an AA breakdown truck. He just wasn't looking properly, and, well, that was that. Yes . . . awfully sad. Well, I always thought he was a hopeless driver. Lucky I didn't marry him, wasn't it? It could have been me!'

Charlie? She was talking about Charlie. This was terrible. Terrible.

'Yes, *awfully* sad,' she repeated. 'But there you go.'

'Amber, is Charlie . . . dead?' I asked, horrified, when she'd put the phone down.

'Well, no,' she said guiltily. 'Not exactly.'

'But you were just telling someone that he was dead. I heard you.'

'Well . . .' She narrowed her eyes. 'I was exaggerating slightly.'

'Is he injured?'

'No. No, I don't think so.'

'Is he hurt in any way?'

'Um . . . don't believe so.'

'Amber, why are you telling people that Charlie's dead?' This was outrageous.

'Oh, I'm just *pretending,*' she said, irritably. 'It helps me get over him, you see.' This was beyond the pale.

'Amber,' I said, 'I really don't you think you should go round telling people that Charlie's dead when he isn't.'

'Well,' she said petulantly, 'he's dead to *me*.'

'I'm sorry, but I think that's awful,' I said, as I went upstairs to get ready for the party at the Candy Bar.

'Minty?' Amber called out, as I ran the bath. 'If Charlie were, you know, dead, do you think he'd want me to go to the funeral?' I didn't grace her with a reply. 'And if so,' she added, 'what do you think I should wear?'

I shut the door, undressed, stepped into the hot water, and lay back in the glistening, scented bubbles. And I found myself reflecting, not for the first time, on the quiet pleasures of the single life. No one dictating to me, for example. I was enjoying that. Being able to go to bed at midnight, or even later. That was lovely, because Dominic always went to bed so early. Usually by ten, and often before, because he didn't sleep at all well. This meant we had to leave parties early, and I'd be lying if I said I didn't mind. I did. But he couldn't help it. I understood that. And of course I never said anything, because you have to accept everything about your partner. That's what Dominic always said. He'd say, 'You've just got to let me be my*self*.' But now, gradually, as time had begun to pass I'd given myself up to some of the simple joys of singledom. No need for constant compromise. Not having to shop and cook. Not having to sit on the Northern Line for hours at a time. The freedom to make my own rules. No longer having to align all my tastes to coincide with Dominic's. No longer changing colour, like a psychic chameleon, to suit or anticipate his moods. I could do my own thing. I could be completely selfish. I could lie in the bath, like this – just like this – for half an hour or more. I could wallow and let my cares drift away. Yes, maybe the single life wasn't so bad, I realised as I relaxed. It was certainly nice not being pushed around any more by anyone. It was really lovely in fact. It –'

'Minty!' Amber shouted from the other side of the door. 'Hurry up in there, will you – I need to get a Tampax!'

Oh God, I thought with a sinking heart, not more period drama. I hauled myself out, grabbed a towel, then opened the door.

'Thanks, Mint. And don't be too long, because I'd like a bath too.'

'Oh, I didn't know that.'

'And we ought to leave in half an hour, so chop chop.'

'Oh, OK,' I said wearily, as I pulled out the plug. Still, I told myself, I was very fond of Amber, and she was only here for a short while. Although, well, it had been three months, actually. Doesn't time fly when you're . . . ? Well, doesn't time fly.

Forty minutes later, we were ready to leave. Amber was wearing her new William Hunt trouser suit. Very sharp. It's navy with the hint of a pinstripe and she looked fantastic. She's so tall and slim that she can wear trousers well. I had put on a Katharine Hamnett calf-length silk dress, which was one of the many things Dominic absolutely hated. He said I was much too short for it.

'You see, Minty, you're a little, tiny person,' he'd said. And this had taken me aback, because I'd never thought of myself as short before. Not tall, of course. But not short.

'Well, actually, I'm five foot five,' I'd said. 'And five foot five isn't really short. It's medium. You just *think* I'm small, because you're tall. But actually I'm not really small at all.'

'Oh, darling, you *are,*' he said, and he wrapped his arms around me. 'You're really a very sweet, *tiny* little person.'

'I really don't . . . think I am, actually.'

'Yes, you are,' he said. 'And tiny little people shouldn't wear long things, should they, darling?'

'Er . . .'

'Should they?'

'Well . . .'

'Should they, darling little tiny Mintola?'

'Um . . . no,' I heard myself say.

I'd tried to wear it once more after that. When we were on holiday. In the Lake District, last summer. But he'd got very cross about it. Very, very cross indeed. And I was determined to stick up for myself a bit, so I asked him why he was so angry, and wasn't it a bit ridiculous, and why couldn't I wear it, and wasn't it my holiday too, after all? He'd had such an angry expression on his face, but I'd stuck to my guns and told him that the dress was perfectly OK, perfectly acceptable, and I just didn't understand his objections to it. At this he'd gone bright red in the face and started waving his arms about – which is what he does when he's angry, which is quite often . . . well, very often – and his voice had started to rise. And to distract myself I did what I usually did on these occasions: I mentally declined his name, from the Latin *dominare*, over and over again. '*Domino, dominas, dominat, dominatum, dominatis, domin*ant*! Domino, dominas, dominat . . .*' But still his voice was rising from its normal light tenor to a near-soprano, a sort of strained, falsetto whine, and suddenly he had shouted, 'Clothes are very IMPORTANT to me!' And, faced with his hysteria, I'd backed down. Because I didn't know how to cope. I'd never encountered it before. So I reminded myself, as I changed, that he's a very, very insecure man, and that's what I have to understand. And to understand is to forgive. Isn't it? But even so, it was very hard. Just a quiet life, I'd thought to myself wearily. A quiet life. An Equitable Life. That's all I'd ever wanted, but with Dominic the premiums were too high.

But now, I could please myself. So this evening I fished the dress out of the box under my bed and, with a naughty sense of liberation, put it on. And the funny thing is that even though Dominic had dumped me and everything, I felt guilty about wearing it. Isn't that silly? It doesn't matter any more! It was rather loose, of course, as I'd lost so much weight. But it looked fine. In fact, I felt quite glamorous in it as Amber and I walked over the railway bridge and entered Chalk Farm Tube. I glanced at the cream-painted wall on the southbound platform. 'CHARLIE EDWORTHY IS A SHIT!!' was still visible, in fuzzy, red letters, about a foot high. They really ought to remove it, I thought. Amber was lucky that no one had seen her.

'I'm going to do a course next Sunday,' I announced, as we waited for the Tube.

'Next Sunday?' she said. 'That's your birthday.'

'I know.'

'It's your thirtieth.'

'Yes. And I'm going to spend it doing a course called the Nice Factor.'

'What's that?'

'It's for people who are too nice for their own good,' I explained. 'It's for people who tend to get pushed around.' Amber's face lit up.

'What a *brilliant* idea, Minty,' she said. 'I think I need it myself.'

'Do you?'

'Yes. I do,' she reiterated above the roar of the arriving train. 'I mean, if I hadn't been so *nice* to Charlie,' she announced, as we rattled southwards, 'then he wouldn't have dumped me, would he? Yes, I see it all now,' she said, as we got out at Leicester Square and walked up Charing Cross Road. 'I was just too bloody *nice* to the bastard!'

The Candy Bar was hard to miss as the sign was in large, loopy neon letters in gaudy pink and green. On the pavement, a woman bouncer stood guard.

'Good – that's to keep the beastly men out!' said Amber vehemently, as we were waved inside.

The party was in progress downstairs, and as we descended the steps into the Stygian darkness we realised, with some surprise, that everyone was in fancy dress. Milling around in the sepulchral gloom were about a hundred women. They were wearing either period dresses, or trouser suits and cravats.

Funnily enough, and quite by chance, Amber and I fitted in quite well.

'Hello, I'm Melissa,' said a beautiful blonde in a pale turquoise satin evening dress and matching elbow-length gloves. 'I run the Candy Bar.'

'Great costumes!' I said admiringly.

'Well, on the first Sunday of every month we try to recreate the glamour of a more sparkling era,' she said. 'We wallow in the nostalgia of the twenties, thirties and forties. Now, would you like a drink?' she added. 'We have a range of really thrilling and seductive cocktails at the bar.'

A girl in a French maid's uniform mixed me a 'Greta Garbo', which seemed to contain a lot of Blue Curaçao. Then she made a 'Marlene Dietrich' for Amber, which contained Cointreau and cranberry juice. Above the mirrored bar a glitterball rotated slowly, sending refracted beams spinning and spangling across the walls. We sat on high stools and surveyed the feminine throng. Feathered fans fluttered in the warmth. Gloved hands reached for powder compacts. Pretty girls in miniskirts and fishnets circulated with trays of exotic cigarettes and shining foil-wrapped sweets. In one corner was the DJ, a big, bespectacled twenty-something woman in a blue silk flapper's dress.

'You've got to ac-cen-tuate the positive . . .' crooned Peggy Lee, *'e-lim-in-ate the negative . . . '* Amber bought a Russian cigarette and lit it. I watched the thin spiral of pale blue smoke pirouette in the spotlight over the bar. I glanced at the two women standing next to us. One was in a vintage forties dress, and her friend was in a black trouser suit. She smiled at me, so I smiled back.

'I like your bow tie,' I said, by way of conversation.

'Well, I wanted to wear my tuxedo,' she replied, 'but unfortunately it's at the cleaner's.'

'I wish I could carry off a trouser suit like that, but I'm not quite tall enough,' I said regretfully, as I sipped my drink.

'Well, I think the main thing about wearing trousers,' she

said, 'is that one should look like a *gentleman*.' We all roared with laughter at that.

'Minty and I are cousins,' Amber explained, as she drew on her cigarette. 'We live together in Primrose Hill.'

'Isn't that a bit . . . awkward,' said one of the women, whose name was Viv. 'I mean, being cousins and everything.'

'Oh no!' said Amber, with a laugh. 'Minty and I are very happy together, aren't we, Mint?' I nodded. 'I moved in a few weeks ago, and we get on like a house on fire, don't we!' I nodded again. 'Never a cross word, eh, Minty?' She gave me a hug, and I nodded again, blankly, and laughed. Amber really seemed to be enjoying herself. She'd already told them about her books, and made them write all the titles down, and now they were having a jolly good bitch about men.

'I've just been dumped,' Amber confided, tipsily. 'By Charlie.'

'Not Charlie Smithers?' said Viv.

'No, no – Charlie Edworthy. Do you know him?' she enquired, as she knocked back her drink. The two women shook their heads. 'He's ruined my life,' said Amber. 'Completely ruined it. But I'm not bitter. I'm getting over him now. I mean, you've got to move on, haven't you? You can't let it hold you back. And so I'm really making strides. I'm not one of these idiotic women who just go on and *on* and on about their exes. I mean, it's a bit stupid, isn't it?'

'Yes, it is,' I said quickly.

'You have to be realistic,' she went on. 'You have to be positive. You have to look ahead, not back; in front, not behind, because, let's face it, what's done is done.'

We all nodded in agreement. And then Viv said, 'I was going out with a dreamboat called Alex for a while. I thought it was going really well, but then, out of the blue, I got the Big E. It took me *eight months* to get over it.'

'And Sam – God, Sam was a *disaster*,' said Viv's friend, Sarah, rolling her eyes. 'I really thought that relationship was going somewhere,' she said with a drunken sigh. 'We had so much in common. Then one day I got this "Dear Jane" letter, totally out of the blue. It hit me so hard I had to check into a health farm.'

'How awful,' said Amber sympathetically, as she bought us all another drink. 'Well, Minty's got an even worse story.'

'No, I *haven't*!' I hissed. I refused to tell complete strangers about my disastrous wedding day. Just the memory of it made me feel sick. Amber's so damn insensitive at times.

'Go on, Mint,' she persisted, 'tell them.'

'No.'

'Well, I will, then.'

'Please don't,' I whispered hoarsely. 'It's very personal.' But by now the other women were agog.

'Well, you see,' Amber began, but she was interrupted by Melissa, who had stepped on-stage and was clapping her hands.

'Ladies!' she began, above the murmur of female voices. 'Ladies! The cabaret is about to begin. Would you please put your hands together for Lola and Dolores from Argentina, who are going to dance a tango for us!'

There were whistles and cheers as Lola and Dolores entered in figure-hugging dresses, clasped each other at shoulder and waist, and snaked seductively around the floor. We all clapped and cheered as Lola threw Dolores on to her back, then flicked her up again. It was brilliant. They strode off-stage on their vertiginously stilettoed heels to a chorus of wild approval. Someone got us another drink, then the DJ put on 'In the Mood', and everyone took to the floor. Everyone, that is, except Amber and I. We watched, mesmerised, as the women paired up, clasped each other in a ballroom pose, and spun and shimmied round the floor. And even though most of them danced very well, this looked a little odd, to be frank. Then the music changed again to 'The Boogie-Woogie Bugle Boy of Company B' and they all jitterbugged wildly to that, flinging one another across the crowded floor. And then the tempo changed again. We heard the opening bars of 'Blue Moon' and Viv and Sarah had wrapped their arms round each other, and Viv's hands were roaming over Sarah's curvaceous behind.

And everyone else was slow-dancing too. And long, lingering kisses were being exchanged. And now I realised that that sharp tang in the air was aftershave.

'Oh Christ,' said Amber, drunkenly. And then she laughed. 'I should have guessed,' she added. 'I should have guessed when I saw . . . *that*!' She waved her hand at the large black-and-white poster for the Emma Peel Fan Club.

'Aren't you two darlings going to dance?' said Melissa, as a black woman in a white tie and tails cradled her in her arms.

'Well, we might do – in a minute,' I said, cautiously.

'I'm sure everyone will want to dance with *you*,' Melissa added, seductively, to Amber. 'But first, there's a little surprise!'

The music faded, Melissa clapped her hands again, and announced: 'Ladies! Your attention please. For your further entertainment I am delighted to introduce Miss Suzie Saucisson!!!' Her right hand swept to the end of the room where a young woman was standing, bathed in the spotlight. She was draped in a floor-length feathery white coat, her face concealed behind a fan. The trombones struck up with familiar, brassy bravura. *Dee dee deee*! She wiggled forwards, dropped the fan, then the coat, and – good God! *Dee da dee da!* Underneath she was wearing nothing but a white basque, stockings and suspender belt, and long white, sequinned gloves. *Dee dee deee*! She put the index finger of her left hand in her mouth, and teased it off with her teeth. *Dee da dee da!* Then she pulled the glove off, and twirled it round her head to appreciative roars before flinging it into the crowd. *Dee dee – boom boom! Dee da – boom boom!* Then she did the same with the right. *Dee dee – boom boom! Dee da – boom boom!*

'Get 'em off!' all the women shouted. *Dee di dee! Da di da! Dee dee, da da*!

'Phwooargh! I'd like to give her one,' I heard Viv shout. *Dee dee deee!* Next Suzie kicked off her swansdown-trimmed mules and slowly unclipped her suspenders. *Dee da dee daa!* She rolled a white stocking down her left leg. *Dee dee deee!* She played with this for a few moments then hooked it round the neck of a woman in a tuxedo, laughing and throwing back her head. *Dee da dee da!* Her pale blonde hair shone in the spotlight as she wriggled out of her corset, held it up, then dropped it to the floor. *Dee da – boom boom*! *Dee da – boom boom! Dee da – boom boom! Dee da – boom boom!* All that was left was a white feather boa, the two ends of which were covering her breasts. *Dee di di, da di da, di dee dee DA DA!* She was doing the splits! And now – oh God – she was coming towards us. Writhing and wriggling. And she was looking at Amber. *Dee dee dee! Dee da dee da!* I turned my face away. I was almost catatonic with embarrassment. *Dee dee dee. Dee da dee da!* I mean, really, hadn't she noticed me? *Dee dee – boom boom! Dee dee – boom boom!* Amazing figure, though, I thought. *Dee dee – boom boom! Dee da – boom boom!* Amber remained as rigid as a plank as the girl removed her feather boa with a theatrical flourish then draped it round her neck. *Dee di dee, dee di dee, di dubity DO!* A tumult of applause arose as she threw her arms round Amber, and kissed her smack on the mouth. Then she drew back, squinted at me, and a look of shocked recognition crossed her face.

'Oh, gosh! Hello, Minty.'

'Hello, Sophie,' I said.

'Feel confident with the Re-Usable Incontinence Pad!'

'I hope you weren't too embarrassed,' Sophie giggled, as we stood in front of the mirror the following morning. She'd followed me out to the ladies loo.

'Provides Practical Protection, Day and Night!!!'

'No, of course not,' I lied.

'Can be re-used hundreds of times . . . '

'You see, I wasn't wearing my glasses. That's why I didn't recognise you.'

'I see.'

'The absorbent 2-ply material keeps moisture away from the skin.'

'I never wear them because it doesn't look sexy. And I like the fact that I can't see anyone properly – it makes me feel less inhibited.'

'Of course. You're terribly good at it.'

'The outer layer is waterproof nylon for added protection!'

'Thanks. I must say, your cousin's gorgeous.'

'Just £14.95. Please allow twenty-eight days for delivery.'

'Yes, but she's straight. We both are.'

'Then why were you there?'

'We didn't know what it was. I saw the press release on the fax and decided to go.'

'Oh, Melissa was just sending that to me to check,' Sophie explained. 'I'd been busy and hadn't picked it up.'

'But we had a great time.'

'Oh, good. Will you come again?'

'Er, don't know.'

'And now the travel news, brought to you by Skoda. There are delays at Putney Bridge while serious jams in central London have reduced speeds to three miles per hour . . .'

'And you won't tell anyone?' said Sophie, anxiously, as I dried my hands.

'Of course not. No.'

'Because I don't know what Jack would think.'

'Well, Jack's pretty distracted these days, so I doubt he'd think anything,' I said.

'I've GOT one!' shouted Melinda triumphantly as we went back into the office. She was holding up a letter, and grinning broadly.

'He's called Wobert. He's witten to me – look!' She waved the letter about, then began to read it aloud: *'Dear Melinda, I only listen to London FM because of you*!' she read. 'Isn't that fantastic?' She was beside herself with joy. *'I love listening to you on Capitalise. And in particular I love the way you can't say your 'R's.'*

Melinda's face suddenly expressed puzzlement. Then she burst into loud laughter. 'How widiculous!' she said. 'Of *course* I can say my R's. The man's obviously wight off his twolley!'

'Stalkers usually are,' I said. 'I'd throw it away, if I were you.'

'Oh no!' she said. 'I'm going to keep it. I'll show it to Uncle Percy,' she added. 'He'll hoot!'

'How is Uncle Percy?' Wesley enquired. We never get to see him. He hardly ever comes into the office.

'Oh, he's fine,' she said. 'Now, he thinks I ought to take the full maternity leave allowance,' she went on, as she clasped her expanding middle.

'Oh yes. Yes. Yes. You definitely should!' we all cried.

'I'm not sure,' Melinda went on, obtusely. 'I think our watings might go down if I do. I don't think Uncle Percy's thought of *that*!'

'I really would take the full amount,' said Sophie diplomatically. 'Those early months are absolutely crucial for a baby's healthy development. It's now been established that being parted from the mother in early infancy can have devastating psychological consequences, leading to a variety of behavioural problems in adult life.'

'It could even be the trigger for stalking,' I suggested. 'Breaking the maternal link in those critical first six months could lead to a later obsession with people in public life.'

'Oh, I'll think about it,' Melinda said. 'I'm not due to go until mid December.'

'I don't know *how* we'll cope, Melinda,' said Jack, who'd just walked in. 'But I'm sure we'll manage somehow. I'd like to see your script in half an hour, by the way.'

'Minteeee,' Melinda whined as Jack left the room.

'What?'

'Minteeee, will you help me?'

'Well, what is it? I've got to make some calls.'

'OK, just a quickie. Now: the Northern Ireland peace pwocess . . . tell me again – it's the Pwotestants who live in the south, isn't it? Or is that the Pwestbytewians? Could you just explain it all again?'

'We are not going to teach you to be nasty,' said David Chadwick, one of my tutors on the Nice Factor course the following Sunday morning. 'We are going to teach you how not to be so "nice". Because being nice gets in the way of doing what you want, doesn't it?'

Five heads nodded vigorously as we sat in the Business Design Centre in Islington. There was a middle-aged managing director whose secretary didn't like photocopying, so he ended up doing it himself. There was a thirty-something blonde who always got stuck with party bores because she was too nice to hurt their feelings; there was a retired dentist on the verge of a nervous breakdown because his wife was so domineering; then there was Amber, and me. Plus a woman called Jo who was running late and who was still on her way.

'Nice people tend to fall in with other peoples' wishes,' said David's co-tutor, Elaine. 'They want to keep everything smooth and "nice" in order to avoid offence. This means they are constantly sublimating their own desires.'

'Is it OK if I put my coffee on the floor?' I enquired, looking anxiously at the pale carpet.

'Oh dear. You've just been nice,' said Elaine, shaking her head sadly. 'You asked permission.'

'Sorry. I was only being polite.'

'That's the most common justification people use,' said David wearily. 'We don't mind what you do with your coffee,' he added. 'You can spill it all over the floor if you like.'

'Look, I'm awfully sorry but –' began Ronnie, the managing director.

'Please don't preface everything with "I'm awfully sorry",' interrupted David. 'That kind of "I really hate to bother you . . ." "I'm sorry to make a fuss . . ." is excruciating and immediately puts you at a disadvantage. Now, what do you want to ask?'

There was a pause while Ronnie struggled to ask a simple, direct question in a non-apologetic way. He ran his left hand through his thick grey hair, and fiddled nervously with his tweedy tie.

'I'd like to ask . . . what sort of people you've helped?' he said.

'Very good, Ronnie. Well, we've had divorcées who've given away everything to former spouses because they were too nice to claim their rightful share,' said David.

'We had one man who travelled from York to London every day because his wife refused to move south,' added Elaine. 'He was too nice to insist, but he'd had a heart attack because of the stress of commuting so far. We've helped people like that,' she went on. 'And we can help you.'

'The point is that we don't have the power to change other people,' said David, 'but we can change our*selves*. Of course, it won't change you overnight,' he went on, 'but it will give you a vocabulary which you can use to help you become less compliant. Now, Amber,' he said, 'you haven't told us all why you're doing this course. Would you tell the group?'

'Well, it's professional and personal,' she replied. 'I was too nice to my boyfriend, so he dumped me.' I kept quiet. If that's what Amber wanted to believe, so be it. 'And I've got real problems with my work,' she added. 'I'm a novelist. But my publishers just don't look after me. They don't market my books properly,' she explained, 'and the net result is that I've never won any literary prizes. It's outrageous. So I thought this course might help me give them a bloody good kick up the arse.'

'Ah,' said Elaine, thoughtfully. 'Well, it's not really about that,' she explained. 'It's about finding the middle ground, the ground which lies in between being nice and being nasty. Above all, it's about learning how to say "No". How about you, Minty? Why did you decide to do the course?'

'Well . . .' I said, feeling dreadfully exposed now and wishing I wasn't there.

'Yes?' prompted David, gently.

'Well, people push me around,' I began.

'*Do* they?' said Amber, her eyes round.

'Yes,' I said. 'They do. In a number of ways. For example, at work, at London FM, my colleagues are always asking me to do things for them, even though I'm very busy myself. But somehow, however firm I try to be, I find I can never refuse.'

'Why not?' said Elaine. 'Are you worried that they might think you're not nice?'

'Yes,' I said dismally. 'They make me feel obliged to help

them out, because they all think I'm nice. In fact, they're always telling me I'm nice. So I feel I have to *be* nice, and then of course I resent it.'

'And do you ever ask them to help you?' said David.

'Oh *no,*' I said, shocked. 'I wouldn't *dream* of it.'

'That's funny, isn't it, Minty?' said Elaine. 'You would never inflict on them what they inflict on you. That's typical. Because you're "nice". Oh, hello, Jo!' she said as the door creaked open behind us. 'We've only just started. Come in and pull up a chair. Carry on, Minty.' And I found this rather difficult to do, because the person who had just walked in wasn't 'Jo' at all. It was 'Joe'. Joe from Paris. He was obviously taken aback too, because he'd gone red. He gave me a faint smile of recognition as he sat down.

'The other thing,' I said, 'and this is the main reason for my coming here – is that three months ago I had this . . . terrible experience. I was getting married you see and . . . and . . .'

'Yes?' said Elaine encouragingly.

'In fact . . . it was my wedding day . . . and . . .'

Oh God, this was so embarrassing. Especially in front of Joe. I could feel my heart pound and the heat rise to my face.

'What happened?' David asked gently.

'My fiancé ran off,' I replied. 'In church. Just as we were about to make our vows.'

'My *God*!' said the woman who suffered from party-bores. The others were all staring, dumbfounded, and shaking their heads. I glanced at Joe. But he didn't look shocked at all. He obviously knew all about it, from Helen. And that made me feel a bit odd, to think that I'd been the subject of a conversation between Helen and Joe.

'What a dreadful thing,' said Elaine.

'It was,' I said bleakly. 'It was terrible. And it's only really now that I'm beginning to try and find out why it happened.'

'Why *do* you think it happened?' Elaine enquired.

'I don't really know. That's what's so awful. That's what makes it even harder to get over. Because I don't know the answer to that. Perhaps I never will. Because I'm too proud to get in touch with my fiancé again, after what he did to me. And he's never contacted me to even try and explain. All I can tell you is that he just – ran off. In front of two hundred and eighty people.' My throat was aching. The carpet had begun to blur. Joe passed me a tissue. That was nice of him. Especially as I hadn't been very friendly in Paris.

'Carry on, Minty,' said Elaine quietly.

'Well, it was a massive shock,' I continued. 'And I'm trying to get over it. I'm trying to rationalise it. Because otherwise I know I won't be able to move on. And I think maybe the reason why it happened is because I'd allowed Dominic – that's his name – to push me around so much before . . .'

'He was domineering, was he?' asked David.

'Yes,' I said. 'Extremely. And I think because I'd never set parameters with him – I didn't like to, you see – I subconsciously gave him permission to do anything he liked. Even to jilt me. I think that's a big part of it. He had all the power. And so I've come to realise that at work, and in my relationships, I need to set boundaries. To keep a bit of power for myself. But however hard I try, I find it almost impossible to do. Anyway, that's why I'm here.' Thank God. It was over. Now they knew.

'Thank you for being so honest, Minty,' said David. 'We'll work on that with you today. But first, Joe, please introduce yourself and explain why you decided to do this course.'

I looked at him. He was wearing off-white chinos and a crumpled checkered shirt, and deck shoes with no socks. He hadn't shaved. His hair had been cut very short. And though I knew Helen was seeing him, I was also aware, in an academic kind of way, that I found him a very attractive man.

'My name's Joe Bridges and I'm a writer,' he began.

I saw Amber's face tense up and her eyes rise to the ceiling.

'I've adapted my first novel into a screenplay, which I'm trying to sell,' Joe went on quietly. 'And I've just sacked my agent, because he'd made some serious contractual errors. So I've decided I'm going to do things on my own. And getting a film project off the ground is notoriously difficult. So I thought this course might give me some psychological armour to deal with the tough times ahead.'

'Good,' said David. 'And now, we're going to stand up for the first exercise, which we call the "Nice–Nasty Circle". What happens is that we each say one nice thing to each other, then one nasty thing. And the nasty thing can be as insulting as you like.'

'Now, Minty,' said Elaine, who had caught my appalled expression. 'That feeling you've just had about not being nice, that sinking of the heart, that fear of giving offence, that's what we're going to be dealing with here, OK?'

'OK,' I said, nervously, though my pulse was racing and my face was hot. We stood in a circle, smiling nervously at each other, then David started it off. He was standing next to Elaine. And I was between her and Joe.

'You've got lovely blue eyes,' David said to the party-bore magnet whose name was Anne. Then he turned to Elaine. 'And you've got *appalling* dress sense!'

'But I think *your* dress sense is wonderful,' she replied serenely. 'That shirt really suits you, David.' Then she turned to me, and looked me up and down. It was excruciating. I braced myself for her insult as I might brace myself for a bomb. But suddenly Amber intervened:

'Look,' she said. 'Sorry to interrupt, but I don't think you should be *too* nasty to Minty because, actually, it's her birthday today.' I threw my eyes to the ceiling. I could see that Elaine was struggling to control herself.

'Amber,' she said slowly, 'this is only an exercise, OK? Right, Minty. A very happy birthday. And now I'm going to say something unpleasant. Ready?'

'Ready,' I said, as she scrutinised me once more.

'You're terribly scrawny, aren't you?' she said. 'Don't you think you're too thin?' That was it. Phew. Could have been a lot worse. My turn now. I had to say something nice back to her, because she'd just been nasty to me. I looked at her. Large hazel eyes. Quite tall. Nice dress. Oh God. What on earth could I pick?

'I really like your earrings,' I said. 'They're very attractive and unusual.' Then I turned and looked at Joe. I had to say something unpleasant to him. How embarrassing. I'd much rather be insulted than dish out insults myself. My heart was thumping so loud I was sure everyone could hear it. I looked at his handsome face, his open expression and his short dark hair which was receding slightly into a widow's peak. He was smiling at me. He was smiling because he was embarrassed because he knew I was about to say something rude.

'Er . . . you're starting to lose your hair,' I said. His face fell a mile, and I felt sick.

'Oh God, did I hurt your feelings?' I asked. 'I'm really sorry. It isn't really receding, you know, only a tiny bit, and most men lose a little at the front, don't they, so I really wouldn't worry abou–'

'Minty, this is only role-play,' said David. 'I don't think you really hurt Joe's feelings.'

'Yes she did,' he said. 'I'm shattered. I'm heartbroken!' Then he grinned. And I relaxed. And now he had to pay me a compliment, when I'd just been nasty to him. Poor chap. He looked me up and down for what seemed like ages, biting thoughtfully on his lower lip. And then he said, 'I think you're *very* pretty, Minty.' My God! I felt a punch of adrenaline and the blood rushed to my face. I'd better not tell Helen he'd said that. Still, it was only an exercise. He didn't mean it. He was looking at Amber now. 'And you're too tall,' he announced.

'And you're too short,' she spat. '*And* your book's crap, by the way. Complete crap! And what's more –'

'Amber, you're supposed to say something *nice* to Joe,' said Elaine.

'Why?' she whined. 'He's just been horrible to me.'

'Exactly. And that's what "nice" people do,' she explained. 'People are rude to them, but they say something nice back. People hurt them, and *they're* the ones who apologise. Because nice people take the blame. So please say something complimentary.'

'OK. Well . . .' Amber smiled, as she tried to think of something. 'I think your book's really *sweet,*' she said.

Sweet? That wasn't a compliment at all! Then Amber turned to Ronnie.

'And you're a pathetic WIMP if you can't even get your own secretary to do the bloody photocopying.'

Ronnie blenched. Then swallowed. 'And you're a refreshingly forthright young woman,' he said, by way of a compliment.

On it went, until the circle was complete, and then we went round again the other way. At first, we all seemed to find the exercise excruciating. Our insults were accompanied by stifled giggles and red faces, averted eyes and shuffling feet. But then, thanks to Amber, everyone got into their stride – and soon the slights were flying like surface-to-air missiles.

'– your shoes are filthy!'

'– your teeth are a mess!'

'– I hate your voice.'

'– your ears are huge!'

'– you're too fat!'

'– what a cruddy tie!'

So it was rather strange, when, at lunchtime, we all reverted back to type, competing to fetch and carry, and pass each other things and look after each other in the way that nice people do.

'– After you with the water.'

'– Oh, of course. Terribly sorry – I was hogging it.'

'– Another piece of bread for anyone?'

'– Well, yes, but what about *you*?'

'– Does anyone mind if I have this last lettuce leaf?'

'– Oh no, no, not at ALL!'

Excessive consideration can be so wearing. Joe came and sat next to me.

'Would you help me with my insults, please, Minty,' he said, as he picked up his knife and fork. 'I'm not very good at being nasty.'

'I thought you were doing OK,' I said.

'Oh no, I really found it *very* difficult. I think I need a little extra practice.'

'Um. OK, then,' I said, cautiously.

'Right. Your hair's a mess, Minty.'

Oh. Thanks very much.

'And your shirt's horrible,' I replied.

'Your face is perfect for radio!' Bloody cheek!

'And you're crap at table football!'

'Oxfam suits you *so* well,' he said, but by now he was smiling.

'Your teeth remind me of Stonehenge!' I pointed out pleasantly.

'Your hair's much too long.' He was grinning now.

'Your aftershave smells like cat's piss!' I smiled. He was looking at me, out of the corner of his eye. He was thinking up something really awful. And though he was trying to look serious, he was stifling laughter.

'You're a big fatso – don't you ever stop eating?'

And I laughed too. Though it was true. I *had* eaten quite a lot. For the first time in three months.

'You're quite right,' I said. 'I'm stuffed!'

'The Full Minty,' he quipped, with a smile. And then he poured me some coffee.

'How's Helen?' I asked.

'She's fine,' he said.

'She was my bridesmaid,' I added ruefully.

'Yes,' said Joe, 'I know.' And I found myself wondering what else he knew about my disastrous wedding day.

The afternoon session began with role-play. Joe role-played being in Hollywood, convincing a famous film director of the merits of his script. And every time the director said 'no', Joe would have to turn it round, by sheer persistence, and get him to say 'yes'. It took him five or six tries. But he got there. And then it was Anne's turn.

'You get mugged, socially,' said David. 'You've got this "I'm a nice person" expression on your face, so life's losers and the walking wounded stick to you like flies.' He then role-played a party-bore.

'Tell him you find him boring,' prompted Elaine, as David wittered away.

'I can't,' Anne said, 'it's rude.'

'Go on. Get rid of him.'

'But I might hurt his feelings,' she wailed.

'Just do it. Say something that will put him off!'

Within ten minutes Anne had graduated from, 'Well, it was very nice talking to you . . .' and, 'Excuse me, I must find the loo,' to, 'You're a human anaesthetic. I am not remotely interested in what you're saying. I'm going to talk to that *fabulous*-looking man standing by the olives.' We all cheered.

'But I couldn't *really* say that,' she said, as she sat down.

'No, you couldn't,' said David. 'But if you practise being rude, if you play at it in your mind, then your body language will change and the social muggers won't find you such easy prey.'

Then it was me. Joe had to pretend he was Wesley, constantly whining at me for help. And I had to say politely, but very firmly, 'no'. But I found this rather difficult because the fact was that by now I thought Joe was really rather nice and so I didn't want to refuse him. Then David made me do some role-play about Dominic. I had to pretend that he was screaming at me about my clothes, shouting at me for wearing the 'wrong coat for the country' – that was a favourite complaint – or wearing something he disliked. And instead of saying, 'Oh, OK then. Anything for a quiet life,' I'd be shouting: 'No, I won't bloody well change my clothes, you domineering, inadequate, shallow BASTARD!' And everyone was clapping and laughing and cheering. And it was very funny. Terribly funny. And then I burst into tears. And it wasn't quite so funny any more.

'Well, it's working,' said David, after a minute. Joe looked upset. And I thought that was nice. Because, let's face it, he hardly knew me. And then we had to do an exercise where we were all seated in front of a big blank blackboard, and we could draw, or write on it anything we liked. Anything at all. One by one we all went up. Amber drew her initials and a book. Then I did my usual doodle, of a big, closed box, with a dot trapped inside. And Joe had got up, and drawn on to it two windows, and an opening door. And then he'd added a roof, the sun, and some flowers. And when I saw him do that, I felt something in me . . . unfurl. And the tightening screw in my chest relaxed.

Finally, we came to the end of the day. We all had to give each other advice, one by one, to help us find the way forward.

'Take yourself back,' said Joe, simply, when it came to my turn.

'– throw out the clothes Dominic made you wear,' said Anne.

'– buy new things, things you know he'd hate.'

'– No, just buy whatever *you* like!'

'– Do something radical – change your life.'

'– Remember who you are!'

Who you are?

'I'm Irene Araminta Malone,' I said.

'I-A-M?' said Joe. 'I *am*.'

'I really got a lot out of that course,' said Amber happily, as we made our way back to Primrose Hill on the bus. 'No more Mrs Nice Guy. No more accepting a pile of shit from men, or allowing my publishers to neglect me. I'm really not putting up with it any more. I'm going to change, Minty. *Change*! Minty, you haven't said a thing – are you listening?'

'What? Sorry – no, I shouldn't say sorry, should I – er, I didn't hear what you said, I was thinking.' I was slowly working something out. I'd had a mental breakthrough, you see. An epiphany. A revelation. A Damascene flash. And now I knew why Dominic had done what he'd done. I was right. It *was* because I was too nice. So he'd lost all respect. Doing the course had shown me this. Seeing everyone being so nice. It was pathetic. It was pathetic that they couldn't stand up for themselves. Or, worse, that they *could* stand up for themselves – they all knew how – but had been too nice, too weak, rather, to do it. And the reason why they didn't was fear of rejection. Being nice was a kind of insurance policy. And though I understood it, because I'm like that myself, I couldn't respect it at all. And that's what had happened to me. I now saw that I *had* been nice to Dominic – but in a negative way. Jumping to it every time he barked, simply in order to avoid a conflict. Meekly doing what he said, to earn his approval and keep things 'nice'. How *abject*! I was appalled. Seeing my behaviour objectified like that had shocked me to my core. I'd been an independent, confident person when he met me, and look what I'd become! A spineless people-pleaser. A wimp. A sap. And so Dominic had lost all respect. I didn't blame him now. I blamed myself. It was *my* fault, I now realised. That's why he'd dumped me. Because he no longer had any respect for me. He'd taken one look at me in church, wearing a dress that he had picked out, and he knew he just couldn't go ahead.

Now, I'm not letting him off the hook here, you understand, because what he did was terrible. But I was involved in it, because I didn't have to *let* him do it. And so at last I understood. I could see that I was largely to blame. And perhaps, armed with this new self-knowledge, I'd be able to start moving on.

'Minty,' said Amber, 'what are you thinking?'

'Oh nothing,' I said. 'Nothing.' I didn't want to tell her my theory – she never agrees with me. Anyway, I was ashamed of it. I was ashamed to acknowledge what a meek, compliant creature I'd become.

'I feel *inspired*,' said Amber, as we got off the bus. 'I really feel uplifted by what I've learnt.'

I felt uplifted too. By what I'd discovered about myself. And I realised how vital it was for me to be more assertive. To say what I really wanted. To set boundaries. So now I felt emboldened to bring up a subject with Amber that I'd been hitherto afraid to discuss. And that was how long she was going to stay. It had been almost three months. And in the beginning she'd told me she was only going to stay for a few days. And my flat's full of her things. The half-landing's choked with her furniture, and there's stuff spilling out of her room. And although I'm very fond of her, it was beginning to get me down.

'Amber,' I said, as she turned the key in the lock.

'Yes.'

'Amber . . . how much longer do you think . . . um . . . you'll be staying with me?'

She looked at me. Oh God. Oh *God*. I should have kept my big trap shut. There'd be an awful scene now. I'd hurt her. I'd made her feel rejected. My face flushed red, and I instantly regretted having mentioned it.

'How long am I going to be staying with you?' she repeated.

'Yes,' I said, my heart pounding. 'How long?' To my astonishment she broke into an enormous smile, then flung her arms round me.

'Oh, Minty,' she exclaimed. 'Just as *long* as you want me to!'

'Ah.'

'Don't worry,' she said, 'I've got *no* intention of moving out yet. I'm not going to abandon you while you're still getting over Dom.'

'Oh, jolly good.'

'And you're really helping me get over Charlie.'

'Great.'

'So you've got me for *quite* a while,' she said, happily. 'And in any case, it's such *fun*, sharing a flat, isn't it, Mint?'

'Oh yes,' I said. 'Yes. It is.'

'Do you know,' she went on, as we took off our coats, 'it reminds me of that lovely canal holiday we had in 1983.'

Oh God. That was awful. I was on a barge with Amber, Auntie Flo and Uncle Ed, and their miniature dachshund, Mungo. It rained every day, the boat was freezing, and I had to share a tiny berth with Amber. Then one morning Mungo was standing on the deck, and he saw another dog on the towpath. And he started barking at it. And he barked so hard that he fell off the boat, into the canal. And Amber had made me jump into the water and save him. She was hysterical. She adored that dog. 'Go on, Minty!' she screamed. 'You've got no alternative!' And before I could point out that it wasn't my dog, and why couldn't *she* rescue him, I had jumped in after Mungo, only to see that he was happily swimming for the bank. But I was too nice to refuse. So I jumped. I think I've been jumping all my life.

'No, I really *love* living with you Minty,' said Amber, warmly. 'But you must let me contribute to the bills,' she added, as she picked up the phone.

'OK,' I said quickly. 'Yes. Yes, I will. That would be nice.' Then I went upstairs. I went into my bedroom, opened my cupboard and all the drawers, and confronted my clothes. I removed all the things that Dominic had given me. The Sloaney skirts, and shoes with silly buckles and bows; the headbands and the silk scarves. The green wellies and the waxed down jacket, the neat twinsets and the plaid. Into a black bin-liner it went. And yes, even the Hermès bag. That too. It all had to go. Every stitch. Every thread. 'Take yourself back' – that's what Joe had said. And that's what I would do.

So on Saturday morning I dropped my bulging bin-liner off at the Camden branch of Oxfam, then I got the Tube down to Covent Garden. In Neal Street I darted in and out of the shops, surveying the rails of trendy clothes. I bought things I'd never bought before – a black leather jacket, Ally Capellino jeans, Red or Dead kick flares, and apron dresses and cropped T-shirts and floaty, calf-length skirts. Then I went to have my hair trimmed at my usual salon, Headlines.

'So how's married life?' asked Chris, my friendly stylist, as he put a shiny black gown round me.

'I don't know,' I said, truthfully. 'It all went wrong.'

'Did it?' he said, aghast. 'You poor darling. Want to talk about it?'

'No, thanks,' I replied. I sat before a tall blue mirror, near the window. Before me on the counter was an array of brushes; the hairdryers were slotted into their holsters like sleeping guns. Chris picked up my hair, feeling the weight of it in his hands.

'An inch off?' he enquired. I looked at myself long and hard.

'Yes,' I said. 'At least.'

'Maybe two?' he suggested, as he began to brush it through.

'Yes. Two . . . two would be fine.' It hadn't been trimmed since July. Maybe he should take three inches off, I thought. Or four. Or five. I scrutinised my reflection. Or six inches, or seven. Dominic liked it long. Perhaps Chris should take off eight or nine.

'Cut it all off,' I announced. 'I don't want long hair any more.'

'Are you sure?' he said. He looked shocked.

'Yes,' I said, giddily. 'I'm sure. And then . . . I'd like it coloured. Streaked. With some, I don't know, reddish highlights.'

'Total transformation, then?'

'Yes. Total transformation,' I agreed. 'I want to reinvent myself.'

'Are you *sure* you want it short?' he said as he lifted his shears.

'Yes,' I said. 'I'm sure. I want it really, really short.'

And as Chris's scissors flashed in the spotlights, shining black loops fell to the floor, like the links of a chain. I may not be light-hearted, but I'll be light-headed, I thought as the long tendrils fell away. The other stylists were looking, and grinning as Chris sliced into my hair. Occasionally he straightened my head with his hands, checking that the length matched exactly on either side. And now he wasn't shearing, he was snipping, grasping the hair between index and middle finger, and cutting it, straight, across his comb. Samson's strength drained away when his hair was cut – but I felt mine return. For the first time in months, I felt invigorated, strong.

'This looks great!' Chris exclaimed. 'We can really *see* you now.' It was true. There was my jawline, and my ears. And the curve of my cheekbones. And how strange to feel the air on the back of my neck. I began to laugh. I felt elated, slightly intoxicated, as this unfamiliar image emerged.

'Movin' on up,' blared from the salon hi-fi. *'Movin' on up. Movin' on up. Nothin' can stop me . . .'* I looked at the mass of black hair, lying on the floor at my feet like a tangle of discarded tape. My hair had been edited, cut, chopped down into a short, boyish bob. Chris passed a soft brush over the nape of my neck, and held up the mirror for me to see. I liked it so much, I almost clapped. Then the colourist, Angela, came over with her chart of swatches. What should I have? Topaz? Mahogany? Burgundy, or Garnet? Cyclamen? Safari? What exotic options, I thought. I chose Cayenne – a coppery colour. Hot, peppery, Cayenne. My highlights would look like flames. I was rekindling my fire. Angela brushed on the pink paste, then neatly folded the hair into tiny tinfoil parcels. My eyes smarted slightly from the ammoniac tang of the dye.

'Movin' on up, Movin' on up, Movin' on up, Nothin' can stop me.' I felt great. I felt fantastic. Do something radical, they said. And I was. I glanced out of the window, on to Shaftesbury Avenue, as the lunchtime shoppers hurried by. Then I flicked through *New Woman, Zest, Self* and *OK!* Yes, I thought, I *am* a New Woman, with Zest, and I'm going to look after my Self and then I'll be OK!

I reflected on how much Dominic would hate my new style – good. I wished he could see it. But I knew this was very unlikely. There was no contact between us, and our social circles did not overlap. We lived in different parts of town and we never went to the same places. So the chance of an unscheduled encounter was practically nil. This meant I'd had to satisfy myself with idle fantasies of revenge. I had played them over and over in my mind, like favourite videos. As Angela coloured my hair, I replayed these revenge dramas again. I imagined turning up at his house, in a dawn raid, and forcing him, at gunpoint, to tell me why he'd run out on me in church. Then I visualised meeting him, by chance, in the street, and looking right through him, as though he didn't exist. And now I was driving along, towards a zebra crossing, and suddenly Dominic was stepping out. But in my dream I was not slowing down and coming to a complete stop, as recommended by the Highway Code. No, I was accelerating towards him, fast. And then, here I was arriving at the Opera House with my extremely successful new man, who probably runs the World Bank or something of that kind. And to my astonishment, as our car pulls up, I see Dominic standing outside. He's obviously waiting for someone. Clearly someone far less attractive and intelligent than me. And he's looking a little bit down at heel, his clients having all deserted him in disgust at his ghastly behaviour. So he's not looking too good. He hasn't shaved recently. His coat could do with a clean. His blond hair has receded somewhat, no doubt due to all the stress. Whereas I am looking radiant. In fact, I have never looked better. And as my new beau escorts me up the steps to our waiting box, I'm generous enough to turn and give Dominic a sweet but pitying smile . . .

I sighed, then glanced at the girl sitting next to me. I'd been far too self-absorbed to notice her properly before. Her long blonde hair had been washed and trimmed. Now it was being Carmen-rollered into big, fat, bouncy curls which were being swept up on top of her head. She looked as though she were about to step on to the set of some lavish costume drama. By contrast, I looked like a human colander, with my layers of tinfoil pockets, like armour plating, rattling gently against my head. I looked absurd. I wanted to laugh out loud. So I did. I laughed. And then I glanced at my neighbour again, and I immediately stopped laughing, and a dull pain filled my chest. A garland of fresh flowers had been placed on her head. Tiny rosebuds and gardenia, jasmine and stephanotis had been threaded on to a base of ivy, which was being carefully pinned in place. She looked radiantly lovely. And this was her wedding day. I told myself that it was all right. That I didn't mind. Because I was getting over Dominic now.

'Are you OK, Minty?' said Angela.

'What? Oh, yes, I'm fine. Fine.'

'The vapour from the dye stings the eyes,' she said.

'Oh yes,' I nodded. 'Yes, it does.'

'Well, almost done,' she added, 'and then we'll leave it to take.' I smiled at her, blankly, then looked at my neighbour again. Now I noticed the sapphire glinting on her ring finger, and caught snatches of her conversation:

'About a hundred . . . finger buffet . . . Berkatex . . . quite simple . . . three, and two pages . . . Mombassa.'

Suddenly she seemed to fade from view, and I took her place, in my Neil Cunningham dress, and my tiara, and my veil, and next to me, standing there, was Dominic. And he was saying, 'No . . . no, John . . .'fraid not.' And the memory of it made me feel sick. But then I thought, What's done is done. I can't put the clock back. I've got to accept what happened, and move forward. And in any case, I thought expansively, would Dominic have made me *happy*? No, of course not. I knew that. And that was a key to moving on. Self-knowledge. Accepting and recognising. Having the good sense to realise that though it was extremely painful and of course desperately humiliating, it was, strangely, all for the best, because Dominic wouldn't have made me happy at all, in fact. Dominic . . . *DOMINIC*! I shot to my feet. That *was* Dominic! Walking past the window. I'd just seen him. I'd know that blond head anywhere. *Dominic*! In a flash I was out of the shop, and running down the street. I was conscious that my hair was covered with forty pockets of tinfoil, but I simply didn't care. The adrenaline rush made me fly as though I were running for my life. I was aware of my black nylon gown flapping in the wind and of the bemused stares of passers-by.

'– It's the caped crusader!'

'– Nah! Halloween innit?'

'– look at that hairstyle! Crazy cow!'

I passed the Shaftesbury Theatre and came to St Giles' Circus but the pedestrian traffic light turned red. Damn! There was Dominic striding along, fast, and now he was passing the Oasis Health Centre and turning left into Endell Street. Taxis chugged past, with a foul eructation of diesel fumes; Lycra-clad cyclists rang their bells and ranted at cars; a bus thundered towards me, then stopped. The lights had changed again. Thank *God!* But where was Dominic? I couldn't see him now. I couldn't. But I had to speak to him. I *had* to. I had to talk to him and tell him that I was really getting over him and was hardly even affected by it any more. That's what I wanted to say. I flew down the street, heart pounding, and there he was, already well towards the bottom. I wanted to shout out, 'Dominic! Look! I'm getting over you! I'm really moving forward! Can't you see? And I understand what happened, Dominic – well, I think I do – and I'm *really* sorry if I made you lose respect for me by being so pathetic, it must have been awful for you, but I'm not like that now!' And I passed Henry's wine bar, and then came to the Rock and Sole fish and chip shop, and now Dominic was turning right. And he passed the Armani Emporium, but didn't stop to look in the window, which surprised me, as he can never normally resist. And I could see his blond head bobbing down the street as he strode along; and I could smell freshly ground coffee beans as I passed Coffee Republic, and I was panting and I had a stitch. I hadn't sprinted like this in years. Now he was crossing James Street, and heading into Covent Garden Tube. And I was gaining on him, because he'd stopped to put his ticket in the automatic barrier. And I wanted to talk to him, I just wanted to ask him whether my theory was, in fact, correct. 'Dominic!' I wanted to shout. 'Please could you confirm that the reason you dumped me on my wedding day was because you no longer thought highly enough of me? I'd just like you to confirm that for me, Dominic, so that I can really move forward. Not that I'm *not* moving forward, Dominic. In fact, I'm almost completely over you now. As you can see.' Oh God, he was going through the barrier.

'Dominic!' I shouted. 'Dom!' And I saw him pass through, and I had my ticket in my pocket, and I put it in, but it beeped and said 'Seek Assistance'. But the only person who *could* give me assistance was Dom. So I called out, 'Dominic! Dominic! Please *stop*!' But still he didn't seem to hear. And I was *so* out of breath, and feeling very conscious now of what a bizarre figure I cut. And I shouted again, much louder now, 'DOMINIC!! DOMINIC!! COME *BACK*!!!' And it worked. He heard. Because from the other side of the barrier he turned round – at last, at *last,* he turned. And he looked utterly astonished. Gobsmacked. Thunderstruck. Not because of my bizarre, tin-foiled hair, or my flapping salon gown. But because it wasn't Dominic at all.

'Er . . . can I help you?' said this man, on whom I'd never set eyes before. Same hair. Same build. Approximately same age. That was all. Of course it wasn't Dominic. How could I have thought it *was*?

'Are you all right?' he enquired politely, though he was clearly aghast.

'I'm . . . fine,' I said weakly. 'I'm . . .' I could feel the familiar ache in my throat, and my eyes began to swim. 'I'm sorry,' I said, hyperventilating from exertion and shock. 'You see, I thought, I thought . . .' But he was already heading for the lift. Then I leant against the station wall, and covered my face with my hands.

November

'*Minty*?' Jack enquired when I went into the Monday morning meeting. I gave him an enigmatic smile. 'Good God,' he enunciated, slowly. 'Suits you,' he added admiringly. 'Bit radical, though.'

'Yes,' I said. 'Precisely.' I ran my hands through my inch-long coppery hair which I had slicked down with a little gel. They'd go wild for me at the Candy Bar. I was almost sorry not to be going back. Suddenly, Suzie Saucisson appeared in her normal bluestocking mode. She peered at me through her pebble specs.

'*Wow*!' she breathed. 'Different! I'm amazed Tom let you in.'

'He was a bit doubtful at first.'

'Nice colour,' she added. 'Hey! Great jacket too.'

'Thanks.' I was wearing my Ally Capellino suit.

'You look so . . . *modern*,' she went on, wonderingly, as she took her place at the table.

'Thoroughly Modern Minty, that's me!'

'Well, *we've* got to be thoroughly modern too,' she said with a vehement air. 'Jack,' she went on, 'before we begin the meeting, can we talk about digital training?'

'Oh, some other time,' he replied, irritably. He picked up a piece of yellow leader tape and began twisting and stretching it in his hands. He was as coiled and tense as a watch-spring. And it was only ten o'clock.

'We've really got to crack on with it,' Sophie announced, as she consulted her clipboard.

'Yes, yes,' replied Jack testily.

'But some people round here don't want to know. Wesley, for example,' she added indignantly. 'He's refusing to go on the training course. Aren't you?'

'It does sound awfully *difficult,*' Wesley whined. 'And you *know* I don't like computers.'

'But we've *got* to get to grips with the new technology!' Sophie exclaimed. 'We're like the toffs on the *Titanic,* gaily kicking up our heels while the digital iceberg looms.'

'Oh, I'm sure we'll get round to it sometime,' said Jack, with forced casualness. He seemed, as usual, to have other things on his mind.

'No, we must get down to it now,' she repeated. 'We're a laughing stock at *Broadcast* – they can't believe we still use tape.'

'Sophie,' said Jack carefully, 'as you're blessed with such a remarkable intellect, perhaps you could explain where we're going to get the money to pay for all this new equipment?'

'I'll ask Uncle Percy,' said Melinda. 'He's got thwee million in his cuwwent account.' Then she burped, loudly. 'Oops! Sowwy!' she giggled. 'Wind,' she confided, as she patted her mountainous bump.

'I think the changeover to digital technology should be a priority,' Sophie persisted. 'We're at the dawning of a new century. A new *age*.' Her eyes shone with evangelical fervour.

'I said I'll sort it out,' said Jack with scarcely concealed annoyance. 'But first we've got to get the ratings up. Why? Because we have to deliver the . . . ?'

'Listeners,' we all said, wearily.

'Who attract the . . . ?'

'Advertisers.'

'Who provide our . . . ?'

'Rev-en-ue!'

'Right. So, let's hear your ideas.'

'Look, I really don't think it can wait,' Sophie went on with an exasperated air. 'We're dinosaurs,' she added desperately. 'And we all know what happened to *them*!'

'Sophie!' Jack replied with frosty hauteur. I could hear the scraping of rank being pulled. 'May I remind you that you're not in charge here.'

'No, but –'

'And I am. So I'll decide.'

'Yes, but . . .'

'So please don't push your luck.'

'OK, but –'

'And I, for one, won't be dictated to by you.'

'Yes, but we've got to move ahead, adapt . . .'

'Bugger off!' said Jack.

'What?'

'Go on. Just bugger off! Bugger. Right. Off.'

There was a short, shocked silence. Sophie reddened, then fled in tears. We shifted uncomfortably in our seats, and exchanged subtle glances.

'Gosh, that's a bit *wude,*' I heard Melinda whisper to Wesley. And it was. It was incredibly rude. Jack was very short-tempered these days. Sophie may have been a bit pushy – but then she was very young. More to the point, she was right.

'OK, let's get on with the meeting,' said Jack. And though his tone of voice was calm, his face had gone a deep shade of red. 'Let's just . . . get on with this,' he repeated with a sigh. 'And your ideas had better be good.'

'*Diarrhoea*?' enquired a soothing voice, over sound effects of a flushing lavatory. I stared at my bowl of Mulligatawny.

'*Keep on running to the loo*?' I pushed the soup away, and picked at my plate of congealing macaroni.

'*Put diarrhoea on the skids with Bung*!'

'Can I join you, Minty?' It was Jack. I nodded. He sat down with his sandwich and a cup of coffee. He looked tired and strained, as usual.

'Sophie all right?' he asked.

'Yes. Think so.'

'I shouldn't have lost it like that,' he said guiltily, 'but she really was being incredibly annoying.'

'Well . . .'

'Coming on the Head Girl with me,' he said bitterly. 'I sometimes think she's a bit too strait-laced for London FM, you know.'

'I'm not so sure,' I said. 'I think she may have hidden depths.'

'Was I too hard on her?' he asked suddenly. He gave me a piercing, almost imploring look.

'Oh, well, no, not really . . .' And then I remembered what I'd learnt on the course. 'Actually, yes,' I said. 'You were.'

'I can't help it,' he sighed. 'I just don't have the same reserves of patience any more.' This was true. Despite his sardonic exterior, Jack used to be easy-going, concealing his sharp managerial skills under a soft blanket of laissez faire. Now he was sharp, and cold. Worse, he seemed not to care. He bit into his ham and cheese sandwich and chewed thoughtfully. Then he rested his head on his hand.

'Are you all right, Jack?'

'No,' he replied. 'I'm not.'

'Anything I can do?' I pushed my plate away. He smiled, and held my gaze. Then he shook his head, and looked away.

'It's too late,' he said wearily. 'I've just got to face up to it. I've got to face up to the fact that I've made a terrible mistake.'

'Oh, I'm sure if you speak to Sophie and explain, she'll understand,' I said. 'She is a bit bossy, but she's very young and probably doesn't realise that –'

'Oh, it's not *Sophie,*' he cut in. 'It's *Jane.*'

Jane? His wife of eight months. He heaved another huge sigh. And I was just going to ask him whether or not he wanted to talk about it, because Jack and I have always got on so well, when he went on, quite unprompted:

'It's my step-daughters, Topaz and Iolanthe. They make my existence hell.' He swallowed hard. 'I've just had one of the worst weekends of my life.'

'Oh dear.'

'They hate me,' he whispered.

'How could *anyone* hate you?' I replied. He smiled a rueful smile, then rubbed his temples with the tips of his fingers.

'Well, they do,' he said with a sigh. 'In fact, they loathe me. They always have. I'm the enemy. The object of their detestation. All I get is abuse.'

'Doesn't Jane stick up for you?'

'That's the last thing she'd do,' he replied with a bitter laugh. 'They're Mummy's little darlings – but they're thirteen and fifteen now. That's why I lost it with Sophie,' he went on, quietly. 'She reminded me of them. Trying to push me around. Trying to undermine my authority. I couldn't take it. It's bad enough getting that at home.'

'I see.' Poor Jack. 'But . . . you put your foot down with Sophie,' I pointed out.

'Yes.'

'In fact, you *really* put your foot down there.'

'Yes,' he conceded, again.

'So why can't you do it with your step-daughters?' There was a pregnant pause.

'Because . . . I just . . . *can't,*' he said at last. 'I'm not their father, as they constantly remind me. And they'd go bleating to Jane if I did. Things are bad enough between us as it is,' he added ruefully. 'That's why I went for Sophie.'

'It's called "Kicking the Cat",' I said.

'What?'

'That's what you're doing,' I explained. 'You're kicking the cat. I learnt that on a course I did recently. If you get a load of grief at work, you take it out on people at home. With you, it's the other way round, and so you're taking it out on Sophie. You're kicking the cat. Do you see?'

'I suppose so. To be honest, I just can't think straight at the moment. In fact, Minty, I'm at the end of my tether.'

'O SOLE MIO . . .'

I'm at the end of my tether too.

'. . . STA 'NFRONTE A TE!'

I've been listening to this all day.

'QUANNO FA NOTTE . . .'

And it's really loud.

'O SOLE MIO!'

And every time I try and turn it down a touch, Amber turns it back up. I just can't think.

'Couldn't we have it a little softer?' I said. 'Just a bit.'

'No. It doesn't work unless it's at full volume.'

It's therapy, you see. For Pedro. At this time of year he tends to get a bit down in the beak. Amber says it's Seasonal Affected Disorder. It's certainly SAD. He won't leave his cage, his little head droops, and he refuses to utter a word. Worse, he plucks at the feathers on his chest – a sure sign of psittacine distress. And the only thing that can snap him out of it is Neapolitan love songs. Though he's *very* picky about the artistes. Mario Lanza rather than Tito Gobbi, for example. Caruso rather than Carreras. He also appreciates the more subtle Neapolitan intonation of Toni Marchi. Just like Granny did. But he has absolutely no time for Pavarotti. Believe me, it's been tried.

'CHE BELLA COSA, 'NA IURNATA 'E SOLE, N'ARIA SERENA DOPPA 'NA TEMPESTA!'

'He's a very sentimental bird,' said Amber, as she picked up my mahogany occasional table and moved it to the other side of the sitting room. 'He likes music that comes from the *heart.* I ought to knit him a stripy fisherman's jumper,' she added with a laugh. She placed her long, elegant hands on her slim hips, and scrutinised the sitting room. Then she said, 'Give me a hand, Mint.'

'What?' She had grabbed the arm of the small sofa.

'Let's move it into the window.'

'Why?'

'Because it'll look better there. That's why.'

'But I don't really . . . *want* it to go there,' I said cautiously.

Amber looked at me incredulously. I braced myself. My heart was pounding. My palms were damp. I felt the familiar panic and tried to remember what they'd said on the Nice Factor. What was it? Oh yes: 'Does a fear of rejection make you say "yes" when you really mean "no"?'

'You don't want it to go there?'

'N-no,' I said. 'No, I don't.'

'Oh, don't be so ridiculous, Minty!' she replied with a burst of snorty laughter.

'But I like it as it *is*,' I tried again. She was so maddening. So bossy. She must have driven Charlie round the bend. And despite everything she'd heard on the Nice Factor she was *still* doing it to me! I could feel my blood pressure rise. I experienced an overwhelming urge to clean. Then I remembered something else I'd learnt on the course: excessive niceness can be dangerous. Too much self-restraint builds up a munitions dump of resentment which can explode at some totally inappropriate moment, often with completely the wrong person. And I didn't want to blow up at anyone. I just wanted to be able to state my rights and say 'no'.

'Look, Amber,' I said, 'I really don't –'

'Oh, come on, Minty!' she said again. Half an hour later, the sitting room had been completely rearranged. My two sofas had swapped sides, my standard lamp was next to the fire; my rosewood desk had vacated its nook, and the Persian rug had been moved. I hated it.

'Now,' she said, as I involuntarily put on my apron, 'those curtains – awful!'

'I *say*!' screeched Pedro.

'Oh good, he's cheering up!' exclaimed Amber.

While she crooned over Pedro, I surreptitiously turned down the hi-fi. And as Mario Lanza subsided, other sounds filtered in – the crack of an occasional firework, and shrieks of childish laughter. The big display was taking place tonight, on Primrose Hill. I had no plans to go, though I thought I might watch it from the garden. Amber was trying to get Pedro to eat a piece of apple. He took it in his scaly, outstretched claw, then held it up to his beak and nibbled it. Oh God, I wish she'd find her own place, I found myself thinking as I reached for the Jif. It's not even as though she pays me any rent.

'I need more space,' she announced. Hurrah! At last! Telepathy.

'My bedroom's very small,' she went on. This was true.

'Yes, it is,' I replied. 'It's very cramped.' Not least because it's full of her own books. She keeps buying them in a futile attempt to get into the bestseller lists. She must have two hundred at least.

'I just don't have enough room,' she went on.

'Well, there is a solution to that.'

'Yes, but it would be quite tough.'

'I think I'll get used to it,' I said.

'I do hope so.'

'Don't worry. All good things come to an end.'

'So you don't mind if I have your bedroom then?'

'Sorry?'

'You see, you're out at work all day, so you only need a bedroom to sleep in. But I have to work in mine. Think in mine. *Create* in mine. So I thought we might swap.'

'*What*?'

'Because I've got to deliver my manuscript by January . . .'

'Yes, but . . .'

'. . . and, frankly, the lack of space here is a bar to my creativity.'

'Now look . . .'

'And, let's face it, yours is twice the size.'

'Amber!' I said. 'I . . .' This was it. I'd had enough. I was about to go off like Mount Etna. But all at once Amber had rushed up to me and kissed me on the cheek.

'Oh, Minty, thank you! Thank you! *Thank* you! Darling Minty, I *knew* you'd say yes – you're so NICE!'

By now Pedro's recovery was complete. Moreover, he was bored, and had started shouting.

'Wah, wah, wah!' he went. '*Waaaah*!'

'Oh! Look, Minty – he's better,' crooned Amber. 'Isn't that *lovely*? He's yelling. Let's see if he'll sing.' She turned up the hi-fi and soon Pedro began to singalongaMario.

'*O SOLE MIO . . .*'

'Oh God.'

'*STA 'NFRONTE A TE*!'

'DELICIOUS ICE-CREAM . . .' sang Amber.

'. . . FROM ITALEEEEEEEE,' crooned Pedro.

From somewhere, far away, above the cacophonous combination of Mario Lanza, a woman and a parrot, I could hear the telephone ringing. I went into the hall.

'Yes?'

'You pile of rubbish!'

'What?'

'You waste of space!'

'Who *is* this?!'

'Call yourself a radio reporter?'

'Now look here –'

'Come on, Minty! Your turn.'

'Joe!'

'Precisely. Do you fancy a drink?'

Did I fancy a drink? Well, no. No, I didn't. In any case, what was the point of having a drink with Joe? He was seeing Helen. I knew that.

'Do you want to come out?' he asked.

'Um . . .'

'*JUST ONE CORNETTO . . .*'

'Go on.'

'GIVE IT TO ME!'

'Well . . .'

'*QUANNO FA NOTTE . . .*'

'Come on, Minty.'

'*. . . O SOLE MIO.*'

'Do you want to have a drink . . .'

'Oh, Minty, he's so much BETTER!' Amber yelled.

'. . . or don't you?' said Joe.

'Yes,' I said suddenly. 'I do.'

Half an hour later Joe and I were sitting in the Engineer, my local. He lives close by, you see, in Camden – just one stop on the Northern line or a fifteen-minute walk.

'How did you get my number?' I asked him. 'Did Helen give it to you?'

'No, it was on the contact address list, for the Nice course.'

'Oh.'

'Now, I hope you haven't been too nice recently,' he said, avoiding, I thought, the subject of Helen. He sipped his beer, and looked at me seriously.

'I'm afraid I have,' I replied. 'I've just been terribly nice, actually, to Amber.'

'Oh dear,' he said, ruefully. 'That's very disappointing.'

'But I have done something radical,' I said, touching my hair. Joe nodded. 'Amazing!' he exclaimed again.

'And how about you?' I asked. 'Are you squaring up for your struggles with the studios?'

'I'm working on it,' he replied. 'I'm determined to get my film made.'

'Well, the book's wonderful,' I said truthfully. 'I'm halfway through it. You write really well.'

He smiled. And where Amber would have launched into a long discussion about her characters, their motivation, how long it had taken her to write, what such and such a critic had written, and how big her print run was, Joe simply said, 'Thanks,' and changed the subject. All of a sudden we noticed that everyone was beginning to leave. I looked at my watch. It was seven thirty-five. The firework display was due to start in ten minutes.

'Shall we watch it?' he said.

'Well, if you'd like to.'

'Well, I would. But only if *you* want to,' he said, with exaggerated niceness.

'I must say, it does sound rather pleasant. But are you quite sure *you* want to go?' I replied, in kind.

'Quite sure.'

'Because I wouldn't want you to do anything you didn't want to do,' I said.

'May I say how very considerate that is of you,' he replied, happily.

'Oh, thank you.'

'But let me assure you that I would indeed very much like to watch the display, Minty. But only if *you* do too.'

'Oh, I do.'

'Sure?'

'I'm sure. Are you sure.'

'Sure.'

'Please feel free to change your mind at any time.'

'OK, that's enough niceness, ed!' he said. 'We're going to the fireworks, and that's it. Come on!' And I found myself laughing. He was very amusing. In fact, he was enormous fun. We walked on to Regent's Park Road where a human stream, scarved and anoraked, was flowing towards the Hill. Children were carried aloft on shoulders, gumboots waded through leaves, sparklers hissed and flared in the darkness like electric dandelion clocks.

'Ten, nine, eight . . .' the crowd roared. 'Seven, six, five . . .' We turned in through the gates. '. . . Four, three, two, one . . .'

BANG!!! KER-ACK!!! BOOOOOOOM!!! Vast, incandescent chrysanthemums exploded against the night sky. We craned our necks as their long silvery trails hung in the air like spray. PHUT! PHUT! PHUT! went the Roman Candles. WHEEEEE!! WHEEEEE!! squealed the rockets. Then a spangled meteor shower burst with a sound like the pinching of cosmic bubble-wrap. 'OOOOOOOOO!!' went the crowd, then 'AAAAAAAAHHHH!!!!' as a gigantic, hyacinth-shaded sea anemone flowered, trembled, then dissolved. I glanced at Joe. His upturned profile was bathed in light as a fiery fountain cascaded over our heads. Below us, flames as high as houses leapt from the huge bonfire into the dark.

'Glow circles a pound!' we heard a tout shout, as the show ended, and we clapped and cheered.

'Would you like one?' said Joe. I nodded. He put some money in the bucket for Crisis, then he selected one of the coloured phosphorescent strips. It looked like a tiny rainbow as he carried it back in his hands.

'Here.' He snapped the two ends together, then placed the luminous circlet on my head.

'You look like Titania,' he said with a smile, as we began to walk back down the hill.

'Didn't she fall in love with a donkey?'

'Yes.'

'What happened?' I asked. 'I can't remember.'

'Well, she was so besotted, so unlike her true self, that she just couldn't see that the man was, in fact, an ass. When she realised her mistake, of course, she was appalled.'

'Well, she would be.'

'However, it all ended happily. And everyone ended up with the right partner.'

'How nice. I wish life was like that.'

'It could be,' said Joe, as we drew up at my gate. 'Gosh, what's that din?' From inside the flat, we could hear screeching and singing.

'It's Amber, her parrot, and er . . . yes . . . Placido Domingo. I'd ask you in,' I added, 'but I don't think it's quite the right moment . . .' Joe gave me a hug, which astonished me, and then he kissed me on the cheek.

'I do hope we can get together again, Minty,' he said.

Did he? Why? I was totally confused by now. What about Helen? And why hadn't he been with Helen this evening? Maybe he was going to see her later on. Maybe . . . maybe I shouldn't be too 'nice' about this, I thought. Maybe I should just grasp the nettle and ask.

'Joe, can I ask you something?' I said hesitantly. 'It's been bothering me all evening.'

'You can ask me anything you like.'

'OK. Um, are you . . . ?' I laughed, then looked away. 'I feel really silly asking you this,' I tried again. 'But, er, are you seeing Helen?'

'Helen? No,' he said. 'We're just friends.'

'Ah.' Then why was she being so secretive with me?

'She's great,' said Joe.

'Yes,' I replied, 'she is.'

'I like her a lot.'

'Me too. But I haven't heard from her for ages. In fact, she's gone a bit funny on me; and she usually only does that when she's seeing someone, and I kind of thought that someone might be you.'

'No! Why did you think that?'

'Because . . . when we met in Paris,' I explained, fiddling with my scarf, 'you asked me for my number.'

'Yes, I did.'

'And I refused because, well, I don't want to hurt your feelings, Joe, but you see, I didn't want to go out with you be–'

'Minty –' he interrupted before I could go on to explain that I didn't want to go out with *anyone* at that time. 'Minty . . .' he repeated.

'Yes.'

'I think you've got the wrong end of the stick here.'

'Have I?'

'Yes. I didn't *want* to go out with you.'

'Didn't you?

'No.'

'Oh.'

'I was just being . . . friendly.'

'Ah.'

'I'm a friendly person.'

'Yes, I know.'

'And you looked so sad, you see.'

'I was sad,' I said with a sigh.

'You looked terrible, actually.'

'I felt terrible.'

'In fact, you looked distraught.'

'I was distraught,' I said.

'And Pierre and I needed partners for the table football, and you and Helen were there, and you both seemed very nice.'

'I see.'

'And I only asked for your number because I thought we might remain, you know, friends.'

'Oh, right. Well, I've got it straight now.'

'And in any case, Minty, I don't want to hurt your feelings, but I wouldn't go out with you in a million years.'

'Oh. Why's that?'

He looked at me seriously.

'Because of what you've just been through. You're not ready.'

'Aren't I?'

'No. I don't think you are. Some time ago I went out with a woman who was on the rebound,' he explained. 'She'd had a very bad time. But . . . she really hurt me. In fact, it was a disaster. So I vowed I'd never make that particular mistake again.'

'I see.'

'Too much baggage, Minty. I saw that on the course.'

'Well, yes, but . . .'

'You've really got to recover before you go out with anyone new.'

'Yes, of course,' I said. I was feeling slightly irritated by now.

'You've got to move on a bit more.'

'Yes. Yes, I know that.'

'But I'd love to see you – just as a friend.' Ah. 'I mean, I was really glad when you turned up on that Nice Factor course, because – can I tell you something?'

'Yes.'

'Now, promise you won't get too conceited?'

'Promise.'

'Well . . . I think you're a horrible old bat.' A feeling of inexplicable happiness came over me, as though I'd dived into a vat of warm toffee.

'Thanks,' I said with a shy smile. 'I think you're ghastly too.'

'Do you really mean that?'

'Yes, of course I do.' Gosh, he really was *very* nice-looking.

'So we're friends now, aren't we, Minty?'

'Yes.' I sighed. 'We're friends.'

'So, no more misunderstandings, then?'

'No.'

'That's good. In fact it's excellent. Well,' he added brightly, 'I think I'll be off.' Then he smiled, and walked away. And I was suddenly very sorry when he turned the corner, and I couldn't see him any more.

'And now to family matters,' said Melinda into the microphone the following Tuesday. 'With me in the studio is Mike Hunt –'

'I told her to say *Michael*!' said Jack, furiously.

'– the newly appointed Minister for Family Values. Now, Mike, could you tell the viewers – sowwy! I mean *listeners* – how you hope to stwengthen family life?'

We were on air, live. Wesley was producing, Jack was supervising, and I was frantically cutting down a feature. I glanced at the clock – we'd gone on air at two. It was now twelve minutes past, and the piece I was editing was scheduled to go out at two fifteen. My knees felt weak and my pulse raced as I pressed the 'Fast Forward' button, stopped at the place I'd marked, then yanked out lengths of tape. Damn Wesley, I thought as I spooled back and forth, heart pounding, frantically slashing and splicing. He'd managed to exploit my good nature again. When *is* the Nice Factor going to kick in? I wondered, as the seconds ticked relentlessly away. I got to the end, then spun through it one more time to make sure there were no glitches.

'Done it!' I said, breathlessly, as I removed my 'phones.

'Thanks,' said Wesley, as he sat at the switch-and-flashing-light-studded console. 'Is it de-ummed?'

'Yes. Smooth as a baby's bum.'

'Oh, thanks, Mint. Oh God, my timings are out,' he whined. They always are. He peered at his stopwatch. 'Er . . . what's one minute twenty plus two minutes fifty-three?'

'Four minutes thirteen,' I said.

'Well of *course* the Labour Government is committed to family life,' I heard the Right Honourable Michael Hunt say. 'That's why we're going to make it compulsory for divorcing couples to seek counselling. And when it comes to the issue of single mothers, we strongly feel that the taxpayer should not have to pick up the tab.'

'Quite wight!' said Melinda. 'Now, I'm pwegnant myself, Mr Hunt.'

He gazed at her enormous bulge.

'So I see.'

'One more minute, Melinda,' Wesley whispered into her headphones on 'talkback'. She nodded to show that she had heard.

'Now, I'm not a single mother. I'm mawwied. My husband Woger's a stockbwoker. But even if I were a single mother with absolutely no money, I'd never expect anyone else to cawwy the can for me.'

'Ha!' I exclaimed.

'I work hard for my living. I support myself . . .'

'With the aid of Uncle Percy,' said Jack.

'. . . because I think that's *wight*. And I think nothing of working wight up to the end of my pwegnancy,' she went on. Oh God, she was getting carried away. 'My baby's not due for another thwee weeks, but I fully intend to go –' Suddenly she gasped, and the electronic monitoring levels on the desk popped up like toast. Her lips compressed. Her eyes goggled. Then her features crumpled like an old sheet, and she opened her mouth and went 'AAAAAAAHHHHH!!!'

'Oh God!' said Jack, standing up.

'Good heavens!' said the minister.

'OOOOOHHHHHHH!!!!! Oh Chwist!' she yelped. 'My waters have just bwoken!'

'Get her out of there!' said Jack. He flew to the talkback.

'Just sign off, Melinda! Sign off, and we'll put on a tape.'

'No!' she said. 'No! I won't! I want to share this with my fans. Do you think a few contwactions are going to stop *me*?' We all gawped like goldfish through the glass.

'It's my duty to stay at this micwophone until the pwogwamme's over!' she announced. 'If necessawy, I'm pwepared to give birth on air.'

'Please don't!' said the Minister as he leapt to his feet.

'Why not?' said Melinda. Then she was felled by another spasm. 'OOOOOOHHH! I mean . . . we've had death on air, haven't we, listeners?' she went on, as she clutched the green baize table. This was true. The octogenarian vicar who did *Prayer for the Day* had croaked – live, as it were – just a few months before. 'So we can have birth on air too,' she went on. 'London FM is the station where *anything* can happen – OOOOWWWWWWWW!!! – the whole of human life! And as the Minister for Family Values is actually here, in the studio, he might even give me a hand. Do you know what to do, Mr Hunt?'

But Mr Hunt had already gone. He had rushed out of the studio, then disappeared, at a run, to his waiting ministerial car.

'Now don't wowwy, evewyone!' Melinda shouted into the mike. 'It's not as bad as it sounds – Oh fuuUUUUCCCKKK!!!!'

'Shut the microphone!' shouted Jack. 'Shut it! And put on that tape!'

The engineer shut the fader, put on the tape I'd edited, then Jack and Wesley went through to the studio, and hauled Melinda out.

'But I want to stay!' she screamed. 'Think of the watings we'd get! We could get a Sony Award for this. Think of the splash in *Bwoadcast*!'

'That's exactly what I am thinking of,' said Jack, as he helped her into a chair.

'Wesley, call an ambulance. Minty – get in that studio.'

'What?'

'You'll have to finish the programme for her. You've got two minutes left on this tape.'

'I don't *want* Minty to pwesent the pwogramme,' wailed Melinda. 'It's *my* pwogwamme – not hers!' But I was already pushing on the studio door. I was on my way.

Melinda's waters breaking three weeks early like that was my lucky, well, break. You hear about this kind of thing happening. Disaster strikes the star, and the understudy steps on-stage.

Only, I wasn't actually the understudy. Jack had booked Nina Edwards from Chat FM's drive-time show to stand in for Melinda. But when he heard me do it, he changed his mind. And so now, it's me – it's me! Me! *Me*! Presenting London FM's flagship show. Thank you, God! Thank you very, very much. Thank you for letting something NICE happen to me at last! This goes some way, may I add, God, to counteracting the disastrously negative effects of my nuptial catastrophe. Oh yes, I really think you're getting the hang of it now. And you've decided to give me the chance to shine. Mind you – that's not hard. A Guatemalan goat with a cleft palate could have presented the programme better than Melinda. And of course, I had the added advantage of having written her script. So when I stepped into the studio that fateful afternoon last week, I already knew it inside out. Because I'd written every word. All I had to do was read it. It was quite a lively show one way and another, and when I signed off and stepped out of the studio, everybody clapped! And Jack hugged me and said, 'Well done.' And I felt a bit tearful then, because I do really admire Jack and, well, it had been a stressful afternoon. And Melinda had her baby that evening, a little girl, and we all sent her some flowers.

'Before the news, a reminder that at 2 p.m. you can hear today's edition of *Capitalise*,' I heard Barry the announcer say, 'presented by Minty Malone.' And I got a warm glow inside, mingled with a burst of adrenaline. And the feeling that for once, just for once, all was well with my world. Because this is my launch pad. I'm determined to fly. And I can cope with anything, even having to swap bedrooms with Amber. Which I don't really mind. I can afford to be generous, after all. I mean, my career's going *so* well now. I'm feeling so much more confident. I've worked out why Dominic left me. And I'm going to work on that. And I've cleared up my misunderstanding with Joe – his book's *wonderful*, by the way. Though I did find myself wondering why, if Helen *isn't* dating Joe, she'd gone to Paris again . . . But then I put it out of my mind.

Because my priority now is my career, and myself. My brand *new* self. New Mint.

'My darlingest Minty,' wrote Ron the Stalker, on pink paper strewn with silver hearts. *'You stepped bravely into the breach, as it were, and saved the day for London FM. What a star performance, sweetheart. I couldn't fault you. You were as smooth as silk. But DON'T YOU GO GETTING IDEAS ABOVE YOUR RADIO STATION!!! Don't go getting any BIG IDEAS just because you've landed yourself a LUCKY BREAK, you stupid girl!! You're still MY Minty, OK? You belong to ME. So don't forget it. Your ever-loving, ever-listening, Ron.'*

Eeeuuuughhh. Yuk. Oh well. I didn't mind, because I'd had some genuine, non-nutty fan mail too. About five letters so far, which isn't bad for a week's work. And all highly complimentary. What balm to my battered ego. And when we're in the studio, Sophie and Wesley and Monica and the others run around after me as though I were some film star. They offer to get me tea and biscuits, and of course I always refuse because I wouldn't want to put them to any trouble, but it does amuse me because it's as though my status has completely changed. Everyone's so respectful. And I keep saying, 'No, no, don't worry, I don't need a thing.' But on the other hand, their attention is nice.

'Would you like some coffee, Minty?' said Wesley, as we prepared to start the run-through for the programme earlier today.

'No, thanks.'

'Something to eat?'

'No, thanks. I'm fine.'

'Or a cold drink, maybe?'

'It's OK, Wes. Thanks.'

'Happy with the running order?'

'Yes. Fine.'

'Oh, Minty, it's so nice working with you,' he said, with a simpering smile. He came a little closer. And I thought, why doesn't he get some new clothes? His gear's as outdated as a Rubik cube. 'You're so professional, Minty,' he breathed, 'you don't ask anyone for help, you just get on with it and you're so lovely and –'

'How's Deirdre?' I cut in strategically.

'Well, actually, Minty, it's funny you should mention Deirdre, because –' He stopped. Jack had come into the studio, with Monica and Sophie, ready for the run-through.

Jack gave Wesley a pointed look, then we sat and made a few last-minute adjustments to the script.

Beep. Beep. Beeeeeep. 'This is London FM and it's two o'clock,' said the continuity announcer an hour later, 'time for today's edition of *Capitalise* with Minty Malone.'

'Hello,' I said, as I leant towards the mike. 'Today, Russia's mafia: how extensive is their network in London? We meet the singer whose haunting voice helped make *The English Patient* a global hit. We preview the Preacher of the Year Award, and take a serious look at sermons. But first: the masculinity crisis – has feminism broken men? With me to discuss this issue are radical feminist Natalie Moore, who writes for the *Guardian*, and Bob Ladd, editor of *Loaded*. And we're keen to hear *your* views too, so do call the *Capitalise* hotline on 0200 200 200 and join us, live, on air.'

To begin with, the discussion was very polite:

'– do you really think so, Natalie?'

'– I'm not quite sure I agree with that, Bob.'

'– yes, yes, I see what you mean.'

'– mmm, with respect, I have a different view.'

But then it got a little more heated, and within a couple of minutes, they were at each other's throats.

'Masculinity crisis! What a joke!' spat Natalie.

'Come off it!' replied Bob Ladd. 'Men have it tough these days.'

'Oh yeah? My heart bleeds.'

'What are blokes supposed to do?'

'You've subjugated us for centuries and now you're trying to get us to feel sorry for you too!'

'You should!'

'Well, the vast majority of us don't!'

'With respect, Natalie,' I intervened, 'don't you think Bob has a point when he says that men feel they no longer have a role?'

'All I know,' she said, conceding not a micron of ground, 'is that men have had it all their own way for aeons, and now, at last, it's *our* turn.'

'OK, open it out,' Wesley whispered into my headphones. I glanced at the callers' names beginning to flash up on my computer screen.

'Well, on Line 1 now we have Malcolm from South Croydon. Malcolm, welcome to the show.' He was patched through and we could hear the amplified phone line buzz and thrum.

'Erm,' Malcolm began, and his voice was shaking, 'I'm having a masculinity crisis.'

'Oh dear. Why's that?'

'Because my wife upped and went last year. She took the kids, cleared out the house, and took me to the cleaners. I live in a bedsit now.'

'Well, Malcolm, I'm very sorry,' I said. 'What an awful story.'

'It's a *typical* story, isn't it?' Bob Ladd cut in. 'You women, you've got it all your own way now. We're just sperm banks. You take us for what you can get, then throw us away like shells.'

'Yes, but we don't know *why* Malcolm's wife left him, do we?' Natalie interrupted. 'Women don't leave unless there's a good reason. He was probably violent,' she said, thumping the soundproofed table with an audible 'thud'. '*Were* you violent, Malcolm?'

'I'm sorry, Natalie,' I intervened, 'but we can't expect Malcolm to answer a question like that.'

'No, I *was not!*' said Malcolm indignantly. 'Hardly ever!'

'Thank you, Malcolm. Now, on Line 2 we have Frances, calling from Dulwich.'

'We know there's a masculinity crisis,' Frances began,

'because the Samaritans are receiving record numbers of calls from depressed men, and this suggests that they're not adjusting well to a world in which women seem not to need them.'

'That's a very good point, Frances,' I said. 'Thank you. And now on Line 3, calling from Battersea, is . . . Mrs Dympna Malone.' Dympna Malone? Oh God.

'Hello, everyone,' Mummy crooned. In the background we could hear barking, yapping and whining. She giggled. 'Sorry about the noise, but it's my day down at the dogs' home. DOWN BOY! DOWN! Ooh, you are a *naughty* puppy! Anyway, I'd just like to say that I'm having a car boot sale next Saturday at my home in Maida Vale in aid of the new Willesden refuge for battered men.'

'Battered men!' Natalie spat. 'They don't exist!'

'Oh yes they do,' said Mum. 'And we've got some. So that's 28 Churchill Road W9 . . .' I made frantic, slashing gestures across my throat to Wesley.

'. . . next Saturday at two.'

'Thank you for that, er, Dympna,' I said, as they faded her out. 'And on Line 6 now we have . . . ah . . . a retired accountant. Called, um, *Bob*. Hello, Bob,' I said. 'Are you having a masculinity crisis?'

'I certainly am,' said Dad pointedly. 'Because I never get to see my wife. I retired two months ago,' he went on. 'And I've seen her about three times since then. She's rather taken up with her fund-raising,' he went on meaningfully. 'So I don't get much of a look-in.'

'Oh dear,' I said.

'In fact, there are times,' Dad went on darkly, 'when I seriously wonder whether my marriage can survive.' Oh heavens. I really hoped Mum was listening to that, but the chances were she'd gone straight back to her stray dogs.

'Well, Bob, I hope you can get your wife to, er, scale it down a bit. And now on Line 4 . . .' Oh *God*.

'Right, everyone, just listen, it's Amber Dane here. Author of *A Public Convenience*, which, incidentally, is a brilliant novel

– I do recommend it – published by Hedder Hodline at a very reasonable ten pounds.'

'What's your *point,* caller?' I said.

'Well, Minty, I agree with everything Natalie Moore has been saying.'

'Oh good!' said Natalie with a smirk.

'Men have treated women appallingly for centuries,' Amber went on. 'My ex-boyfriend, for example. He dumped me four months ago. Just like that. For no good reason. Just because I don't want to have children. Outrageous! Obviously I can't tell you his name . . . Oh, all right then, it's Charles Edworthy and he lives in Parson's Green and he works in the City and he –'

'Thank you *very* much for joining us today,' I said brightly as Amber swam into libellous waters and was swiftly faded out. 'And now, on Line 6 we have, er . . . Joe Bridges.' Oh, why couldn't they put through some people I *didn't* know? On the other hand, it was lovely to hear Joe's voice.

'Hello . . . ?' I heard him say. He was clearly on a mobile phone.

'Hello, Joe,' I said. 'What's your view on all this?'

'Well . . . I'm in a cab, and the driver has your programme on and we were both very interested in what you've all been saying so we decided to call. I mean . . . I do think it's a hard time to be a man, because, well, a lot of women don't seem to like men much any more.'

'Yeah!' we heard the cabbie say. ''Ere, give us the phone, mate.' There was a clunk as the mobile phone changed hands. 'Look, right, I agree with my passenger and I fink the problem *is,* right, that men and women just don't communicate nicely with each other – know what I mean? OI! GET OUT THE FRIGGIN' WAY, YER STUPID COW!! Sorry 'bout that. Bleedin' women drivers! Where was I? Oh yeah, communication. Respect. I mean, granted, geezers 'ave given women a hard time, right, but now they ain't 'alf gettin' their own back.' There was a grinding sound as the phone changed hands.

'That's right,' we heard Joe say. 'Women seem insensitive

to how hard it is for men these days, when we often don't know what women really want.'

'There does seem to be enormous distrust now between the sexes,' I said, adjusting my headphones.

'But too many women have, say, one bad experience with a man,' he went on, 'then assume that we're all the same. That's what women say. That men are "all the same". But we're not.'

'Oh yes you ARE!' shouted Natalie Moore.

'No, hear me out,' said Joe. 'This is a debate. And my main point is that women should be more generous in their attitudes to men, because they can afford to be, because at last things are going their way . . . Hang on, Minty.' There was another awkward clunk.

'Right, it's me again,' said the driver. 'Now, my wife left me too. Absolutely no good reason. I'm not difficult – OI! WHY DON'T YER INDICATE, YER STUPID WANKER?!! – And I really don't know what she saw in the other bloke. I mean, she's a housewife of forty-two, and he's a twenty-five-year-old construction worker! I ask you. Anyway, even though she left me, right, she got the 'ouse and the kids. What did *I* get? The bleedin' record collection . . .'

There was more hand noise as the phone was passed back again.

'I'll tell you what I think would help in this conflict between the sexes,' said Joe feelingly. 'What would help is if we told each other the truth. That's all I want to say, really. Anyway, I've got to go now – this is Terminal 3, isn't it? Anyway, thanks for listening. Bye.'

Oh. Damn. He'd gone. Pity. It was just getting interesting. And it was so nice to hear his voice. And I thought how much I liked his voice. Then I thought how much I'd like to hear his voice again. After the programme I found myself wishing that Joe would ring me back, but he didn't and I didn't have his number, and I'd lost my contact address sheet from the course and I wondered about phoning the Nice Factor to get it, but decided not to. And then I remembered what he'd said:

'This is Terminal 3, isn't it?' Ah. Oh. I wondered where he was going. And why. And who he might be with. And how much he liked them. Then I resolved to put Joe to the back of my mind, because he's obviously very busy, and so am I.

You see, after I'd saved the day when Melinda's waters broke, a colleague of Natalie Moore's phoned me from the *Guardian* and said she was writing a feature on new voices in radio, and she included a bit about me. And then *that* got picked up by the media editor of *The Times*, Rosie Brown. And she rang and said she'd like to do a short interview with me, which she did, and it appeared, complete with a rather nice photo of me sitting at the microphone. And Jack put it up on the noticeboard, and I must say every time I walk past it my heart does swell a bit. It was headlined 'Fresh Mint', which made me laugh. And Rosie Brown had described me as one of a new breed of independent young women working in independent radio. 'Minty Malone is single, successful, and utterly dedicated to the job,' the article read. 'Her relaxed style on air, and user-friendly demeanour masks a steely determination to succeed.' And I felt hugely flattered, though I'd never have described myself as 'steely' in a million years. Strong, perhaps – yes, I think that's what I'd have said: 'Strong Mint.' Definitely. 'Extra-Strong', in fact. And it was strange to see my face looming out of the pages of a newspaper, and to know that hundreds and thousands of people had read it including, perhaps, people I knew.

Of course, I wondered whether Dominic had seen it, and what on earth he'd thought. It would have been a bit of a shock. One or two friends did phone to say they'd spotted it, but Helen didn't contact me, though I know she reads *The Times*. And I just don't know *what*'s going on there. Or why she's being so remote. It's all a bit of a mystery, to be frank. But I couldn't beat myself up about it. Things were going so well for me now. I wallowed in the knowledge that I'd be presenting the programme for the next six months. And of course, Jack was paying me more. Not as much as Melinda – she got £500 a show – but a lot more than what I'd been getting as a reporter. And the word from Sir Percy was that he was happy for me to present *Capitalise* in Melinda's absence. In any case, with all his business interests he hardly ever has time to listen. So I was on a kind of high. I felt that I was living in a fairy tale as for three weeks I presented the programme and felt my horizons spread and expand.

'Thank you very much for joining us today,' I said, as I watched the second hand judder towards the figure '12' on the studio clock. 'Don't forget to make a date with us tomorrow at the same time, on 82.3 FM. So until then, from me, Minty Malone, and from all of us on *Capitalise*, goodbye.' I removed my cans and pushed through the sound-proofed double doors.

'Well done, Minty!' said Jack. 'The duty desk have just rung to say they've had some more nice calls about you from listeners.'

'Ooh, good.'

'You're really getting into your stride with it now. I'm very impressed.'

'Thanks. I feel quite at home with it all, really. It doesn't take long.'

'I knew you could do it,' said Jack.

'Oh yes, Minty, you're brilliant at it,' said Wesley. 'You're a natural. And it's really *great* that you don't have a speech impediment.'

'I must say, it does help,' I said with a grin. And we collected up the scripts and tapes and took them back to the office, and sat down to have the usual post-mortem meeting on the programme. And we were all laughing and joking and congratulating ourselves on how well everything seemed to be going and how the ratings were beginning to lift, when we heard rapid footsteps in the corridor and a strangulated cry. Suddenly the door burst open, and there was Melinda, red in the face, and clutching her three-week-old baby.

'Melinda!' said Jack.

'Melinda?' said Sophie.

'What are *you* doing here?' Wesley asked.

'Well . . .' she was out of breath. She'd obviously been running. 'I've been listening to the pwogwamme wecently, and I thought I'd better come back. So I've decided not to take my maternity leave after all – I've swapped it for a parking space!!'

Jack did what he could. He politely told Sir Percy that it was in Melinda's interest to take time off and that, whereas he valued her highly as a presenter, he felt that her return to work was too soon. He also pointed out that, although I had been doing an excellent stand-in job, Melinda's position was secure. But Sir Percy said it was up to Melinda what she did, and he didn't have the time or inclination to get involved. So she did come back. And there was nothing anyone could do. And she brought her baby, Pocahontas, with her. And her nanny.

'Successful working mums like me can't afford to take time off,' Melinda announced at the Monday meeting. 'And I'm afwaid to say that I thought the pwogwamme was suffewing duwing my absence.'

'Thank you, Melinda,' I said. My face prickled with suppressed rage. I wanted to weep and wail.

'Oh, no offence to you, Minty,' she said. 'It's not your fault. But of course you don't have my long expewience of pwesenting.'

'Minty's been doing a brilliant job,' said Jack, reddening with indignation. 'No one could have done it better.'

At that, Melinda looked annoyed. And everyone knew the real reason why she'd come flying back – she was worried because she knew I was doing it well.

'Please don't feel you've failed,' she said, looking at me.

'I don't feel that at all,' I replied.

'Anyway, Minty, there's nothing *wong* with being just a weporter,' she went on with sledgehammer tact. 'And I don't want you to be jealous of me just because you're not going to be pwesenting the pwogwamme *any* more. And I am.'

I looked at her and felt my tears subside. *Right.*

'Oh, I'm not jealous, Melinda,' I corrected her calmly. 'What an absurd suggestion. I'm *furious*!' I said. 'I'm furious that a fifth-rate fatso like you should get the plum presenting job purely because of her connections!'

There was a collective gasp. Everyone was staring at me, slack-mouthed. Did Minty say that? I could almost hear them thinking. Did Minty *really* say that? Jack's eyes were on stalks. So were Wesley's. So were my own. I did say it. I actually said it! I said something completely and utterly not nice. I stared at Melinda. The colour had drained from her face. But instead of erupting, as I thought she would, she seemed determined to remain composed.

'I'm pwepared to overlook that nasty wemark,' she said carefully, 'because I know you must be vewy disappointed that things haven't worked out. You were getting cawwied away, Minty. You were getting big ideas. It's all vewy well being in *The Times* and all that, but, quite fwankly, that was just a flash in the pan.'

'Waaaaaah! Waaaaah!' The nanny passed the bawling baby to Melinda, who opened her shirt, flipped out a breast the size of a football and marbled like Stilton, then carried on talking.

'I think I'm a sort of wole model weally,' she went on happily. 'Citwonella Pwatt's wong. Modern working women *can* have it all – and I'm living pwoof!'

And so I was demoted. The Harpies had swooped down and scooped up my feast. I had managed to snatch defeat out of the jaws of victory. On the game board of life I had not passed 'Go'. In fact, I had shot up the longest ladder, only to hit a huge python with my very next throw. I thought my heart would break as I went back to being a reporter. Or rather, to being the marriage and maternity correspondent of London FM. I seemed to get nothing but features on nursery provision and civil Christenings, and fostering and dropping sperm counts . . .

'Child benefit,' I heard Jack say the following Monday.

'What?' I said. He'd caught me by surprise. I was reading the job ads in the *Guardian* media pages.

'Child benefit,' he repeated as he came and stood by my

desk. 'I think we ought to do something on it and –' he stopped, and peered at the paper, where I had ringed three adverts in red. I felt my face flush as I folded the *Guardian* away.

'Minty . . .' said Jack quietly. He looked rather depressed. 'I hope you're not going to leave.'

'Well . . .' I began awkwardly. I didn't want Jack to know I was looking around, but I had to move on, and my recent presenting experience, although abbreviated, would stand me in good stead.

'Please don't go,' said Jack, twisting a piece of tape.

'I might have to,' I replied. 'I'm not getting very far here.'

Jack sighed, then pulled up a chair.

'Look, I know it's hard for you now,' he whispered, with a subtle glance at Melinda. 'My hands are tied, as you know. But the situation could change.'

'How?' I whispered back. 'Melinda's never going to leave. And there's nothing else here I can present. *Capitalise* is the only feature programme we do.'

'Well, I intend to bring in some new shows,' Jack explained. 'Just as soon as our ratings pick up. And when that happens you'll be my first choice to front one of those.'

'But how likely *is* that?' I asked. 'Our ratings are terrible. I love it here,' I went on, 'but I can't hang around for some golden opportunity that may never arise.'

'Well,' he said with a sigh as he stood up, 'you must do whatever you feel right.'

Though it didn't feel right to be looking for other jobs. In fact, it felt utterly wrong. It felt like a betrayal. And the thought of actually leaving London FM filled me with dismay. But I didn't know how else to cope with the sharp disappointment of what had happened. The jagged graph line of my life had taken another downwards dive. I felt like Sisyphus, pushing a huge boulder up the steep mountainside. And every time I'd almost reached the peak, the rock would roll back down. '*Dum spiro, spero,*' I said to myself vainly. And sometimes, '*Dum spero, spiro.*' But the fact was that I was *dis*pirited. Dismayed.

Which is why I was very glad, a few days later, when Joe called me again.

'Sorry I didn't ring you after that phone-in,' he said, 'but I was on my way to New York. I thought you were very good, by the way – you're a brilliant presenter.'

'No I'm not,' I said flatly.

'Oh yes you are!' he said confidently.

'Oh no I'm *not*!'

'Oh . . . I see, you want me to insult you. OK, you're a crap presenter.'

'I'm not a crap presenter.'

'God, there's no pleasing you, is there?'

'I'm not a crap presenter,' I reiterated crisply. 'I'm a crap *reporter*.'

'What?'

'I'm just a reporter again. Melinda came back early.'

'Oh. Bad luck.'

'Quite.'

'So you must be feeling a bit low.'

'Yes,' I said wearily. 'I *am*.'

'Then let me take you out to dinner, to cheer you up.'

'You'll take me out to dinner?' I said, brightening. 'Where?' And I hoped he'd suggest Odette's, in Regent's Park Road, because Odette's is expensive and chic. But instead he said, 'Would Pizza Express be OK?'

So on Saturday evening I set off for Camden to meet him. I could have got the Tube or a bus, but I preferred to walk. The dismal weather matched my mood. A dense fog filled the streets. A clammy rain was starting to fall. The broad brown plane leaves lay like severed hands, and the air smelled of mould and decay. I turned my collar up as I crossed over Regent's Canal, where a solitary barge, lamps aglow, belched woodsmoke into the night. As I entered Parkway the blue neon lettering on the restaurant cut through the mist like a knife. I pushed on the glass doors and there was Joe, reading, beneath an enormous mirror. Suddenly he looked up and smiled.

'Nasty to see you again,' he said delightedly, giving me a friendly hug.

'Ditto with bells on!'

'Drink?'

'Yes. Drink,' I replied, with a meaningful air. 'I've got a whole lot of sorrows to drown.' I glanced around as Joe ordered a bottle of wine. There were small, marble-topped tables and simple wooden chairs and, nearby, some tall, potted palms. Their curving fronds fanned out over our heads, framing Joe and me in the glass. He poured the Chardonnay as we studied the menu.

'I'm going to have either the Veneziana, or the American,' he said judiciously.

'It'll be the Four Seasons for me,' I said. And with each successive sip of wine I felt my cares drift away, like clouds. Joe was looking so attractive, I thought, as he told me about his trip to New York.

'I met Julian Jones. He scouts for Paramount.'

'That sounds promising,' I said.

'He likes my book,' Joe explained. 'But he says the script needs some more rewrites before he's prepared to pitch it to Hollywood.'

'And will you do that?'

'Yes. Because he's right. He gave me some other advice too. He said I should move to LA.'

'Oh.' *Oh*. 'Why?' I asked, aware of a sudden sinking of my heart.

'Because if I go there, and hassle people, I stand a much better chance of success.'

'So, will you go?' I asked, apprehensively.

'I might,' he replied. 'But not yet.' And the surge of relief I felt when he said that took me by surprise. 'Now, what about you, Minty?' he went on. 'What are *your* plans?'

'I don't know,' I said with a shrug. I had another large sip of wine. I knew I shouldn't drink too much – it always goes right to my head – but today I felt like it. 'My boss wants me to stay,' I explained. 'But I feel I've got to move on.'

'Yes,' said Joe with a funny little smile. 'I think you have.' And at that, we looked at each other and, emboldened by the booze, I held his gaze for a moment.

'What did you mean?' I said. 'When you rang the phone-in?'

'What did I mean? Nothing. I just felt like having my say.'

'No, I mean, what did you mean when you said we should all "tell each other the truth"?'

'Well . . .' he exhaled and fiddled with his fork. 'I . . .' He paused while the waiter put our pizzas on the table.

'Tell me,' I said again. I poured us both some more wine.

'Well, we'd all hurt each other less if we told each other the truth. That's what I meant,' he explained. 'You see, my ex, Lucy, she didn't tell me the truth. And I really wish she had, because I wouldn't have got so involved.'

'What happened?'

'I don't want to talk about it,' he replied flatly. 'We're having a nice time, Minty.'

'But you know all about me,' I pointed out with a tipsy sigh. 'Why can't I know something about you?'

'OK then,' he said wearily. 'I met Lucy two years ago. She was separated from her husband. He'd been having an affair. Her marriage was over. That's what she told me, and I fell for her hook, line and sinker. I was absolutely besotted. She'd been on her own for almost a year and told me she'd be divorced by the following spring. So we got more and more involved, and I proposed and she said yes. I was just so incredibly happy.'

'What went wrong?'

'She went back to her husband. His affair ended unexpectedly and he said he wanted her back. So back she went, despite the fact that she'd assured me that she never, ever would. But it wasn't true. The truth was that she still loved him and hoped to be reconciled. And if I'd known that from the start, I'd never have got as involved with her as I did. She really . . . hurt me,' he said. 'She didn't mean to,' he added quickly. 'But she did. There,' he concluded with a shrug. 'Now you know.'

'I'm sorry.'

'It's history.'

'Does it still hurt?'

'Sometimes. Not so much. I've recovered, really. Just as you'll recover from Dominic one day.'

'Oh, I'm getting over him already,' I said airily as I sliced into my pizza. 'He wasn't a very nice person, so that makes it easier.'

'Why on earth did you want to marry him then?' said Joe with an expression of surprise.

And I hate questions like that so I said, 'I suppose I was confused.' By now the bottle of wine was empty – I'd drunk most of it, and my head had done several lengths. But I was starting to enjoy myself. Joe had never looked more attractive, I thought, even if he didn't wear good clothes like Dom. He had lovely, curving lips, I noticed now, and a broad physique. And the fact that he wasn't seeing Helen freed me to feel something dangerously like desire.

'Let's have another drink,' I said with a drunken giggle.

'No thanks,' he said. 'I've had enough. I think you have too.'

'No I haven't,' I retorted. 'I haven't had nearly enough. Now, where do you live?' I added boldly.

'Round the corner,' he replied.

'That's convenient!' I said with a throaty laugh.

'Convenient for what?' he shot back with a slightly discomfited air.

'Convenient for you!' I said. I leant across the table, and fixed him with a seductive stare. 'Take me back to your place,' I breathed.

'Minty, would you stop flirting with me,' he said wearily. 'It's rather tiring.'

'Why shouldn't I flirt with you?' I flung back. 'I *like* flirting with you. You're nice. You should be flattered that I'm flirting with you. I don't just flirt with anyone. Like some flighty . . .

flibbertigibbet. Take me back to your place,' I whispered again.

'OK, then,' he said. 'I *will* take you back to my place and I'll –'

'– rip my clothes off?!' I suggested gaily.

'Make you some strong coffee,' he corrected me crisply. 'And then I'll call you a cab.'

'I've been called worse things than that!' I said with a guffaw. I really was being *so* amusing! So we ambled out into the misty night, and I tucked my hand under Joe's arm. And despite his affected nonchalance, I could feel the rapid beat of his heart. We turned right into Albert Street, and stopped outside an elegant white terraced house. A wisteria had coiled and wreathed itself through the wrought-iron railings. I traced its twists and turns with my index finger as Joe groped for his keys. Then we descended the steps to the basement and he unlocked the door. Here I was, in Joe's place. I'd sometimes wondered what it was like. And now I knew. It was . . . small. *Very* small. I thought, with a pang, of Dominic's spacious house in Clapham. And Dominic's house was always incredibly tidy, but Joe's flat was a tip. Books were stacked up everywhere, like stalagmites; the carpet needed a clean. The double-glazed windows were grimed with dust, and a pile of laundry lurked in one corner. It was sobering – literally – to see the gulf between Dominic's elegant lifestyle and Joe's. I felt my desire subside in a cold shower of sharp reality.

'Sorry, it's a bit of a mess,' I heard Joe say as he clattered about in the tiny kitchen.

'You're right!' I called out. 'It's disgusting!'

'Minty!' said Joe, reappearing. 'That wasn't very nice.' Then he laughed and shook his head. 'You and your insults,' he said with an admonitory wag of his finger.

'Oh. Yes. That's right,' I said, backtracking madly. 'When I said "disgusting", what I really meant was – creatively chaotic.'

'Still, at least I've got some decent coffee,' he shouted above the buzz of the grinder. And soon we were sitting side by side on a battered old sofa which, I couldn't help noticing, did *not* co-ordinate successfully with the décor. And by now, depressed by my surroundings and by Joe's evident poverty compared to Dom, I had stopped flirting and was struck, instead, with a kind of awkward diffidence. This was a mistake. I'd nearly got carried away. I would get a cab, and go home.

'Thanks for supper,' I said quietly as I sipped my coffee out of a rather chipped mug. I gave him a sideways smile. 'Sorry I was being such a pain.'

'You weren't,' he said gallantly. 'You were being funny.'

'I was being an idiot – I drank too much.'

'You were a bit . . . overpowering.'

'I know,' I agreed, guiltily. 'Flirting like that. I ask you! *Ridiculous,*' I added with a soft laugh. 'It's because of all my stress.'

'So you didn't mean what you said?'

'What did I say?'

'You invited me to rip your clothes off. That was a joke, I assume.'

'Er . . . yes,' I said. 'Of course.'

'Fine,' he said. 'Don't worry, I won't.'

Oh. I experienced a stab of disappointment.

'You won't?' I reiterated, quietly.

'No, I won't.'

'Oh.' I looked at him. 'Why not?'

'Well, it wouldn't be right, would it?'

'Wouldn't it?' I said shyly.

'No. Because you're on the rebound. I told you that before.'

'I'm not on the rebound any more,' I pointed out. 'Frankly, Dominic's old news. He no longer makes the headlines for me!'

'Can I tell you something?' said Joe seriously. He turned towards me, and I took in his lovely mouth and his strong, lightly stubbled jaw, and his large, hazel eyes which seemed to gaze into me with a lighthouse intensity. 'Can I tell you something?' he repeated.

'Anything you like,' I said softly.

'I like you, Minty.' He sighed. 'In fact, I like you an awful lot. But I'm not going to be someone's comfort blanket ever again.'

'Look, I *am* over Dominic,' I repeated. 'I know you think I'm not, but I am. I mean, Dominic was not nice. Very. But you *are* nice,' I said with what I hoped was a beguiling smile. And now I didn't want to go home after all. I wanted to stay here with Joe. He looked so strong, and his aftershave smelt so nice. It wasn't Chanel, like Dom's. But it was lovely. Clean and fresh, with the scent of lime. I had an overwhelming urge to snuggle up to him and sniff his neck. And now I wanted him to put his arms round me and hold me. Just hold on to me. That's all he had to do. So I took his hand in mine, realising, as I did so, that I hadn't held a man's hand for months. Joe was single and sexy and kind. Joe was here. With me. So I did something daring. I held his hand to my lips and kissed it, once. But he didn't react. So I stood up.

'Well, I'd better be getting back,' I said. 'Let's call that cab.' But Joe didn't reach for the phone. He sat there staring at me. Just staring. But I knew I'd pushed things far enough. So I went over to the phone and started dialling. And suddenly Joe's hand was on mine, and the receiver went back down.

'Oh, Minty,' he said, as his lips found my own. 'Oh, Minty.' Then his hands were cupping my face, and now they were unbuttoning my shirt, and he was leading me down a narrow corridor to the back of his flat. And within a minute we were naked, and moving together, in the silence of his darkened room.

'Oh, Minty,' he kept saying. Just like that. 'Oh, Minty.' Over and over again. This was wonderful. I needed this. I needed him. He was so . . . *good.* 'Oh, Minty,' he said again.

'Oh, *Dominic,*' I sighed.

'*WHAT?*' Joe was out of that bed like a sprinter out of the blocks, and the room was flooded with light. I sat bolt upright, clutching the sheet.

'What did you just call me?' said Joe. His face was thunderous.

'I didn't call you anything,' I said.

'Yes, you did. You called me Dominic.'

'I did not.'

'Yes, you did.'

'Did not.'

'*Did*!'

'Did I?'

'Yes.'

God how *awful.*

'Oh. Well . . . sorry,' I said, beginning to panic. 'I didn't mean to. I really didn't. Look, I'm sorry. I'm really very sorry. Please, Joe, don't be cross.' But it was too late. He was clambering into his boxer shorts and had pulled his jumper over his head.

'I *told* you!' he went on as he stormed out into the sitting room. 'I told you, you've got too much baggage. You've got tons of it – your trolley's stacked up high.' He grabbed the phone and started dialling. 'Oh, Easicabs? A passenger for Princess Road, please, from 160 Albert Street. Basement flat. Of course you're not ready,' he reiterated, as he came back into the bedroom and pulled on his jeans. 'You're still obsessed with that bastard. Well – *be* obsessed with him. That's absolutely fine. But don't get involved with me.'

December

I was very shaken by my encounter with Joe. In fact, I felt terrible because I knew I'd really fouled up. Just when I was getting close to him. Just when I realised how much I liked him, and just when I *needed* him, too, given the disappointment I'd had at work. And he was wrong to say I wasn't getting over Dominic. I was. It was a simple mistake, that's all. The kind of mistake anyone can make. A momentary lapse. But I regretted it with all my heart. I picked up his book, lying on the bedside table in the spare room which *I*, and not Amber, now occupied. I turned to the inside back page, looked at his photo and was filled with remorse once more. I'd phoned him the next day, horribly hungover and very anxious, but his answerphone was on. So I'd left him a message, but he hadn't rung me back. I was upset about this, and was going to call him again, but then I decided not to. I knew I was in a hole, and that I should stop digging, and that in due course, he might come round. But ever since it happened, I've been feeling miserable, and jumpy – in stark contrast to Amber, who has discovered an inner calm. For if I've just taken a huge step back, she appears to have taken three strides forwards.

'I feel really tranquil,' she said this morning, as we walked round the Camden branch of Sainsbury's. 'I really don't know why, but for the first time since Charlie dumped me, I feel relaxed and positive, glowing with an inner wellbeing.'

'Lucky you,' I said ruefully. I'd decided not to tell her about my catastrophic encounter with Joe.

She grabbed a ticket at the delicatessen counter. 'I feel like my old self, Minty. Like my *best* self. I feel ready to face the world. The book's going really well now that I've swapped rooms with you. I'm *brimming* with creativity and optimism, I really feel –'

'NUMBER FORTY-THREE!'

'Oh, that's us. Half a pound of feta, please. Yes, I feel so *happy*, Minty, so fulfilled now, so . . .'

'Sorry, we've run out of feta,' said the woman on the Deli counter. 'How about a nice bit of smoked mozzarella instead?'

'Smoked mozzarella?' Amber gave her a frigid stare. She looked as though the woman had just offered her a 'nice bit of smoked parrot'.

'Yeah,' the woman reiterated, 'smoked mozzarella – £8.42 a kilo.'

'But I don't *want* smoked mozzarella,' said Amber. And her lower lip began to tremble with incipient rage.

Oh, for God's sake, I thought, it's not worth making a fuss about. It's just cheese, isn't it?

'It's OK. We'll take the smoked mozzarella,' I said to the woman, trying to assert myself in reasonable, non-aggressive, Nice Factor fashion.

'No, we bloody well *won't*!' Amber spat.

'Why on earth not?' I said. 'It's nice.'

'Minty, I don't know how you could be so insensitive!' she hissed, and her eyes began to fill. What on earth was going on?

'Amber,' I said quietly, out of earshot of the delicatessen counter, 'what, please, is the problem?'

'The problem is, Minty . . .' she began. By now tears were streaming down her face. 'The problem *is*,' she tried again, then sobbed. 'The problem is – uh uh – that smoked mozzarella was Charlie's *favourite cheese*!'

'Oh,' I said.

'And now I've been reminded of him. And it's like a knife in my heart. And that annoying woman was trying to force me to have smoked mozzarella when I had deliberately asked for Feta, and then you not even understanding –'

'I didn't know!' I exclaimed.

'Well, you know me better than anyone else,' she wept. 'So you *should* have known that Charlie always preferred mozzarella to feta in salads. And not just *any* mozzarella,' she added, almost hysterical by now. 'Not that squishy, watery, yukky, rubbery stuff in little plastic bags. No! *Smoked*! It had to be smoked!! *Now* do you understand, Minty? Now have I got through to you?'

'Isn't this a bit over the top?' I said, as Amber took off furiously with our trolley. 'All you had to say was, "No thanks. I'll have the Edam."'

'It's more complicated than that,' she wailed as she hurtled down the aisle towards Preserves. 'What you don't realise,' she said, stopping to grab a tin of pineapple chunks off the shelf, 'is that it takes a very long time to get over someone. In fact, it takes ages,' she sobbed as she set off again. '*Ages*!' Oh God, everyone was staring. 'And I'm not over Charlie yet,' Amber blubbed as she sped passed Hot Beverages. 'It's a very long process, Minty. I've got to mourn.'

'I know,' I acknowledged irritably.

'But you don't understand that!'

'I think I do,' I retorted, as we turned right into Chilled Foods. 'You seem to forget what I've been through myself with Dominic.'

'Oh, I know,' she acknowledged irritably. 'But you're getting over it quicker than me, because you're a happy, simple, sort of person.'

'Oh, thanks.'

'It's true, Minty,' she said, as she scrutinised the Dairy Spreads. 'Let's face it, you're Apollonian, you're light and bright. "*Un Coeur Simple*," as Flaubert might have said. But I'm Dionysian: dark, creative, and yet destructive' – she grabbed a carton of plain yoghurt – 'I *feel* things more than you.'

'You have no IDEA what I feel!' I flung back, outraged.

'Yes I do!'

'No you don't.'

'Oh *yes* I do,' she said.

'Oh no –' I stopped myself. People were staring. 'You *don't,*' I said with quiet emphasis. 'Because you never ask.'

'Well, why don't you tell me?'

'Because – haven't you noticed? – I don't tell *anyone*.'

'Well why not?'

'Because a) I don't want to and b) it's very boring for other people.'

'Minty!'

'But you!' I hissed. 'You talk about nothing else. You parade your feelings – your oh-so-*fine* feelings – for everyone to see.'

'I don't.'

'Yes you bloody well do. You wear your heart on your sleeve, and your guts. You're like one of those silly buildings by Richard Rogers. Your insides are on your outside!'

'Minty!' Amber's huge green eyes were goggling. 'I really don't know what's got into you lately – that wasn't very *nice*!'

'Good!' I said. 'I don't *want* to be nice. I've *had it* with being nice. Why do you think I did that *course*? Being nice gets me nowhere,' I went on fiercely, as I reached for a packet of ginger snaps. 'Being nice means I get dumped on my wedding day! Being nice means doing everyone else's work! Being nice means I always come second. No, not even second. *Last*! Being nice,' I hissed, 'means giving up my own bloody BEDROOM!'

'Well, yes, that *was* nice of you, Minty,' Amber conceded, aware now that we were an object of considerable curiosity. 'Anyway,' she went on, as we passed Crackers and Crispbreads, 'the point *is* . . . I still love Charlie. And I want him back!'

'WHAT?' Now she had *really* lost the plot.

'I want him back,' she repeated carefully. 'And I'm going to get him back. In fact,' she went on, with quiet menace, 'I'm going to make him come *crawling* back.'

'Amber,' I said, 'do you see those women sitting at the check-out?'

'Yes,' she said cautiously.

'You have bored them all, every single one, once a week for the past five months, about what a "bastard" Charlie was to you. And do you see that man stacking shelves over there?'

'Yes.'

'You've done the same to him, ditto. And to that bloke, over there, in Household Accessories. And you've shopped Charlie to every single person walking their dog on Primrose Hill. And you've graffitied abuse about him on the walls of at least six underground stations – maybe more.'

'Oh, so what?' she said, crossly.

'Aren't you afraid of looking a little . . . hypocritical here?'

'Not really,' she said.

'And do you know why our post is now arriving an hour and a half earlier than normal?' I enquired.

'No,' she said with a sniff.

'Because the postman is sick of you hijacking him every morning and bending his ear about Charlie. He's changed his shift so that he now delivers our mail before you're up.'

'Oh.'

'And have you forgotten the number of times you've called the phone-ins at London FM?'

'Oh, well . . . that . . .'

'Amber, you have slagged off Charlie to a minimum of five million people across London. The only thing you haven't done is to berate him from a soapbox on Speakers' Corner. And now you say you want him back?'

'Yes,' she said. 'I do.'

'WHY? Why do you want him back?'

'Because . . . because . . . I haven't got over him.'

'Well, he's got over you!'

'That's not true!' she exclaimed. 'He probably wants me just as much as I want him.'

'Amber, if he did, he'd have asked you. But he hasn't. Get *real*, you idiot! Get a LIFE!'

Yup, I think the Nice Factor's definitely starting to work now, I thought to myself, as Amber and I made our way back to the flat. They said it would take a while to kick in, and they were right. I'd stuck it up Melinda. And I'd enjoyed an uncharacteristically frank exchange with Amber. She was still snivelling as I opened the front door. But at least she could see my point of view.

'OK, OK, so I may have been a little . . . hard on him,' she acknowledged as we unpacked the shopping. She went over to her dartboard, and took down the heavily punctured photo of Charlie. 'But that's only because I was so *upset*. Because I love him *so* much. But I do want the bastard back, Minty . . .'

'I say!' screeched Pedro. And then he laughed.

'. . . and I've thought of a way to do it. But I'll need your help,' she added.

She needed my help??

'NO!' I said. There, I'd said it. And I was sticking to it. 'NO,' I said again.

'Pleeeease, Minteeeeee,' she whined.

'No. Absolutely not. No way.'

'Oh, go on.'

'*Nein. Non.* Negative.'

'You see, I've got this brilliant plan . . .'

'*Niet. Ochi. Nej.*'

'Let me tell you about it . . .'

'NonononononononoNO!'

'I want to go to the Anti-Slavery International Gala Ball,' she said. Oh.

'That charity do you went to with Charlie last year?'

'Yes. His father's on the board, so I know that Charlie will be there too. He always goes. It's in ten days. At the Savoy. Will you come with me, Minty? Please. *Please.*'

Oh *God*. Oh God.

'*N-o,*' I said.

'Go on.'

'No. No. *No.*'

'Ple-ea-ea-ea-ease,' she bleated.

'I just don't think it's a good idea.'

'It *is* a good idea,' she said.

'Look, if you want him back, why don't you just ring him up?'

'Well, because it wouldn't work. But if he *saw* me,' she said, suddenly brightening, 'wearing some *fantastic* ballgown, then it might.'

'Look, I . . .'

'Please, Minty,' she said. She put her arm round me. 'I'm sorry I was beastly. I really am. But I need your support.' Damn. I'm a pushover when people apologise. However horrid they were before.

'Please,' she implored me again.

'Oh . . . oh . . . *all right*,' I said, crossly. 'But we don't have partners,' I pointed out. However much I wanted to, I could hardly invite Joe. 'Who on earth could we go with?' I said.

'Ah. I've thought of that,' she replied.

When Amber said that she wanted us to hire men for the evening from a new escort agency called Boys'R'Us, I nearly backed out of the whole thing.

'It sounds absolutely hideous!' I said.

'No, it's not. It's very sensible,' Amber insisted. 'It's a new agency which enables successful independent women like you and me to hire a bloke for the evening. Everyone does it in the States.'

'But it sounds appalling,' I said. 'Hiring men?'

'No,' said Amber. 'We're not "hiring men". That makes it sound sordid. We're engaging the services of a walker. And a walker is the ultimate accessory for the successful single woman. Choosing him should be as simple as selecting a frock off a rack . . .'

'. . . I think you need someone who's entertaining and a bit trendy, Amber,' said Shirley Birley, the woman who ran Boys'R'Us. 'Vivienne Westwood, I'd say, rather than Norman Hartnell.' We were sitting in her tiny office in Oxford Street three days later. I'd rushed up there in my lunch hour.

'How many men have you got for us to choose from?' I enquired.

'Three hundred,' she replied. Mmm, not bad. I thought again of Joe. But I couldn't invite him. It was just too awkward. Amber was flicking through Shirley Birley's bulging files.

'Now, *he's* good-looking,' she said, as she gazed at a photo of a dark-haired man called Dustin.

'He's absolutely gorgeous,' Shirley agreed. 'He's a model. But the problem with him,' she added judiciously, 'is that he's stupendously boring.'

'Oh,' said Amber. 'Well, I don't want that. I mean, why would I pay £200 for a man to bore me, when I already know several men who'd do it free of charge? What about this one?'

'Oh, that's Jez,' said Shirley. I craned to look at the photo of a pleasant-looking man in a sports car. 'He's currently studying to be a hypnotherapist and amateur mystic,' Sheila explained. 'But I think his adenoidal voice would get you down.'

'Hhmmmm,' Amber said, thoughtfully. 'Him!' she said excitedly. '*That* one!' She scanned his profile. 'He fits the bill.'

'Yes,' said Shirley, with a funny little smile. 'That's Laurie. Yes . . . I think he'll do very nicely for you.'

Laurie was six foot two – he had to be tall, of course, for Amber – with dark brown hair and blue eyes, and he was thirty-six. I decided to go for someone slightly older. Someone with a bit of *savoir-faire,* who might be able to talk about opera, theatre and art. If I had to go through with this, then I was determined to have a reasonably entertaining man on my arm. My walker was called Hugo and he was forty-two. He looked as though he knew how to dress and he claimed to have a 'lively interest in the performing arts'.

'Book him,' I said, to Shirley. Then Amber paid the bill.

'I think this is very empowering,' she said afterwards, as we walked down the stairs.

'I just hope it's all worth it,' I said. After all, it was going to be incredibly expensive. The hire of the two men was £400, and we had to pay their expenses on top. Even their cabs home. With the tickets for the ball selling at £100 each, Amber's total bill was going to be over nine hundred pounds.

'I don't mind the cost, Mint,' she said. 'Anyway,' she added with a smile, 'I've got a feeling it's going to be money well spent.'

I certainly hope she's right, I thought as I sat in the office two days later, editing a feature on the Child Support Agency. I considered Amber's strategy risky and misguided, but she was not to be deterred. Once she decides on a course of action, that's it. She's just like Dom in that way. I sat, hunched over my tape recorder, spooling my material back and forth. By now I'd been editing for three hours without a break and my headphones were giving me hell. So I stopped to rub my ears and uncrick my neck and, as I straightened up, I glanced into the car park. And I saw an old Ford Escort pull up in the space now designated exclusively for Melinda's Porsche. Out got Deirdre – she was collecting Wesley – and there was nothing odd about this. Deirdre often fetches Wesley. Except that today she looked *different*. Her straggly brown hair had been cut into a glossy bob which swung about her flamboyantly bejewelled ears. She was wearing a short, chic suit, rather than her usual cheap separates, and for the first time, I could see her legs. And I realised that she had very good legs, and they were encased in glossy tights. And on her feet were heels, rather than her normal, dreary, flat lace-ups. She looked transformed. Her face was nicely made-up, she was clutching a smart matching bag, and as she bounced into Reception, she glowed as if lit by an inner flame. And I thought, I know why she looks like this. Her fertility treatment has worked. She's pregnant. And now she's happy. That's why she's taking more care of herself. So this morning, when I was chatting to Wesley about a piece I was doing for his programme, I casually tried to find out.

'I, er, saw Deirdre in the car park last night. She looks so well.'

'Oh, yes,' he said. 'She looks great.'

'She really seems to be . . .' How could I put this politely? '. . . making the most of herself.'

'Oh, yes.'

'She's so attractive, Wesley.'

'Yes,' he said wonderingly. 'She's really smartened up recently. Even her underwear. She used to be perfectly happy with Marks and Spencer's cotton knickers, and now she keeps buying all this, you know, sexy stuff.'

'Sexy stuff?'

'Yeah, lingerie. I keep finding little bags of it. She can't seem to get enough. She's asked me to get her some for Christmas. What's it called? Oh yeah, La Perla. Still,' he added with a shrug, 'as long as she's happy.'

'She certainly looks it,' I said. In fact, Deirdre had never looked happier.

'Let's hear the news,' said Wesley. He turned on the speaker, and there was Barry, pissed as a newt, as usual.

'. . . company cars . . . air-strikes . . . United Nations . . . Blair . . . and some news just in,' he added, audibly rustling his script. 'It's been reported at Westminster that the Minister for Family Values has resigned. Rumours have been circulating all day that Michael Hunt would quit, after it was revealed that his Commons secretary is expecting his child.'

'I feel really nervous,' said Amber as we got ready for the Anti-Slavery International ball the following Saturday.

'Well, at least you look fantastic,' I said. And it was true. In fact, she looked traffic-stoppingly beautiful. She was wearing a new ballgown from Thomasz Starzewski. It was in pale green satin with a bottle-green velvet bodice, and she had accessorised it with Granny's diamond earrings. I settled for a black velvet dress, size ten, ballerina-length, which I dressed up with a silver devoré shawl. To my surprise, I found myself feeling quite excited, though I wished that it was Joe who was going to partner me. But there'd been no contact at all. I resolved to send him a friendly Christmas card, in the hope that he'd start to soften. His coldness was getting me down. But as we set off in the cab for the Savoy I felt my mood begin to lift. It was an adventure, after all, though I thought Amber was mad to expose herself to the possibility of being rejected by Charlie again.

'Well, if that happens, it's my funeral,' she said, with a shrug of her lovely powdered bare shoulders. 'But at least then I'll *know*.'

When we arrived at the hotel, our walkers were already there, waiting, by the reception. They seemed genial, polite and friendly, and they both looked good in their DJs. As we walked downstairs to the Champagne Reception in the Lincoln Room I felt my spirits lift.

'A writer, eh?' said Laurie to Amber. 'So you're one of these Ladies who Launch.' She gave him a weak, disinterested smile, but I thought he was quite amusing. Perhaps the evening wouldn't be too bad. It might even be fun. The room was packed, making it hard to spot Charlie amongst the throng.

'– fabulous dress, Cressida.'

'– the merger's been sheer bloody hell.'

'– more champers, Peregrine?'

'– the Red Cross Ball was fab.'

'– where are you going for Christmas?'

'– *super* stuff in the tombola.'

'– LADIES AND GENTLEMEN – DINNER IS SERVED!'

The gilded, mirrored Lancaster Room looked lovely. Silver cutlery gleamed on damask cloths, flowers bedecked every table. Candles flickered romantically in the half-light, and expensive scents perfumed the air. So far our walkers had impressed us with their attentiveness and finesse. I was confident that, were I a smoker, Hugo would light my cigarette for me, and that if a bread roll were to fly my way he would gallantly intercept it. As for Amber, she was already bickering with Laurie as though he were one of her oldest friends.

'You put your knife in your mouth and you're in big trouble,' I heard her hiss as the starter arrived.

'Is it OK if I lick my plate?' he shot back with a smile, as he poured her a glass of Chablis. She gave him an evil look. Then she removed a pair of tiny, mother-of-pearl opera glasses from her evening bag and began to survey the huge room. Where was Charlie? I glanced at the souvenir programme. There was his father, Lord Edworthy, in the list of the Charity's board of governors. But no sign of Charlie himself. We were on a mixed table with an assortment of other 'odd' couples. There was a thin, bald, bespectacled man in his mid fifties who said he was the City Editor of a broadsheet. I looked at his ratty, calculating face and felt sorry for his partner, a rather large brunette called Cindy. Next to them was a couple in their mid forties, who said they dealt in antique silver. And opposite us was a retired industrialist, who I thought I vaguely recognised. He was accompanied by a blonde less than half his age and about twice his height. We all began to make polite small talk as we tucked into our vegetable terrine.

'So, how do you two know each other?' Mrs Antique Dealer asked Amber and Laurie. Ah. Oh dear. We'd all forgotten to do what clients and walkers should: concoct a convincing little story.

'Amber and I were at school together,' said Laurie, with a smile.

'Where was that?' the woman persisted, and I hoped that Amber would have the presence of mind not to say 'Cheltenham Ladies College'. But Laurie had got there first.

'Stowe,' he said. Amber's eyes opened just a little wider than normal.

'Yes, we were in the same A-level physics set,' said Laurie, warming to his theme. 'Amber got a C,' he confided. 'You didn't work hard enough, did you, darling?'

'Er . . . no, um, I suppose I didn't,' she replied with careful brightness.

'She was awfully naughty at school, weren't you, poppet?'

'Ha ha ha!'

'But I got an A,' he said.

'Oh, congratulations!' said the woman. 'I was always useless at Science.'

Amber's face was reddening with her burgeoning wrath. She'd have Laurie's bollocks for breakfast. I couldn't bear to watch. In any case, Hugo was chatting to me now.

'So, do tell me about your work,' he said with studied politeness. 'Working in radio must be absolutely fascinating.'

'Oh, it is. Most of the time,' I said. 'It has its ups and downs, though,' I added ruefully. 'What do you do?'

'Well, I was an estate agent, but I had to retire early on account of my poor health.'

'Oh dear,' I said.

'Yes, it was awful.'

'Oh, bad luck.' Whatever it was, I didn't want to know.

'You see, it all started with a bout of what I thought was indigestion,' he explained, as the waiters cleared away our first course. 'I had a lot of discomfort here –' he tapped his sternum.

'Really?' I thought he was going to talk about art.

'And my doctor insisted it was indigestion, but I was convinced it was an ulcer.'

'Isn't that easy to find out?' I asked as the grilled chicken breast stuffed with pistachio mousse arrived.

'Yes, but my symptoms were quite complex . . .'

'Well . . .'

'And then I began to have . . .' he lowered his voice '. . . terrible wind.'

'Oh dear.'

'Yes, it was appalling. Beans?'

'Er, no thanks.'

'And I thought maybe I had bowel problems.'

'I see.'

'I mean, I was spending a *long* time in the loo . . .'

'Really?'

'Oh, yes. I was in there for hours.'

'How fascinating.'

'I was convinced I had trouble with my colon.'

'What *lovely* flowers!' I exclaimed. And they were. On each table was an informal, Christmassy arrangement of yew, variegated holly and white anemones, loosely tied with a red tartan ribbon – just the kind of thing that Helen might have done.

'Anyway, so I went back to the doc and *insisted* on a scan . . .'

God, this man was *awful*. And to think he was being charged out at two hundred quid a go! I'd get Amber to insist on a refund. But then, to my joy, Hugo began chatting to Cindy and established that she was a GP. Now he was boring her instead of me, which gave me an opportunity to scan the room for Charlie, of whom there was still no sign. What a waste of a grand if he wasn't even here! I glanced at Amber, she was evidently trying to extricate herself from Laurie, but with limited success.

'I don't want to talk to you all evening,' I heard her say. 'I've got to find someone.'

'That's fine,' he said, soothingly, as she picked up her opera glasses again. 'And if you see someone you fancy just go straight ahead,' he said. 'Tell you what, we'll have an arrangement. If you're having a nice time being chatted up, you just pull on your left ear, like this, to indicate that you're fine.' She lowered her glasses and stared at him. 'BUT,' he went on with mock earnestness, 'if you get stuck with a bore, just touch the end of your nose, like this –' he touched her nose – 'and I'll come running over and rescue you.'

'Thanks,' said Amber uncertainly. Her sharp tongue seemed to have deserted her. She was clearly slightly unnerved. Oh God, this really wasn't going well.

'Coooeeeeeeee!' I heard someone call. 'Cooooeeeeee! Minteeeeeeee!' Christ, it was Mum!

'Hello, darling!' she said. 'I'm helping out with the raffle. Are you and your friends going to buy a few tickets – I'm sure you are, it's such a good cause. Would you like some?' she asked the hideous City Editor. 'They're only ten pounds each and we've got some *lovely* prizes!' He shook his shiny head.

'Oh, go on, Niall,' said Cindy. But he refused. He'd obviously calculated that the odds were a little long.

'I'll have some,' I said, with crisp crossness. I hate it when people are mean. 'I'll have ten,' I said. 'Oh, Mummy, this is Hugo; Hugo, er . . .'

'Smith.'

'Hello, Auntie Dympna!' said Amber. 'Didn't realise you'd be here.'

'Hello, Amber darling,' Mummy began, then she looked at the retired industrialist, and froze.

'Ivo!' she exclaimed. He was trying to hide behind his menu. 'Ivo – how *lovely* to see you. And WHAT a surprise! Now, I'm sure *you* want to buy *lots* of raffle tickets for your young, er, friend here, don't you?'

'Oh . . . er.'

'Oh, I'm *sure* you do, Ivo,' Mummy persisted. 'It's an excellent cause. All those poor little children forced to make bricks and carpets.'

'Well, er, I'm really not . . .'

'And often working in the most hazardous conditions.'

'Harrumph!'

'And how's Fiona, Ivo? Haven't seen her for weeks. I must give her a ring. Tell you what – I'll give her a ring tomorrow.'

'Well, er . . .'

'Why don't you buy a strip of ten, Ivo? I'm sure your young, er, lady friend, here would think that awfully generous of you . . .'

'Oh, I would! Ya!' squealed the girl.

'Or, even better – twenty!'

'Oh, ya! Ya!' squeaked the girl, clapping her hands like a performing seal.

'Yes, yes, of course,' Ivo grunted as he opened his dinner jacket and reached for his wallet.

'That's *so* nice of you, Ivo!' said Mum as she relieved him of four fifty-pound notes. 'I knew I could rely on you . . . Good luck, dear!' she whispered to the girl with a facetious smile. And then she was gone.

By now, pudding had arrived, and been eaten, and we were on to coffee and petit fours. And there was still no sign of Charlie, and the MC was announcing the start of the charity auction. On a podium at the front of the ballroom, illuminated by a spotlight was the auctioneer, Nick Walker. According to the souvenir programme, he was a furniture specialist from Christies.

'And our first lot is this magnificent Panama hat from Ecuador,' he began, as a hush descended. 'This one is of the finest quality, and will have taken around three months to weave by hand. You may be interested to know, ladies and gentlemen, that Panama hats are so called because Teddy Roosevelt wore one when viewing construction of the Panama Canal.'

Amber leant over to me and hissed: 'Any sign of Charlie?'

'No. I don't think he's here.'

'Oh God!'

'And let's start at a hundred pounds,' said Nick Walker. 'Am I bid one hundred pounds? Thank you, sir. At one hundred – thank you – and ten. And twenty. And thirty . . .'

'What a waste of money!' Amber spat.

'I think it looks rather nice,' said Laurie. She glared at him.

'I mean, hiring *you*, you idiot!'

'Oh, darling, you say the sweetest things.'

'. . . one hundred and forty . . . at the back there. Any advance on one hundred and forty?' At the table to our left, a hand went up.

'Oh, well done, sir! We have one hundred and sixty over there to my left. This is a fine Panama hat. Perfect for summer days and cricket matches. Any advance on a hundred and sixty? Thank you, madam. One hundred and eighty. With the lady at the back there, at one hundred and eighty pounds. And two hundred. Well done, sir. Two hundred pounds. And twenty. And forty. And sixty. Against you, sir. Thank you, sir. And eighty. Three hundred, sir?' The atmosphere was intensifying with the pace of the bidding.

'Thank you, madam. Three hundred and *fifty*.' Everyone gasped, then laughed.

'And it's with you at three hundred and fifty pounds, madam. At three hundred and fifty, once . . . twice . . . and –' the gavel came down – '*Sold*!'

'Why don't you ask your mum if he's here?' Amber whispered, as the next lot, a day at Wentworth Golf Course, went under the hammer. 'She's been going round all the tables. She might have seen him.' By now the bidding was well up as the auctioneer teased and cajoled people into putting up their hands.

'And that's two thousand pounds,' we heard him say. 'Any advance on two thousand pounds?'

'She's too far away,' I pointed out.

'So I had a stool test . . .' I heard Hugo drone as he sipped his coffee. 'My doctor said it was normal, but to be honest . . .'

'Still at two thousand pounds. Once . . . Twice . . . Thank you very much! And the next item is our star lot. Showing here.' Two of the waiters had lifted it aloft. 'It's a magnificent painting by Patrick Hughes – one of this country's most important contemporary artists.'

We all craned to see the picture, with its strange eye-bending perspective. It was a huge canvas of a maze.

'And I'd like to start the bidding for this at eight thousand pounds – a snip, may I say, for a Patrick Hughes. So, starting at eight thousand . . . And I have eight thousand on my left. Thank you, sir. And eight thousand five hundred at the back there. And do I have any advance on eight thousand five hundred pounds?' I looked to see who was bidding for the Patrick Hughes. And then, suddenly I saw Charlie. There he was. Right on the other side of the ballroom. He'd been obscured by the huge centrepiece of flowers, but now he'd pushed back his chair, and was just visible in the semi-darkness.

'He's over there,' I whispered to Amber. She trained her opera glasses in Charlie's direction.

'Oh yes. There he is. There he *is*!'

'Nine thousand pounds. And nine thousand five hundred.'

'Oh, Charlie,' Amber murmured. 'Oh, Charlie. *Oh*!'

'What?'

'He's with a *woman*!' Oh God.

'Well, who is it?'

'Can't see.'

'Let me look.' Amber's left hand went up in an elegant arc as she passed the opera glasses over Laurie's head.

'*Thank you*, madam!' shouted Nick Walker happily. 'Ten thousand pounds from the young lady in the fetching green ballgown.' Oh God. Oh God. 'At ten thousand pounds,' he repeated. 'Any advance on ten thousand pounds? Still less than the market value for a painting by Patrick Hughes.'

Amber looked stricken.

'Sit on your hands!' Laurie hissed.

'And it's still at ten thousand pounds. A bargain, may I say. With the lady in green . . . Ten thousand.'

'Oh God!' Amber moaned.

'Going once!'

'Oh no!'

'Going twice! At ten thousand pounds now. Last chance. LAST CHANCE! At ten. Thousand. Pounds . . .' Amber was white. The gavel was raised. It might as well have been a guillotine about to descend on her neck. 'And going now at ten thousand pounds . . . At ten thousand pounds. Again, once . . . twice . . . and – Oh, *thank you,* sir! Ten thousand *five hundred*! With the gentleman at the back there.'

'Never mind, darling,' said Laurie with a smirk.

'Oh, why don't you belt up!' she said, giving him a look that could cremate. 'Who's Charlie with, Minty?' she asked.

I peered through the glasses.

'I don't know,' I said. 'I can't see her face.' All I could see was a blue strapless dress, and strawberry blonde hair. Then the blue strapless dress and strawberry blonde hair stood up, and their owner slipped across the back of the room.

'Oh God, she's moved now. She's moving towards the door. She must be going to the loo.'

'Quick, let's follow her!' said Amber. 'Come on, Minty.' She had grabbed my hand.

'And at twelve thousand pounds now. Still with the gentleman at the back . . .'

'. . . God, I'll *kill* her,' Amber hissed as we squeezed our way through the tables. 'Stealing my boyfriend like that.'

'And last chance now at twelve thousand pounds. Last chance. It's your very. LAST. CHANCE. And at twelve thousand pounds . . . going . . . *going* . . . GONE!'

As we pushed through the double doors we heard the crack of the gavel, and a burst of applause, like sudden rain.

'The loo's this way,' said Amber, as we hurtled down the stairs. Inside, we found a small queue of women, their long taffeta skirts rustling as they waited. They were tut-tutting, and shaking their heads.

'– did you see that girl in the blue dress?'

'– disgraceful!'

'– pushing in like that!'

'– no manners.'

'– must have been desperate.'

'– must have been drunk, you mean!'

For through the wooden door, we could hear the sounds of strenuous regurgitation. And then it stopped. And we heard the cistern flush. And then Helen emerged, looking white, clutching a length of folded toilet-paper to her mouth.

'I'm awfully sorry about that,' she said, weakly, as she made her way to the basin. 'But actually, I'm not drunk. I'm pregnant.' An embarrassed hush descended, while she splashed water on her face. Then she looked in the mirror, and our eyes met.

'Oh, Minty,' she said, with a wan smile. 'Hello.' And I turned to look at Amber. But all I saw was the end of her green silk skirt before the door swung shut behind her with a firm, resounding 'click'.

She cried, of course. Not at first. At first she didn't say anything. She just waited outside the hotel while I collected our coats, and then a doorman hailed us a cab. And when we got in the back, she was silent. She just stared out of the window at the rain-soaked streets. But then she started to sniff, and by the time we were halfway up Great Russell Street she was sobbing. And she sobbed all the way to Primrose Hill. I didn't blame her. It was a terrible shock. A door had been slammed shut in her mind. After five months of anger and obsession, Charlie had finally been consigned to the past.

'You should have talked me out of it!' Amber wailed. 'You shouldn't have let me do it.'

'I did *try* to stop you,' I said. 'Don't you remember?'

'No,' she howled. 'Oh, all right, yes. Yes, I do remember now. Oh, Minty –' she laid her head on my right shoulder, and I could feel her tears on my skin. 'Oh God, I wish I'd listened,' she sobbed. 'I feel so bad.'

I felt bad too. I felt bad for Amber, though she'd brought it on herself. I also felt bad about the fact that we'd left the ball without saying a word to our escorts. It seemed rude, even if they were being paid. I wanted to dash in and explain that we were leaving. But Amber wouldn't wait. She wanted to get out of there as fast as possible. When we got back to the flat, we just sat, very quietly, in the kitchen.

'How come you didn't know?' she whispered.

'Because she didn't tell me. I had no idea.'

'Well, if you *had* known,' she croaked, 'would you have told me?'

'No,' I said, after a moment. 'Almost certainly not. Unless there was a particular reason why you *had* to know. But if I'd known before the ball, well then, yes, I would have told you. But I didn't know. For a long time I thought she was keen on Joe.'

'Hello!' squawked Pedro. I went into the hall and picked up the phone. It was Laurie.

'I'm sorry we left so abruptly,' I said, 'but Amber wasn't feeling well. Hang on a moment . . .' I covered the mouthpiece with my hand. 'Laurie wants to know if he can have a word with you.' Amber was hunched over the kitchen table. She shook her head.

'She'll ring you another time,' I said.

'Bloody well won't,' I heard her say.

'Laurie sounded very worried about you,' I explained. 'I think it was nice of him to ring. He didn't have to do that.' She didn't reply. She just gave me this strange, blinkless, stare.

'Money well spent,' she whispered.

'What?'

'I said it would be money well spent,' she repeated, and then she emitted a bitter, mirthless laugh. What an evening it had been. What a shock. And it was as much of a shock for *me*.

'I'm sorry,' said Helen again as we sat in her shop two days later. 'But I simply couldn't tell you.' I watched as her fingers quickly threaded the stems of red freesia and white roses through a moss-covered frame. 'I didn't know what to do,' she went on, as she snipped and split the ends. 'I didn't want Amber to know, because I knew she'd be hurt and furious, and, to be honest, I was worried about what she might do. I mean, I know she's your cousin and everything, Minty, but, well, you know what she's like.'

'Yes,' I said. 'I do.'

'And that's why I couldn't say anything to you.'

'I wouldn't have told her,' I said, with slight indignation. 'I'm not one to blab, you know.'

'Well, to be honest, I didn't want to tell anyone,' she explained. 'Because I didn't know what was going to happen.'

'How did you meet Charlie again?'

'A couple of days after you and I got back from the honeymoon, he came into the shop. He didn't know it was my shop, but he was passing and, on the spur of the moment, he decided to send Amber some flowers.'

'Oh yes,' I said, remembering the valedictory wreath of pink roses.

'He felt bad about breaking up with her, even though he knew it was right. And he seemed so pleased to see me again, although we'd hardly spoken at your wedding. Then, with everything that had happened in that previous week, he just wanted to talk. So he asked me out to lunch. Then a few days later, he asked me out to dinner. And that's how it all began.'

'I see,' I said, as I fiddled with a discarded carnation. 'So that's why you were being a little – distant.'

'Yes. Because of Charlie. It was *very* awkward. And then six weeks ago I got pregnant. I didn't mean to. And I was desperately worried in case he thought I was trying to trap him. So I wasn't talking to anyone while I made up my mind what to do. And I decided to tell him, and he was thrilled about it. In fact, he was so thrilled about it he took me to Paris for the weekend and proposed.'

'Ah. So *that's* why you went back. But why did you keep the engagement a secret?'

'Because Charlie didn't want to hurt Amber's feelings, that's why. So we didn't tell a soul and we didn't announce it in the papers. But I suppose the cat's out of the bag now, so it doesn't matter any more.'

'You see, I thought you were being a bit funny with me because you were keen on Joe.'

'Why did you think that?'

'Because you'd bought his book, and you were talking about him so enthusiastically.'

'Well, that's because he's terribly nice, Minty. He's stable,' she added pointedly. 'He's creative, he's good-looking, and he's fun.'

I looked at her and said nothing.

'OK,' she said, putting down her secateurs. 'OK, OK, OK – I confess. The reason I was so positive about him and the reason why I kept in touch with him was because I thought that when he came back to London you two might . . .' Her expression was full of meaning.

'We did,' I said bleakly.

'You *did*?' she said.

'Yes.'

'Well, good. That's wonderful.'

'No, it isn't,' I said. 'It's terrible.'

'Why? Don't you like him?'

'Yes. Yes, I do.'

'Then what's the problem?'

'The problem is that when we were . . . you know . . . I accidentally called him Dominic.'

'Oh,' said Helen, seriously. 'Oh dear, you insulted him.'

'Yes, but not in the way he likes.'

'What?'

'Oh, sorry,' I said, 'it's a kind of private joke. Anyway, he was *very* upset,' I went on. 'And he won't speak to me now. He says I've got too much baggage. He says I haven't got over Dom.'

'Well, you obviously haven't,' she said. She pulled a feathery spray of gyphsophila out of an aluminium tub. 'It's five months now, Minty,' she went on, as she sliced the end. 'Nothing stays the same. I wish you *could* get over Dominic. It's not even as though he's worth it.'

'I *am* getting over him, in some ways,' I replied. 'But the problem is that what he did was so hard to understand.'

'Well, your friends understand it, Minty. We all thought he was . . . flaky. Neurotic. It was so obvious. A man too scared to step on a plane? And so domineering,' she went on. 'You were so loyal, but we could all see how controlling he was. Those little jokes of his at your expense if you ventured an opinion. Rolling his eyes at us, if you talked for more than a minute at a time. Charlie said that Dominic was always making cracks to him about how "opinionated" you are, when you're not.'

'At dinner parties he used to tread on my toes, under the table, if he thought I was saying too much. Or he'd discreetly squeeze my hand, to shut me up.'

'How horrible!' she said crossly. 'How could you *stand* it? Who the hell did he think he *was*? And he just talked about insurance all the time,' Helen added contemptuously. 'Didn't he realise it's simply not the done thing?'

And I thought no, despite all his etiquette books; despite all that acquired polish; despite that gleaming patina, that glitz, that gloss – Dominic had never learned how to behave.

'Charlie didn't like him,' said Helen. 'He told me he didn't really want to be best man. And look at the mess he was left with! Dominic phoned once or twice, to try and sort of apologise, but Charlie pretended to be out. You're *well* out of it, Minty,' she went on vehemently. 'I mean, why would you want to be with a man who treated you like that *before* you were married?'

'Why?'

'Yes, why? I mean, why did you stay with him?'

Why. *Why*? God I *hate* that question. That's what everyone asks me, and, quite frankly, I wish they *wouldn't*.

'Well, relationships are . . . complex, aren't they?' I replied, carefully. 'People are in them for all sorts of things. And nothing's ever *all* bad. Sometimes Dom was nice to me, and he took a great interest in my career.'

'He just thought it looked good,' said Helen, cutting off a length of Cellophane, 'to have a wife with a glamorous broadcasting career. That's why he was interested. I bet if you'd been a teacher, or a nurse, or a florist like me, he wouldn't have looked at you twice.' This had the ring of truth. 'And you changed, Minty,' she went on. 'You went all quiet, as though you were a dog that's scared it's going to be beaten. You became –' she waved her secateurs at me – 'not your true self. In fact, Minty, you were a bit of a doormat.'

'I know. And I think, ironically, *that's* why he dumped me.'

'But he *wanted* you to be a doormat! That's *exactly* what he wanted.'

'Yes, but then he lost interest. In becoming a doormat I'd lost his respect. You see, I think that, in a way, what happened to me was my fault, for being too nice. For agreeing to all that crap.'

'But you're still doing it!' she exclaimed. 'You're *still* being too nice to Dominic. I mean, my God, Minty – you're even taking the *blame*!'

'Well, a relationship's about two people,' I said. 'I was one of them. And it can't have been *entirely* his fault.'

'He's shallow and inadequate, Minty. He's ruthlessly selfish and he's cruel. That's why he did what he did.'

'But what I don't understand is, why would a man plan a wedding to the degree that Dominic did – draw up a pre-nuptial agreement, and even take out wedding insurance – if he didn't intend to go ahead with it on the day? It just doesn't make *sense*, Helen. That's what gets me down. Not fully knowing why. *That's* what's holding me back. And that's why I messed up with Joe.'

'Then ring Dominic and demand to know. Demand a satisfactory explanation.'

'I don't want to ring him.'

'Then go round to his house and *make* him explain. You have a right to do that, Minty, because what he did was terrible.'

'I'm not going to do that,' I said firmly. 'My pride won't let me. Anyway, it's too late.'

'Then you may never find out, which means you'll never move on. It will fester for years,' she added, as she snipped off a length of yellow ribbon. 'Joe's right – you do have too much baggage. Sorry to be so forthright,' she said. 'This is the first time I've really spoken to you about Dominic since Paris. And I couldn't say all this then because it was too soon. And because of what's happened to me, I didn't have the chance to talk to you before.' I looked at Helen's engagement ring. It was a large, dark pink ruby, surrounded by small diamonds.

'So, when's the wedding?'

'February the fourteenth.'

'Valentine's Day,' I said.

'Charlie's a stupid bastard,' said Amber, again. 'Go on. Say it. Charlie. Is. A. Stupid. Bastard.' Pedro stared at her blankly, then blinked.

'You're wasting your time,' I said. Amber secured a length of silvery tinsel to Pedro's cage, which he duly started to shred.

'Do you want to put the fairy on top of the tree – or shall I?' she said. She'd spent all morning decorating a small conifer which was now positioned, baubles twinkling, in the window.

'You can do it,' I said. I was reading the *Weekly Star*. What did Sheryl von Strumpfhosen's horrorscope predict for me today? I turned to Libra. The scales. The sign of partnership and balance, I thought with a bitter little smile. 'Libra, your optimistic outlook is about to be restored,' wrote Sheryl. 'You'll be inundated with opportunities to enjoy yourself. The skies are brightening ahead.' Hmmm. I allowed myself to feel cautiously optimistic. Then I looked at Cancer to see what lay in store for Dom. I can't break the habit. I always read his sign as well. I found myself hoping it was bad. 'Cancer,' wrote Sheryl, 'after a turbulent and difficult time, you are shortly to get everything you deserve.' My heart leapt. Good. Something bad was going to come his way. And then I found myself wondering what Joe's star sign is, but I didn't know. I looked at the Christmas card I'd just written to him. I'd simply signed it, 'Love, Minty'. Yes, please love Minty, I thought.

'Isn't Christmas *fun*?' I heard Amber say. She genuinely seemed to be enjoying herself. In fact, all things considered, she'd recovered remarkably well from the trauma of the ball.

'You know, Mint, it's a relief,' she said again, as she hung up some paper chains. 'And the reason it's a relief is because it just goes to show how shallow Charlie is. Just waltzing off with your friend Helen within *minutes* of dumping me.'

'Er . . . yes,' I said.

'It proves he has no fine feelings. None. And *what* a cliché!' she exclaimed, contemptuously. 'Best man goes off with bridesmaid. I *ask* you!'

And when she said that I realised that something had been salvaged from the ruins of my wedding day. Some human happiness at least, though not my own.

'In fact, I'm so disappointed in Charlie,' I heard Amber say, 'that I'm taking him out of the book.'

'Oh, good,' I replied.

'I mean, I wouldn't like him to believe I was even *thinking* about him,' she went on with a tight little laugh, 'let alone *immortalising* him in a work of art.'

'Oh, quite. I don't think he'll be too disappointed.'

'And now that I know what a shallow, spineless drip he is, well – I just think, what a lucky escape. And I've had an epiphany, Minty. A revelation. I mean, Charlie was *OK*, but he was a bit boring. What I *really* need is a sparky kind of bloke.'

'Sparky?'

'Yes,' she said, as she flicked on the fairy lights and they began to wink and flash. 'A witty bloke. That's what I need. A bloke with a bit of bottom.'

'I couldn't agree more,' I said.

'Oh, hel-lo,' squawked Pedro as the phone rang out. 'Hello!' he screeched again. Amber picked up the phone. 'Yes,' she said. 'Who? . . . Oh Christ – not you again!' She rolled her eyes theatrically at me. 'Look,' I heard her say. 'How many times do I have to tell you? No . . . No, I don't want to go out to dinner with you. I've got better things to do with my time . . . Like what? How dare you!' She rolled her eyes at me. 'I've got a novel to write here . . . No, you can't be in it. There's a waiting list, you know . . . Well, it's two years if you want to be portrayed sympathetically; if you want to be portrayed *un*sympathetically, I'm afraid it's three . . . Yes, I'm *quite* sure I don't want the pleasure of your company . . . No, I'm not tempted in the slightest. In fact, I think you've got a bit of a nerve after your performance at the Savoy . . . Yes, yes, I do understand that you wouldn't charge me on this occasion . . . Yes . . . Yes, I agree that two hundred pounds down to nothing represents an excellent discount. But I'm afraid you'll just have to offer this unrepeatable bargain to someone else, because I'm just not interested. Got that? Thank you *so* much for calling. And a very Happy Christmas to you too.'

'Some people!' she giggled as she came back into the sitting room. She heaved an exasperated sigh. 'What on earth makes Laurie think I'd have anything to do with a man who hires himself out to strange women?'

January

'Hello?' I called as I turned the lock in the door on New Year's Day. 'Anybody home?' That was funny, Amber said she was going to be here over Christmas, working on the book. Where on earth was she? 'Hello! Amber?' I called again. No reply. How odd. There was Pedro, in his cage, asleep, his head tucked into the nook between his wings. But there was silence elsewhere. Perhaps she was working upstairs and hadn't heard me come in. Maybe she'd gone out. But I could see her coat, on its peg. I opened the sitting-room door. The television was on. And there was Amber, sitting in front of it, with tears streaming down her face. On the screen was a brown, floppy-eared rabbit, lying on a table at the vet's. The camera closed in on its back leg, which looked damaged. Then the shot widened to reveal Rolf Harris.

'Well, poor little Fluffy's in a right old state here,' said Rolf cheerfully to camera. 'That encounter with the neighbour's lawn mower has left him rather the worse for wear.'

'Uh – uh . . .' Amber sobbed quietly.

'His left hind leg's broken in two places and I'm afraid it looks like bad news. We could even be talking amputation.'

'Oh *no*!' moaned Amber. Her cheeks were stained with dark rivulets of mascara, her chin was dimpled with distress. The rabbit stiffened as the vet injected it. I sat down quietly on a chair.

'Now, will Fluffy make it – or won't he?' said Rolf, pushing his glasses a bit further up his nose. 'Well, personally I'm not putting any money on it. Sometimes small animals don't come out of the anaesthetic,' he went on in a confidential whisper. 'Their little systems just won't take it. So we've got a very tense wait ahead of us, folks . . .'

'I can't watch,' said Amber, standing up. 'Just . . . tell me what happens, will you, Minty?' I heard her footsteps creaking up the stairs.

'In the meantime,' said Rolf, 'let's see how Willy the Wallaby is doing down at the animal sanctuary after that fight he got into with Pat the pot-bellied pig . . .'

'It's OK, Amber,' I called up the stairs, five minutes later. 'The rabbit's better now.' I heard her door creak open.

'It's better,' I repeated.

'The bunny?'

'Yes.'

'And did they . . . ?' she asked tremulously.

'No,' I said. 'They didn't. They put two steel pins in, and he's hopping about again now, good as new. Come and look.' She flew downstairs, and stared at the screen, a damp Kleenex clasped in one hand. And there was Fluffy, limping slightly as he moved gingerly around his pen.

'Thank God,' she breathed. 'Thank *God.*' She smiled, and wiped her eyes. She's just like Pedro, I thought, again, as the credits rolled. She's a sentimental old bird too.

'Anyway, Happy New Year,' I said.

'Oh, Happy New Year!' beamed Amber, now fully recovered. 'How was Christmas?' she enquired, as she turned off the TV and took my coat.

'It was fine,' I replied, as we went into the kitchen. 'A bit quiet, though. Mum spent the whole time down at Crisis, dishing out turkey to the homeless. So it was just Dad and me.'

'Oh,' said Amber.

'There was a bit of a row, actually,' I confided, as she put on the kettle. 'Dad told Mum that *he* was having a Crisis at Christmas, but it made no difference. She refused point-blank to come home.'

'Minty,' said Amber, 'why has Auntie Dympna got this, you know, obsession about good works?'

'I don't know,' I replied. 'Maybe it was discovering that Saint Dympna was the patron saint of lunatics. That might be the answer. Or it could be something to do with her frontal lobes. All I know is, Dad's at the end of his tether. He threatened her with divorce.'

'My God!'

'Mind you, he's always doing that. And usually it's a joke. But now that he's retired, I'm not quite sure that it is a joke any more.'

'Oh dear.'

'He's very unhappy. He never sees her.'

'What does he do with himself?'

'He goes to the golf club. He reads. He listens to the radio. But he's really fed up. He says he doesn't want to go into his dotage alone.'

'Don't blame him.'

'He's all for giving to charity,' I added. 'But he told Mum, yet again, that she should leave some room for us.'

'Poor Uncle David,' Amber murmured as she made me a cup of coffee. 'You know, Auntie Dympna's just like Mrs Jellyby in *Bleak House*,' she went on authoritatively. 'Madly raising money for the poor of West Africa while her own children run around half-starving and in rags. *Bleak House* is such a wonderful novel,' she went on expansively, as she passed me a biscuit. 'A scathing portrayal of a society permeated with greed, hypocrisy and guilt. A masterpiece of narrative art.' And when she said that, I thought, yet again, how interesting Amber is when she's talking about classic books, and how I could listen to her all day. And I thought, too, how strange it is that such a clever and perceptive critic should write such tosh herself.

'Anyway – here it is!' she said. 'Ta-dah!' She plopped her latest manuscript down on the kitchen table with a theatrical flourish. 'I proudly present *Animal Passion*!'

'Gosh, you've finished it – congratulations!'

'No! *Really?*' squawked Pedro, waking up. He blinked, then shook himself, and began to preen his wings.

'I worked on it all over Christmas,' said Amber excitedly. 'Twelve hours a day. I felt driven, uplifted and inspired. And I really think that, with this one, I'm finally going to break through.'

And so we cracked open a bottle of champagne to celebrate the completion of her ninth book and the start of a New Year which would bring – we knew not what. For some people, of course, it would bring weddings, and babies. Helen, for example. And hundreds and thousands of others, I thought, as I surveyed the 'Forthcoming Marriages' column in *The Times*. There are always so many engagements at this time of year – just as there are always so many divorce petitions too. Christmas seems to be a fault line, causing domestic upheavals, either for better or for worse. And I was just idly going through the announcements – Mr R. McDonald to Miss B. King, Mr S. Bingley to Miss A. Bradford, Mr J. Collins to Miss L. Harper, Mr T. Firkin to Miss K. Frog – my eyes lazily scanning downwards – Parker to Knoll, Marks to Spencer, Harvey to Nicholls, Fortnum to Mason – blah, blah, blah, Oh, *so* many – Whites to Lilly, Ede to Ravenscroft, Laurent to Perrier, Lane to Park . . .

Lane? My heart began to beat wildly, and I felt blood suffuse my face. '*The engagement is announced,*' I read, '*between Dominic, only son of Mr N. Lane of Birmingham South, and Mrs M. Lane of Sutton Coldfield, and Virginia, elder daughter of Mr and Mrs C. Park of Highview House, Melton Mowbray, Leicestershire.*' Dominic? Dominic? *Engaged?* And then it was my turn to burst into tears.

'How *could* he?' I sobbed. 'How *could* he, so soon?'

'It's fucking outrageous,' said Amber. 'Bastard,' she added for good measure. 'Mind you,' she went on bitterly, 'that's what Charlie did.'

'Yes, but Charlie had a good reason, Amber. Let's face it, he wanted children, and you didn't.'

'Too bloody right. They ruin your figure, and you can't go out for eighteen years. And by the time you can, none of your friends want to see you because you're both incontinent *and* moronic.'

'OK, that's how *you* feel,' I said, rolling my tear-filled eyes. 'But Charlie didn't agree. So you had to part. That's quite understandable. But I don't understand how Dominic could find someone else so quickly, let alone know them well enough to propose.' I wept. '*Unless* . . . ?' A cold hand clutched at my heart.

'You don't think that he . . . and she . . . ?' Amber said. Her eyes had narrowed to slits. I could see the mental wheels grind and turn.

'I don't know,' I murmured hoarsely. 'I hadn't thought of that.'

'Well, maybe *that's* the reason,' she said, quietly. 'Maybe *that's* your answer, Minty.'

'Maybe it is,' I croaked. I felt sick. How naïve of me, how very naïve, to think he hadn't been unfaithful.

'*Or*, she's up the duff, like Helen,' Amber suggested. 'On the other hand,' she added judiciously, 'I can't quite imagine him doing the decent thing if she were.'

And the awful fact is, Amber was right.

'No, *that* wouldn't be it,' I wept. 'He probably – uh – uh – *loves* her. He was probably – uh – having an affair. But then, why didn't he break it off with me *before*?'

'Minty . . .' said Amber, quietly. She was peeling an apple for Pedro.

'What?'

'Well, I don't know whether this is the right time to tell you this, but I know Virginia Park.'

'Oh,' I whispered. I was shocked.

'Do you want to know?' she asked. 'Shall I tell you?' I looked at her. I wasn't sure.

'Yes,' I said quietly. 'Tell me.'

'Well, she's from quite a rich family,' Amber began.

'You can tell that from the address,' I said miserably. I looked at the announcement again. 'Highview House, Melton Mowbray.'

'She's a pork-pie heiress.'

'Oh. Well. Good for her. But how do you know?'

'Because she was at school with me.'

'Ah.' Fear gripped my heart. I thought I was going to vomit. 'Is she pretty?' I asked.

'Well, pretty ordinary,' said Amber, expansively. 'She's got a horsey-looking face, ankles thicker than Hillary Clinton's and no perceptible upper lip. And she must be thirty-eight if she's a day, because she was four years above me.' This cheered me up, a bit. Though it also surprised me greatly.

'It's not like Dominic to go for an older woman,' I pointed out. 'He said he could never understand why some men married women a few years older than themselves. He said he thought it was wrong and that he'd never do it.'

'Ah, but Virginia's loaded. So maybe he's been generous enough to make an exception in her case.'

'But he's got money of his *own*,' I said. 'I just can't quite see that swaying him. Of course they're smart,' I added bitterly, 'he'd love that. A bit of background. Mixing with the county set.'

'Oh, they're not really smart,' said Amber dismissively. 'At school we used to tease her for being such a *nouve*.'

'Oh.'

'We called her Porky Parky. And Miss Piggy. Her family were very . . . aspiring.'

'Just like Dominic, then.'

'She had this really over-elocuted voice,' Amber went on. 'It was bizarre. And the family had no taste. We used to scream with laughter when the gold Porsche turned up on Speech Day.'

'Really?'

'And she was a real bossy boots. She was a prefect – just loved ticking me off. How extraordinary to think that he's marrying *her*,' said Amber with an uncomprehending shrug.

Marrying her. My God. This was all too much. I buried my head in my arms.

'Happy New Year,' said the postman as I left the house for work. I just gave him a grim little smile. Because it wasn't a

Happy New Year. It was a miserable one. In fact it was the worst one I'd ever had. Yet again, Sheryl von Strumpfhosen had got it completely and utterly wrong. 'The skies are brightening ahead,' she'd predicted. Bullseye, Sheryl! Oh yes, things are *really* looking up. And as for Dominic's – he was getting 'everything he deserved', was he? Did he really deserve to be happy with someone else, I thought bitterly, let alone so soon? I mean, it was one thing to have been abandoned by him on my wedding day. It was quite another that he'd gaily gone on to someone else – *and* made a commitment – within a mere five months! The pain, which had begun to ebb away slightly, now flooded back, redoubled. My wound stung anew, as though it had been sprinkled with sulphuric acid.

Going into work the next day was agonising. I felt intolerant and sharp. And my disappointment at losing out to Melinda grated on me even more.

'Minteeeee,' she said, in her wheedling, 'help me' tone.

'Yes?' I said, trying not to breathe in through my nose. She was changing the baby on her desk.

'Chwist!' she said. 'It's the nappy fwom hell!'

'Why don't you get your nanny to do it?' I snapped. 'Preferably in the car park!'

'Because I sacked her. She was useless. And I haven't got another one yet. Do you know, Minty, I've alweady been thwough *thwee* nannies. Can you believe it?'

'Yes,' I said matter-of-factly. 'I can.'

'Anyway, Minty,' Melinda went on, blissfully oblivious to my Arctic *froideur*, 'I just wondered whether you could tell me about the Euwo again. I haven't quite got the hang of it yet.'

'I'm awfully sorry, Melinda,' I said with formal pleasantness, 'I'm afraid I don't understand it myself.'

'Minty,' said Wesley. He looked excited as he came into the office with a pile of tapes.

'I'm sorry, Wesley,' I said. 'I don't have time to help you edit your tapes, so you'll just have to do it yourself.'

'I wasn't going to ask you to help me,' he said. 'I just wanted to tell you something. I wanted to tell you something about –'

'I'm sorry, Wesley,' I said, putting on my headphones. 'I'm really busy and I don't have the time.' Zero Tolerance. That's what I had. And Maximum Misanthropy. I didn't want to know about anyone else's problems. My heart had calcified. And round it I'd installed a drawbridge, a moat and six Rottweilers. The Nice Factor would be proud of me.

Jack looked dismal too, but I didn't try to find out why. I was determined simply to keep my head down and quietly slog away; to bury my memories of Dominic and this latest development under fathomless layers of work.

Over the next few days I churned out features on – Oh God – civil weddings, and teenage mums, and fifty-five-year-old women expecting Petri-dished-up twins. I'd rather do boring financial stories, I thought crossly, or sport, or fashion or hedgehog racing in Milton Keynes – *anything* rather than all this marriage and maternity stuff which only exacerbated my pain. And having to trek off to see Citronella Pratt was an added sore.

'Did you have a good Christmas, Araminta?' she enquired.

'Yes, I did,' I lied.

'Just you and your parents, I suppose.'

'Yes, yes, that's right.'

'How lovely,' she said. 'We had *so* many people here,' she confided smugly. 'I mean, this is a pretty big house, but even so it was a bit of a squash. Still,' she went on softly, 'we managed. And how about New Year?' she said over her shoulder as she reached down for a book. 'I suppose your New Year Resolution was to find yourself a husband?'

'No,' I said. 'Actually, my New Year Resolution was to kill and then dismember you.' She turned and gave me a quizzical stare.

'I'm sorry, what was that?'

'I said my New Year Resolution was to *remember* what *you* said.'

'Ah. You know, you single women are so *brave,*' she crooned, as she lowered her huge backside on to a nearby chair. 'I really don't know *how* you cope.'

I just gave her a blank-eyed smile, then mentally counted to ten in order to prevent myself from clubbing her to death with the microphone or strangling her with the lead. In the papers this week there'd been a debate about working mothers. In her column, Citronella had bravely leapt to their attack. I pressed the 'Record' button with a sinking heart.

'I do think women who have small children and who work are *terribly* selfish,' she announced in her low, deceptively sweet voice. 'We all know that the first five years of a child's life are the most formative years,' she went on smoothly. 'And children *need* to be with their mothers during that vital period. Now, I'm a feminist,' she added. Of *course*. 'But I think that on *this* issue, feminism has got it wrong.'

'But most women don't have the luxury of choosing whether or not they go back to work,' I said. 'They *have* to go back. Their income is essential.'

'Oh, I *know* that old argument,' said Citronella with an indulgent smile. 'But the fact is that sacrifices *have* to be *made*.'

'But you don't have to make those sacrifices yourself, do you?' I said with unfamiliar boldness. She blinked. Looked at me. Then gave me a *faux*-guilty smile.

'Well, no,' she conceded, 'I don't. I suppose I *am* in a very fortunate position in that my husband is so successful. And then of course I'm doubly lucky in that I have always been able to pursue my career from home.'

'Career?' I said, archly. 'What *was* your career, exactly, before you began writing your column?'

'Oh, childcare consultancy,' she said confidently, though her large behind shifted on her chair. 'But I really don't want to brag about my past accomplishments, Araminta. And though it's not always easy working at home, with a very boisterous and *particularly* demanding toddler, I am in the very fortunate position of having help in the home.'

'Yes,' I said, crisply, 'you have a nanny, and a cleaner, I believe.'

'*And* a gardener,' she added with a smirk. 'Oh yes, I know how *lucky* I am,' she continued, fiddling with her voluminous frock. 'Terribly, terribly, lucky. But that's not the point here. The point is that small children need to be with Mummy.'

'Well, thanks very much, Citronella,' I said breezily, as I pressed the 'Stop' button. 'Another very thoughtful contribution to our programme.' Citronella showed me to the door herself today. And I glanced at the beautiful Françoise, playing with the infant Sienna, and wondered how she could stick working for this dreadful woman and why on *earth* she stayed.

'Anyway, chin up, Minty!' said Citronella as I stepped on to their drive.

'Chin up? It's not down,' I replied with a breezy smile. But of course it was. It was in the gutter. Scraping along with all the stones and the dirt. I half expected to wake up one morning and find it had double yellow lines. I was miserable. I was in despair. This was the bleakest of all midwinters. My rock had rolled down the mountain again and lodged in a deep crevasse. At work I coped by being businesslike, crisp and unfriendly. Nor was I any fun at home. I stayed in my room, reading *Great Expectations* and reflecting on my bad luck. I brooded on it; I luxuriated in it. I nursed it as though it were a glass of vintage port. And I must have been really desperately unhappy, because when, at last, Joe phoned, I didn't want to know.

'This is the third time he's rung,' said Amber from the other side of my door two days later. 'Why won't you speak to him?'

'Because a) I don't want to,' I replied. 'And b) I don't want to.'

'He says he wants to talk to you.'

'Well, he didn't before. He ignored me for over a month.'

'May I remind you, Minty,' said Amber, 'that the Season of Goodwill is not yet over.'

'It is for me.'

'Why won't you have a word with him, Minty?'

'Because he hurt me. That's why.'

'Well there's no need to hurt him back.'

'Why not?' I said airily. I *wanted* to hurt men. Miss Havisham got back at them by educating her ward Estella to despise them. And now I would despise them too. It wasn't difficult.

They *were* despicable. All of them. An inferior breed. With no feeling. Jilting one woman and then gaily going on to the next. I had no faith in them. None. I didn't want to know. In fact, I didn't want to know about anyone. In just a few days I'd grown a brittle carapace of unconcern. My shell was as hard and unwelcoming as the frosty January ground. I didn't need the Nice Factor any more. I wasn't 'nice' at all. And when, on the sixth, Amber called out that we'd better take down the Christmas decorations because otherwise we'd incur bad luck, I emitted a bitter, hollow laugh. So she said she'd do it herself. And she told me she was going to plant the Christmas tree in my little garden, as she'd deliberately asked for one with roots. But I didn't offer to help her. I was hard and heartless. Because Dominic had been so heartless to me. So when, later that day, I heard Amber calling, I simply groaned, and turned back to my book:

> *Miss Havisham beckoned Estella to come close . . . 'Let me see you play cards with this boy.'*
>
> *'With this boy! Why he is a common labouring-boy!' I thought I overheard Miss Havisham answer – only it seemed so unlikely – 'Well? You can break his heart.'*

'Minty!' I heard Amber call again. 'Come down here.'

'Why?' I shouted back.

'Just do it.'

'Don't want to.'

'Come on!'

'No.'

'Please.'

'Go away.'

'But I want to show you something.'

'I'm not interested.'

'Something exciting.'

Oh. Curiosity drew me downstairs. I found Amber in the garden. She'd planted the Christmas tree, which was remarkable, as the earth was frozen hard. And now, there on the wall, rubbing itself against her, was a dainty little black cat. I'd never seen it before.

'Isn't it *sweet*?' she said with a rapt smile. Her breath came in little clouds.

'Yes,' I said. 'It is.' It was tiny, and slightly chinky-looking, as though it had some Siamese in it, and it had a funny little kink in the end of its tail like a question mark.

'It's so *thin*,' Amber observed, as I stamped my feet in the knife-like cold. 'I don't know how it's survived in this freezing weather. It obviously hasn't eaten for ages.'

Oh. *Poor* little thing. I felt the ice around my heart begin to crack and tears sprang into my eyes. I went up to it, and stroked it. It stood up on its hind legs and rubbed its face against my hand, like a wave.

'We must give it some milk,' I said.

'Come on – puss puss!' Amber called, though it needed no encouragement. It had shot through the open back door, into the kitchen and was now winding itself in and out of Amber's ankles in a restless figure of eight. We put some milk down for it, and then some ham, cut up small. And then a little smoked salmon.

'I've got a pot of Russian caviar,' said Amber excitedly. 'I'm sure it would like some of that.'

'I'm sure it would,' I said. 'But I think we ought to give it proper cat food.' So I went to the corner shop and bought a couple of tins of Whiskas, and when I got back it had had Amber's caviar, and was lying across her lap, dribbling with happiness, and purring like a tiny tractor. And that was that.

'What shall we call it?' I said later, stroking its tiny, triangular ears. 'We've got to give it a name. How about Epiphany?'

'Why?'

'Because today's the Feast of Epiphany, when Christ was revealed to the three wise men.'

'Mmm,' said Amber thoughtfully.

'Or we could just call it Cat,' I suggested. 'Or Catalogue. Or Catalonia. Or Catatonia or Catalyst or –'

'Perdita,' said Amber suddenly. 'That's what I'd like to call her. It's from the *Winter's Tale*,' she explained, 'in which the infant Perdita was lost, and then found. It's a wonderful play,' she went on, dreamily. 'It's about redemption, and resurrection. It's about being given a second chance when you thought you'd really buggered things up.'

'Perdita,' I said. 'Or rather Purr-dita,' I punned. 'But how do you know it's a girl?'

'Well, she looks like a girl. She's got a pretty, girlie face.'

'We ought to check. Let's ask Laurie.'

'Oh, he's such a pain,' said Amber crossly.

'No he isn't,' I said quietly. 'He's fun. In fact, he's sparky,' I added, pointedly.

'He's an idiot,' she insisted.

'OK. If you say so. But he's a trainee vet,' I pointed out. 'So he can tell us what sex Perdita is, and he can also examine her to make sure she's all right.' Put like that, Amber thought it was a good idea. So Laurie came round that evening and declared Perdita to be a healthy female 'queen' of about four months.

'She's just a big kitten,' he said. 'She's terribly thin. But that's all that's wrong. Maybe her owners moved house, and forgot her, or she wandered out and got lost.'

'We'll put a notice in the "Lost and Found" column of the local paper,' said Amber. 'I hope no one claims her,' she added wistfully. 'She's lovely.'

Pedro was cross, of course. We knew this because he stopped saying, '*Super*, darling!' for a while. And he wasn't cross because he was jealous – though parrots can be jealous – but because he has nothing but contempt for cats. Now, dogs he likes. Dogs he can respect. But with cats he has always affected a superior, icy disdain. Granny had a Burmese called Binky, and Pedro ignored it for fifteen years.

'Pedro will just have to get used to Perdita, won't you, Pedro?' said Amber cheerfully. 'Because I think' – she crossed her long slim fingers – 'she's here to stay.'

So was Laurie, at least for supper, and he told us about his latest exploits as a male escort.

'On Monday I did a Bar-Mitzvah with a divorcée of forty,' he said. 'On Tuesday I went to a Law Society drinks party with a widow of fifty-three. And last night I had to go to a British Medical Association dinner with a single woman of thirty-five.'

'Oh,' said Amber, a little suspiciously, I thought. 'Was that fun?'

'Yes,' he replied.

'I see. A lot of fun?'

'Yes. But not as much fun as the Anti-Slavery International Ball,' he added gallantly. 'Now, some of these women ask me for sex,' he confided, as we ate our pasta.

'And what do you say?' Amber enquired, somewhat nervously, I thought.

'I say that it's absolutely out of the question,' he replied. 'And then I explain that sex is extra. However,' he added pointedly to her, as she rolled her eyes, 'I'd like to point out that it's free for friends.'

'Oh, jolly good,' she said, in a bored kind of way which I knew – I *knew* – masked something else.

'All these women are so *exhausting*,' he said with extravagant indolence. 'I'll be glad when I can give it up. But I can't afford to at £200 a throw – well, £150 after Shirley's taken her cut. And it's so easy. All I have to do is put on a suit and be charming.'

'Charming?' said Amber archly. 'Is that what you call it then?'

'Yes.'

'I don't remember you being charming to me.'

'Oh, you're so negative.'

'Well, you weren't,' she insisted.

'Look, I pulled out your chair. I told you my best jokes. *And* I consoled you when you narrowly lost the auction. I know how *devastated* you were by that,' he added with a facetious smile.

'Mmm.'

'And had you not left the ball so precipitately – like Cinderella herself, I couldn't help thinking – I would have invited you on to the dance floor.'

'Oh yes?'

'I would have looked deeply into your eyes and said, "Wanna shake?"'

'What a pity to have missed *that,*' she said, sardonically.

'And I'd just like to say that if you were to hire me for the rest of my life it would work out at a mere five million quid, assuming that I make it to seventy.'

'I see.'

'But we could of course negotiate a good discount – it's always cheaper if you buy in bulk.'

'Well, that's very flexible of you,' she said, with a tiny smile. 'Now, why did you change career?' Amber enquired, seriously. 'I meant to ask you that at the Savoy, but I had other things on my mind.'

'I'd always wanted to be a vet,' he explained. 'But my father persuaded me to go into chartered surveying, like him. And later I regretted not having held out for what I truly wanted. So when I was thirty, I went back to college. But this time, I didn't get a grant. And I've used up all my savings. So that's why I became a walker. To subsidise my final year.'

He's a risk-taker, I thought, like Joe. Striking out from the safety of the harbour for strange and possibly hostile shores.

'And have you got a place in a practice yet?' Amber asked him. 'For when you qualify.'

'Yes,' he said, 'at the Canonbury practice in Islington, where I'm doing my placement now. I'll join them officially when I qualify in July. *If* I qualify,' he added, standing up. 'On which note, I really must get back to my revision. Equine Obstetrics – fascinating. Thanks for supper,' he added. 'Bring the cat into the surgery and we'll sort out all her jabs. We don't want her getting 'flu. And in a couple of months you'll need to think about having her spayed.' He stroked Perdita, then smiled at Amber, and me, then quietly let himself out. 'Isn't he an annoying fellow?' said Amber, hugging the cat.

'Terribly,' I said.

'Really, really annoying.'

'Mmmm.'

'A very, very irritating man.'

'Absolutely. Shall we ask him round again?'

'Did you know that the Dreck Furniture Warehouse is having a New Year Sale?'

'A New Year Sale?'

'Yes. There's 75 per cent off everything – even leather suites.'

'I just can't believe it – 75 per cent off?'

'Yes! An incredible 75 per cent off! I just can't believe it either!'

'At prices like that, it's just too good to be true!'

'Wow! 75 per cent off? That's just AMAZING!!!!'

'It's amazing, Minty!' exclaimed Wesley.

'What?' I took off my headphones.

'It's amazing. I've been trying to tell you for days, but you just didn't seem to want to chat.' This was quite true.

'I'm sorry Wesley,' I said guiltily. 'I've been rather . . . preoccupied lately.'

'I noticed. We all did. Look, are you all right, Minty? You seemed to be in a bit of a state.'

'I'm . . . fine,' I said with a sigh. 'I'm OK – really.' This was more or less true. The first white heat of my anger had cooled now, leaving hot, but bearable embers. And somehow, having that little cat around had taken the edge off my pain.

'I've got some wonderful news!' said Wesley. 'It's Deirdre – she's pregnant! She's four months gone.'

'How *incredible*!' I said with involuntary wonderment. 'I mean, how fantastic! When's it due?'

'June!'

'Congratulations.'

'Yes,' he said excitedly. 'I'm going to be a father.'

'That's unbelievable . . . I mean, that's lovely.'

'Yes, I'm thrilled about it,' he went on. 'And Deirdre's so happy. I can't believe it – I'm going to be a Dad.' He opened a drawer in his desk and took out the *Mothercare First Baby Guide*.

'We're going to get 20 per cent off everything,' he confided, 'because Deirdre gets the staff discount.' He opened the catalogue at the pushchair section, then placed it in front of me.

'What do you think?' he asked as I surveyed the array of colourful buggies. 'Should we go for the Seville, or the Verona, or the Classico?' They all seemed to have Italian names. 'On the other hand,' he went on thoughtfully, 'the Dolce Vita would be nice.'

'Yes,' I said ruefully, 'the Dolce Vita would be *lovely*.'

'Oh, Minty,' he said wistfully, 'the mysteries of procreation. It's just so amazing. I'm going to be a father!'

'So did you . . .' I began. But the words died on my lips. Shut up, Minty, I said to myself. It's none of your damn business.

Wesley glanced round the office to make sure he couldn't be overheard. Then he leant towards me and said, 'We had trouble, you know.'

'What?'

'We had trouble. Having the baby.'

'Oh, I didn't know that,' I said innocently. 'Well, lots of people have trouble, don't they?'

'No, we had *real* trouble.'

'I see,' I said seriously.

'It was very hard for Deirdre because of course it was . . .' he lowered his voice a little further, '*her fault*.'

'Really?'

'Yes. Her eggs. Not too hot.'

'Oh dear.'

'Pretty much hard-boiled. So she went to get some help.'

'Well, good. Um did you . . . go too?'

'Oh yes,' he said, 'of course I did. Just to hold her hand. You have to give your partner moral support, don't you?'

'Yup.'

'And luckily the fertility doctor was able to sort her out.'

'Well, that's great.'

'And now, at last, I'm going to be a *father*.'

*

'"You're not my father." That's what they say,' said Jack, in his office after work. He'd been nervously twisting leader tape all day – the floor was strewn with it – and then, when everyone had gone, he'd asked for my advice, again. '"You're not my dad," they say.' He sighed. 'Christmas was sheer bloody hell.'

'Scummy breath? Try the new, revolutionary Thompson Tongue-Scraper!'

'Why are they so nasty to you?'

'The ultimate in oral care!'

'Because they blame me for the divorce.'

'Eliminates bacterial build-up!'

'But it's not my fault.'

'Only £7.99!' Jack wearily turned off the speaker.

'What the girls don't know,' he continued, 'is that their father had been fooling around with other women for years. And that's why Jane finally kicked him out. But she's never told them that because she didn't want to lower their regard for him.'

'That's decent of her,' I pointed out. 'Lots of wounded wives wouldn't hesitate to shop their errant husband to the kids.'

'I know that,' he conceded, wearily. 'Except that it means I get all the blame. So, in protecting her children, Jane leaves me exposed to their wrath. They're like the Furies, Minty. They're bloody vicious.'

'Well, maybe when they're older, she might tell them the truth. Or maybe they'll have got to like you by then.'

'I can't wait that long, Minty. To be honest, I'm not sure I'll still be around. I think the whole thing's been a huge mistake.'

'But you can't just give up on your marriage after less than a year.'

'But I'm not sure I'm prepared to put up with all this hostility. It's hard enough adjusting to married life when you've never been married before, let alone having so much grief from your wife's kids.' He sighed. 'They really know how to hurt.'

'What do they do?'

'When they're not abusing me verbally, they take my clothes out of the laundry basket, and dump them on the floor. They take my coat out of the coat cupboard, ditto. They also remove my shaving things from the bathroom cabinet, and my toothbrush from the "family" rack.'

'How nasty.'

'They send me to Coventry,' he went on ruefully. 'They also send me to Wolverhampton, Watford, Manchester and Stoke. Do you know what else they do? Steal.'

'Steal?'

'They stole my credit card out of my jacket . . .'

'My God.'

'And went to Harrods. Three hundred quid! And the last phone bill was four hundred.'

'Christ.'

'And the drugs I've found lying around!'

'Really?'

'I've found grass, Thai sticks, E – no heroin yet, thank God, but it's extremely worrying. I'm sorry to burden you,' he added with another painful sigh. 'But I've got to talk to someone about it.'

'Don't you discuss it with Jane?'

'I've tried. But I don't get very far . . . she doesn't really understand.'

'Well, she ought to, she's a counsellor.'

'But she listens to people moaning all day, I don't feel I can do the same when she gets home. In any case,' he went on, as he began to twist and stretch another piece of tape, 'Jane doesn't believe in disciplining young people.'

'Oh.'

'It's all this "positive parenting" stuff – her parents were incredibly strict with her, so she always vowed she'd be the opposite. And she is. Anything goes. Her children must be allowed to "express themselves", apparently. And at the moment they express themselves by hating me.'

'Well, you've got to show Topaz and Iolanthe that you're part of their family.'

'A nuclear family,' he sighed. 'With nuclear warfare. Cruise missiles, SS20s, the works. How appropriate that we live at the Arsenal. I just don't know what to do,' he said despairingly.

'Well, do something family-ish. Go on a holiday.'

'I suggested it. But the girls said they'd only come if I didn't.'

'How about ten-pin bowling?'

'I tried it. They refused. They said they could do that anytime with their mates.'

'Well, why don't you have a party? You and Jane could invite your friends, and the girls could invite a few of theirs.'

He looked thoughtful. 'A drinks party?'

'Yes.'

'A winter drinks party. Actually, that's not a bad idea. In fact, Minty, it's a very good idea. And would you come, if I did?'

'Yes,' I said. 'I would.'

And so, ten days later, I set off for Jack's. He had moved into Jane's house, her former marital home – another mistake on his part, I suspected. He'd wanted to pool their resources and buy somewhere new, but Jane had thought it would upset the girls to move so soon after the divorce. It put Jack at a huge disadvantage, though. He was on their patch. In their father's place. It made the girls hate him even more. You could understand it, in a way. Still, at least it was quite a nice house, in a quiet road not far from where he'd had his flat on Highbury Hill.

He and Jane had met in the launderette. Their respective washing machines had broken down. They'd eyed each other up over the spin cycle and then she'd asked him to help her fold her sheets. Amazing. There's so much luck involved in how you meet someone. Charlie had met Amber at one of her book launches. And then he'd met Helen again when he'd gone into her shop to buy flowers. And Mum and Dad had met ice-skating. And Wesley and Deirdre had met in a Wimpy

Bar. And Dominic had sold me an insurance policy. Perhaps that's how he'd met Virginia Park too, I wondered bitterly. Probably was. I wondered whether he'd had the courage to tell her what he'd done to me? Unlikely – the man was such a coward.

As I turned right out of the Tube at seven o'clock, I resolutely banished thoughts of Dominic. I found the house halfway up Plimsoll Road. The house that Jack built, I thought ironically. Or rather, the house that Jack was trying to build. *Ding. Dong*. The door opened, and there was Topaz, the older girl. I remembered seeing her at my wedding, giggling. I eradicated that image from my mind and resolved to be friendly, for Jack's sake.

'Hello, Topaz,' I said, with a smile. She was wearing an inch of eyeliner, a silver Lurex crop-top and a black leather miniskirt which barely covered her pants. 'I'm Minty. Remember?'

'Oh yeah!' she said, with a smirk. 'How could I forget? You were the one who got –'

'Minty,' Jack cut in, 'hello! How nice of you to come.' He gave me a warm, but slightly nervous smile. 'Now, I'm sure Topaz will take your coat.'

'Bleedin' well won't,' she said.

'Right,' said Jack. 'That's fine. Fine . . .' And he took my mac and ushered me into the large double living room. I seemed to be the first to have arrived.

Chakka chakka chakka chakka chakka chakka chakka.

'Hello, Iolanthe,' I called to the younger girl, who was sitting in a corner of the room, with headphones clamped to her ears. 'Hello!' I tried again.

Chakka chakka chakka chakka chakka chakka chakka.

She lifted them off briefly, and looked at me out of narrowed eyes. 'Hi!' she said, with a vague smile. Then she replaced her headphones. Jack nervously poured me some champagne, and turned up the Bach partitas.

'How's school going?' I asked Topaz.

'Skanky!' she replied.

'Sorry?'

'Oh, that means "bad" doesn't it, Topaz?' Jack enquired. She gave him a granitic glare.

'You have to know the code,' he explained. 'Teen-talk. It's a whole new language. Like Esperanto, only harder.'

'This music's bleedin' gnarly,' she added.

'Ah,' said Jack. 'Translation: I don't care for your choice of CD.' The atmosphere was already icy, despite the fire burning brightly in the grate.

'Are some of your friends coming this evening?' I asked her pleasantly.

'Yeah,' she said. 'But not f'rages. It's not cool to arrive early, like you've done.'

'Ha! Well, I didn't know how long it would take to get here,' I said. 'I came by Tube.'

'Don't you have wheels, then?' she exclaimed contemptuously.

'Um . . . no. No, I don't.' She rolled her eyes.

'Oh, hello, Minty.' Jane appeared, carrying a plate of canapés. 'Nice to see you, er . . .' I knew she was going to say 'again', because the last time she'd seen me was in my wedding dress '. . . with such a lovely new haircut,' she finished. I smiled. And I thought how nice she looked. She's the same age as Jack, nearly forty-three, but she looks a lot younger than that.

All of a sudden there was the sound of a match striking against sandpaper, and then the smell of a Silk Cut filled the air. I looked at Topaz as she inhaled, expertly, then released a silvery plume with a practised toss of her head.

'I keep asking her to give up,' Jane confided with a wry smile as I skewered a cocktail sausage. 'But she won't. Still, I do think young people have to make their own mistakes, don't you?'

'Oh, um, yes,' I said.

'And she is fifteen.'

'Jack's always telling me to stop,' Topaz confided, as she drew on her cigarette. 'But it's none of 'is business. And if my real dad don't mind, I don't see what it's got to do with Jack.'

'Yes, I'm afraid if Jack asks the girls not to do something, they go right ahead and do it, don't you, you two?'

'Yeah.'

'Yeah!' said Iolanthe.

'But then I think it's better to use emotional reasoning on teenage children. For example, I say to Topaz, "Darling, did you know that smoking can cause cancer?" And she says –'

'I don't give a flying fuck!' Topaz cut in, with a guttural laugh.

'Exactly.' Jane rolled her eyes with mock-exasperation. 'Kids today! I don't know. Still, we were all young once, weren't we?'

'How's work?' I asked Jane. 'Are you busy?'

'Oh yes!' she said, gaily. 'There's a steady stream of anorexics, bulimics, depressives, delinquents and embryonic axe-murderers.'

'Just like we have at home,' said Jack, with a hollow laugh. 'Just joking, Jane.' She was giving him the beady eye. 'That was just a joke, OK?'

Ding. Dong. Saved by the bell. Jane went to the door. Jack went back on coat duty. I sat in a corner of the sofa and looked at the sitting room. It was very . . . Ikeatat. Bright, but undistinguished. Stripped wooden flooring covered with bright kilims. A wrought-iron candle chandelier. Colourful screen-prints on the walls. Gaily chequered curtains on decorative poles. I wondered where to place my drink. Not on the antique mahogany side table to my left; its delicate top was inlaid with a chessboard. Now that was obviously Jack's. In fact, looking round the room again, it was easy to identify his things, because they didn't really fit in with the rest. A pretty oil painting of an alpine pass hung awkwardly alongside a Hockney print. A pair of beautiful cut-glass candlesticks looked out of place on the pine mantelpiece. All the things that were less obviously 'serviceable' I was sure belonged to Jack.

In front of me was a low, wooden coffee table. I put my drink on that, then picked up one of the books, *Communicating With Your Teenager* by Sheila Munro. Beneath it was a well-thumbed copy of *You Just Don't Listen: You Just Don't Understand*, and *Other People's Children* by Joanna Trollope.

Ding. Dong. Ding Dong. The room had almost filled up. The fizz was flowing and I was introduced to neighbours, and friends, and counsellor colleagues of Jane's. Jack hadn't asked anyone else from London FM. But it was all rather jolly, though the two girls could not be induced to join in. They sat on the stairs reading their copies of *Sugar* and *Shout*! And by ten the party was at its height, and we were all feeling nicely merry, when there was the sound of tyres screeching to a halt outside, the slamming of car doors, drunken male laughter, and then, *Ding Dong.*

'Avon calling, hur hur!' shouted a loud male voice through the letter box. 'Come on, Topaz, open the friggin' door!' Topaz and Iolanthe flew to open it, and in walked a gang of denimed, black leather-jacketed youths. The room seemed swamped by testosterone. Topaz and Iolanthe's faces were shining with joy. Their heroes had arrived.

'Evenin',' said a boy of about fifteen with a loud, dirty sniff. It was hard to tell which was the greasier, his Brylcreemed hair, or his gleaming, sebum-coated face.

'Hello, er . . . Wayne, isn't it?' Jane enquired with a welcoming smile. 'And Pete.' Pete held up a tattooed hand by way of a greeting. On his chin was a purulent eruption like a mini Krakatoa. 'Jack, do get them some drinks,' said Jane. 'We've got quite a choice of beer, boys.'

'Great,' they said, and they made for the kitchen.

Ding Dong! Another group of teenagers had arrived. Three more boys, and a couple of girls. They stared at us as though we were aliens from the planet Zog.

'Cor, what a bunch of skanky antiques!' said a girl called Dawn with purple hair and ears so be-ringed that they resembled curtain tracks.

'Now, "skanky antiques", that's us,' Jack explained to me, knowledgeably. 'Just in case you thought Dawn was expressing reservations about the furniture.'

'Bleedin' rentals,' said her friend.

'Rentals?' I said.

'*Par*entals,' Jack explained.

'Now, what would you like to drink, Dawn?' Jane asked.

'Vodka and orange,' she replied.

'Yes, of course,' said Jane. 'Same for you, Tyler?'

Tyler nodded. 'Make it a double,' she said.

'Just help yourselves, girls,' Jane called out benignly as they headed for the drinks table. 'We trust you young people not to overdo it.'

'No, we damn well don't,' Jack hissed.

Ding Dong! In came girls with pierced eyebrows, and girls with black fingernails; girls in knicker-length dresses, and girls with strange footwear. I couldn't help staring at the bizarre things on their feet: trainers with sling-backs; platforms with flip-flop thongs; clumpy leather casuals spangled with pink glitter.

'– Like my new platforms?'

'– I *luv* Prince William.'

'– Nah, I prefer Leo.'

'– Oh, he's a right Kevin.'

'– Mum's stopped my pocket money.'

Ding Dong. In came more boys – boys with long greasy hair; boys in baggy shirts; boys with fluffy moustaches; boys whose faces were measled with acne. Within half an hour the fifteen-year-olds had outnumbered us 'antiques' by two to one, someone had changed the CD, and the sitting room had begun to resemble a fifth-form disco. The lights had been turned low and a grope-a-thon was now in progress. The atmosphere was becoming oppressive as the hormonal soup was stirred.

'– come on!'

'– nah! Don't want to.'

'– go on.'

'– Oi! Thass disgusting!'

'You know, there's nothing worse than inhibiting a young, vulnerable person,' said Jane, as Topaz grabbed a passing boy, pulled him on to the sofa and started snogging him enthusiastically. 'Did you know,' she went on seriously, 'that teenagers who are stamped on by their parents find it hard to form successful relationships in later life?'

'Oh, really,' said Jack, wearily.

'I think it's a mark of civilisation,' Jane crooned, 'if the older generation can be tolerant and understanding of the young. I mean, my parents were *terribly* strict with me . . .'

''Scuse me –' A girl pushed past Jane into the downstairs loo, her hand clapped to her mouth. In the sitting room two boys were holding a spitting competition, trying to see who could hit the centre of the mirror, from the sofa, with the greatest accuracy.

'Goodness, is it eleven?' I heard one of the 'rentals' say.

'Well, must be off.'

'Thanks for a great party, Jane.'

'See you, Jack.'

In the meantime, Dawn and Tyler, now on their sixth double vodka and orange, were giggling hysterically. And every time Tyler opened her mouth to laugh, her silver stud glinted on her tongue. Suddenly she seemed to topple on her six-inch platforms and, as she lost her balance, she grabbed at one of the boys.

'Oi, Pete! Keep yer 'ands OFF 'er, OK?' yelled Wayne from the other side of the room.

'I never touched her,' protested Pete.

'You just WATCH IT!'

'OK,' said Pete again. 'I don' even *fancy* 'er,' he added, waving his can of Carlsberg. 'Your gnarly girlfriend's an old dog.'

'WOT? You come 'ere and say that!'

'Nah,' said Pete.

'You come right here and –' Wayne grabbed Pete and lifted him up by the shoulders against the wall. Jack's dainty oil painting was dislodged, and slid off its hook to the floor.

'Careful of that!' said Jack, rushing to rescue it. 'What do you say?'

'Yeah – WOT do you SAY?!' shouted Wayne, still pinning Pete to the wall.

'OK. OK. Sorry,' mumbled Pete.

'Thass better,' said Wayne, dropping him with a thud. 'You've got ter show a little REESPEC.'

'– Well, we *have* enjoyed ourselves.'

'Because if you don't show any REESPEC . . .'

'– it's been awfully nice.'

'. . . I'm gonna bash your bleedin' 'EAD IN!

'– we'll give you a ring soon.'

'– INNIT?'

'– no, no, we'll let ourselves out.'

'OK. OK,' said Pete.

Ding Dong! My God – more. Another knot of adolescents, drunk as skunks, charged into the house. Word had clearly got round, and by now a discreet drinks party had become a rave. The windows rattled as the kids all began dancing to the mindless techno-beat.

'This is "Trance",' shouted Iolanthe happily, as she bounced up and down with a boy.

'Don't you mean, "Coma"?' said Jack. 'Look, Iolanthe, we've got to turn it down,' he shouted, 'or we'll have the police coming round.'

'Bog off!' said Iolanthe with a drunken giggle. 'Mum says she doesn't mind.'

'No, I don't really,' Jane agreed. 'This is how young people express themselves.'

'Well, I'd rather they didn't express themselves like this in our house. My *God*!' he exclaimed. 'What are those white pills?' A tall thin boy with shadows under his eyes was handing out small, white tablets. The floor was jumping, the pictures were shaking as the kids bounced up and down to the beat.

'I think we ought to go upstairs,' said Jane, 'so that we don't get in their way.'

'Well, I really ought to go home,' I said.

Ding. Dong.

'Oh, please, Minty, I need your moral support,' whispered Jack.

'We really shouldn't spoil their enjoyment,' crooned Jane.

'But it's got nothing to do with me.'

'After all, they're only young once. My parents wouldn't let me go to parties at all.'

'I need your help, Minty,' Jack hissed, again. I could feel his hand pressing on my arm.

'But it's between you and Jane.'

Ding. Dong.

'I won't renew your contract!'

'Jack!'

'I'm sorry,' he whispered hoarsely, as Jane made her way upstairs. 'But I'm so desperate. I'm just so, *so* desperate.'

'Oh, OK. But what am I supposed to do?'

'Just try and get through to my wife.'

'No, of course they won't damage anything,' said Jane, serenely, as we sat at the top of the stairs. 'I feel sure of that. The point is that if we show them we trust them, then they'll behave in a trustworthy way.' From below came the sound of wood being split.

'OI! PETE, LOOK WOT CHEW DONE NAH!'

'I think something's broken,' I said.

'Oh, no no no,' said Jane. 'I can't believe they'd be so thoughtless of other peoples' property.'

Then there was another 'KER-UNCH!', followed by the distinctive tinkle of falling glass.

'My God!' I said. 'Did you hear that?'

Suddenly the sitting-room door flew open. We saw a boy rush into the hall, minus his shirt, his hair streaming with beer.

'Perhaps we should just keep out of their way,' said Jane, as we retreated further up the stairs, 'so that we don't inhibit them. And of course I don't want to embarrass the girls in front of their friends by coming over the heavy parent.'

I glanced into the bathroom; it was a towel-strewn swamp, someone having tried, unsuccessfully, to clean up a pool of sick at the base of the loo. 'I LUV IAN' had been sprayed, in shaving foam, over the mirror, while the contents of the medical cabinet had been strewn across the floor.

'Tsk tsk,' Jane tut-tutted. 'They *are* naughty. Still, it won't take long to clear up.'

'YER WANKER!' we heard from downstairs, as we opened the door to the spare bedroom. Then we heard, once again, the unmistakable fracturing of furniture.

'Oh my God,' said Jack, his head in his hands. 'We've got to do something – they're trashing the house.'

'Mmm,' said Jane, 'but we must be careful because they're very sensitive young people.'

'Sensitive young people?' said Jack. 'Sensitive young people, my arse!' He stood up. 'I've had *enough*!' he hissed. 'I've had enough of your lily-livered liberalism, Jane. These "sensitive young people" are thugs and they're destroying our house.'

'Yes, but –'

'But NOTHING!' Jack went on furiously. 'You must be out of your MIND, Jane,' he yelled. 'You must be stark, staring MAD! I'm going to put a stop to this – RIGHT NOW!!'

He flew downstairs. Then he threw open the sitting-room door, and stood, dumbstruck, looking in.

'Oh my God!' we heard him moan as we peered over the banister. He shook his head. 'Oh my God,' he said again. And we noticed in the distance, but growing louder now, the whoop and wail of the sirens. 'Oh my GOD!' he exclaimed a third time. And then he turned on the light and yelled, 'RIGHT, YOU LOT – OUT!!!' The music slammed to a stop and several boys ran out of the house like rats fleeing a burning barn. The party was over. The carriages had arrived. And now Jane and I ventured downstairs and stood surveying the wreckage.

'Oh no,' said Jane. 'Oh *no*.' The overmantel mirror was crazy-paved with fractures. The pale green sofa was marbled with red wine. The curtains had been slashed in three places and there were cigarette burns in the rugs. On the walls, pictures hung at odd angles, as though drunk, while the wrought-iron candle chandelier had been half pulled out of its rose. Worse by far, for Jack, his chess table had been thrown across the room. It was missing half of one leg and its elegant, checkered top was cracked in two.

'RIGHT!' Jack shouted. And as Kevin and Wayne attempted to exit, fast, he grabbed them by their collars.

'You two are going to help me clear this *UP*!' he yelled. He was holding them at arm's length, as though they were dangerous dogs. 'And if you don't give me your assistance, I shall give your names to the police.' Because by now the sirens had stopped, and the Panda cars had drawn up, their flashing blue lights penetrating the house and spinning across the walls.

'Right. Will you assist the police with their enquiries, gentlemen?' Jack enquired acidly. 'Or are you going to help me put this mess straight?'

'Er . . . I fink we'll help you,' said Wayne.

'Yeah, we will.'

'Yes, you will, WHAT?' said Jack, simmering with rage.

'Yes we will . . . sir,' Wayne replied.

Jack released the boys. Then he went outside, and we saw him conferring with the cops. We thought they might come inside, but within two or three minutes they'd driven off. Suddenly Topaz and Iolanthe emerged, with two boys, from the garden, their hair and clothes awry.

'Oh my gawd,' gasped Iolanthe.

'Christ!' Topaz breathed.

'This is what your friends have done,' said Jack, fixing them with a contemptuous stare. 'The friends your mother and I thought it would be nice to invite. The friends you encouraged to behave like total pigs. I trust you're both quite satisfied.'

Topaz had started to sniff. Iolanthe looked utterly distraught.

'And now you're both going to help me clear up. And so are you,' he said, addressing the four boys who remained. 'Right,' he said to the shortest, 'collect up all the bottles. And you – you're going to clean the floor. Iolanthe – go and get him a mop. Topaz,' Jack commanded, 'you can clean the sofa. And as for you,' he said to Wayne, 'you are going to help me take the mirror down from the wall.'

'Yes. Yes, er, sir,' said Wayne. 'Sorry, sir . . . no offence.'

I looked at Jane as we all cleared up, aware of the sour smell of vomit, and the sweet stench of dope. She seemed to have been struck dumb. And I glanced at the girls, who were also quite silent. They looked ashamed and appalled. But as Jack took charge, in a way he'd probably never taken charge before, I thought I also detected what I can only describe as a kind of admiration in their eyes.

February

'Of course I don't mind,' said Amber. 'Don't be silly, Minty.'

'That's a relief,' I said, as I put some snowdrops in a tiny vase. 'I didn't know how you'd take it,' I went on. 'But I decided you'd have to know soon.' I'd kept the invitation in my room, of course. I was hardly going to display it on the mantelpiece. But I didn't quite see how I could attend Helen and Charlie's wedding without Amber finding out. And so, this morning, I decided to tell her. She appeared to take it well.

'Obviously I knew they'd be getting married, Minty. She's up the duff, after all, and the bastard's the decent type.'

'Yes. But that's not why they're doing it. They just clicked, I suppose.'

'Well, Charlie always wanted kids, and now he's going to have them,' sighed Amber. 'You know, he was the wrong man for me,' she said. 'He didn't have enough . . . oomph! I can see that now.' I saw it long ago. 'He was a pushover, and that was dull. As for Helen,' she added expansively, 'well, good luck to her. Did you know that a quarter of all babies cry between three and four hours every day?'

'Really?'

'Worse – they do most of their crying at night!'

'Oh dear.'

'They take all your energy, Minty. All your creativity. They sap your very life-force. And of course they consume *vast* amounts of cash.'

'You always talk about what they take,' I said quietly. 'Never about what they bring.'

'No, I really don't want brats,' said Amber, picking up Perdita and cuddling her. 'I can't imagine anything worse. And it would *ruin* my literary career.'

'Mmm.'

'Statistics say that 20 per cent of British women born after 1960 are going to remain childless,' she added, 'and one of them is going to be me.'

'It's a free country.'

'Do you know they've just got a cat next door,' Amber added as Perdita lay, purring, across her shoulder.

'Really?'

'Yes. I mean it's *quite* nice,' she added as she patted Perdita's back, 'and of course I was *very* polite about it. But, to be frank, it's not *nearly* as pretty as Perdita. And it's not nearly as clever. Quite slow, in fact. There's absolutely *no* comparison. Have I shown you what Perdita can do?' she went on animatedly. 'Just watch *this!* Still clasping the cat to her left shoulder, she went into the sitting room and came back with a ball of pink wool. She put Perdita down, then jiggled the wool up and down in front of her. In a flash, Perdita had pounced, pinioning it to the floor.

'Isn't that *fantastic,*' breathed Amber, her eyes like saucers.

'Er, yes,' I said.

'Her reactions are just amazing, you know. I think she's very advanced for her age. Aren't you, dinkums? Mummy thinks you're de most clever, most beeau-oot-iful puddy tat in de world.'

'Pass the sick-bag,' I said.

'No, she really *has* got an exceptionally high IQ, Mint.' Amber gazed into Perdita's huge, emerald eyes. 'Would 'oo like some more milky den, darling?' she squeaked. Yuck. Though at least Amber's constant ministrations had improved Perdita's health. She had put on quite a bit of weight, and she'd grown in height by more than an inch. Her emaciated little face had filled out and her coat now gleamed like jet. And in just a month she had made herself quite at home. During the day she sits on Amber's lap as she writes or reads, blissfully extending and retracting her claws. At night she sleeps on Amber's bed, curled round her head like a feline Astrakhan. She never leaves her side. And despite all our efforts to trace her owner, no one has come forward to claim her. And that's just as well, because Amber is completely enslaved.

'He's my slave!' said Melinda.

'Who?' I enquired. It certainly wasn't me any more. I was sticking to my New Year resolution to be mean and unhelpful to Melinda.

'Wobert,' she said, waving his latest letter. 'He says he's my slave. At least that's what he wites. Isn't it a scweam?'

'What does your husband think?' I asked.

'Oh, he doesn't think anything,' she said. This was probably true.

'I wonder what he's like,' I said. 'Not your husband,' I added quickly. 'I mean, your stalker, Robert.'

'I don't know. Maybe he's tewwibly attwactive,' she exclaimed. 'Perhaps I should twy and meet him!'

'I wouldn't do that,' I said. 'He might be an axe-murderer, for all you know.'

'Oh, don't be silly, Minty!' said Melinda, with a little laugh. 'Now,' she said, changing the subject, 'I'm a bit stuck on this single cuwwency business – the pwo's and cons of EMU. Could you take me thwough the arguments again?'

'I'm sorry, Melinda,' I lied. 'But I'm working flat out on this piece about child labour. Why don't you ask Jack?'

'You *know* I can't do that,' she hissed theatrically. 'He'll think I'm completely *useless*!'

'You are,' said Jack. He had just come in.

'I am what?' said Melinda, indignantly.

'Ready with the script? You are ready with the script?' he repeated. 'That's what I said. I'd like to have a look, you see.'

'Oh,' she said, suspiciously. 'Well, I just need a little more time. I've got to wite my Euwo link.'

'Well, don't be long,' he replied. 'I've told Wesley I want a proper rehearsal. I want everything to go smoothly today because Sir Percy's coming in to watch.'

'Oh Chwist!' said Melinda. 'I'd forgotten. It had better be good then, I suppose.'

'Yes,' said Jack, crisply. 'It had. Now, if you're stuck on the EMU cue, ask Sophie. She's hot on that sort of thing.'

'I'm rather busy myself,' Sophie groaned. She was organising the rotas for our digital training sessions. Jack, mollified by his recent victory on the home front, had finally caved in.

'Please, Sophie,' whined Melinda.

'All right,' she agreed with a sigh. Sophie put down her pen, then came and stood by Melinda's desk, folding her arms in magisterial fashion. 'Now, it's really not difficult, Melinda,' she began, pushing her small wire-rimmed glasses a little further up her nose. 'Basically, the Euro, having replaced the ECU, is the common currency of EMU and the new cornerstone of EU fiscal policy. The member states which have joined so far are, in alphabetical order – Austria, Belgium, Finland, France, Germany, Ireland, Italy, Luxembourg, The Netherlands, Portugal and Spain. This "Eurozone", as it's called, forms a market of about 300 million customers, accounting for one fifth of the world economy. The key benefits of joining,' she went on smoothly, 'are greater price transparency, more efficient capital markets and reduced risk to business from exchange-rate volatility. Some analysts also claim that the long-term effect of membership in supply-side and commercial terms will be lower prices, the realisation of a real common market, as well as wider competition. Now, the *anti*s,' she added, 'Lord Owen, for example, argue that Britain's entry into EMU would mean accepting a "one-size-fits-all" interest rate which would entail a concomitant loss of national control as well as a reduction in labour flexibility. They also point to the spectre of higher taxes and increased unemployment, while highlighting the fact that several key conditions for EMU's success are still not yet in place. The convergence criteria, for example, have undoubtedly been fudged, and several countries have entered the Euro with debt levels too high for comfort. How*ever*,' she went on seamlessly, 'the pro's – and this actually includes the CBI – whilst acknowledging that conditions are not yet perfect, are in favour of Britain's eventual entry, believing as they do that it will promote further development of the single market, thereby reducing internal costs and barriers to expansion. Got that?'

Melinda looked as if she were going to cry.

'I never understand Sophie's explanations,' she whined, as Sophie returned to her rotas. 'But I can understand yours, Minty, because you're not as clever as her.'

'Thanks,' I said, tartly.

'I mean, you *explain* things better than her,' she corrected herself. 'Please, would you give me a hand?'

'All right, then,' I said looking at the clock. 'We'll swap. You cut down this piece for me – you've got twenty minutes, by the way – and I'll write your link for you.'

'But you know I don't know how to edit, Minty,' she whined.

'Well, I'm sorry, but I simply can't do two jobs.' She looked at me resentfully, but I didn't soften. I hadn't forgiven her for what she'd said about the programme 'sufferwing' while she was away. Anyway, why *should* I help her? She never did a thing for me. A few minutes later we all went down to Studio B, ready for the rehearsal.

'And in an hour from now, *Capitalise*, presented by Melinda Mitten,' said Barry.

'Are the tapes all ready?' said Jack, as he scrutinised the script.

'Yes,' said Wesley.

'De-ummed?'

'Yes. All clean.'

'Got the sound effects?'

'Yes.'

'And music?'

'Yes.'

'Wesley,' said Jack wearily, 'I'd rather you didn't practise your paternity skills during working hours. Would you kindly put Melinda's baby down?'

'Sorry.' Wesley stopped dandling Pocahontas and put her back in the car-seat, which he then proceeded to rock with his left foot, rather too violently, I thought. I had visions of one of us having to catch her, but luckily she was well strapped in.

Five minutes later, the studio door opened and Monica showed in Sir Percy. He looked affable enough, though a little out of breath.

'Now, don't get oop, lads and lasses,' he said in his broad Yorkshire brogue. 'I'm quite 'appy to be sat 'ere.' He took a seat on the padded bench by the door, then smiled benignly at Melinda as she waved at him through the studio glass. 'Don't mind me, folks,' he reiterated. 'Youse all got work to do fer t'programme and, anyroad, I don't need nowt.'

'Are YOU shamed by your grammatical mistakes?' enquired a cultivated male voice, as we waited for the programme to start. *'Does YOUR poor command of English let you down? Then try our stunning correspondence course! Here's what one satisfied customer had to say:*

'Six months ago I couldn't even spell ''executive'',' announced a Michael Caine soundalike. *'Now I ARE one.'*

'Just £69.99,' explained the first voice again. *'Payable in three easy, interest-free payments. Most major credit cards accepted.'*

Beep. Beep. Beep. 'And now time for today's edition of *Capitalise,'* said Barry, 'presented by Melinda Mitten.' Sir Percy was grinning approvingly.

'Hello, evewyone,' crooned Melinda. 'Today we look at attitudes to the Euwo – are the pwo's now gaining gwound? We have a sobewing weport on the spwead of child labour. We pweview the new Steven Spielberg film, and we'll be talking to the distinguished architect, Sir Norman Foster, about his wonderful new ewection.'

We all suddenly expressed an interest in the carpet, but Sir Percy hadn't noticed a thing. He seemed to be enjoying himself and, overall, the programme wasn't too bad. The mix of items was good, the tapes were all fine edited, and the programme finished bang on time with the 'live' interview with Sir Norman.

'Well, it's been an honour talking to a man who's cocked up so many fine buildings,' Melinda concluded happily. 'Sowwy – *clocked* up!' she corrected herself as she peered at her script again. 'Do join me again tomowwow, listeners, but for now, fwom me, Melinda Mitten, goodbye.'

'Bah gum, that were a right interestin' programme,' said Sir Percy appreciatively as we all trooped out of the studio. 'Right interestin'. But I would like to see t'office too, seeing like as 'ow I never really cum down 'ere. And I'd like to 'ave a word with you, Jack, about future of t'station. Ratin's, an' all that.'

'Of course,' said Jack. 'We'd be delighted to show you round.' And so we all went up in the lift to the third floor, and Jack put on the coffee machine, and someone went to get nice cups and saucers. And then Sir Percy said he'd like to nip to the gents, and Monica poured us all some coffee, and Melinda opened a box of rather delicious-looking cakes. There were nine dainty little sponges, in pleated wrappers, each with a pool of snow-white icing, topped by a glistening, crimson cherry. We were all starving because we never have time for lunch. But we politely waited for Sir Percy to return from his ablutions.

'Melinda, m'duck, well done!' he exclaimed warmly as he came back into the office. 'I thought that script of yourn were right good.'

'Thanks vewy much, Uncle Percy,' she said. 'I wote it all myself.'

As Monica handed Sir Percy a cup of coffee, his eye caught the open box of cakes on Melinda's desk.

'Fairy cakes, eh?' he said. 'My favourites. There's nowt like a fairy cake. Very thoughtful of you to bring those in, Melinda, m'duck. Don't mind if I do.' And he grabbed one, and sank his teeth into it, and began chewing. And chewing. And Melinda had taken one, and had just offered the box to me.

'Did you make them yourself?' I enquired.

'Oh no,' she said. 'I'm a hopeless cook. Wobert sent them to me.'

'WOBERT SENT THEM TO YOU?' we all cried.

'Yes,' she replied. 'Awfully sweet of him, wasn't it? He said he wanted to give me a pwesent.'

We all stared, aghast, at Sir Percy, whose face had suddenly frozen. And now his eyes were registering a combination of puzzlement and shock. And he had stopped chewing. And he was choking. And spitting. He began to spit the cake out of his mouth. And out it came in damp, half-masticated bits, with vivid red flecks of maraschino cherry. And as he pebble-dashed Melinda's desk, his coffee cup fell from his hand. Then, with an astonished expression on his bucolic face, Sir Percy crashed to the carpet-tiled floor.

'Dearly Beloved,' said the vicar, 'we are gathered here today . . .' I couldn't help thinking about it. Not even the sight of Helen and Charlie smiling blissfully at each other in front of the altar on their wedding day two weeks later could eradicate the awful scenes at London FM. 'Dearly Beloved . . .' That's what the vicar had said at Sir Percy's funeral on Thursday . . . What a shock. What a sensation. What an absolute bloody nightmare. I sighed, and tried to distract myself by reading my Order of Service: 'St John's Church, Holland Park, London. Saturday February 14th.' And in the bottom left-hand corner it said 'Helen', and then, to the right, 'Charles'. The church was full. It was a freezing day, with light snowfall, and we were all in our winter gear. But however hard I tried to concentrate on the wedding, the dreadful events at work kept springing into my mind. It didn't take the police long to trace Robert. He'd made a fundamental error, you see. He'd put his address and phone number at the top of all his letters. So they paid him a visit and told him he was nicked. And in his statement he insisted that he hadn't meant to kill Sir Percy. He said this was a vile slur. He'd intended to kill *Melinda*, as a punishment for 'ignoring' him.

'I loved her,' he told the police. 'I loved her despite her screechy voice and her speech impediment, and her glaring factual errors. But she didn't appreciate my devotion. She took it for granted, failing to reply to a single one of my ninety-four letters. Yet despite her callous rejection, I continued to love her. But I could only take so much. It was a *crime passionel*,' he added, knowledgeably, 'so with a bit of luck, I'll get away with a couple of years.'

Poor Sir Percy. Robert had injected the maraschino cherries with cyanide. It's very quick. But what an awful way to go. We felt terrible for him. He seemed so amiable. And of course Melinda was distraught. *Distraught.* She was very fond of him. He was her uncle. Her favourite uncle. More importantly, he was her patron. And I fancied that the tears she shed at Putney Crematorium were for herself, as much as for him.

What would happen now, we all wondered, as the shock quickly gave way to consternation about the future of London FM. Jack attended an emergency board meeting with Sir Percy's MG consortium, and was told that it would be business as usual for the time being.

'Thank God,' we heard Melinda murmur, when Jack answered our fearful questions in the boardroom later that day. 'I think we should keep things *just* as they are,' she announced. 'As a twibute to Sir Percy. It's what he would have wanted,' she went on confidently. At that Jack maintained a significant silence. None of us were prepared to lay bets on anything. Our future seemed as fragile and complex as a cobweb. London FM might be sold. We could all lose our jobs. The number-crunchers might close it down, or turn it into a music-only station. Anything could happen. Anything at all.

The story was in the papers, of course. In fact, it made quite a splash. 'PRETTY PENNY BARON POISONED!' screamed the *Sun*. 'TIGHTS KNIGHT MURDERED!' said the *Mail*. Sir Percy was obituarised in the *Telegraph* and *The Times* as a 'man of vision' whose contribution to the hosiery industry could not be underestimated. 'He swiftly climbed the ladder in ladies' tights,' declared one commentator. 'He was always on the run,' claimed another. 'He filled more stockings than Santa,' announced a third. Poor, poor Sir Percy. He was only sixty-four. How sad. And it could so easily have been Melinda, I thought with, yes, I admit it, just a soupçon of regret.

I adjusted my fur hat and glanced discreetly around. I'd never been to a wedding here. The church was early English Gothic, the brown brickwork exterior stained black by exhaust fumes and acid rain. But inside it was light and bright, painted a creamy white, with two rows of battered mahogany pews. This was the first wedding I'd been to since my own. Helen said she would quite understand if I didn't feel like coming to the service, but I wouldn't have missed it for the world. After all, I had started the chain of events which had led to it. Or rather, Dominic had. It was the Dominic effect, again, I thought ruefully. Not that he was invited, of course. And I found myself wondering whether he'd have the nerve to marry Virginia Park in church, and whether she'd have to wear a Neil Cunningham dress too. How much would *their* reception cost? As much as twenty-eight grand? She was loaded, so perhaps it would cost even more. And would Dominic offer her father a comprehensive insurance policy to cover them in case of disaster? And would he have the gall to make a speech? And if he did, what on *earth* would he say?

Behind us, from the gallery, the choir sang 'God Be In My Head'. And I found myself wondering how long it would take me to get Dominic *out* of my head. And I found myself wishing that I could press a 'Fast Forward' button like I do when I'm editing tape, and spin right through all the pain and the crap. But I couldn't. I knew I'd have to endure it, in real time, minute by minute, day by day, until at last it began to recede. I looked at the flowers. Helen had done them herself, of course. They were red for Valentine's Day. On either side of the steps leading up to the altar were two spectacular displays of scarlet amaryllis, relieved by sprays of large white orchids. And she'd attached a hand-tied bunch of red ranunculus to the end of every pew. In front of her, she had carried a huge bouquet of crimson roses, designed to cover, as far as possible, the swelling curve of her bump. Helen has Great Expectations, I thought with a bittersweet smile.

Amber had been a bit down this morning, not surprisingly, when she saw me getting ready. But her mood lifted when she opened her mail. She had a card. A Valentine's card. It had a little black cat on the front. She read the inscription, and snorted.

'That's very sweet of you, Minty,' she said. I looked up, surprised, from my toast.

'Very thoughtful of you,' she said, laughing gently, and shaking her head. She handed it to me.

'To Amber, with lots of love and kisses from your little pet,' it was signed. And there were several crosses and four tiny paw prints.

'I expect Perdita asked you to buy it for her, didn't she?' She planted a kiss on the cat's nose.

'What?'

'It was a little conspiracy between you and Perdita, wasn't it?' she said with a knowing grin.

'No,' I said truthfully, 'it wasn't. Amber, I really can't guess who it's from . . .' I lied. 'Can you?'

'Oh,' she said. 'Oh yes.' And the penny crashed to the floor. And she suddenly looked disconcerted.

I don't say anything to her about Laurie and how suitable he is, and how witty and amusing and nice. If I did, she'd run a mile, because she's perverse like that. I mean, Laurie's ideal. But she just can't see it. I don't know how anyone can be so blind.

'Marriage was ordained for the mutual society of man and wife,' I heard the vicar say, 'and for the procreation of children.' I braced myself. And then it came – the awful moment when Charlie was asked to make his vows. And the memory of Dominic's reply to the very same question made me feel physically sick.

'I will!' Charlie said it so loudly that there was a slight echo. 'I *will*,' he said again. He was smiling. And so was Helen. Despite my current problems at work, and my bitter marital memories, I couldn't help smiling too. And it's true that the more you smile, the more you feel like smiling, so by the time Helen and Charlie were walking down the aisle together, my mood had lifted once more.

As we shuffled out of our pews to the strains of the Widor Toccata, I turned and glimpsed a familiar figure. It was Joe. He was looking at me, warily. I anticipated that he'd be as cold towards me as the February day – after all, we hadn't spoken for over two months. I didn't know what to do, so I gave him a tight little smile. The kind of smile that indicates neither hostility nor overt affection. The kind of smile that, in the right circumstances, can simply open the door. And now he was coming towards me. But then we could hardly avoid each other, and so it was inevitable that we'd have to speak.

'Hello,' we said, in unison.

'How are –? ' we both tried again.

'I –' we said, simultaneously. And then, all of a sudden, we laughed. That's all it took. From a distance the ice had looked thick enough to stand on, but we'd decided to skate on it instead.

'What a hideous hat,' said Joe. My heart leapt.

'Thanks,' I replied happily. 'I hate your coat.'

'Do you really mean that?'

'You know I wouldn't say it if I didn't.'

'Your singing voice is awful,' he added, as we walked out of the church, getting, here and there, I have to admit, some rather odd looks from other guests.

'Is my voice really that bad?' I enquired.

'Like a bagful of cats,' he said. 'No, let me re-phrase that: like a bagful of cats on their way to the gravel pit to be drowned.'

'That's awfully nice of you,' I said warmly. 'I've been having lessons, actually.'

Joe and I stood side by side in the churchyard while Helen and Charlie posed for photographs, happily thinking up sweet-and-sour nothings to say to one another. Beneath our offensive badinage, I was thrilled that our rapport had been restored.

'Your hair looks like a bog brush,' I pointed out, as we walked down the path in the sunshine.

'Thanks. Your lipstick's vile.'

'I'm afraid your socks do not harmonise with that suit.'

'And your telephone manner is dire. That is,' he went on pointedly, 'if you deign to come to the phone at all.' Ah. Game over.

'I didn't feel like it,' I said as we turned left into St John's Gardens.

'Do you two want a lift to the Belvedere?' Helen's sister Kate called out as she unlocked the door of her car.

'Oh, no thanks,' we both said simultaneously, 'we'd like to walk.' And then we looked at each other and smiled. It wasn't far to Holland Park. And in any case it was a fine morning. The birds were singing and the crocuses had begun to pierce the frozen earth like tiny spears. Though it was bitingly cold, there was the hint of a thaw. And on the overhanging branches we could glimpse slivers of green as the tight brown buds began to unfurl.

'Why wouldn't you speak to me?' asked Joe, serious now, as we turned into Lansdowne Road. 'Was it because I was so unfriendly to you after . . .' He sighed. 'You know?'

'Oh, no,' I said, 'that wasn't the reason. Though at least we're quits now, I suppose. The fact is that when you phoned, I wasn't talking to anyone at all.'

'Why not?'

'Because I was just so . . . miserable.'

'Why? No, let me guess: it's Dominic, I suppose?'

'Yes, it is,' I said wearily. 'He's getting married. He's otherwise engaged.'

'That's quick work,' said Joe.

'It certainly is,' I replied.

'Are you all right now?'

'I suppose so. Whatever "all right" means.'

We walked on in silence now, past huge white stuccoed houses, our feet crunching into the thin layer of sugary snow.

'I know we've fallen out a bit, Minty,' said Joe after a minute or two, 'and I'm sorry about it, but I hope you understand.'

'Of course I do,' I said.

'I just can't afford to get myself in a mess again,' he explained. 'I was protecting myself, that's all.'

'I don't blame you,' I said. 'In any case, you're right. I did have too much baggage. I still do.'

'Well, it'll get lighter,' he said, as we crossed the road. 'Timing,' Joe added.

'What?' I said.

'It's all a matter of timing,' he explained. 'The fact is, we met at the wrong time to be anything other than friends.'

I nodded my agreement, but the word 'friends' made me feel very depressed.

'Any job prospects?' he enquired.

'Not yet. London FM's been in turmoil.'

'I read about it,' he said. 'Death by fairy cake. Awful.'

'I know. No one knows what's going to happen. How are your re-writes?' I enquired.

'Coming along,' he said. 'But the bad news is . . .'

'Yes? We turn left here.'

'That 90 per cent of film scripts never get made.'

'Well, I'm sure yours will. I bet it's brilliant.' He gave my arm a grateful squeeze. 'Where did you get the idea for your novel?' I asked him as we entered Holland Park.

'My mother's Polish,' he explained, as we walked through a dense copse of silver birches. 'The story's a true one, based on what happened to her elder brother. He was autistic. He was very disturbed and destructive. And no one knew anything about autism then, so they just wrote him off. He couldn't, or rather wouldn't, even talk. Anyway, when he was nine he befriended this stray dog and it changed him. It seemed to unblock a part of his mind. And within a few months he began to speak, and "*Pios*" was the first thing he said.'

'I loved the book,' I said truthfully, as two squirrels bounced across our path. 'In fact, it made me cry. It's easy to imagine it on the screen.'

'But it's going to be very hard getting it there,' he said. 'Which is why I've decided to go to LA.'

'Good idea,' I replied, with a thin smile. 'When are you off?'

'In a few weeks. But we could insult each other long-distance.'

'Fine,' I said, with a stab of regret.

'I'm sure you could write me some offensive E-Mail, Minty.'

'Yes, I'm sure I could.'

'We could continue to exchange gratuitous abuse.'

'That would be nice. I could do it from the computer at work.'

'But I hope I'll see you again before I go,' he said as we walked up the gentle slope into the Belvedere. He went ahead to the door, and held it open for me.

'I know we've had our ups and down, Minty,' he added as I walked through. 'But I'd just like you to know that I still think you're appalling.'

She really is *appalling*, I thought, as Melinda staggered into the office with a tray the following Monday morning. She'd been to get us all coffee. This was such a rare occurrence that I had seriously wondered whether she'd be able to find the canteen without assistance.

'Here you are, Minty,' she said soothingly as she placed a cup on my desk. 'You did say milk, didn't you?'

'What? Oh, yes please. Thanks. Can I give you the money?'

'Oh no, of course not, Minty!' She rolled her eyes and laughed. 'This one's on me.'

'Gosh, well, thanks.'

'Anyway,' she added with a giggle, 'it was only a few Euwo's! I've weally got the hang of that now.'

'Well, good.'

'Are you *sure* you don't want me to get you some biscuits to go with it, Minty?'

'I'm sure. Thanks.'

'Because I weally like to help my colleagues. In any way I

can. In fact, I'm going shopping later, Minty, so do let me know if there's anything you need fwom Harvey Nicks.'

'Thanks, but I don't need anything. Honestly.'

'Well, just ask,' she said with a smile. 'And what a *vewy* nice dwess you've got on, Minty,' she added with tropical warmth.

'Oh, thank you. It's new.'

'And that scarf goes *weally* well with it.'

'Oh, er, thanks,' I said again. The constant compliments were a little wearing. They'd been flowing for over a week. We all knew why, of course. To be frank, we found her sudden charm offensive.

'Sophie, here's *your* tea,' she crooned. 'With lemon, and half a teaspoon of sugar, just like you always pwefer.' The ice caps were in danger of melting at this rate.

'Oh, thanks, Melinda,' Sophie replied, as she stood by the fax machine.

'And what *nice* shoes!' Melinda exclaimed. 'Are they new, Sophie?' She was as transparent as a trout stream.

'Er, yes, they are,' Sophie replied as she tapped in the number.

'Well, I think they're *gweat*. Kurt Geiger?'

'Ferragamo, actually,' said Sophie. Gosh.

'I love your suit too,' said Melinda. 'It almost looks like Chanel.'

'Um . . . it *is* Chanel, actually,' said Sophie with a self-conscious grin. Good Lord. I'd noticed Sophie's startling sartorial transformation of late, but I didn't like to comment. Like me, she had changed her image. But in her case she had upgraded herself from Next and River Island to bank-breakingly expensive designer wear. I had concluded that the Candy Bar was paying her well, because London FM certainly wasn't.

'I do like that jacket you're wearwing today, Wesley,' said Melinda, as she put a cup of coffee down on his desk.

'Well, that's very sweet of you to say so,' he said. In fact, it was quite a smart sports jacket.

'And how's Deirdwe?' Melinda enquired solicitously. 'How's it all going on the bump fwont?'

'Oh, the bump's really going very well, actually,' he replied with a rapt smile. 'She's just had another scan.'

'It's *so* exciting having a baby,' Melinda went on with a beatific smirk. 'Perhaps your baby and mine can play together. We could ask the bosses to install a cweche.'

'Mmmm,' he said. 'Perhaps.'

Then Jack swept in. He'd just come back from a pow-wow with the Board. As he hung up his coat, we anxiously scrutinised his face, trying to read in it signs which might give away what had been resolved. Would there be a merger? A takeover? A buy-out? A bye-bye?

'Hello, Jack – what a *super* tie!' gushed Melinda. 'I've just got evewyone some coffee. Would you like me to go and get some for you too?'

'No, thanks,' he said. 'But I would like to have a word with you, Melinda, in my office, if that's all right.'

'Oh, of *course* it's all wight,' she replied benignly. 'I'm just coming.'

Jack went into his office, held the door open for Melinda, then shut it firmly behind her. We all exchanged meaningful glances. What was going to happen? There was silence for about five seconds. And then we knew.

'NOOOOOOO!!!!' we heard her scream. 'NO! NO! NO! NO! NO!' This was followed by violent sobbing.

'You can't do this to me!' we heard her blub. 'You just CAN'T.' We craned to hear what was going on. In between Melinda's ululations, we could hear Jack's muted interjections.

'YOU CAN'T DO THIS TO ME!' she screamed again. 'Don't you wealise who I *am*? Uncle Percy would be FUWIOUS.' And then the door crashed open, and Melinda came flying out, her tear-stained face contorted with rage.

'He's twying to sack me!' she exclaimed. 'He's twying to get wid of me. As if it isn't enough having lost Uncle Percy in such twagic circumstances.'

We all returned her beseeching looks with blank ones. What on earth did she expect us to say?

'I want you all to stand *up* for me!' Melinda almost screamed. 'It's totally unfair. He's twying to victimise me.'

By now, Jack had emerged from his office and was standing in the doorway, his face reddening with suppressed rage. In his hands he was twisting a length of yellow leader tape. But his voice, when he spoke, was calm.

'Melinda, would you please come back into my office, so that we can discuss this in private?'

'NO!' she shouted. 'I won't. I want evewyone to hear how badly you've tweated me.'

'I would like to resume this conversation in the privacy of my office,' he reiterated.

'NO!' she shouted. 'If you've got anything to say to me, say it in fwont of the team! Or are you *afwaid* to, Jack?' she taunted. That did it.

'No, I'm not afraid of anything,' he said quietly. 'I'm just trying to do my job. And part of my job, Melinda, is to inform you that your contract has not been renewed. Right, everyone,' he said, 'since Melinda insists that we discuss things in here, I'm happy to tell you that, after lengthy deliberations, the Board of MG have decided, on balance, to keep the station on.'

'Thank God!' Sophie shouted. We breathed a collective sigh of relief.

'They have also appointed me Managing Director, with total responsibility for the output. One of my priorities now is, of course, to lift the ratings. And I intend to accomplish this by replacing Melinda with Minty, as presenter of *Capitalise*.'

My heart sang. I struggled to suppress an ecstatic smile.

'You can't do that!' Melinda spat. 'She's not vewy good.'

'Yes, she is,' said Jack. 'She's very good indeed.'

'I've still got some power awound here, you know,' Melinda hissed.

'No, you haven't,' said Jack simply. 'Now that Sir Percy is no longer . . . with us, you don't have any power at all.'

'But . . .' she was wheedling now, aware that aggression had failed, 'I'm the most popular pwesenter that London FM's ever had.'

'Melinda,' said Jack, with magnificent serenity, 'you delude yourself. You're about as popular as a fart in a crowded lift.'

'That's vewy *wude*!' she spat.

'Your voice is atrocious,' he went on calmly. 'You have a conspicuous speech impediment. And you make so many fluffs I'm surprised we don't have a special vacuum cleaner to hoover them up. But worst of all, you are incapable of writing a simple link without your colleagues' help. Melinda, let me be quite blunt here. As a professional broadcaster, you are "cwap".'

'I don't have to listen to this,' she hissed.

'No,' said Jack. 'You don't. What I was going to tell you, before you insisted on continuing our conference out here, was that in recognition of the two years you have worked for the station, you will of course get an appropriate pay-off, to be negotiated with the accountants. Thank you for your contribution to London FM, goodbye.' Jack returned to his office and shut the door.

'I was lying about your tie!' she shouted at the closed door. 'It's howwible. Just like you!' Then she picked up her bag, and the baby, and came and stood in front of my desk.

'Well, I hope you're satisfied, Minty,' she spat. 'I hope you're *weally* happy.' And of course I was. Ecstatically. But I was careful to say absolutely nothing.

'And as for the west of you,' she snarled, 'I . . . I . . .' Words, never her strong point, suddenly deserted her. She gave us a valedictory glare, and was gone.

'More Turmoil at London FM!' trumpeted *Broadcast*'s front page a few days later. They love us. They absolutely love us. We provide them with great copy, you see. It's like a soap opera. And Melinda's furious departure was another dramatic twist in the tale. On the inside pages they did a big piece about the station, and described the changes that have been made in the past week – including a very tough new stalking policy. All letters from nutters are now sent straight to the police. And the article praised the way Jack had promoted Sophie to edit *Capitalise* and how, at twenty-two, she's the youngest editor in the programme's history. They did a big number on me, too; about how I was Jack's first choice to present the show. And – get this – they called me 'The New Voice of London FM'. I nearly died.

Then the next morning the *Evening Standard* phoned up and said they wanted to do a feature on us too. It was to be a 'Day in the life of' kind of piece, and so this woman came along with a photographer and they trailed us at work, from the morning meeting at nine thirty, until we came off air. The piece came out this morning – in fact, I've got it in front of me now – and it really does look good. It's a double-page spread, entitled 'The Retuning of London FM'. There's a photo of Sophie chairing the meeting; and there's one of me with my headphones on, and there's a fun photo of us all laughing and joking after we've just come off air at two forty-five. And there was a very nice one of Jack sitting in his office, taking a phone call, looking very relaxed – well, he *is* a lot more relaxed these days, since he kicked *derrière* at home. He says the girls – and Jane – are now treating him with considerably more respect. And he was quoted as saying that he wants to keep a strong current affairs element in the programme, and that he hopes to avoid the dumbing down of news which goes on all too often elsewhere. He also said it was his intention to introduce a number of new programmes to the schedule in due course. And that before long he would steer the station into the brave new digital age.

So finally things are starting to go well, and the programme's going like a dream. To top it all, I got a call from Joe, which I was thrilled about. And the reason why I was thrilled was because he's not in London at the moment. He's with his parents in Manchester while he does some extra research for one of the characters – I think she's the little boy's teacher. Joe told me he's been going through all the old family photos and letters with his mum. And he's there for ten days, but he gave me a call. So I was feeling incredibly happy. In fact, I was having a very good day.

'What a super piece in the *Standard*, Minty,' said Mum, when she rang me at work after the show. 'Now, I can't talk for long because I'm at the Badger Trust AGM, but I just wanted to tell you what a lovely photo it is of you, darling. I wonder if Daddy's seen it?' she added vaguely.

'Haven't you spoken to him?'

'Oh no, I've been so busy recently,' she replied. 'I haven't seen him for *days*. Ships in the night, and all that!'

'Mum,' I said, 'you told us you'd tone it down.'

'Tone what down, Minty?'

'All your charity stuff. You said you'd tone it down when Dad retired.'

'Yes, darling, I know.'

'Well, he's been retired for nearly five months.'

'*Has* he?' she said, dumbfounded. 'Good Lord! I've been so busy, I hadn't even noticed. Of course he's retired, that's right. Anyway, if you want to talk to me later, ring between six and seven because I've got a bring-and-buy for the Red Cross before that, and a drinks party for Action on Addiction afterwards.'

'I wish someone would take some action on *your* addiction,' I said crisply. 'You're just a hopeless philanthropolic!'

March

It's great being a presenter. I love it. Not just because of the obvious advantages that go with the job – i.e. career progress, higher job satisfaction, increased earnings, elevated professional status and occasional media interest. No, I love it for the following very specific reasons: a) I don't have to interview Citronella Pratt any more; b) I can go home earlier; and c) I'm a lot happier. So much so that some of my anguish about Dominic and his new engagement has lifted. I do feel more cheerful. For the first time, I feel I'm able to cope. The pendulum has swung back in my favour. And that's what life is like. The rich tapestry and all that. The ineffable multiplicity. What Emily Dickinson calls 'The mixing bells and palls' of existence. Something utterly dreadful happens – being dumped on your wedding day, for example – and then, to balance things up a bit, a piece of good luck comes along. Like my promotion. Though I was sorry that it only came about because of what happened to poor old Sir Percy.

Anyway, what I'm really enjoying, apart from the work itself, is the fact that, once the programme's over, I'm free to leave. No longer do I have to stay at my desk, editing features late into the night, then walking around with eyes like peanuts the following morning. It's Monica's turn to do that now. She said she'd always wanted to be a reporter, and so in the general reshuffle that went on, Jack promoted her too. She's thrilled. She's young and keen and she's got the broadcasting bug, so she doesn't mind the hard graft. Anyway, my job is simply to present the programme. And it's great not having to help everyone any more. So once we come off air, that's it. I can go. Usually, however, I don't. I like to hang around in the office for a while chatting to everyone, though Wesley does nothing but talk about his impending fatherhood – he's a total baby bore these days. And I read the papers and make a couple of calls, and then, at about four thirty, I toddle off. So today I arrived back home at about five fifteen, and there was Amber, on the phone, as usual.

''ello,' I heard her say, 'eez zat Borrrders boo-ookshop? Ah. Zees is Sylvie Dupont speekeenger.' Oh God, not *that* old trick again. 'Ah em joost reenging to pless an orrrrder for a vairy gooder boook zat all my frrrenz 'ave bin telleeng me to bah. Eet eez colled *A Public Convenience* by zat vairy good rrrriter, Amber Dane. I would lak to orderrr *dix*, er, I min, ten copees, *s'il vous plaît* . . . *Oui, oui* . . . *Merci* . . . *Au revoir* . . . HA!' She was laughing as she put the phone down.

'Don't tell me,' I said. 'You'll accidentally on purpose forget to go and collect the books.'

'Yes,' she said, with a smirk. 'And then they'll have to sell them.'

'How many bookshops have you done this in?'

'Thirty-three,' she said. 'In a number of different foreign accents. I'm particularly proud of my Russian one. Do you want to hear it?'

'No, thanks. I hope you remember whether you're Russian or French when they phone you back to say the books have arrived.'

'Oh, don't be so silly, Minty. I always give a false number.'

'You're dreadful,' I said with a laugh.

'Look, it's hard enough being a writer as it is. You've got to pull every trick in the book.' Suddenly Perdita appeared and jumped, purring and mewing, on to Amber's lap.

'She looks so well,' I said, stroking her head. 'She's really put on weight.'

'Yes, but not too much, because we don't want her becoming a little fatso, do we, darling? Now, Perdita, shall we show Auntie Minty what Mummy bought you from Harrods today?'

Amber gave me a beatific smile, then disappeared into the kitchen and came back with a fur-lined basket, and a personalised porcelain cat plate.

'These are the *dernier cri* in feline accessories,' she announced, happily. 'Nothing but the best will do.'

'Lucky Perdita,' I said, 'that someone loves you so much.'

Amber opened a tin of pilchards in aspic, then piled the new plate high.

'Don't overdo it,' I said. 'If she eats too much she'll be sick. Anyway, I think she looks just right.'

'No, I think she's still growing,' said Amber, as Perdita got stuck in. 'And remember, Minty, we've got to compensate for her unfortunate start in life.'

'Hello!' squawked Pedro. The phone was ringing. It was probably one of Amber's bookshops. 'How are you?' Pedro screeched as I went into the hall. 'Yes . . . yes . . . yes,' I heard him say in a bored sort of way as I picked up the receiver.

'Hello,' I said.

'Is that Minty Malone?' said an unknown female voice. Whoever she was, she sounded distressed. I was so taken aback by her tone, I didn't answer straight away.

'Is that Minty Malone?' enquired the voice again, more urgently now.

'Er, yes. It is,' I replied. 'Who is it?' There was a moment's silence, which unnerved me.

'We don't know each other,' the voice went on, carefully. It was a very posh voice. 'But I really need to talk to you.' She pronounced it 'rarely'.

'Why?'

'My name's Virginia Park.'

The hall carpet rushed up to greet me as I sank on to the adjacent chair. My face seemed to have heated to boiling point, and my heart was banging like a drum.

'Do you know who I am?' she enquired in a voice which quavered with emotion.

'Yes,' I said quietly. 'I do.'

'I rarely need to talk to you,' she repeated.

'What for?' I said. I felt sick.

'Because I think you'd want to know.'

'Know *what*?' I heard myself say. I was fearful and yet agog.

'It's Dominic,' she said, quietly. 'I'm ringing about Dominic.' Well, I knew *that*. Why *else* would she call? What was this about? Oh God. A sudden fear gripped my heart. Oh God. Oh no. Please, no. He'd been hateful to me, but I wouldn't wish him any harm. Visions of Dominic plastered all over the M1, or being bagged up after some unpleasant accident, sprang into my mind. That's why she was calling me, because his mother was too distraught.

'Is he dead?' I said. I felt sick. 'Just tell me. Has something happened? Is he dead?'

'No he *isn't* dead,' she spat. 'I bloody well wish he was!'

'Then why on earth are you ringing?'

'Because . . .' and now there was an audible sob. 'Because the bastard's just broken it off.'

'We were supposed to get married in May,' I heard her say between teary gasps. 'My dress was almost ready. All the hotels had been booked. And we'd posed in *Leicestershire Life*.'

'I see,' I said.

'But last week, we were having dinner, and all of a sudden Dominic said – uh uh – that he didn't want to get married. That he couldn't – uh uh – go through with it. He said that he *wouldn't* – uh uh – go through with it. He said that he'd made a stupid mistake, and that everything had changed.'

'Oh,' I said. I was too shocked to say anything else.

'I haven't slept,' she said. 'I feel suicidal. I just don't know what to do. And I knew about you,' she continued. 'I'd asked him about you once or twice. I'd seen your name and phone number in his address book. He'd crossed it out, but it was still legible.'

'Oh,' I said, again. I found myself wishing she hadn't told me that.

'So when I was collecting my things from his house, I wrote your number down. And then this morning I saw that piece about you in the *Evening Standard,* and I just *had* to talk to you.'

'Why?' I said.

'Because, I thought, after what he did to you, you might be able to give me some advice.'

'How do you know what he did to me?' I asked. 'I can't imagine him volunteering the information. In fact,' I went on, and now a cold fear gripped my heart, 'I'd like to know when you met him.'

'Oh, years ago,' she replied. 'We went out briefly, in the early nineties.'

'Oh,' I said, 'I didn't know that.'

'I was crazy about him, but it didn't last long. And then last July I bumped into him again, in Harrods. And he seemed in a real state. He mentioned that he was getting married and told me he had wedding nerves. And I wished him good luck, and thought no more of it. But then, to my surprise, he contacted me in early August – he still had my number from before. And so I asked him how the wedding had gone.'

'What did he say?'

'Well, he didn't really want to talk about it.'

'I'm sure he didn't. But what did he say? How did he explain it?'

'He said that he hadn't got married after all because, how did he put it? Oh yes. Because there'd been "a problem with the church" . . .'

A problem with the church? A problem with the *church*??? Was *that* what he told people? That there'd been a problem with the church! I nearly choked.

'The only problem with the church,' I said with icy emphasis, 'was Dominic's sudden departure from it, mid marriage, in front of two hundred and eighty people.'

'Oh my God,' she said. 'He didn't put it like that.'

'Of course he didn't,' I replied. And then something cracked inside me. Something finally broke. Gone was my suppressed sadness. In its place was rage.

'It's so humiliating,' I heard Virginia Park say. She was crying again.

'You're dead right,' I said. 'It *is*.'

'The engagement was in the paper,' she wept. 'Absolutely everyone knew. I just feel so, so, awful,' she said. She pronounced it 'say'. 'I don't know what to do,' she sobbed. 'I haven't done a stroke of wark.'

'I'll tell you what to do,' I said.

'What?'

'I'll tell you what to do,' I said again, louder now, as I rose to my feet.

'Yes? What?'

'REJOICE!!! That's what you should do. REJOICE!'

'I don't know what you mean!'

'Rejoice that you have been spared from marrying a man so low, so, so . . . contemptible, so craven, so caddish . . .' My God, all these words seemed to begin with 'c'. 'Such a coward, such a cur, such a . . .'

'Chicken!' interjected Amber, who had been sitting quietly on the stairs. I could hear Virginia Park sobbing.

'I'm sorry for you,' I said. I was clutching the side of the hall table now. 'I'm sorry that you're suffering. Because I suffered too. But you asked me for my advice. And I'm giving it. Let me repeat it. Let me shout it from the rooftops: REJOICE!! I say unto you – REJOICE!! And be GLAD!! Praise the Lord! Hallelujah! For He has delivered you. GOODBYE!!'

I put the phone down. I felt sick and faint. Despite my bravado, I found tears coursing down my face while unanswered questions raced through my mind. How many guests were they going to have? What proportion of them were his clients? Was she the reason Dominic jilted me? And why had he dropped her too? Was this simply Olympic-level commitment-phobia, or was there method in his marital madness? I sat on the hall chair, staring wild-eyed into space, pressing my mental 'Rewind' button, and replaying what she'd said.

She said she'd met him in July, just before our wedding,

and that he'd seemed very nervous. He *was* very nervous. I'd noticed that too. But then, when he isn't trying to sell someone something, he does appear nervous and neurotic. Because he's pretty insecure. So I'd simply attributed his anxiety to pre-marital tension and, God knows, I'd had a bit of that myself.

I looked at Amber. She was waiting for me to tell her what was going on. But I was so shocked by this latest twist in the tale that I hardly knew where to begin. And I was just about to inform her that Dominic had jilted Miss Piggy too when the phone suddenly rang again. I let it ring once. Twice. Three times. And then I picked it up.

'Yes?' I said, with weary wariness.

'It's me again,' said Virginia Park miserably. She was still crying. I visualised her fleshless upper lip covered in tears and snot.

'I feel so awful,' she moaned. 'I just need to talk to you.'

'I'm sorry,' I said. I felt exhausted.

'Please.'

'Look, I can't add anything to what I've just said. I don't want to get involved. It's too painful. I'm sorry. I've been through enough and I want to protect myself now. I'm sorry, Virginia. I really am. Goodbye.' I put the phone down. Ten seconds later, it rang again. Oh God, I *wished* she'd get the message. Some people are just so thick-skinned! I picked it up.

'Look!' I said. 'I really *can't* help you. I'm *very* sorry for you. But I can't enlighten you about Dominic's behaviour any more than I have. And although you want to talk about him, I'm afraid *I* don't, because, to be quite honest, I'd simply like to forget that I *ever* met him.'

There was silence at the other end. Thank God. I'd got through to her, at last. I could do without all this. Life was stressful enough as it was. And I looked at Amber and sighed and rolled my eyes, and was just about to hang up when I heard an all-too-familiar voice say, very quietly, 'Actually, Minty, it's me.'

*

'Don't,' said Amber, when I put the phone down on Dominic three minutes later. 'Please, don't meet him.' I looked at her.

'Has my hair gone white?' I enquired. 'Have deep cracks appeared on my face?' She shook her head. 'I feel I've aged fifty years in the last ten minutes.' I was shaking. My palms and brow were damp. Hearing his voice again had seriously disturbed me. But hearing him ask to meet me had shocked me to my core.

'I don't think you should see him,' she said again, more forcefully now. She passed me a tissue. 'What's the point?' We went into the kitchen, where she reached up for what was left of the cooking brandy.

'I have to see him,' I croaked. 'Because then I might understand. He says he's going to explain everything. He says that there are things I don't know. Things he couldn't tell me at the time.' Amber was rolling her eyes and had stuck two fingers to her temple. I looked at her. 'He said he felt awful about what happened.'

'About what *happened*?' she exclaimed. 'That's a typical Dominic construction, isn't it? About what he *did*, you mean!'

'Yes, that's what he meant. That he feels sorry about what he did. But he says there was a reason for it.'

'The reason is,' said Amber, vehemently, 'that the man's a flaky fuck-up with no moral fibre.' I looked at her bleakly. 'He has all the backbone of an earthworm,' she added. 'No, I'm sorry, that's unfair to earthworms. He has less.'

'Don't be so hard,' I sobbed.

'Why not? He deserves it. He's a long, winding Lane, Mint, leading nowhere.'

'Oh, Amber.' I was in floods.

'He's a fucking liability,' she went on angrily. 'So he's dumped Virginia Pork-Pie too?' I nodded. 'They should attach a government warning to him,' she said. '"Associating with this man, ladies, may seriously damage your mental health." It's a very bad idea,' she said again, shaking her head and pursing her lips. 'I think you should ring him back and say no. Anyway, why do you *want* to see him?'

'Because I was very attached to him,' I replied quietly. 'And he . . . it . . . what happened on my wedding day has obsessed me for the past nine months. And because I didn't understand why it happened, I've been largely blaming myself. And now, at last, I have the chance to find out the truth, and I'm not going to turn that chance down.'

Amber sighed. 'Well, as long as he doesn't try and get you to go back to him.'

'Don't be ridiculous,' I said wearily. 'Of *course* that's not going to happen.'

'I want you to come back,' said Dominic, the following Thursday, at about twenty past eight. 'I think we should give it another go.'

We'd met shortly after eight, in the Ivy. He hadn't taken long to say what he had to say. It was as though he wanted to get it in, quickly, at the beginning, in case this tense encounter got out of hand. I just stared at him, and said nothing. I'd mentally rehearsed this moment many times. The moment when he and I would meet again. But it was an event I had not believed would ever come to pass. Because once Dominic's made a decision, he *never* changes his mind. Oh yes, Dominic always knows what he wants – 'exactly'. But, to my amazement, he had proved me wrong. And now here we were. Face to face once more.

What would you have done? Refused point-blank to go? Agreed, then stood him up? Gone to the restaurant and hurled abuse, or tipped soup all over his head? Perhaps you'd have denounced him in public. Or turned up with another bloke. I'd run all these options through my mind over the past couple of days. I'd tried them on for size as I might try on clothes in a shop. In the end, I'd rejected them all. They didn't suit me. I'd simply decided to be cool. That's what I would be – very, very cool. So I packed ice around my heart. But my legs were shaking as I entered the restaurant.

The waiter offered to show me to Dominic's table, but I went straight to it, unassisted, as though I were a heat-seeking missile. I got a jolt, naturally, when I saw him – a burning surge of adrenaline. He looked the same, I thought, but at the same time he somehow looked different. His eyes were just as blue, of course, though his hair was darker, from the winter. But I was irritated to see that he looked slightly heavier. This suggested an easy conscience, or perhaps it was all those pork pies. He stood up, and there was an awkward moment when I could see he was going to try and kiss me. So I was careful to turn my head, inhaling as I did so, with a sharp pang, the familiar aroma of his Chanel. He was drinking a gin and tonic and offered me one. But I ordered a Perrier, because I knew that if I had any alcohol, I'd cry. He was very well turned out, as usual, not in the sackcloth and ashes I'd hoped for, but in a dark suit, and a discreetly striped shirt, with double cuffs, in which were visible a pair of silver links I'd given him for his birthday. He was wearing a pale yellow silk tie, which I didn't recognise. Perhaps that was from Miss Piggy. Anyway, he looked very smart. And the funny thing was, when I was getting ready to meet him, I'd felt the usual panic that I wouldn't look good enough for him. That he'd complain about my appearance. That he'd say my bag was 'wrong' with my suit, or that my jacket was too baggy, or the wrong colour, or too cheap. And I'd felt a sudden stab of guilt at throwing away all the clothes he'd given me. Then I'd sat down on my bed and slapped my brow, twice, with the palm of my hand. And I'd put on a pair of Red or Dead chinos, because he doesn't like women to wear trousers, and a black jacket by Comme des Garçons. All my most un-girlie gear. And I'd slicked down my hair with a little gel. He'd looked slightly taken aback when he saw me. I saw his eyes flicker with surprise. But he made no comment about my Eton crop, or my conspicuous change of style. Maybe he'd seen the photo of me in the *Standard*. Maybe he'd been prepared.

We sat there, eyeing each other nervously for a few seconds. He tried to smile, but I met his eyes with a steady, disinterested gaze, despite the clamour in my heart. Because for the very first time in our relationship, I was the one with the power.

And this was because of the simple fact that it was Dominic who had asked to meet me. We perused the menu for a few moments in silence. Then the waiter came to our table.

'I'll have the tricolore salad of vine-ripened tomatoes, followed by pan-seared swordfish,' I said.

'I'm sorry, madame,' he replied, clearly confused. 'But zat is not on ze menu.'

'Oh, silly me!' I exclaimed softly with a benevolent smile. 'I was getting confused with the Waldorf. I'll have the Sevruga caviar, please, followed by the roast mallard with *foie gras*.' I was only sorry they didn't have any Beluga caviar.

'And for sir?'

'Smoked salmon, and shepherd's pie.'

'Or should that be humble pie?' I said pleasantly, as the waiter walked away. 'I presume that's what you're going to eat this evening?'

'I know I ought to,' he said quietly. 'And you have every right to be angry, Minty. It's no more than I expected.'

'Do you know,' I said, smiling brightly, 'today, I'm not actually angry. Not at all. I *was* angry, of course,' I went on calmly. 'To be perfectly honest, Dominic, I was so angry I thought I'd get cancer.'

'I'm sorry,' he said. And he looked it.

'In fact . . .' I went on, being careful to keep my voice low, because Dominic's very self-conscious and can't bear 'scenes' of any kind.

'What?' he said.

'I had a kind of breakdown, because of what you put me through.' He was silent. 'Just thought I'd tell you that,' I added, with a smile. Then I sipped my gently fizzing Perrier. 'Still,' I said cheerfully, 'no hard feelings, eh? Isn't that what you said? No hard feelings? I'm afraid I can't say the same for Virginia Park.' Dominic reddened at that. 'Yes, Dominic, I'm sorry to say that, despite my extensive experience in this field, I was quite unable to help her. Oh, I gave your engagement ring to a Parisian busker, by the way.'

'Minty –' Dom blurted. His face expressed a strange

mixture, of annoyance and contrition. Not many people have the kind of face that can do that. But Dominic's can. 'Minty,' he tried again. Oh, I do wish he wouldn't keep repeating my Christian name, I thought to myself. He's not trying to sell me an insurance policy now. 'Minty,' he repeated, 'I understand that I may not be your favourite person at the moment, but I hope you're not going to make this evening hard for me.'

'Oh, Dominic, I wouldn't *dream* of it,' I said, pleasantly. 'I was always very kind to you, as you know.'

'Yes,' he said, 'I do know that.'

'I was always very, very sweet to you.'

'Yes,' he said wistfully, 'you were. You were always very sweet and, well, nice. And that's why I wanted to see you again.'

'So that I could be nice to you? Well, I think I might find that rather difficult.'

'No. Of course I don't expect you to be nice to me, straight away. That will take time. I wanted to meet you, because . . . well . . . I'd like to try and put things right.'

'I have two questions for you, Dominic,' I said, helping myself to a roll. 'a) What makes you think you *can* "put things right", and b) why do you *want* to?'

'Because . . .' he sighed heavily. He was clearly finding this stressful. Oh God, his eyes were shining. Were those incipient tears? To my dismay, I felt the coronary ice begin to drip. 'Because I'm so fond of you, Minty,' he said.

'Really?'

'Yes. And I think I *can* put things right,' he went on, 'because of what we once had. And the reason *why* I want to do it, Minty, is because I know I made a terrible mistake.'

I made a terrible mistake. A terrible mistake? Why didn't he say, 'I know I did something terribly wrong?' My heart chilled over again.

'You certainly did make a bit of a mistake there,' I said. 'But never mind, Dom. It's all in the past.'

'Is it, Minty?' he said, with a faint smile. 'I hope it is. And I think we can only consign it to the past' – *We?* – 'if I explain to you what happened. If I explain,' he went on, 'how I came to get everything so wrong.' *How I got everything so wrong?*

'I'll tell you how you got everything so wrong,' I said. 'I mean, this is just from my own selfish point of view of course, so you have to bear that in mind. But how you get everything so wrong, *I* think, is by abandoning me in church on my wedding day in front of almost three hundred people. You also got everything wrong by never once apologising to me, or even contacting me to see if I was all right. You *also* got everything wrong,' I added, 'by leaving my parents with the bill, which, incidentally, in case you've forgotten, was twenty-eight thousand pounds. And then you *also* got everything wrong, and again this is just from my own self-centred perspective, by getting engaged, within a mere five months, to someone else.'

'I hope you're not going to be too hard on me, Minty,' he said. 'And, yes, I *am* eating humble pie. Which is what you want. And it's no less than you deserve.'

'Thank you, Dominic.' Our starters arrived. He picked up his knife and fork and I found myself looking at the gold crest ring on the little finger of his left hand. He'd bought it, second-hand, when he was twenty-five. I'd always thought it much too big. It depicted a hind with an arrow through its throat. That's what he'd done to me.

'It was all a terrible mistake,' he said, as he squeezed lemon on to his smoked salmon. A mistake. *Mistake*? That word again. 'I made an appalling error of judgement,' he continued. 'And I take full responsibility for what happened. I'd like to stress, Minty, that you were not in any way to blame.'

'Really?'

'No.'

'Well, that's a relief,' I said, without irony. 'Because, actually, I did think I was at least partly to blame. In fact, Dominic, I've been in agonies about it all for months.'

'No,' he said, 'it was entirely my fault. But there are extenuating circumstances, which I want you to know about.'

'I should be very interested to hear what they are,' I said.

Because that, dear reader, was the only reason I was sitting there. Out of a simple need to know.

'Why did you do it?' I asked.

'I was up shit creek. That's why.' He sighed heavily. 'My whole world was about to cave in.' This was news to me. I was intrigued. 'Something . . . horrendous had happened,' he explained. 'Three weeks before the wedding . . . it was dreadful.' The memory of it, whatever it was, seemed to make him feel ill. His eyes looked dead and blank. I felt a sudden wave of sympathy. I couldn't help it. I put my knife down.

'I don't know what it was, Dom, but you know I would have helped you.'

He looked at me, and smiled. 'Yes,' he said, 'I know. But the trouble was that you couldn't help me – no one could, because it was . . .' he emitted a little groan '. . . too awful. It was too big. And I didn't want to get you involved.'

'So you weren't having an affair with Virginia Park, then?'

'No' he said, 'I wasn't. She's irrelevant.'

'Not to me. Before you carry on, could you tell me why you got involved with her?'

'That was a . . . mistake,' he said, with an exasperated shrug. 'I wasn't thinking straight. I was on the rebound.' Rebound*er*, he should have said. 'She's irrelevant,' he insisted again.

'So what was it then? What had happened that was so terrible?'

'I'd been threatened . . .'

'Threatened?' I repeated. My God. By who? The mafia? The Triads? The Yakuza? The IRA?

'I'd been threatened with losing everything,' he went on quietly. 'Every penny of what I'd built up. Everything was going to be taken away from me. And I was going to be left with nothing.'

'Why?'

'I'd have had to sell my house, and my car, and it still wouldn't have been enough. I'd have had to surrender my Peps, my Tessa's, my endowments, my premium bonds, my Post Office Savings accounts – everything.'

'Why?' I said again.

'Because of a . . . mistake I made at work.'

'You did something wrong?'

'No, no – not *wrong*. It was a grey area.'

'A grey area?'

'It was about pensions,' he explained.

'Pensions? What about them? You sold them all the time.'

'Yes, I did. Very profitably. But then we all ran into problems. There were investigations.' Investigations? Suddenly, it clicked, and I knew.

'Mis-selling,' I said. 'You were mis-selling pensions! That's why you were in trouble.'

'Yes,' he said with a sigh.

'You were advising people to take out private pensions, rather than staying in their company scheme. That's it, isn't it?'

'Well, that's the nub of it. Yes.'

'And you were advising them to do this, even though you knew the new scheme would be less profitable than the occupational one they were in.'

'Well, that's putting it rather bluntly.'

'And the reason *why* it would be less profitable – do correct me if I'm wrong – is because all the commission that they had to pay you would take a big chunk off the value of the fund.'

'Ye-es. Yes, it would.'

'And that it would take these people years and years to catch up, if they ever did. So it was like starting with a massive handicap.'

'I suppose so. Yes,' he conceded.

'Whereas, if they'd stayed in their company scheme, as you should have advised them, they'd have been better off in the long run.'

'You seem to know rather a lot about it, Minty,' he said warily.

'Well, there's been quite a lot about it in the papers. And one of our business reporters has been following the story. He says three million people were conned.'

'I didn't con anyone,' Dominic insisted.

'Didn't you *know* that you were selling them something less valuable than what they already had?' He was silent.

'No. Not really.'

'I find that hard to believe. Didn't you tell them about all the commission?'

'Yes, of course I did. I didn't pull the wool over anyone's eyes.'

'Ah, but did you tell them that your commission wasn't being paid by the insurance company? That it was coming directly out of their premiums? Did you tell them that?'

'Well . . . as I say, it was a grey area.'

'Seems pretty black and white to me.'

'Yes, but it wasn't my fault. Remember, when this all started, the Tories had been really pushing private pensions. I genuinely felt I was helping my clients. And of course the Robert Maxwell business gave company pensions a very bad name. People *wanted* private pensions. Anyway,' he went on, 'it was the industry's fault for failing to regulate it properly.'

'And you got into trouble.'

'Yes,' he confessed, 'I did. And it's been a nightmare.' He shuddered at the memory. 'A nightmare,' he said again. 'It had been rumbling on for months,' he explained. 'And there are these plans to pay compensation. The insurance companies are going to be shelling out twenty *billion* pounds for this.'

'Surely that's their problem, not yours.'

'Yes. But then in early July, a rumour began to circulate that some independent financial advisers might be made personally liable. And I learned that I was one of them.'

'You would have had to cough up?'

'Yes. To the tune of around twenty thousand pounds per client. Minty –' he leant forward – 'I have nearly two hundred clients.'

'Yes, I know. Half of them were at our wedding.'

'That works out at four *million* pounds.'

'Yes, I suppose it does.'

'I genuinely believed that I was about to lose everything,'

he said. 'Every last penny that I'd earned. Everything I'd built up from such a tough start in life.'

'Oh, don't give me the sob story.'

'But you don't understand, Minty, because your life was so much easier than mine.'

'Not once I'd met you.'

'It's not fair of you to judge me, when your background was so different from mine. You had private education. Then you went to university. And your grandmother's legacy enabled you to buy your flat. I didn't have any of that. I'd built up everything entirely by myself.'

'Look, I know that. I respected you for it. In fact, it was always a strong point in your favour. But that's not the issue here.'

'Yes, it is,' he insisted. 'Because it was the threat to what I'd built up which was gnawing away at me. I can't tell you how terrified I was to think I'd lose it all. And so I got myself in a *total* panic. I don't know how I managed to function normally.'

'You didn't function normally. You jilted me.'

'I'm sorry,' he said again. 'I'm truly sorry for what I did to you.'

'Thank you. I accept your apology. Though I think you could at least have had the "decency" – if that's the right word – to call it off beforehand. Like you've done with Virginia Park.'

'But the wedding was just so . . . unstoppable,' he said. 'It was like a juggernaut. And every time I wanted to say, "I'm sorry, Minty, but I can't go through with it," you'd tell me something about your dress, or the catering details, or the flowers or whatever. You were so happy. How could I cancel it?'

'Well, you should have done,' I said. 'It was rather embarrassing having it cancelled like that on the day. It's passed into local legend in Primrose Hill,' I said. 'They sing ballads about it in the pub: "The Jilting of Minty Malone".'

We paused while the waiter removed the plates from our

first course. Dominic couldn't resist taking the opportunity to do a little discreet rubber-necking.

'Isn't that Stephen Fry,' he said, 'just coming in?'

I glanced to my left. 'Yes.' And as Stephen Fry passed our table, he caught my eye and smiled politely and said, 'Hello, Minty.' I smiled back.

'Do you *know* him?' said Dominic, agog.

'Not really. I interviewed him on Tuesday. But I'm going to his book launch next week.'

'Oh, so Radio-Biz is obviously going well.'

'Yes,' I replied. 'It is.'

'You've made it,' he said. 'You're a presenter.'

'Yes,' I said. 'I never thought it would happen. But I am.' The waiter appeared and placed the duck in front of me and the shepherd's pie in front of Dominic, then retreated. 'So where were we?' I said brightly above the gentle babble of the other diners. 'Ah, yes, you were facing financial ruin, and you wanted to call off our wedding.'

'Yes.'

'Now, *why* did you want to call it off, Dominic?' I enquired. I felt that, now, we were getting to the crux. He dipped his fork into the shepherd's pie, then looked at me.

'To protect you,' he said. I almost choked.

'*Protect* me?' I enquired.

'Yes. How could I put you through all that?'

'You *did* put me through "all that",' I said.

'I mean, how could I put you through all the worry and anxiety of my financial ruin. It just wouldn't have been *fair* to you.'

'But I had a job, Dominic.'

'Yes, but, with respect, Minty, you weren't earning much. Then.' *Then?* 'I was so proud of what I had to offer you,' he added. 'And it was all going to be taken away.'

'Yes, but I wasn't marrying you because of what you'd *got,*' I said. 'I was marrying you because I believed I loved you. That's what I believed. Then.'

'But I didn't feel it was fair to put you in a position where

I wouldn't be able to support you properly. Pay for anything. Buy you anything.'

'I didn't *need* anything.'

'We wouldn't have been able to afford a house in a good area.'

'But I have a nice flat in Primrose Hill. We could have lived there, Dom. Or we could have sold it and bought a house somewhere less fashionable until you were on your feet again. There's no mortgage on my flat, Dominic. I'm not a pauper, you know.'

'No,' he said. 'But . . .'

'But what?'

'But . . . our standard of living would have been so much lower than what you were expecting. And I just didn't feel that it was *right* for me to expose you to all my problems. In any case,' he continued, 'I was in a complete panic. I wanted to tell you, but could never find the right moment. Then before I knew it the wedding day had dawned, and I was standing there in the church, and I just knew I couldn't go through with it.'

'So you didn't. We were about to make our vows,' I pointed out. 'But then, to my utter astonishment, you *dis*avowed me.'

'Oh God, Minty!' he said. 'Do you think it was easy for me? Do you think it was easy, doing what I did? Running out on you in front of all my clients?' *All my clients*?

'But the other problem that I have, of course, is that you said such nasty things to me. In front of everyone. You said – and do correct me if I'm wrong, Dominic. You always do correct me if I'm wrong. And even if I'm right, you still like to correct me – but you said that I was very untidy.'

'But, darling, you are,' he said, with an indulgent smile.

'And you said that I talked too much and never knew when to shut up.'

'Well, I was in a state,' he said. 'I didn't know *what* I was saying. I was trying to come up with reasons, excuses, for what I was about to do. And in any case, darling' – he reached for my hand – 'you *do* talk too much. You love talking, don't you, darling. Talking, talking, talking. Little Minty Mintola just loves to talk. And it *is* annoying, darling.'

'It isn't annoying. It's *normal.*'

'Oh, darling,' he said again.

My knife hovered over my plate. I put it down.

'You know, Dominic, you've always portrayed me very falsely. I really don't know why.'

'I don't know what you mean,' he said peevishly.

'You've made out, right from the start, that I'm this garrulous idiot, jabbering away nineteen to the dozen, unaware that no one's listening. That I'm "boring" everyone, as you always liked to say. That I'm droning on and on, like some tedious, uninvited guest.'

'But you *do* talk a lot, darling.'

'It's called conversation, Dominic. It's called making conversation. That's what normal people do. And that's what I was trying to do with you. To oil the wheels of our relationship, because you were often so quiet. Is it because you have so little to say yourself, that you crush conversation in others?'

'No, it's just that you *do* like to chatter on, and it can be quite exhausting. And you know I don't sleep well, and I work very hard and I need to relax when I'm at home.'

'But too much silence can be a strain. You see, Dominic, you talk very little, unless you're actively trying to sell someone something. Then, of course, you talk. Out comes the patter. But you don't really have a lot to say for yourself otherwise, do you?'

'I . . .'

'You don't really ever express any opinions or views on anything. You're not interested in any exchange of ideas.'

He rolled his eyes, theatrically. 'That's because you're talking so much I can't get a word in edgeways.'

'Rubbish!' I said. 'It's because you don't have much to say. Or you can't be bothered to think of anything. You're quite uninformed. Perhaps because you've spent the last fifteen years making money during the day, and watching Sky Sports by night. And apart from a few relationships and a few golfing holidays, that's really all you've done.'

'I . . .'

'You're not an entertaining or thoughtful person, Dominic. In fact – can I be frank here? – you're boring. Did I ever tell you that? You're a very boring man.'

'I . . .'

'You've never taken any risks. Or done anything daring. You've never even travelled.'

'Only because I'm terrified of flying. It's a phobia.'

'No, it's not, it's an excuse. It's not the *flying* you were scared of, Dom. It's what you might find at the other end. You've never challenged yourself in any way. And you certainly never challenged me. You're just so, so boring, Dominic. You're very attractive,' I added. 'But you're so boring. I thought I'd die of boredom when I was with you.'

'Now look here, Minty, I –'

'And I wouldn't have minded so much if you'd at least been decent and kind. But you weren't. You were the *opposite*. You spent most of the time undermining me. You took my kindness for granted. You sapped my confidence and sense of self. You controlled what I said, what I did, and what I wore.'

'Then why didn't you complain, if it was as bad as you say?'

'It's extraordinary, isn't it? You're quite right. Why *didn't* I complain? Because I was too nice, that's why. Because I wanted to keep everything nice and smooth. Because I hated scenes. Because I was afraid to confront you. But I'm not afraid of that now.'

'So I see.'

'I've changed, Dominic. Haven't you noticed? You were always telling me to go and change – and now I have.'

'Yes, I know. I first noticed it when I read those articles about you. You do look different.' He reached for my hand again. 'But I don't mind, Minty.' *I don't mind*???

'I'm not talking about my *appearance*, Dominic. I'm talking about my *self*. Who I *am*. And I'm quite different now – changed, changed utterly, to coin a phrase. I used to be nice,

Dominic. Too nice. But I'm not quite so nice any more. I'm not nasty,' I added quickly. 'Though you may now think I am. But I'm certainly not nice. Because being nice got me nowhere. And it's taken me thirty years to find that out.'

'Minty, you're saying all this because you're so angry,' he said. 'You're punishing me for what I did. And I knew this might happen, I was ready for it. You don't mean it, Minty. Let's face it.'

'No, let's face *this*,' I said, calmly. 'Let's face the fact that you're a wanker. And let's face the fact that I *do* mean every word. And if my comments have been a little negative, it's because I now know that you've been lying.'

'No, I haven't,' he said indignantly.

'Yes, you have. Just as you lie to people about your name and about where you went to school. I'm not suggesting that you were lying about the pensions thing, or the fact that you were in a terrible state about it all. But you've been lying about your motives for doing what you did. And now, at last, I've worked it out.' I put down my knife and fork. And I looked at him, still careful to maintain the pleasant expression I'd worn all evening.

'The reason why you wanted out was not because you didn't want to "put me through" the financial crisis you thought you were going to suffer. It was because you realised, no doubt with some regret, that I was no longer rich enough for you to marry in your newly impoverished state.'

'That's not true.'

'I think it *is* true. And you said that Virginia Park was irrelevant. But she isn't. Because she told me that she'd met you three weeks before our wedding. And I think – and again, do correct me if I'm wrong – that you decided, then, in your hysterical state, that you were going to ditch me, and marry her. Because even if you lost everything, with all Virginia's money, you'd be able to maintain your smart lifestyle. But you couldn't have done that with me. With me you would have had only a Standard Life. We wouldn't have gone shopping in Bond Street for quite a while.'

'You're wrong,' he said again.

'I think I'm right. You see, I didn't talk to Virginia for long. But it was long enough. And she told me that she knew you before. She also let slip that she'd been very keen. And then you met her again, in July, and there she was – still single. And you knew you'd only have to snap your fingers to have her come running back. But, crucially, you knew that with her you could be Park Lane. And it wouldn't matter if you couldn't bring home the bacon for a bit, because she had enough rashers of her own. I think it's very appropriate, Dominic, that you're telling me such pork pies.'

'I didn't want to marry Virginia,' he said. 'It was just a temporary insanity. A moment's madness. She'd have driven me round the bend.'

'No, the reason why you decided you didn't want to marry her after all is because you knew you were off the hook. The crisis was over. I've just remembered something she told me that you said. You told her that you'd made a stupid mistake, and that "everything had changed". And what had changed is that you were in the clear, so you didn't need her cash any more.'

'If it was money that motivated me, as you say, I'd have married her anyway. Then I'd have had a fantastic lifestyle, wouldn't I, with all her money, and mine?'

'That's true. But you obviously didn't *want* to marry her, and that's why you cancelled the engagement.'

'You're right,' he said, bitterly. 'I didn't want to marry her.'

'Why not?'

'Because she's a *pain,*' he said vehemently. 'I'd forgotten just what a pain she is. She's so bossy,' he went on.

'Unlike you, of course.'

'She was trying to tell me what to do.'

'Heaven forfend.'

'And correcting me.'

'Fancy that.'

'And laying down the law. Trying to set the agenda. But I warned her about this,' he said, his voice rising. 'I warned her

– but she wouldn't listen. She wanted to go to the Caribbean and she knew I couldn't fly, but she said to me, "Look, I don't give a stuff about your bloody phobia. We're going to Barbados." And I said, "No, we're not. Don't you realise that half the world's Jumbo jets are now twenty years old? Don't you realise that air crash deaths have now reached record levels?" And she said, "If you think I'm never going to Sandy Lane again, you've got another think coming, Dominic. No arguing. We're going. And you're flying." Can you imagine, Minty!' He ran a nervous finger round his collar. 'She's not like you, Minty,' he went on quietly. 'She's not sweet and nice, like you.'

'That's why you wanted me back. You remembered, once your crisis had passed, how sweet and nice I'd been. How compliant. How uncomplaining. What a dull little doormat I'd become.'

'Oh God, I wish this nightmare had never *happened*,' he whined. 'It was all a false alarm. I wish we could just put the clock back. We *can* put the clock back, Minty.'

'No, we can't. I'd never realised quite how shallow you were, Dominic, until today. Until today I had never really fathomed the bottomless depths, as it were, of your shallowness. And now I have.'

'Don't you understand? I was in a state, I wasn't thinking clearly.'

'On the contrary,' I replied, 'you were thinking with calculated clarity. It was just the timing of it all you got wrong. And to think, all this time I've been blaming myself, Dominic! But it wasn't my fault at all.'

'No,' he said. 'It was mine. Mine.' He raked his right hand through his hair. 'Oh God, I'm a silly arse.'

'Oh no, Dominic. You're not,' I said. 'That's unfair.' I leant forward, and whispered, 'You're much, *much* worse.' He didn't reply. 'It was all about money,' I went on quietly. 'That's what it was about. That's why I was totally humiliated in front of two hundred and eighty people. That's why I've spent most of the last nine months in a state of acute mental distress.

Because you thought you were going to lose your *money*.' He stared at the table cloth. And then I remembered something else he'd said in church.

'And that lie you told, that lie about being "deeply religious".'

'I *am* deeply religious,' he said. 'It's just that you've never bothered to find that out.'

'But it was a part of you I never *saw*, so how on earth was I to know? Do forgive me, Dominic, for misjudging you. And as you're so deeply religious, I'm sure you'll be able to tell me what day it is today.'

'What day? It's Thursday, of course. What do you mean "what day"?'

'Ah, but it's not just any old Thursday, Dom, it's Maundy Thursday today. Do you know what that commemorates? You're deeply religious, so you'll know.' He looked blank.

'Christ's last supper,' I informed him. 'That's what it commemorates. It's our last supper too, by the way. And do you know what traditionally happens on Maundy Thursday?'

'No,' he said testily. 'I don't.'

'The monarch distributes special, newly minted coins to the poor.'

'You're so knowledgeable,' he said sarcastically.

'Well, I confess we covered it in the programme today for one of our Easter reports so that does give me a head start. Newly minted coins,' I said, again, wonderingly, now. 'New-mint, Dominic, like me.'

'Well,' he said, 'this evening hasn't been much of a success.'

'On the contrary, Dominic. It's been wonderful. I'm *so* glad I saw you again. But now I'm going to go home.'

'Look, I made a terrible mistake,' he said, as he saw me stand up. 'What more do you want me to say?'

'What more? Nothing. I'm quite satisfied.'

'Minty, think of what a nice life we could have.'

'A nice life?'

'Yes. We could have a lovely house in Wandsworth.'

'No thanks.'

'We could be a powerful couple, Minty.' Powerful? *Ah*. He did a little scribble in the air for the bill.

'I don't want to be powerful,' I said as I picked up my bag. 'I just want to be happy. And I could *never* have been happy with someone as low as you. Thanks for supper, Dom,' I added with a smile. 'I'm *so* glad I saw you again. CU next Tuesday!' I exclaimed happily. Puzzlement furrowed his brow.

'See you next Tuesday?' he said. 'See you next Tuesday?'

'Think about it,' I said. Then I left.

April

'APRIL FOOL!' I said to myself this morning when I glanced at the calendar. 'I'm the biggest April Fool there is! And I'm a May fool too, and a June Fool, and I was especially foolish in July, when I very "Nearly Wed" that contemptible man.'

Well, I'm not going to be a fool any more, I determined as I stood under the shower. Because at last I'd got everything sussed. I'd worked it all out. I'd suffered in the process, but it was worth it. Because I was reborn. I was new-Mint. At last, at last, I could move on. I said I was going to come through this, and I had. I felt as new as an Easter chick. I'd pecked my way out of my hard little shell, and I was going to stand in the sun, and thrive. 'It was *all Dominic's fault,'* I said to myself wonderingly. It was *nothing* to do with me. I'd tortured myself for months, but I wasn't to blame in any way. In the end, the answer was simple – money. Cash. Lucre. Loot. Moolah. Profit and loss. It was as easy, and as brutal, as that. I was simply a casualty of his cupidity.

Thank *God* for Virginia Pork, I realised as I got dressed. Without her intervention I'd never have known just how low – how *shal*-low – Dominic was. Her unexpected phone call had been crucial. She had saved my psychological bacon. And so I smiled benignly at my fellow travellers as I rattled southwards on the Tube. Though there were fewer of them than usual because it was Good Friday. Indeed it was. A *very* Good Friday. It was a *fantastic* Friday because, at last – *at last* – I'd been set free. I glanced at my watch. Five to nine. I didn't have to be at work until ten. So I didn't go down to the Angel.

I got off at Embankment instead. And I walked along the Strand in the lemony sunshine with only a slight pang as I passed the Waldorf. But today it felt different. It wasn't a stab of regret for what might have been. It was simply a pang for all the pain and crap that Dominic had made me endure. I crossed the Aldwych then carried on down Fleet Street, past the Law Courts and the old *Express* building, past Prêt à Manger, and then I turned right, into St Bride's. I knew it wouldn't be easy, but it was something I had to do. It was an essential part of the process – the final act of letting go.

After hovering for a moment in the porch, I went inside. It was empty. Completely empty. And it felt as warm as breath. Today the flowers were yellow for Easter joy – a sunburst of daffodil buds and creamy tulips, and stiff stems of golden forsythia. I walked up the aisle once more, hearing my footsteps tap across the tiles, then I halted at the very same spot where I had stood with Dominic in July. And as I inhaled the honeyed scent of the beeswax, the echoing voices returned, like ghosts:

'– Wilt thou?' *Wilt thou?*

'– No.' *No. No.*

'– sickness and in health.' *Sickness.*

'– just *can't.*' *Just can't, just can't.*

'– Come on, Dom.' *Come on.*

'– bound to come unstuck.' *Unstuck.*

'– Sshh! Madame!' *Ssshhh*!

'– Don't slip!' *Don't slip, don't slip*!

And then I looked up at the ceiling and tried to imagine seeing sky instead, and the walls all blackened and charred, and every pew on fire. That's what happened to me, I thought. I was bombed too. I was reduced to rubble, left a gaping, broken shell. And I thought I'd never recover. But now I knew I would. I had been restored. I would be just as I was, yet different. A reconstruction of my former self, using fabric that wasn't there before. I thought I ought to say something, but I didn't quite know what. So I simply said, 'Thank you!' quite loudly, and then I decided to go. And as I made for the door

I passed a noticeboard marked 'Intercessions'. It was thickly plastered with little handwritten requests for prayers. 'Please pray that Julian and I will see each other again,' said one; 'Please pray for Alice, who is gravely ill,' implored a second; 'Please pray for my son, Tom, who is worried about his exams,' asked a third; and then I read, 'Please pray for my daughter, Minty, who is very unhappy.' It was in Dad's handwriting. He must have come back, after the wedding, because he wouldn't have had time on the day. And I took it down, because I didn't really need prayers so much any more. Then I wiped my eyes and walked to work.

'From the sublime to the ridiculous.' What an apt expression that is, I thought, as I stared at Wesley half an hour later. He did indeed look ridiculous. In fact, he looked bizarre. Not because he was dressed oddly or had shaved his head, but because he looked nine months pregnant. He . . . *ah*! I remembered what day it was and gave him a superior smile.

'You can't April Fool me,' I said. 'I know what you're up to.'

'It's not an April Fool, Minty,' he replied seriously as he rubbed his protruding stomach.

I stared at him. What else *could* it be? He looked as though he was about to give birth. In fact, he looked like that man in the silly poster ad which was supposed to encourage men to 'take responsibility'.

'Wesley, if it isn't an April Fool, then what *is* it?' I enquired.

'I'm empathising.'

'You're doing what?'

'I'm empathising. With Deirdre. So that I fully understand what she's experiencing.' He lifted his jumper to reveal what looked like a bulging green canvas bullet-proof vest tied with tape to his front.

'It's an empathy belly,' he explained. 'It's for men. So they can really appreciate what their pregnant partners are going through.'

'Oh.'

'They're American,' he explained. 'I bought it on the Internet. You can't get them over here.'

'Thank God you can't,' I said. 'It looks awful. I mean, what self-respecting British man would wear one?'

'Well . . . *I* would,' Wesley replied with a slightly wounded air. 'I think it's a good idea. You can add stuffing to it, as the baby develops. Deirdre and I are six months gone,' he explained. Then he stood up, and pressed his fingers into the small of his back.

'Ooh, me back's killing me,' he said.

'Wesley!'

'I'll be glad when it's all over.'

'Oh, come on!'

'I get these terrible cramps –'

'Spare us!'

'And I keep wanting to puke.'

'Please, Wesley!' I pleaded with a laugh. 'We had enough of that with Melinda.'

'You know she's coming back, don't you?' he said as he got out his Mothercare guide.

'WHAT?' The smile fell off my face and crashed to the floor.

'Melinda's coming back. Didn't you know?' I stared at him, aghast.

'No, I didn't.'

'It's OK, Minty. Don't worry – your job's safe. She's going to be working the graveyard shift.'

'The nutters phone-in?'

'Two a.m. until four. Jack had some gaps in the rota, and says she'll be all right for that because she won't have to write a script.'

'That's true.'

'All she has to do is stay awake and yak to all the crazies.'

'I'm surprised she accepted after the appalling row they had.'

'Well, apparently, she's desperate to come back and "bwoadcast", and Jack was equally desperate to find someone willing to do it. Talk of the devil –' Wesley added.

'Good morning,' said Jack cheerfully. He's *so* much happier these days. 'The office looks very tidy,' he said suspiciously. 'Did the cleaners slip up and remember to come? Wesley, I can't help wondering why you've got a pillow stuffed up your jumper.'

'It isn't a pillow. It's an empathy belly. For pregnant men.'

'I *see*,' said Jack. 'Good morning, Minty,' he added. 'You look happy. In fact, you look blooming.'

'Blooming?' I said, wonderingly. '*Do* I?'

'Yes,' he said, 'you do. Positively blooming.' He picked up Wesley's *Mother and Baby* book, then gave me a sideways smile. 'You're not in love, are you?'

'What? Oh no. I'm just happy,' I explained. 'That's all. I've had an epiphany.'

'I think Deirdre's going to be having one of those too,' said Wesley with a grimace. 'Apparently it's very painful.'

'Is it?' said Jack.

'No, not an episiotomy – an *epiphany*, a sudden flash.'

'Sure it's not your hormones?' Wesley enquired, as he got out his Miriam Stoppard.

'Yes, quite sure. It was a flash of *insight*.'

'You look like you're in love,' Jack tossed over his shoulder, as he went through to his office.

'Yes,' said Monica, suddenly. 'You do.'

'Oh, don't be so *ridiculous*, everyone,' I exclaimed, with a little laugh. Then I picked up the phone and dialled Joe.

I wanted to tell him, you see. I wanted to tell Joe about my breakthrough. I wanted to tell him that I'd consigned Dominic to the waste-disposal unit of my past. So we arranged to meet at the Screen on the Green in Islington at six the following evening.

'You look *repulsive*,' he said admiringly, as he planted a noisy kiss on my cheek.

'You look pretty cruddy yourself,' I replied happily. 'I mean that nicely, of course.'

'I know you do,' he said, as we went inside. I glanced at

him again. And it was as though, today, I could see him clearly, because Dom's dark shadow had been lifted away. I wanted to tell him about my meeting with Dominic, but decided to wait until after the film, a new print of John Schlesinger's classic version of *Far From the Madding Crowd.*

'Please don't rattle your popcorn too loudly,' Joe admonished me as the lights dimmed to darkness and the nylon drapes swished aside.

'I don't *have* any popcorn,' I said.

'And please don't talk to me during the film,' he went on as Julie Christie appeared on the screen. 'It's very annoying for everyone else.'

'Shhh!' said someone behind us.

'See what I mean?' I rolled my eyes.

'And don't grab me in the scary bits,' he whispered. 'I know what you're like.'

'There aren't any scary bits,' I whispered back.

'Well, just keep your hands off me, OK,' he said, as his right arm went round my shoulder. I laughed. And then I blushed. I felt inexplicably happy to find myself so close to Joe again. But soon I was lost on the hills of Wessex, caught up in Bathsheba's struggles to keep her farm going, and her obsession with Sergeant Troy. But *anyone* could see that Troy's a shallow cad, and that Bathsheba's a complete *idiot* to keep on rejecting the wonderful Gabriel Oak. Finally, though, Bathsheba gets it right. 'Whenever you look up,' said Alan Bates to Julie Christie at the end, 'there I shall be. And whenever I look up,' he went on simply, 'there will be you.' And he smiles at her. And Julie Christie smiles back. And then the camera pans out and the credits roll.

'That's what I call a happy ending,' I said as we left our seats. 'She saw the light at last.'

'But Hardy makes her suffer first,' said Joe. 'He was sadistic with his heroines – he liked to give them hell. Right,' he said, and he tucked my arm under his. And freed now from Dominic, I felt something inside me jump. 'Come with me,' said

Joe in a commanding fashion. And then, because he's so nice, he added, 'Please.'

As we walked down Upper Street and along Rosebery Avenue, I just felt so, *so* happy. I was moving forward at last. And now I could move forward too with Joe. Surely we could be more than friends. All I had to do was convince him that at last I was over Dom. And I was. Dominic didn't *matter* any more. I saw him as if in a dark, disturbing dream. Now I was waking up, and he was receding, like a spectre – ethereal, unreal. And here was Joe. All flesh and blood. His arm solid and strong beneath my own. And he was talking away about this film director and that one, which was fine, because he's so knowledgeable, and I'm very interested in the cinema myself. Then we found ourselves passing Sadlers Wells, and people were hurrying inside and, to my enormous surprise, I saw Dad. He was standing outside. He looked slightly agitated, which was strange as he's normally quite calm. I guessed that Mum must be running late from one of her charity do's.

'Dad!' I called. And then I remembered his note on the board at St Bride's and I was filled with filial affection. 'Daddy!' I yelled again. But he hadn't heard. He was just standing there, not waving, but frowning. And then, at last, he saw me – and the astonished expression on his face!

'Minty?' he said wonderingly.

'Hello! What are you going to see?'

'Oh. Erm . . . *Coppelia*,' he replied; slightly edgily, I thought. And was it my imagination, or did he blush?

'This is Joe,' I said. And Joe and Dad shook hands. Then we stood there for a few seconds and Dad suddenly said, 'Well, I mustn't keep you both,' as though he didn't want us to hang around. And I found this more than a little odd.

'Hope you enjoy the show,' I said. 'And I hope Mum turns up soon.' Dad smiled, a rather tense kind of smile, I thought, and as Joe and I went on our way I told him about Mum's obsession with good works. Then we crossed the road and turned left into Exmouth Market and stopped outside a place called Café Kick. Inside, it was simply done, and there were three pub football tables.

'I've always wanted to come here with you,' Joe said. 'But somehow, it just never seemed . . . right. Today it does.'

'Yes,' I agreed. 'It does. In fact, Joe, I want to tell you something. Something important.'

'OK. Fire away.' But he'd already put some money in one of the football tables, and seven cork balls clattered into the tray. I decided to tell him afterwards. First, I wanted to play.

'Now, remember,' said Joe, with an admonitory wag of his finger, 'no spinning.'

'Who do you think I am? Alastair Campbell?'

'And no bananas.'

'As if I would.'

'And every time I beat you, you buy me a drink. And every time you beat me, I buy you one, ditto.'

'Fair enough.'

The game started well. I was playing pretty aggressively, trying to break through Joe's defences.

'Great save!' I shouted. 'You've got very fast reactions. But not –' I added, as I lined up my centre forward behind the ball – 'quite fast enough. Thank you! One–nil!' He bought me a Peroni. And then he scored, and I bought him one.

'You're spinning – stop it!'

'Well, you're taking too long with your shots.'

'Are you accusing me of cheating?'

'Yes.'

'Right, you've had it. Goal! Two–one!!'

I bought him another beer. And then another. We were both pretty merry by now. I was laughing. In fact, I was almost high on happiness, though the beers undoubtedly helped. We were both being very flirtatious.

'I'm glad we're friends again, Minty,' said Joe.

'Are you?' I said with a smile.

'Yes. When we had our Brief Encounter in Paris,' he went on with a mischievous smile, 'you made me feel . . . Breathless.

I was *A Bout de Soufflé*, he added with a burst of inebriated laughter. Ah ha. I could play this game too.

'It was a Fatal Attraction, was it?' I enquired, with a giggle. I had another quick sip of beer.

'Well, in a way,' he said. 'But I didn't do anything about it because . . .' he paused and let the ball idle for a moment in the corner '. . . you were clearly *Un Coeur En Hiver*.'

'Yes,' I conceded. 'I was having a Crack Up because I didn't have A Wedding. Oh, great goal!'

'Right, that's another Peroni. You were a Psycho,' he said.

'I was *not*,' I retorted. 'I was simply one of these Women On the Edge of a Nervous Breakdown.'

'Because you'd been a Fool for Love. But then,' he went on, 'It Happened One Night. We had a rather Dangerous Liaison which left us both Dazed and Confused.'

'I did not exactly feel Dead Calm after that,' I said as my half back connected with the ball. 'So I stayed Home Alone.'

'You were Gone With the Wind,' said Joe. 'You wouldn't even take my calls.'

'Well, by then I was totally pissed off with men. So I decided to concentrate on My Brilliant Career.'

'But that caused me Misery.'

'I'm sorry. Ooh – good goal! That was a sly one, Joe.'

'But now it's OK and we can –'

'– get Back to the Future?' I suggested daringly as I threw in the last ball. The game was almost over. It was time to talk. It was time for me to tell Joe how much he meant to me. Truly, Madly, Deeply. That I wanted us to be more than Friends. That I didn't want him to go to LA. That I wanted him to stay in London, and make me laugh. Everything had changed.

'There's something I want to tell you,' I said, as we ordered a couple of plates of pasta. 'Something important.' He gave me a penetrating stare.

'You're not . . . with child, are you, Minty?' he enquired dramatically. I rolled my eyes.

'No,' I said. 'I'm not.'

'Because I'll stand by you if you are, Minty – I'm not one to evade my responsibilities. You know that.'

'Look –'

'And may I say what a *lovely* mother you'd make,' he added.

'I'm trying to be serious,' I interjected.

'OK,' he said, with a smile. 'Let's get serious.'

Yes, I thought. *Let's get serious.* What a good idea.

'It's about Dominic . . .'

'Oh God,' said Joe, 'not again. I was rather enjoying myself there.'

'I only wanted to tell you that I've got over him *completely*. It's over. Finito. Because I found something out. Something that's changed everything.'

'Really?' he looked intrigued now. We sat down at a small table at the back.

'I discovered that it wasn't my fault,' I announced.

'What wasn't?'

'What happened to me. With Dominic. It was all his fault.'

'What do you mean?'

And as we ate our pasta, I explained, slightly tipsily, about how Virginia Park had called me, and then how I'd met Dominic again, and the things he'd said, and what I'd gradually worked out for myself – that in the end, it had all been about cash.

'It was all about money,' I said indignantly. 'Mammon. He dumped me in a panic, because he thought he was about to lose all his loot. And then when the crisis unexpectedly blew over, he realised he'd made a mistake, and wanted me back.'

'But you're not . . .'

'Oh *no!*' I exclaimed. 'I'm not going back to Dominic. Of course not. But I'm so glad I saw him, just one more time, because if I hadn't, a) I'd never have been able to tell him how despicable he is, and b) I'd never have known the truth.'

'And now you do?'

'Yes. And the truth is that I don't have to blame myself any more. And that's just so wonderful, because it ate away at my confidence – the thought that I might have brought it on myself.'

'Why *did* you think that?'

'Because I thought the reason he'd done it was because I'd been so nice to him, so weak and compliant, that he'd lost all respect for me.'

'But, from what you say, and from what I saw of you on the Nice Factor course, you *had* been weak and compliant.'

'Yes, yes, yes, I know. I'm not denying that. But that's not why he dumped me. But *I* thought it was, and I'd been torturing myself for months. It was really eating away at me. Now I know that theory was *wrong*, and that it wasn't my fault at all.'

'It wasn't your fault?' he repeated. He was fiddling with the fork.

'No,' I said again. And I was smiling. 'It was all Dominic's fault. I understand that now. I hadn't realised quite how shallow Dominic was. And now I do.'

'I see.'

'It was all about *money*,' I repeated. 'It was as simple as that.' I shook my head, and then I said, 'I discovered I'm not to blame.'

'I see.'

'And that's just so, so liberating for me.'

'Well, it must be.'

'And now I feel I can move on. I can truly move forward at last. Don't you feel glad for me, Joe?' I grabbed his hand. But he didn't say anything. He was just looking at me in this slightly funny way.

'Why don't you say something?'

'Well, what should I say?'

'Oh, I don't know. Anything. Say you're happy. Say you agree.'

'Why should I say that? I don't.'

Oh. He'd obviously had too much to drink. Couldn't get his brain round it.

'OK,' I said. 'I'll explain it again, you see –'

'Oh no, I have all the information I need,' he said, with what seemed like a slightly chilly smile. 'But it's the conclusion you've drawn that I don't think is quite right.'

'Look, the conclusion I've drawn is that it's all Dominic's fault. Not mine. He was shallow. But I didn't know quite *how* shallow he was until I saw him on Thursday night.'

'You did know,' said Joe, pursing his lips.

'No I didn't.'

'I think you did.'

'No I *didn't*,' I repeated. And I was feeling slightly irritated by now. 'I thought Dominic was only superficially shallow –' We both laughed at that. 'I mean, I thought he was only shallow about appearances, about clothes, and cars and parties.'

'I see.'

'I thought he was only shallow about surface things. But now I know that he was shallow in a *grievous* way.'

'It sounds like it.'

'Then why don't you understand what I'm saying?'

'Oh, I do understand it. But I just don't agree with you that you didn't know how shallow Dominic was.'

'I didn't,' I insisted. 'How *could* I know? I didn't know about the pensions thing or the compensation plans. That was information I only received afterwards.'

'But you'd already seen how shallow he could be,' said Joe. 'You'd seen it over and over again. So why be surprised when he turned out to be *deeply* shallow, as it were.'

'Well, I was surprised.'

'But that's like being surprised if someone who's previously shown violent tendencies then goes on to commit a murder. The signs were there. It's in the mental make-up, the psychological background. You don't have to be a writer to know that, Minty. We all give ourselves away.'

Gosh, this was really quite annoying. I didn't realise how difficult it was going to be.

'Well, I don't agree, Joe,' I said with an exasperated sigh. 'The fact is that I was really taken aback when at last I saw what had been going on.'

'More fool you,' he replied, as he pushed pasta round his plate. And he gave me this funny, slightly weary look. 'I mean, on the course, there you were going on about how, from the very beginning, you'd thought Dominic was shallow. That he seemed overly concerned with "appearances". And how, from the very outset, he'd started, insidiously, to change you.'

'Oh, it wasn't insidious. It was direct. "Wear this. Don't wear that. Say this. Don't say that. We're doing this. We're not doing that." I don't call that insidious at all.'

'Then I'm even more shocked that you put up with it. It sounds awful. And none of us could believe that someone bright and independent like you would put up with such – crap. But you obviously did.'

'Yes,' I conceded, 'I did. And I regret it with all my heart. And I'm never, *never* accepting that kind of shitty inequality again.'

'Good.'

'Because I've moved on.'

'I'm not sure you have,' he said.

'Joe, sorry, but I think this is a bit unkind of you, to be so unsympathetic to me when I've been through such a lot.'

'I'm not being unsympathetic,' he said, pushing his plate away. 'Not at all. Far from it. I'm just a bit . . . disappointed, I suppose.'

'Disappointed? What do you *mean*, disappointed?'

'In you.'

'Oh! Well . . . thanks very much.' Blooming cheek!

'Because you keep blaming Dominic.'

'Yes, I *do* blame Dominic. Why *shouldn't* I blame Dominic? Dominic does *bad* things. It's all his fault!'

'That's where I disagree.'

'Well, I don't know *why* you disagree, because it's *true*.' I felt really cross now. In fact, I was on the verge of tears. Joe was spoiling a perfectly nice evening with his probing, irritating questions. 'It *is* true,' I said again. The table was beginning to blur. 'I was a victim,' I said. My throat ached with a suppressed sob. 'I went through something terrible. *Terrible*. And it was all Dominic's fault.'

'But it was your fault too.'

'It was *not* my fault,' I insisted, struggling now to keep my voice low. 'I was an entirely innocent party. He was scheming behind my back. Scheming to save his money, and to sell me down the river. And that's what he did. In front of two hundred and eighty people. At exactly a hundred quid a head. So I don't quite see how I'm to blame.'

'You were. In a way. For allowing to Dominic to treat you like that. Don't get me wrong,' he went on, 'what he did was inexcusable . . .'

'Well, hallelujah!'

'. . . but you were complicit in what he did, because you didn't tell him where to get off.'

'I didn't tell him where to get off?'

'No, you didn't.'

'I didn't?'

'No. Doesn't sound like it.'

'Well, no, no, you're right. OK, I didn't.'

'Why not?' I shifted slightly on my chair.

'Because it wasn't worth it.'

'Worth it? I see.'

'He had a very nasty temper,' I explained. 'He'd make such an awful, hysterical fuss if he didn't get his own way. It was horrible. I was afraid to confront him.'

'Why?' said Joe with a shrug.

'Because if I'd confronted him there'd have been a terrible scene and we'd have . . . split up – that's why!'

'And would that have been a bad thing?'

'Yes! I didn't want to split up with him.'

'Why not?'

'Because he was my boyfriend. He was The One. I wanted to marry him. So I was prepared to compromise.'

'Oh.'

'Well, everyone compromises – that's what relationships involve.'

'They don't seem to involve much compromise for Dominic,' said Joe contemptuously. 'No, my question is, why did you *want* to marry him?'

'Why? Why? What kind of question is that? I mean, why does anyone want to marry *anyone*?!'

'But from what you say, you didn't really like or admire him. And so that's what I don't understand. *Did* you like him, Minty?' He held me in his gaze. 'Well, did you?' I found myself staring at his eyes. His pupils were large and hazel, with radiating fibrils of gold and green. There was something hypnotic about them. I heaved a long, weary sigh. 'Did you?' I heard him say again.

'No,' I said quietly. 'I didn't really. And I like him even less now I know the truth.'

'But, Minty,' said Joe, leaning forward a little now, 'why were you prepared to marry someone you didn't *like*? I'm sure I asked you that before, and you just evaded the question.'

'Look, Joe, whether or not I liked him has got *nothing* to do with it. He wanted to marry me.'

'But – let me say it again – you didn't really *like* him, did you?'

'No,' I hissed. 'I *didn't*. I didn't like his behaviour. It made me cringe. I didn't like the way he called everyone by their Christian names and tried to sell policies at parties. I didn't like the fact that he would never do *anything* I wanted. I didn't like his supercilious criticisms of people who weren't "smart" or well dressed. I especially didn't like the way he controlled me and destroyed my confidence.'

'Anything else?'

'Yes. His conversation – or rather, lack of it. It was bloody boring. I'll tell you what else I didn't like – I didn't like his intolerance, his chronic selfishness, and his lack of sympathy for other people. In fact,' I said, 'there were lots of things about Dominic that made me feel absolutely *sick*!'

'How astounding, then, that you would contemplate marrying such a man. A man you seem not to have respected or liked.'

'But whether or not I liked him has got nothing to *do* with it!'

'You don't think so?' he said, rolling his eyes.

'No. Because marriage is different. When it comes to marriage, lots of people marry people they don't particularly like.'

'Do they?'

'Yes, because we don't necessarily marry our friends, do we?'

'Don't we? I'd like to.'

'But friends are friends. They're for friendship. And partners are partners.'

'I don't think Dominic wanted you to be his "partner" in any sense of the word *I* could understand,' said Joe. 'I think he just wanted you to be his decorative doormat.'

'Yes, he did. And that's what I almost became.'

'Right, Minty, let me ask you again: Why did you want to marry Dominic?'

'Oh, I don't *know*,' I heaved an exasperated sigh. 'OK. Yes, I do know,' I conceded, fiddling with the salt pot. 'I wanted to marry him because he wanted to marry me. Yes, I admit it. I was flattered. He chose me. And I was flattered by that. There I was, nearly thirty, and I wanted to get married. Then Dominic came along, and he chose me. And I thought he'd do.'

'You thought he'd do?'

'Yes.'

'Despite the fact that your opinion of him was so low?'

'Well, it wasn't low in every way. I mean, he was very successful.'

'Ah ha.'

'And he was attractive. And he wanted me. Dominic chose me.'

'And that's all there is to it?'

'Yes. Well, it was for me.'

'And he chose you and then tried to turn you into something you're not.'

'Yes, he bloody well did – bastard.'

'And I ask you again, why did you go along with that? Why did you try to become something you knew you weren't? Why did you let that happen, Minty? You weren't a baby, and everyone has a choice.'

'Why did I let it happen? Because I understood his insecurity. I knew where it was coming from, so that made me take a more flexible view.'

'Lucky Dominic.'

'Because to understand is to forgive.'

'Is it? I don't know about that. I mean, you now understand why Dominic dumped you . . . ?'

'Yes. Yes, I do.'

'But do you forgive it?' I looked at him. 'Do you?' he asked again.

'No,' I croaked. 'I don't.'

'So why did you make all these allowances for him?'

Why did I? Why? Why? Why? Why? *Why*?

'All right! Because I knew that if I stood up for myself he'd leave me, because that's what he'd always done before. If his girlfriends made any criticism of him, or pointed anything out to him that they didn't like, he'd dump them. Just like that. On the spot. He told me that, himself. Quite early on.'

'Oh, I see. As a kind of warning.'

'I don't know. All I know is that I didn't want to be dumped. I don't enjoy being dumped. No one does.'

'So a fear of rejection kept you, perversely, with a man you didn't really like?'

'Yes. Yes, that's what it was: fear of rejection. I couldn't bear the thought of being ditched by Dominic. Apart from anything else, I don't like change, and I'd got *used* to him.'

'That's not good enough, Minty.'

'And because, actually, all right, yes . . . there *were* some things I liked.'

'Like what? Not his conversation – or lack of it. Not his behaviour. Not his vicious temper. Not lots of things, from what you say.'

'He was very ambitious, like me.'

'OK.'

'And he was very ambitious *for* me.'

'Are you sure it was for you, Minty?' said Joe. He had a funny little half-smile on his face.

'What do you mean? Of course it was for me. He really wanted me to shine.'

'Did he?'

'He said that I was a "class act".'

'Well, you are – this evening.'

'And he said, he said . . .' Oh God, I remembered what he'd said. I exhaled painfully. 'He said . . . it "looked good" for him to be with me.'

'Oh really, Minty? How flattering for you.'

'OK, he probably *was* a bit shallow about that, but the point is that there *were* things about Dominic that were right. Dominic was suitable for me.'

'*Ah.*' Joe leaned back in his chair.

'We looked . . . good together. People often said that.'

'Mmm.'

'And we had a nice time,' I said as I pushed the pepper mill round the table.

'*Did* you?' I asked Joe. 'I mean, *did* you have a nice time?'

'In some ways. And I would never have had to worry again.'

'You mean, financially.'

'He was attractive, eligible and well dressed.'

'But you weren't even remotely *compatible*, from what you said about Dominic on the course.'

'Compatible? Well, no. I mean, not in every way. But in some ways we were.'

'Like what?'

'Look, Joe, we filled in a compatibility questionnaire. And we *passed*!'

'I detect an element of surprise there, Minty. Did you fill it in truthfully?'

I stared at him, shocked to my core. 'Are you accusing me of lying?'

'Er . . . yes,' he said, carefully. 'I am. To yourself at least.'

'Charming!'

'The game's up, Minty.'

'Don't speak to me like that!'

'You've been rumbled.'

'Rumbled?'

'Well, either you were a complete *moron* to put up with such a load of shite from Dominic, or you were shallow. Which was it?'

'I am NOT a MORON!' I hissed. 'Don't you call me that!'

'No,' he said, 'I don't think you *are* a moron. That's *exactly* my point.' We stared at each other over the table. It was like *High Noon*, but I blinked first.

'I'm not shallow,' I whimpered hoarsely. 'I'm not shallow now, and I wasn't shallow then. I was simply mistaken. OK? I mistook Dominic for a safe bet when he was in fact a very risky proposition. But I suppressed the bad things and allowed my view of him to become distorted.'

'Yes, because you were shallow, Minty. In your own way, you were shallow too.'

'I wasn't shallow.'

'Yes, you were. And that's why you put up with him. Because he had money and a bit of polish, and he looked good in his nice suits. But that's all he had to offer. And then – surprise surprise – he ditched you, and you got hurt.'

'Yes, yes, I did,' I said. 'I was terribly badly hurt. And I don't think it's very nice of you to make me feel awful about all this on the one day when I was starting to understand it and come through it and move on.'

'You still don't understand it,' he said, running his left hand through his hair. 'You *still* don't understand that you were partly to blame.'

'I am *not* to blame,' I said vehemently, as Joe picked up the bill.

'OK, Minty, whatever you say.'

'Just who do you think you *are*, Joe?' I hissed. 'Some *deus ex machina*? The fucking Spanish *Inquisition*?' He didn't answer. He just looked at me, which annoyed me even more.

'You've been preaching at me all evening,' I said.

'No I haven't. I've simply asked you a few questions. I've tried to get you to admit the truth.'

'The truth?' I said. 'Well, the truth's none of your bloody business. How *dare* you!' I suddenly exclaimed, glad that the bar was almost empty. 'How *dare* you question me like that and try and *catch me out*!!'

'I didn't try and catch you out,' he said wearily. 'You caught yourself out.'

That was it. He had lobbed a flaming brand into the huge munitions dump of my resentment.

'I am FED UP with this!' I exclaimed. 'You have been VILE to me, ALL EVENING! All EVENING you've been GOING ON AT ME. On and on and ON! Trying to make me feel BAD about myself. Well, I had that from Dominic – I had that from Dominic nearly ALL the FUCKING TIME and I'm not BLOODY well taking it from a BASTARD like YOU who's supposed to be NICE!!! I've HAD IT! I've HAD IT with your horrible, personal and FUCKING IMPERTINENT comments about me when you don't even KNOW ME VERY WELL!! I mean, I haven't sat here and taken YOU apart. I haven't accused YOU of being SHALLOW and UNTRUTHFUL and a PILL.' I had exhausted my arsenal of expletives, so I stood up, blinded now by tears. 'I thought this was going to be a really *nice* evening!' I said. 'But you've RUINED it. You've RUINED a perfectly NICE, HAPPY evening. And I *was* HAPPY!' I was shouting now, tears coursing down my face. 'But now, thanks to YOU, I'm *UN*HAPPY. And I'm NOT going to stay here and be INSULTED.'

'I thought you liked insults,' he said quietly.

'Not REAL ones! Not like this!'

'I bet you never spoke to Dominic like this.'

'No, I DIDN'T, and I damn well wish I HAD!!'

'I wish you had too,' he said. 'Then you wouldn't need to shout at me.'

'The reason I'm *shouting*,' I whispered, aware now that the barman was staring at us, aghast, 'is because you have driven me to it. It's all your *fault*.'

'Yes,' he said, 'just like it was all Dominic's fault.'

'Yes!' I said. 'EXACTLY!' I stooped to pick up my bag. 'Today I was happy!' I spat as I prepared to leave. 'I was HAPPY for the first time in MONTHS. And I was happy to be seeing YOU! But now I'm NOT HAPPY AT ALL!' I shouted as I made for the door. 'In fact I'm very *UN*HAPPY! So I really hope you're happy, Joe – BECAUSE IT'S ALL YOUR FAULT! AND IF I NEVER, EVER SEE YOU AGAIN, IT'LL BE TOO BLOODY SOON!!'

'He's a BASTARD!' I called out to Amber, as I stamped upstairs at eleven thirty. She was in bed, but I didn't care. The light was on. I opened the door. She was sitting up in bed, reading. She was stroking Perdita with her right hand, and holding *Vanity Fair* in her left. 'He's a *bastard*!' I said again.

'Yes, we all know that,' she said. 'You're well out of it. We've been saying that to you for months.'

'No, not Dominic. Joe. *Joe's* a bastard.' I was so angry I was shaking.

'Is he?' She looked a bit surprised. 'I thought you said he was nice. He seems nice, I must say.'

'Well, he's NOT nice. He's nasty. I got it horribly wrong. I made another big mistake.'

'What's he done?'

'Well, we were having a perfectly nice evening – *perfectly* nice. It was going very well. *Very*. In fact, I was even thinking that at last I'd be able to get it together with Joe.'

'That's a good idea.'

'No, it isn't a good idea, because Joe was horrible. Very.'

'How?'

'Well, I told him about meeting up with Dominic again, and how what happened to me wasn't my fault. And Joe accused me of being shallow! *Shallow*! Unbelievable! He said I'd brought unhappiness on myself.'

'*Did* he?'

'Yes. He said I only wanted to marry Dominic because he

was loaded, well dressed and presentable. Bloody, bloody *cheek* of the man.'

'But it's true, isn't it, Minty?' said Amber benignly.

'No, it's NOT true,' I said, shocked. 'I wanted to marry him because I thought he loved me, and he had chosen me, which was very flattering because I hadn't been out with anyone for ages.'

'But Dominic wasn't very nice to you, Minty. We all saw that.' She put down her book. 'And we assumed that you put up with his ghastly behaviour because he was attractive and had a good job.'

'That's not true,' I said. 'I put up with him because I'm so bloody *nice*.'

'Oh, no one's *that* nice, Minty,' she said, turning the page of her book.

'Well, I am. Or rather, I was. But I'm NOT nice any more.'

'So I see.'

I sat on the edge of her bed, and heaved an enormous sigh. 'You know, I was just very, *very* unlucky to meet Dom.'

'There's no such thing as bad luck, Minty. There are only bad choices. And I always assumed you had your reasons for choosing Dominic. Because, let's face it, he was a bit of a shit.'

'That's not true. He could be nice. Sometimes.'

'Like when?' she enquired, as Perdita stretched out her front paws, like two black elastic bands, then rolled blissfully on to her back.

'Well, he was very generous. He was always buying me things. You know that. Nice clothes and that bag, and . . . well, he bought me lots of things.'

'He didn't buy them for *you*, Minty. He bought them for *himself*. So that you'd look "right". Didn't you realise that?' she said, as she scratched Perdita's tummy. 'You're not stupid. I'm sure you did.'

'And we had lovely weekends away.'

'But not anywhere that *you* wanted to go.' I sighed. 'All

those golfing and fishing holidays, Minty – that must have been fun for you.'

'And he was very good to his mother.'

'So was Reggie Kray.'

'Look, I don't want to talk about Dominic, because Dominic's out of my life. But I object to Joe telling lies about me, libelling me –'

'No, it was slander, Minty,' she corrected me. 'If he puts it in a book, then it's libel.'

'Oh, I know that. And we were having such a nice evening, playing table football. And then it wasn't a nice evening any more. It was a nasty evening, because we had this terrible row. He said some AWFUL things to me,' I went on furiously. 'But of course, I put him straight. In fact,' I went on proudly, 'I cornered the market in expletives.'

'Oh dear. Well, ring him up tomorrow and apologise.'

'Sorry?'

'You can apologise to him, in the morning, for being unfair. It sounds like you were unfair. And rude.'

'But he was unfair to *me*! He was *terrible*. He misrepresented me completely. He got it totally and utterly wrong.'

'Ring him up tomorrow.'

'Absolutely not.'

'Well, ring him the day after, then. But make sure you apologise. Because, to be perfectly frank, Minty, I think he was right. Night night.'

And then she put out the light. Just like that! She left me in the dark. I was livid. So I tried to think of something nasty to say. But I couldn't think of anything sufficiently horrible straight away. And then, as I opened the door, something vicious came to me. Something really hurtful.

'Your cat's overweight!' I spat.

T.S. Eliot was right. April really *is* the cruellest month. Because if you're feeling down, as I now am, then the sight of all those *ridiculously* cheerful-looking daffodils, shaking their gaudy trumpets all over the place like trollops, is enough to make you puke. I mean, it can *really* get you down. That goes for the tulips too, and that sickly, sugary fuzz on the cherry trees which will soon be a blaze of pink.

The joys of spring are completely lost on me. Because I have too many worries: a) My father's behaving in a *very* odd way; and b) I've fallen out with Joe, who I thought I really liked but obviously I don't like now *at all*; and c) it's no speakies with Amber because of 1) her impertinent intervention on Saturday and 2) my spiteful comments about the cat, which I made (i) because I wanted to be nasty and (ii) because it's true. That cat *is* fat. But Amber's livid about it. I really got her where it hurts. So she's treating me to one of her supersulks. She just sits in her room – I mean, *my* room, and that's *another* thing – and I don't know what she's doing. It's been like this for *days*. Maybe she's planning her next novel, God help us, or surfing the Net. But she certainly isn't talking to me.

And so it's all been rather awkward. The stony silence was becoming a strain. But then at last, this morning, the ice suddenly cracked. 'I'm sorry, Minty,' she said, with uncharacteristic but slightly frosty humility as she came downstairs. 'I think I owe you an apology.'

'I say!' squawked Pedro. And I was pretty surprised myself.

'It's OK,' I said, as I gave Pedro a piece of apple. 'You couldn't have known that Joe was a creep.'

'I'm not talking about *Joe*,' she said. 'Anyway, Joe isn't a creep. As far as I can tell. No, I'm referring to Perdita. She *does* indeed have a bit of, well, *embonpoint*.'

'You mean, she's fat.'

'Don't get technical with me, Minty.'

'Well, let's face it, she is.'

Perdita was sitting outside, on the window ledge, in the sun, wearing an expression of benign inscrutability on her glossy little black face. She jumped down, and came into the kitchen, tail at ninety degrees, purring like a fire engine and miaowing for more food.

'Wider still and wider,' I said, wonderingly. She seemed,

almost, to sway. Then she sat down abruptly, with a slight thump, as though it had all been a bit of an effort.

'Yes, too many pilchards,' Amber pronounced. 'That's the problem. She loves them, but I'll *have* to cut down.'

'Perhaps it's premature middle-age spread?' I suggested. 'You did say she's advanced for her age.'

'But it's funny that she's not fat all over, isn't it?' Amber said, looking at me. 'It just seems to be her lower tummy. Oh God . . .'

'What?'

'What if it's a *tumour*?' Amber looked stricken. Tears had sprung to her eyes. 'What if she's got cancer, Minty?'

'Don't be silly. She's not in pain, is she?'

In fact, Perdita had never seemed happier. She lay down, rolled over, and the bump seemed to shift slightly to one side. That was funny. And you could see her nipples, quite clearly, like two rows of tiny pink buttons. And she had this sort of guilty and slightly self-conscious expression on her face. Suddenly a light bulb appeared over my head, and the penny dropped, with a sharp, bright, clink.

'She's up the duff,' I announced.

'Oh, don't be so *ridiculous*!' said Amber. 'She's only a *child*.'

'No, I think she's pregnant,' I repeated. 'And she isn't a child – she's a teenager. From what age do cats get pregnant?'

'I don't know,' said Amber. She disappeared, then came back with the *Complete Cat Book* and started frantically flicking through the pages. 'It says here that it's . . . six months.' She lowered the book. 'Perdita's seven months old, at least.'

'Well, that's it. She's not fat, she's in the family way. Laurie said we'd have to think about having her spayed, and we didn't. We forgot.'

'That's your fault, Minty,' Amber said crossly.

'Since when has your cat been my responsibility?'

'Well, I've had a lot on my mind.'

'And I *haven't*, I suppose.'

'You should have reminded me.'

'I see.'

'OK, OK – joint responsibility.'

'That's big of you,' I replied.

'What shall we do?'

'Wait.'

'How long?'

I consulted the cat book. 'It says here that the gestation period is sixty-five days.' I checked the calendar.

'Yes, but, Minty . . .'

'What?'

'We don't know how long she's been pregnant, do we?'

'Well, let's get Laurie round. He'll know.'

'Yes, let's. You phone him.'

'No, *you* phone him. *You're* the one he likes.'

'Yes, but I don't like him.'

'Why not?'

'Oh, I don't know,' she said petulantly. 'I mean, why does anybody not like anybody? Anyway, give him a ring, Minty. And then I think you should ring Joe.'

'Why should I ring Joe? He said vile things to me.'

'But he only said those things because he's very fond of you.'

'Did he?' I sighed.

'Yes. Obviously – otherwise he wouldn't have bothered.'

'Wouldn't he?'

'Of course not. It's obvious: he cared enough to mind. And he was right, wasn't he, Minty?'

I sat down on a chair by Pedro's cage. 'Yes,' I said quietly. And now the floor had begun to blur. 'He was right,' I croaked. I looked at Amber. 'I *was* shallow. It's true. I didn't like or admire Dominic. In fact, I despised him in many ways. But I gave him break after break after break, because he was so . . . eligible. But the irony is, he wasn't really eligible at all.' This confession left me with the taste of ashes in my mouth. I felt a deep sense of shame.

'Never mind, Minty,' said Amber, putting her arm round me. 'We all make bad mistakes. But at least it's not too late,' she went on cheerfully. 'All you have to do is ring Joe up.'

'OK,' I said, sniffing. 'I will. But you've got to ring Laurie first.'

'Oh, I don't want to ring Laurie,' she said petulantly. 'He's so annoying. He drives me mad.'

'Well,' I said matter-of-factly, 'I'll only ring Joe if you ring Laurie. How about that?'

'Oh, well . . . OK,' she said carefully. And she went to the phone. But do you know what she did first? Before she rang him? She *brushed her hair*! I mean, really! She's so self-deluding, it's unbel*iev*able. She simply will not acknowledge that she likes Laurie. It's a complete joke. And I don't know why she's always so funny about him. He's clever, and witty and nice. And he's as sharp as a knife. I know she does like him, but she just won't acknowledge it, and it really makes me want to laugh out loud.

'Perdita is great with kitten,' I heard her announce. 'Yes . . . at least we think so. Would you come round? If you're not escorting some floozie to a function, that is . . . Why don't we bring her in to surgery? In *her* delicate condition? You must be joking! It would be utterly irresponsible – she could have a miscarriage. We'll pay you, of course,' she added. 'No, not in kind. In cash. A call-out fee . . . Yes, OK. At eight. Do you like red or white?'

'He says he'll come,' she announced. 'He really is *so* irritating,' she exclaimed, yet again. 'Now, what should I cook? We could start with smoked salmon. And then we could have duck, or perhaps my wild mushroom risotto? . . . I could go out and get some *porcini*. And I've got a fabulous recipe for a *tarte au chocolat* . . . and I've a good bottle of Pouilly Fuissé.'

While she got out all her cookbooks and began poring over them, I phoned Joe's flat. I really wanted to make it up with him, not least because we'd quarrelled over Dominic! It's the bloody Dominic Effect again, I realised bitterly. And that thought alone made me want to put things right. So I dialled Joe's number. But it didn't pick up. It just rang, and rang and rang. So I tried his mobile phone. It rang four or five times, and then, suddenly, I heard Joe's voice.

'Hello?'

'Joe, it's Minty.'

'Hello?' he said. 'Who's this?'

'It's *Minty,*' I said, a bit louder.

'Sorry, can't hear a thing,' he said. Which was extremely annoying. Because I could hear *him* quite well. 'Try again,' I heard him say.

'JOE!' I shouted. 'CAN YOU HEAR ME?'

'Sorry, I'm just not hearing anything.'

'JOE, IT'S MINTY!!'

'Damn thing . . .' he said. And then I heard, '*Bong. Last call for British Airways flight BA196 to Los Angeles. Would all remaining passengers make their way to Gate 27 . . .*' Oh God. Oh dear.

'JOE, I'M REALLY SORRY ABOUT . . .'

'Christ!' I heard him say. And then he said, 'Sorry, I don't know who you are, but I've got to go.' Then the line went dead.

That was it. He'd gone. I'd missed him. I put the phone down, with an empty, hollow feeling, as though someone had scooped out my insides with a spoon.

'Did you get him?' Amber enquired.

'Yes, I did,' I replied. 'I mean, no. No, I didn't,' I said bleakly.

Amber looked a bit confused. And then she said, 'Do you think Laurie likes Jerusalem artichokes?'

'Woof woof!' went Pedro, so I opened the door, and then gasped. I couldn't help it. Laurie had a shining black bruise the size of a large matchbox just above his right eye.

'Don't be alarmed by this,' he said reassuringly. 'It feels much worse than it looks. Hello, Amber.'

'My God!' she exclaimed. 'What happened to you?'

'I took part in an experiment,' he said wryly as he took off his coat.

'How?'

'I was escorting this Lebanese girl to a party and I didn't realise that she'd hired me for the sole purpose of making her ex-boyfriend jealous. It worked,' he added. 'You'll be pleased to know that the wedding's in June.'

'Do you want anything for it?' said Amber. She looked rather distraught.

'Oh no,' he replied. 'It's fine. A hazard of the trade. No worse than being bitten by a dog in the surgery. On which subject . . . where's the patient?'

We went into the kitchen, where Perdita was lying on her side under the table, rigorously cleaning her fur. She looked up, blinked at us amiably, and lifted her front paw as if in greeting. Then she resumed her grooming, her tiny pink tongue rasping rhythmically across her coat.

'Your cat has a bun in the oven,' Laurie pronounced expertly. 'Well, more than one, actually.'

'How many will she have?' I enquired.

'I don't know – three or four. Maybe five.' He bent down, and Perdita let him gently palpate her swollen tummy. 'I'd say she's about five weeks pregnant.'

'My God!' said Amber. 'But she's only a kitten herself.'

'They start to call from about this age, sometimes younger,' he said. 'I don't like to say "I told you so", but I did mention spaying three months ago.'

'A gym-slip mother,' said Amber. 'That's what she's going to be. Mind you, it was probably date-rape. I mean, she's not *that* sort of cat.'

'They're *all* that sort,' said Laurie. 'Cats don't have much in the way of morals. "Queen" actually comes from the old word "quean", with an "a", meaning hussy.'

'Oh,' said Amber, clearly disappointed. Then she picked Perdita up. 'Tell me who it was,' she said to her. 'Mummy won't be cross. Just tell me. Oh God, I hope it wasn't that ginger tom,' she went on with an appalled expression. 'We don't want them to have red hair!'

'I've seen quite a handsome tabby hanging about. Perhaps it was him,' I suggested optimistically. 'And there's a very good-looking tortoiseshell at number 31.'

Whoever it was, Perdita wasn't saying. She was keeping mum.

'And what do we do, when she's due?' Amber enquired. 'I mean, we're just not prepared for this.'

'Well, I suggest you book her into the Lindo Wing and ask for Mr Pinker,' said Laurie.

'Please don't be facetious,' said Amber. 'We don't know how kittens are born.'

'Right,' said Laurie. 'What happens is that you need a girl cat and a boy cat and a boy cat's got . . .'

'For God's sake!' said Amber. 'We know about the birds and the bees – just tell us what we have to do.' *We*?

'There's nothing you *can* do,' said Laurie. 'They just slope off somewhere, and give birth. They like warm, dark places – cupboards, for example, or under the stairs. Or perhaps under your bed. Or even *in* your bed. I'm afraid they make a horrible mess.'

'Oh dear,' I said, thinking of the carpets.

'Gestation is sixty-five days,' he said, appraising her again, 'so I reckon she'll have them in mid May. We can help you find homes for them, if you like,' he said.

'Did you hear that, Perdita?' said Amber. 'You'll have to give them up for adoption. To avoid disgrace.'

'Anyway, that's my diagnosis,' said Laurie.

'Right, well, I'd like to pay you.'

'Oh no, it's OK,' he said. 'I'll let you pay me when I've qualified.'

'Well, stay for supper then.' And he did.

By now Amber was quite thrilled about Perdita's delicate condition. She was gassing away to Laurie, as she dished up the *foie gras*, followed by sea-bass with puy lentils and delicately steamed sorrel.

'This is good,' said Laurie appreciatively.

'Oh, Minty and I eat like this every day, don't we, Minty?' said Amber. I felt her toe make forceful contact with my shin.

'Oh. Yes,' I lied. 'This is . . . *nothing*.'

Amber was really enjoying herself. She can say what she

likes, but you can tell when someone likes someone, can't you? You can tell because they smile a lot. And their eyes are open quite wide. Amber's certainly were. And she was laughing like a drain at Laurie's jokes. Happiness seemed to just bounce off her like sunlight off a lake. She reminded me of how I felt when I was with Joe. I felt like that too: smiling a lot, giggling a lot. Expanding, not shrinking. Dominic made me cry. But Joe made me laugh. Dominic filled me with dismay. But Joe made me feel confident. Dominic wanted me to keep quiet. Joe wanted me to talk. And I thought of him 30,000 feet up in the air, on his way to LA. And I thought of how much I'd liked him, and how admirable he was, and how we'd had this really nice rapport, a rapport I'd never had with Dom.

'Coffee?' said Amber, reaching for the jar. 'I'm sorry, it's only instant, but it says it's "rich and smooth".'

Rich and smooth, I thought. Like Dominic. Leaving bitter dregs. And as Amber gabbled away to Laurie, I sat with Perdita on my lap, and thought of Joe. I'd taken two weeks to call him, and now he was on his way to the States. And now I was very sorry that I'd told him that I didn't want to see him again because my wish was coming true. Regret seeped into my soul like damp. You've blown it, Minty, I said to myself. You've really buggered things up. And then my face felt hot, my eyes filled, and there were tears on Perdita's fur.

'Minty!' Amber exclaimed. 'What's the matter?'

'Nothing's the matter!' I wept. 'I'm absolutely *fine*.'

'You're not fine,' said Laurie. 'What's happened?'

'Nothing's happened,' I sobbed. 'And I'm definitely not crying because Joe's gone to LA and I made a mistake and now I'm going to pay for it just like I paid for my mistake with Dom, that's not the reason at all.'

'Ah,' said Amber. She handed me a Kleenex. 'You see, Laurie,' she said, 'Minty's liked Joe for ages; but she didn't realise it because she was still obsessing about Dominic, who'd treated her very badly and then dumped her on her wedding day. So she went on honeymoon with her bridesmaid, Helen, who has since married my ex-boyfriend Charlie, who was, coincidentally, best man, though not the best man for me. Anyway, in Paris, Minty met Joe. And she liked Joe – who's creative and nice and interesting but not rich and flash like Dom – but Minty didn't know how *much* she liked Joe until she understood the awful truth about Dominic, who was despicable in lots of ways that I don't have time to go into now except to say that Minty had a chance with Joe, which she believes she's blown, because he told her the ugly truth and she really lost it. So today she phoned him, only to discover he's on his way to LA, so Minty feels she's missed the bus with Joe – and she probably has.'

'Thanks very much!' I wailed. 'I feel a whole lot better now!'

'Well, just ring him tomorrow,' said Laurie.

'How?'

'On his mobile.'

'But if he couldn't hear me from Heathrow, I don't see how he'll be able to hear me from Los Angeles!'

'His battery was probably low,' said Amber. 'Give him a chance to recharge it and then try him again.'

'Let him recharge his own batteries too,' said Laurie. 'It's a twelve-hour trip.'

'And there's an eight-hour time difference,' Amber added, 'so don't call him too early in the day.'

So at about five the following afternoon I rang Joe's mobile number. And it rang once, and then clicked straight into answering mode. I left a message, asking him to call. But he didn't call. He didn't call back that day, or the next, or the one after that. So I phoned the mobile phone company to ask whether or not Joe's phone would actually work in the States, and they said, yes, it would. So I left a couple more messages for him, but I didn't want to leave too many because I didn't want to sound desperate. Only I *was* feeling pretty desperate, so I called again, and not only did Joe still not answer it, the phone didn't actually ring at all. It had gone dead. And I really didn't understand this. And I couldn't even e-mail him from Amber's computer because I didn't have his address. So I phoned his publishing house and asked to speak to Joe's editor, Francis Jones. But Francis was at a book fair and didn't return my call for three days. And when eventually he did, he wasn't much help.

'I'm sorry, but I haven't heard from Joe yet,' he said, 'so I don't have a contact address. He said he was going to stay in a hotel to begin with and then get himself an apartment.'

'An apartment?'

'Yes. He's going to be there for a few months.'

'A few months!'

'That's what he said. He's got a lot to do.'

'Go round to his flat,' said Amber, later. 'Maybe his neighbours are forwarding his mail.' And so I walked down to Albert Street. Joe's wisteria was now in full bloom, with pendant purple flowers like bunches of grapes. I inhaled the scent as I descended the basement steps, and knocked on Joe's door. But there was no reply. And the two other flats seemed deserted as well.

'Where do his parents live?' said Amber when I got back. 'You could get their number from Directory Enquiries.'

'They live in Manchester,' I replied, aware that she was being extremely helpful and, well, rather nice.

'What's his father called?' she enquired.

'I don't know, and Bridges is quite a common name.'

'Why don't you ask the people on the Nice Factor course if they have a number for Joe?'

'I already have,' I replied. 'But the only numbers they have are the two I've already got.'

I rang Helen too, but she didn't know. So I drew nothing but blanks. Then I hit a busy patch at work and by now it was the third week of April. The daffodils had been superseded by tulips; the lilies of the valley were almost in bloom, and the magnolia trees had already shed their great waxy pink petals. Time was passing. Another season in full swing; there was even a whiff of summer in the air. And I thought maybe he'll ring, or write. But he didn't. Because a) he was obviously extremely busy and b) I'd told him I never wanted to see him again. He was six thousand miles away. And eight time zones. He obviously wasn't thinking of me, but I was thinking of him. I thought of him sitting in the Californian sunshine. I thought of him walking on the beach. I thought of him going to parties and film premières. I thought of him meeting new people. More significantly, I thought of him meeting new women. And I was filled with regret and dismay.

'Oh, bugger it!' I said to Amber as we sat in the Engineer on Friday evening with Laurie. 'Bugger and buggery bollocks.'

'Minty!' said Amber, 'I'm so flattered. You normally only swear at people you really like.'

'I'm pissed off,' I said as I distractedly mangled a beer mat. 'All my attempts to trace Joe have failed.'

'Interpol?' said Amber facetiously. 'MI5?'

'I've missed the bus,' I said dismally. 'I've missed the bloody bus.'

'You've missed the bus?' said Laurie. His beer glass stopped in mid air.

'Yes. I've missed it. I've buggered things up. I'm consumed with regret.'

'Well, why don't you . . . you know . . .' Laurie began.

'What?'

'Catch the bus.'

'Catch the bus? What do you mean? How can I? It's gone.'

'Go to LA,' he said.

'Go to LA? Are you *mad*?'

'No, I'm serious. I mean, you're not getting very far here.'

'How can I just get up and go to Los Angeles, Laurie? I'm working.'

'Oh, well then,' he said with a shrug, 'that settles it.'

'Yes, she's working,' said Amber. 'On the other hand, Minty,' she added judiciously, 'you must have masses of leave left.'

'I do,' I said. 'I've got four weeks.'

'Well, go to LA and find Joe,' said Laurie. 'It's not that big.

Everyone knows everyone and you're a journalist, Minty – I'm sure you could track him down.'

'How? What would I do? Just wander around asking people to point me in the direction of Joe Bridges? It's impossible.'

'Well then, don't go,' said Laurie. 'There's no need, because, at the end of the day, Joe can't be that important to you. Otherwise you would.'

'Joe *is* important to me. He's *very* important. But there are practical considerations to . . . consider.'

'If I'd worried too much about practical considerations I'd still be a frustrated surveyor,' said Laurie. 'Instead of which I'm about to become a vet. If I qualify. On which note, I really must get back to my revision. Canine Endocrinology. It's my pet hate – ha ha. Anyway, that's my diagnosis today.'

'Thanks,' I said miserably.

'Take a risk, Minty,' said Laurie, as he stood up to go. 'I mean it – life's too short.'

'Go to LA? How *ridiculous*!' I said to Amber as we walked back to the flat in the late evening sun.

'Well, why don't you?' she said. 'Just tell Sophie you want some time off.'

'I'd have to ask Jack,' I said.

'Do you *want* to go?' she asked.

Did I want to go? Good question.

'Yes,' I said carefully, '. . . if I thought I'd find him and if I thought I could put things right. But I'm not going to go,' I said, 'because, to be honest, I really can't afford it.'

'Can't you?'

'Well, no. It would cost a bomb, and I don't have much put by.'

'I'll pay,' said Amber, suddenly.

'What?' She opened the front door, and I stepped inside.

'I'll pay,' she repeated. 'I've lived here for ten months, and I haven't given you any rent. And you've never said a word about it. Let me pay, Mint. It's the least I can do.'

'*Would* you?' I said, wonderingly.

'Yes,' she beamed. 'But only on one condition.'

'What's that?'

'That I get to come along too!'

And so the decision was made. But I'd have to clear it with Jack, and as soon as possible, so I called him at home the next morning, but one of the girls picked up the phone.

'Oh, hello,' I said. 'This is Minty Malone. Er . . . is that . . . ?'

'Iolanthe.'

'Oh, Iolanthe, hi. I remember. The, er . . .'

'Party,' she said.

'Yes, that's right. The party.'

'Everything's fixed now,' she said.

'Oh good . . . And, er, how are you all?'

'Pregnant,' she said.

'What?'

'Pregnant,' she repeated. My *God*. But judging by the way those girls carried on in January it wasn't entirely surprising.

'Well . . .' I didn't know what to say '. . . that's pretty serious news.'

'It's OK, actually,' she said quietly.

'What do your folks think?'

'They don't mind. It was a bit of a shock, obviously. But they're cool.'

'Oh. Well . . . good,' I said. I didn't know what else to say.

'Anyway, do you want to speak to Jack?' she enquired.

'Yes. Yes I do. Please. Thanks.'

'Hang on, I'll just get him – he's mending my bike.'

'Jack, hi,' I said. And then I blurted out, 'Iolanthe's just told me the news.'

'Yes,' he said. 'It's a bit shattering.'

'What are you going to do?' I asked, though I know I shouldn't have done.

'Have it, of course.'

'God. But what about her . . . age.'

'Look, this kind of thing happens,' he said. 'She won't be the first, and I'm sure we'll cope somehow, though we'll need a bigger house. But I think we can deal with it all.'

'Good. Anyway, sorry, it's none of my damn business. Can I have some urgent leave?'

'What?'

'I need to take some leave.'

'When?'

'Next week.'

'That's very short notice, Minty.'

'I know. That's why I'm ringing you at home. I'm sorry to spring it on you, but I need to go to LA.'

'Is it vital?'

'Yes, I think it is.'

'Can I ask *why* you're going?'

'Well, it's sort of personal.' I didn't want to tell anyone. I wanted to keep it to myself. 'Please, can I go, Jack?'

'OK,' he said after a few seconds. 'But you'll have to be back by the seventh because we've got such a lot on in May.'

'I know.'

'So I'm afraid I can only spare you for five days.'

'Five days?' I sighed. It was so short.

'I'm sorry, but it's five days or nothing, Minty. Do you want to take it?'

Five days? Oh my God.

'Yes,' I said, 'I do.'

'You see, Mum, we'd need you to come in twice a day at least to look after the animals,' I said the following evening. 'It's only for a long weekend. Five days. That's all I can take.'

'Five days? Los Angeles is an awfully long way to go for five days, Minty,' she said.

'I know, but that's the maximum I can have, because of the short notice.'

'Minty, why are you going to Los Angeles for five days?'

'To meet someone.'

'Who?'

'A man.'

'But there must be lots of nice men you can meet in London.'

'No, this is one I've already met. He's called Joe. But he ran off.'

'Not *another* one,' said Mum.

'Well, he was due to go anyway, but because we'd had an argument and I was horrible to him, he didn't tell me a) when he was going and b) where he was staying. But he's terribly nice and Laurie –'

'Who's Laurie?'

'Oh, Laurie's a vet and part-time male escort who's keen on Amber.'

'Oh, darling, I can't keep up with all these changes in your life.'

'Yes but, Mum, you never ask, that's why. Anyway, Joe's gone to the States, quite possibly for months, and I just wanted to . . .' What? What did I want to do? '. . . I just wanted to try and put it right,' I said. And when I said that, a lump came to my throat, and I felt tears prick the back of my eyes. 'Oh, Mummy, he's the nicest man I've ever met.'

'Darling, you said that about Dominic to begin with.'

'Yes, yes, I know I did. But it was a lie. I was kidding myself. Mum, I'm so glad I didn't marry Dominic.'

'Well, so am I, darling. I always thought he was a rotter, and he'd have been the most *useless* spouse!'

'And Joe's just . . . lovely,' I said. 'He's *real*. And I've made such a mess of it with him. That's why I need to go to the States. So will you look after the animals? There's loads of cat food – Perdita's pregnant, by the way.'

'Oh, heavens!'

'But they're not due until mid May so you don't have to worry. And we'll put a litter-tray down for her and we'll leave out a comprehensive selection of CDs for Pedro.'

'Minty, if I'm going to do this, I'd rather stay in the flat, if you don't mind. It'll be much easier than all the to-ing and fro-ing,' she went on. 'And, to be frank, cat litter is *so* disgusting. I just don't think I could face it, so I'd rather be there to let her out.'

'Of course you can stay here, Mum. That's fine. If Dad doesn't mind.'

'I don't think he'll even notice,' Mum replied. 'We hardly ever see each other these days.'

'Well, whose fault's *that*?'

'But I have so many commitments, darling. Do you know we raised £14,000 for the Blue Cross last night.'

'That's great, Mum, but you have a commitment to Dad too.'

'These charities are depending on me, you know.'

'*Are* they, Mum?' I said, wearily.

'Yes,' she said. 'In any case your father seems so distracted these days.'

'Does he?'

'We rarely get to talk to one another.'

'Still, you went to the ballet together not long ago, didn't you?' I said. 'That must have been nice.'

There was an odd silence. It lasted for about three or four seconds. And then Mum said, 'Did you say ballet?'

'Yes, ballet. I saw Dad waiting for you outside Sadlers Wells.'

'Minty,' said Mum very slowly, 'I haven't been to Sadlers Wells for *years*.'

May

'This is outrageous!' said Amber to the woman at the Virgin Atlantic check-in two days later. 'I shall write to Richard Branson personally on my return.'

'I'm sorry, madam,' the woman replied, 'but I'm afraid we don't give complimentary upgrades to Upper Class on request.'

'But I guarantee to give Virgin Airlines a very prominent and favourable mention in my new novel,' Amber went on. The woman smiled as she fastened labels to our luggage, but said nothing. 'However,' Amber continued with an air of slight menace, 'if you don't oblige, I shall have no choice but to mention some other carrier instead. Pan Am, for example. It's up to you,' she added with a shrug.

'Thank you, madam. But I'm afraid Pan Am no longer exists. I do hope you have a good flight,' she added pleasantly. 'Here's your boarding card.'

'Now look here –'

'Please, Amber,' I said, dragging her away. 'Economy class is fine. It's an eleven-hour flight, so we can just watch a film. Or three. Or you could read a few books, or work on your new plot.'

'Yes,' said Amber, 'that's what I'll do. I'll work on my synopsis.' Which is partly why she wanted to come to LA with me – to do some research for her tenth novel.

'This one's going to be a new departure,' she said enthusiastically as we waited for our own departure in Duty Free. She sprayed a tester of First on to her wrist. 'It'll be unlike anything I've ever done before.'

'I thought all your books are unlike anything you'd ever done before?'

'No – this one's going to be really different: detective fiction.'

'Isn't that a little bit . . . commercial, Amber?' I ventured as we wandered through the dizzyingly long glass corridors towards Gate 2.

'Oh no, it's going to be *literary* detective fiction, Minty. It's going to be tough. Terse. Ironic. Realistic. Think Raymond Chandler. Think Dashiell Hammett. Think Philip K. Dick.'

'Quite hard-boiled, then.'

'Yes,' she said animatedly, 'hard-boiled, that's it.'

It'll probably be roasted too.

'It's going to be very *noir*ish,' she added, as we found our seats on the plane. 'It'll look at the seamy side of Los Angeles, the gritty underbelly of a city racked by riots and earthquakes, forest fires and droughts. It's going to be about life on the fault line. Life on the teetering edge.'

'Won't that be quite hard to research, in five days, from a luxury hotel in Beverly Hills?'

'No. We'll hire a car, Minty, and explore. Now, don't worry,' she added quickly. 'I don't mind driving.'

'Oh great!' I said. Oh God.

'Yes, we'll cruise around town like Philip Marlowe in *The Long Goodbye*.' More like James Dean in *Rebel Without a Cause*. 'And I'm sure we'll find Joe,' she added reassuringly. 'I'll practise my detective skills and help you sleuth him down.'

I didn't think Amber could sleuth down a missing skyscraper, but I didn't like to say. It was very nice of her to come with me to the States and to pay for the whole thing too. And when I'd said we could just stay somewhere fairly modest, she had emitted a derisive snort.

'We shall stay at the Four Seasons,' she announced.

'The *Four eaon$*,' I repeated incredulously.

'I don't mind,' she said. 'I've just had a good little run with the stock market. Some rather nice divi-cheques. Anyone who's anyone stays there,' she added. 'It'll be stuffed with film people, and they might help you find Joe.'

'We don't have any leads,' I said miserably as the stewardess brought us two trays of good plane food.

'What about his mobile phone?'

'I've tried to ring him on it, but it doesn't seem to work.'

'How odd.'

'Maybe it's not connected for the States.'

'Why would he bother to take it with him if it wasn't? Did you ask his editor where he is?'

'Yes – he doesn't know. This is going to be a wild-goose chase,' I added with a bitter sigh.

'Don't worry, Minty,' said Amber yet again. 'I just *know* we're going to find him. It's nice of Auntie Dympna to look after Perdita and Pedro,' she added happily as she sipped her wine.

Yes, it was. But I couldn't help wondering who was 'looking after' Dad. Some other woman, no doubt. Oh, *fuck*. Now I understood why he'd been behaving so shiftily outside Sadlers Wells.

'I'm really looking forward to this trip,' Amber declared. 'And you know, Minty, I've got a funny feeling that it's going to be money well spent.'

Hadn't I heard that somewhere before? I wondered, as I put on my eye mask and dropped off to sleep.

The setting sun glanced off the wing of our 747 as the plane banked steeply into LA. We staggered, exhausted, into the airport, grabbed our bags off the carousel and joined the long queue for Immigration. And we waited. And waited. And then we waited some more.

'My God!' said Amber after we'd been standing there for forty minutes. 'It took us eleven hours to get here and it's going to take us another eleven to get *in*.'

'Purpose of visit, ma'am?' enquired the uniformed woman customs officer, twenty-five minutes later.

'I'm looking for a man,' I replied crisply. Jet-lag and the interminable delay had made me sharp.

'Well, I hope you find one, ma'am,' she replied as she stamped my passport. 'Have a nice day, now.'

'Thank you, and I hope you have a pleasant and successful day yourself.'

Then we stepped into a yellow taxi, drove to the hotel in the gathering dusk, and slept. Because of the time difference, it was dawn when I woke. I stood on the balcony and watched the sun come up in a scarlet blaze of underlit cloud. Now I could see the city spread before me, in a shallow bowl, enclosed by a mountainous ridge. The tall feathery palms stood up like swizzle sticks in a glass of Martini, and the distant cars glittered in the rising sun as though they were waves in a shining sea. Out there, somewhere, was Joe. I didn't know where. I hadn't a clue. But he was there. 'To disappear enhances,' wrote Emily Dickinson. And it was true – Joe's disappearance made him seem all the more desirable. He'd upped and he'd gone. And he hadn't told me that he was going, because I'd been such a beast. It's all my fault, I said to myself, again. And I had five days in which to put things right.

'Contacts,' said Amber, as we locked our room and headed down the corridor to the lift. 'That's what we need – contacts.'

'Well, have you got any?' I asked.

'No,' she said, pressing the 'Down' button. 'But I've got a plan. What we do is go to all the places in LA where the scriptwriters and movie people go.'

'But we don't know what those places are,' I pointed out.

'Oh yes we do,' she said. 'It's all in here.' She waved the *Time Out Guide to LA* at me. 'I studied it assiduously on the plane. And the first place we go is Barneys department store and have breakfast in the rooftop café. It's stuffed with film people and celebrities. So we just ask their advice.'

'Amber,' I said, 'we can't just go up to famous people and talk to them. They don't know us. They won't like it. I wouldn't like it if I was them.'

'Oh, don't be so *silly*, Minty,' she replied with an indulgent laugh. 'They're human beings, aren't they? Like you and me. They'll probably be only too delighted to help. No, I'm really not intimidated by famous people,' she added, as the lift arrived with a bright falsetto 'ping'. 'I'm not intimidated at a –'

The doors drew back. And there was Hugh Grant. We looked at him. He looked at us. Then he smiled, slightly shyly, and said, 'Good morning.'

'Good morning,' I replied, as we stepped in. I glanced at Amber. She was staring at the ceiling, her face bright red. And she was unusually silent as we floated down to the ground floor.

'I thought you said you weren't afraid to speak to the stars?' I whispered to her as Hugh Grant faded from view.

'I've just got to warm up to it a bit,' she said, 'that's all. It's just jet-lag. I've got to get into my stride. But I'm really *not* phased by famous people. Oh my *God*!' She exhaled as violently as if she'd been punched in the solar plexus.

'What? What's the matter?'

'Overthereoverthereover*there*,' she hissed. 'Atthe*desk*!'

I looked. Standing at the reception was a very tall, handsome, dark-haired man wearing wire-rimmed glasses.

'It's Oscar *Schindler*,' Amber breathed. 'Don't stare, Minty,' she added fiercely. 'It's rude.'

'I'm not staring. You're staring. That's Liam Neeson. Great. Come on.'

The hotel foyer was dominated, appropriately enough, by a vast arrangement of stargazer lilies. Smartly dressed guests tapped their way across the marble floor or sat on plumptious sofas, doing deals. We walked out of the front entrance past a battalion of uniformed doormen, then set off down Doheny Drive. Now, I'm useless at map-reading. I just can't do it at all. I'm happy to confess that the depths of my cartographic incompetence are quite unfathomable. But Amber's the opposite. She's brilliant at it. She reads maps with the same facility and speed that she reads books. She can instantly see what's north, what's south, what's what and what's where.

'OK, it's four blocks this way,' she said confidently. 'Then we take a right and it's six blocks to Barneys. It'll be good to walk – to get our bearings.'

The sky was Hockney blue and the pavements a refulgent white as we strolled through Beverly Hills in the startling sunshine. We passed Spanish-style haciendas and miniature mock-Tudor mansions with exquisitely manicured front lawns.

'Unreal estate,' muttered Amber, wonderingly.

'Have you noticed?' I said after a little while. 'There are no other pedestrians. Isn't it spooky?' Indeed the sidewalks were as deserted as the Marie Celeste.

'Everyone drives in LA,' Amber explained. 'This city was built for the car. Angelenos love their cars so much they drive from their bedrooms to their bathrooms.'

Twenty minutes later we pushed on the door of Barneys and wandered around surveying the merchandise with the enthusiasm of a couple of vampires at a blood transfusion centre.

'Lovely stuff,' drooled Amber as we scrutinised some gorgeous velvet scarves.

'Do you have any questions for me today?' enquired a sales assistant. She had descended on us with the same certainty of purpose with which a hawk might swoop on a rabbit.

'Do you have any questions for me today?' she repeated pleasantly.

'Questions?' I said quizzically. What on earth did she mean?

'Yes. Questions.' *Ah*. This was sales patter, LA-style. 'Do you have any questions for me?' the woman tried again.

'Well, is there a God?' enquired Amber facetiously. 'How close are we to commercial space travel? And where might we find the lift to the rooftop café?'

'We must be *polite*,' I hissed as we walked away. 'Americans are very courteous and civil. I don't think we should be sarcastic to them. It's not nice.'

'Don't lecture me about being nice, Minty. If it wasn't for you being *not* nice we wouldn't be here at all!'

This was true. The lift deposited us on the fifth floor at the Greengrass Café. We took a table outside, drank in the sweeping view, then got down to some strenuous eavesdropping while we sipped our Mocha frappuccinos. Amber was right –

this was a good place to start. The air was buzzing with show-bizzy badinage.

'– Kevin will never buy it.'

'– Not less than eight million.'

'– friend of Calista's.'

'– I think it's a really great script.'

'– Not really BO.'

'BO?' I whispered to Amber. 'What's that?'

'Box Office,' she explained knowledgeably, waving a copy of *Hollywood Reporter* at me. 'Not body odour,' she added.

Certainly not. Everyone smelt wonderful. Scentsational. And they were dressed with the easy, affluent elegance you find in Cannes or Nice. They were all Pradaed and Karanned. Guccied and Vuittonned. Bodies toned and tanned, gymmed and slimmed – eyelids and jawlines trimmed. We couldn't approach these people in a million years.

'Oh dear!' Amber exclaimed theatrically, as she 'accidentally' dropped her sunglasses at the feet of the middle-aged man seated at the next table. He politely retrieved them and handed them back, and within thirty seconds she had told him all about the purpose of our visit.

'Can you offer us any tips as to how we might find our friend?' Amber enquired. Her considerable charms were not lost on the man, whose name was Michael, and he seemed only too happy to help.

'Who's his agent?' he asked. 'That's the first thing you'd need to know.'

'Well, he hasn't got one,' I explained. 'He sacked his British agent. He said he was going to sell the film script himself.'

'I see. Well, he'll be lucky,' Michael said. 'That's *extremely* hard to do in this town.'

'But it's a wonderful story,' I said.

'That's what they all say,' he replied with a breezy laugh.

'No, it really is. You see, it's set in Poland after the war, and it's about a little autistic boy who's completely locked in. And what happens, right, is that the boy befriends this stray dog, which has got lost in the snow, and through his friendship with this dog, the boy's condition gradually starts to improve and he eventually learns how to speak. And loads of other things happen too, to do with the aftermath of the war, but basically it's about the way animals can open doors in human minds.'

'It does sound interesting.'

'It's wonderful. And very moving too. It's taken from his novel,' I explained. 'His name's Joe Bridges, by the way. He's English. And I'm trying to find him.'

'Are you in the business?' asked Amber.

'Yes, I am.'

'What do you do?'

'I work at Paramount.'

'Do you have any advice on how we can find Joe?' I said with a sigh.

'Well, you should contact the agencies,' he replied, 'because that's what he'd be doing. He'd be cold-calling them, trying to set up meetings.'

'Which ones?' I asked him as I got out my pen and pad.

'You gotta try CAA – that stands for Creative Artists Agency – they're the tops. They're on Wilshire Boulevard. Then there's ICM and William Morris – just ring 'em all up and ask if any of their guys have been in contact with your friend.'

'We'll do better than that,' said Amber. 'We'll go there in person.'

But first we took a cab to Hertz and picked up a car. Half an hour later we were bowling along in a Ford Mustang convertible with the roof down. I switched on the radio and spun through the dials.

'This is KLSX Talk Radio on 97.1 . . . expected high, 74 degrees/// Call Attorney Frank Cohen – no win, no fee/// . . . smog levels good today . . . long tailbacks on Santa Monica . . . ///And God said to me, "Go forth and slay the devil . . ."///You're listening to KXWQ/// . . . And now these messages: Why not make new friends and find that special someone . . . ?'

I *had* found that special someone, I realised ruefully, but then I went and lost him again.

'Dorothy Parker described Los Angeles as "seventy-two suburbs in search of a city",' said Amber. 'I think that's rather good, don't you?'

Indeed I did. For where was the centre? There didn't seem to *be* one. We just criss-crossed street after palm-punctuated street, all looking roughly the same – low-rise buildings topped by huge billboards with vast, iconic images of the stars. Sandra Bullock and Sharon Stone were projected forty feet high. Harrison Ford seemed to gaze down on us with Pharoanic grandeur. The Marlboro Man loomed as large as Godzilla or King Kong. Overhead, signs directed us to Bel Air and Santa Monica, Venice Beach and Brentwood, Pacific Palisades and Fairfax, Malibu and Hollywood Hills. I stared at the map on my lap, but it might as well have been differential calculus for all the sense it made to me. I hadn't a clue where we were, but it didn't matter, because Amber did. She knew exactly, And it occurred to me, not for the first time, that there's a parallel here with her career. She's so much a better critic than she is a novelist, just as she's a much better navigator than a driver. I mean, she's really *not* very good behind the wheel, but she sure as hell knows the way.

'OK – this is Sunset Boulevard,' she said, stabbing the map with her right index finger as we drove along. 'That's the House of Blues –' she pointed to an artistically dilapidated tin-shack. 'It was owned by John Belushi and Dan Aykroyd. And that,' she said, swivelling her head to the right with an alarming lack of rearwards observation, 'is Spago's, Los Angeles' most famous restaurant.'

'How do you know all this? We've only just got here.'

'By meticulous study of the guide books,' she replied. 'I *love* guide books, Minty, don't you? I read them like novels.'

'Well . . .'

'Now, that black building must be the Viper Room,' she added as we approached a traffic light. She looked at her guide book. 'Yes, it *is*,' she confirmed happily. 'It's the Viper Room –'

'Amber!'

'No, it was still green.'

'It had gone red!'

'Oh well, I just can't find the brake on this bloody car. *Anyway,* the Viper Room's owned by Johnny Depp,' she explained calmly as my soaring pulse began to dip. 'That's where River Phoenix died. Right there. On the pavement. Terrible. OK,' she went on, 'we're going to the top of Sunset. And of course everyone knows what happened to Hugh Grant on Sunset Boulevard, don't they? Poor love! Anyway, we should hang a left somewhere soon and that'll take us on to Wilshire Boulevard, and with any luck we'll find CAA somewhere near the top.'

Five minutes later we slammed to a halt outside a white office building, bowed at the front like the space ship in *ET*. I ran inside and spoke to a woman on reception, and she put me through to someone called Cathy on an internal phone.

'Do you know a British scriptwriter by the name of Joe Bridges?' I asked her. 'He's written an absolutely *brilliant* screenplay.'

'Oh, really?' she said warily. She was as warm as Icelandic cod.

'Yes,' I persisted. 'It's about an autistic boy and his dog. It's set in Poland after the war. It's very, very moving, and it's based on his novel, which was published in Britain last year. He's called Joe Bridges,' I repeated, 'and I'm rather anxious to find him.'

'I'm sorry,' said Cathy, 'I really can't help you. We get so many enquiries from scriptwriters.'

'But I've flown to LA from London specially. I'm in love with him, you see.'

'You've come from London?'

'Yes. Yes, I have.'

'You've no address for him, and you've just flown here from London?' she repeated incredulously.

'Yes,' I said. I suddenly felt silly and rather self-conscious.

'Oh, that is *so* romantic!' she exclaimed. 'Hang on, I'll be right down.' And so she came down to reception.

'Now, I haven't heard of this guy – what's his name again?'

'Joe Bridges. He's only been in LA two weeks.'

'And his script's about an artistic Polish boy who befriends a dog.'

'Not artistic, *autistic*. Like in *Rain Man*. It's absolutely brilliant – incredibly moving. Anyway, as I say, I'm trying to find him. Could you possibly ask your colleagues if they've heard of him?'

'Hmm, I guess I could send an e-mail round to everyone, but I'm afraid they'll take time to get back to me.'

'Well, if you do discover that someone working here knows him, or has even met him, please could you ask them to call me at my hotel?'

'Sure. Oh, this is *so* great – I just love stories like this.'

'Well, thanks very much for your help. If he *does* turn up here in the next five days, could you possibly tell him that Minty's at the Four Seasons and would really like to see him?'

'Sure. Lemme write that down. Minnie's at the Four Seasons . . .'

'No, not Minnie, as in Mouse – Minty.'

'That's what I said, Minnie. Good luck.'

Next stop was ICM, a little further down Wilshire Boulevard, where I repeated my spiel about Joe and his script, only to be told the same thing. And then we drove up to William Morris on El Camino Drive – I drew a blank there too. By which time Amber said she was exhausted and feeling jet-lagged and needed to go shopping in Rodeo Drive.

'Perhaps he's gone straight to a producer,' she said as we wandered out of Versace and into Tommy Hilfiger twenty minutes later. 'Perhaps he's working in a studio. Perhaps he's sweeping the streets.'

'Perhaps he's living on the moon with Elvis,' I said bleakly. 'I mean, where do scriptwriters *go* in Tinseltown?'

'Excuse me,' said the young assistant, 'I couldn't help overhearing you, and I think I might be able to help.'

'*Yes*?' we said.

'I'm trying to break into scriptwriting too,' he said. 'There's a café where a lot of the writers hang out. It's on Beverly

Boulevard, and it's called Insomnia because it's open until four a.m. Maybe you'll find your friend there.'

Amber had parked the Mustang at an oblique angle under a jacaranda tree. She released the handbrake and off we went, her head darting dangerously from road to map.

'It's at 7285 Beverly Boulevard,' she said. 'OK, we go up here to Olympic Boulevard, then cross La Cienega, drive about fifteen blocks, take a left down . . . Cloverdale, all the way up, on to Beverly, and then it should be a couple of blocks down on the left-hand side.'

And she was right. That's exactly where it was. Opposite a synagogue. The café was done up in theatrical, shabby-chic style, with heavy velvet drapes, dusty chandeliers, battered chairs and tables, and shelves groaning with books. It was packed, yet it was silent. This was because everyone – including the waitress – was writing. They sat there in silence with their latte and their lap-tops, or with pens and pads of A4. The atmosphere was as quiet and intense as that in a university library the day before finals. Inhibited by the atmosphere of studious concentration, I idly looked at the books. *How to Sell Your Screenplay*; *How to Hack it in Hollywood*; and *Body Trauma – A Writer's Guide to Wounds and Injuries*.

'Ask *him*!' whispered Amber hoarsely. 'That chap over there, in the blue jumper. He looks like he's taking a break.'

I went up to him, introduced myself, and explained that I was trying to find Joe.

'Joe Bridges?' said the young man thoughtfully. 'Joe Bridges? Mmmmm. Joe Bridges . . . ?'

'You've heard of him?' I said.

'No.'

'Oh. Well, he's written a script,' I explained. 'It's set in Poland. It's about an autistic boy and a dog. It's absolutely brilliant. He's trying to sell it, and I just don't know *where* he is or what he might be doing. His mobile phone doesn't work, and I don't have any leads and I've only got five days and I don't really know LA, so I can't begin to imagine where he might be or what he'd be doing.'

'Well . . .' said the writer, whose name was Jed, 'he'd be hanging out in the bars; crashing the Hollywood parties; trying to get an actor or a director interested in his film. I've got a deal,' he went on as he sipped his coffee, 'and I got it by disguising myself as a waiter at a party where I knew John Boorman was going to be. When I brought him his drink, I gave him a copy of my script. Just like that! And he read it, and hc liked it, and now it's in the early stages of development.'

'Wow!'

'A friend of mine got a job washing the cars of famous directors. He was cleaning Tim Burton's car and he just left a copy of his script on the passenger seat. And Tim read it and liked it.'

'Gosh.'

'And a girlfriend of mine posed as a hairdresser and did Meg Ryan's hair. While Meg was sitting there, she told her all about her script.'

'What happened?'

'Well, you know that messy, just-got-out-of-bed look Meg's got?'

'Yes.'

'Unfortunately that was the best my friend could do. Luckily, Meg liked it. Then someone else I know disguised himself as a dentist and got to do Kevin Costner's teeth, and while Kevin was stuck there, in the chair, he said he'd extract them all if the guy didn't read his script.'

'What happened?'

'He got arrested. So your friend might be doing that kind of thing.'

'I hope not.'

'I mean, he'll be networking like crazy by any means he can, because it's just so hard in this town. I mean, like, every day two hundred people move to LA in the hope of becoming successful scriptwriters. It's desperate.'

'Do you come here a lot?' I asked him.

'Most days. I'm rewriting my re-writes.'

'Well, if you do see Joe Bridges, please would you give him

a message? Would you tell him that Minty's staying at the Four Seasons.'

'Sure: Mindy's at the Four Seasons.'

'No, Min*ty*'.

'That's what I said: Mindy. But if you're staying at the Four Seasons you should ask people there – in the bar. Just go right up to them and ask. It's a small town. Everybody knows everybody. It's like, complete Rumoursville here,' he went on. 'It's Chinese Whispers. People gossip constantly. So if you get chatting, I'm sure someone will have met him. Or you might even see him walk in.'

So that evening, when we got back to the hotel, we changed into our smartest gear. I'd put on a cocktail dress, and Amber was wearing a linen trouser suit. And I was just applying a bit of make-up in the bathroom, because obviously I wanted to look my best when I saw Joe again, when I glanced at my watch and saw that it was eight p.m., which was really four in the morning for us.

'You know, we're lucky the jet-lag hasn't hit us too badly,' I called out as I put on some mascara. 'I mean, to us, it's really the middle of the night, isn't it? But I think we're coping pretty well, aren't we, Amber? . . . Amber? . . . Why don't you say something?'

I stuck my head round the door. She was lying face-down on her bed, asleep. And I felt exhausted too. A wave of fatigue knocked me down like a brick to the head. Joe would just have to wait, I thought wearily, as I put on my pyjamas. Never mind, I said to myself philosophically. Tomorrow is another day.

'Go-od morning, you're listening to KCRW public radio, it's Friday the seventh of May, it's six a.m., and it's another LA day. The sun is ju-st coming up and smog levels are going to be good . . .' I got out of bed, opened the balcony doors and stood there watching the sky turn from russet pink to pale turquoise to a searing Yves Klein blue. Then I heard Amber stir and we went down to the open-air fitness centre on the fourth floor. We lapped

the pool for half an hour, then sat in a cabana sipping coffee.

'Nice, isn't it?' said Amber as a hummingbird hovered by an adjacent orange tree.

'It's lovely,' I said. And then I glanced into the gym, which was already in use despite the early hour. We could hear the whir and bleep of the machines.

'*Sporty Spice*!' I whispered in the hushed, reverential tones David Attenborough uses when he's just spotted some rare species of tropical bat.

'What?'

'Sporty Spice – *there*, in the gym.'

'My God!' breathed Amber. 'So it is. She's up early.'

'So are we. And isn't that . . . no, it can't be . . . but it does look like . . . ?'

'Who?' said Amber, squinting.

'Seinfeld!'

'*No*!'

'Yes. There – on the far jogging machine.'

Amber's eyes narrowed to slits.

'So it *is*. Gosh! I dare you to go and talk to him.'

'Talk to him?'

'Yes, I dare you. To ask his advice.'

'You dare me?'

'Yes.'

'OK then, I will.'

'Go on, then.'

'I'm going to.'

'I'm watching.'

'I'm going to go right up to Jerry Seinfeld and talk to him about Joe.'

'Let's see you.'

'Right.'

'Off you go, Minty.'

My stomach was churning like a cement mixer and my legs seemed to have turned to marshmallow.

'Any day now,' I said.

'Go on. But wait till he comes off the running machine.'

'Oh yes.'

'Don't want to annoy the guy.'

'No.'

Five minutes later Seinfeld's jogging machine slowed, and stopped, then he stepped off.

'Right,' I said, breathing deeply. 'Here I go.' I straightened my hair, wrapped my bathrobe around me, and went right up to Jerry Seinfeld. I did it. At first he looked taken aback, so I said, 'Mr Seinfeld, I really don't want your autograph, but do you mind if I just ask you something?'

'Er . . . sure,' he said uncertainly, still clearly not convinced that I was neither deranged nor a stalker. So I explained. And this time I got my spiel down a bit shorter, because obviously I didn't want to take up too much of the guy's time and irritate him. And now he no longer looked alarmed; he looked interested and was politely nodding his head.

'Well, that sounds like a great script,' he said.

'Oh yes, it is,' I replied. 'It's absolutely brilliant. But I'm just wondering where I might find Joe, because I've only got four days left and I haven't a clue where he is.'

'Well, you've got to go to the places where the movie people go,' he said. 'I'd try the Polo Lounge at the Beverly Hills Hotel, a lot of film people go there. And there are plenty of other places too, like the Sky Bar and the Ivy. What was his name again?'

'Joe Bridges.'

'And he's British?'

'Yes. Anyway, thanks very much for your help,' I said. And then I rejoined Amber by the pool.

'I just talked to Jerry Seinfeld,' I said wonderingly.

'I told you there's nothing to be scared of,' said Amber.

'Absolutely,' I said. 'I couldn't agree more.' Though my right hand was shaking as I picked up my cup of coffee.

When we got back to the room, Amber booked a table for lunch at the Polo Lounge and then I got out the business phone book, looked up some of the other agencies, and made some more calls about Joe. By this time I was getting really good at the spiel – in fact, in a funny sort of way, it was almost as though I was doing the pitch myself: 'English writer/Joe Bridges/brilliant script/Poland/little boy/dog/autism/snow/Joe Bridges/Minty Malone/Four Seasons.' I reckon each call took less than four minutes, and I must have made over thirty. And no, none of them had heard of him, but they all said they'd ring me back if he got in touch.

'At least you're covering a lot of ground,' said Amber, as we headed off to the Polo Lounge at twelve thirty. 'No stone unturned, and all that. Do you know I'm really enjoying this,' she added, as we made our way through the opulent back-waters of Beverly Hills. She'd bought a map – *Movie Stars' Homes* – which she consulted as we drove along.

'Now, that house there – that long, low, white one with the pillars – that's Julia Roberts',' she said knowledgeably. 'And that one with the huge Star of David over the door – that belongs to Shirley Maclaine. Now, the big one with the tall gates,' she said, taking her right hand off the steering wheel to point it out, 'that's Phil Collins' place. And number 927 – where's number 927? – oh yes, there it is! – That belongs to Robert Redford.'

'You should do this for a living,' I said.

Five minutes later we drew up outside the Beverly Hills Hotel, a vast pink plaster palace set in several acres of garden. Amber handed the car keys to the doorman for valet parking, then we walked up the long red carpet, under a green-striped awning into the plushy pink and green interior.

'This place belongs to the Sultan of Brunei,' she said, as we checked our appearance in the lavishly appointed loos. 'According to the guide book it cost 180 million dollars to restore.' She turned on a gold-plated tap. 'Apparently, Elizabeth Taylor spent five of her honeymoons here.'

'Well, I spent *my* honeymoon at the George V!' I exclaimed with a boastful smile. And I realised, then, in that instant, how far I'd come in ten months. Not only had I got over Dominic and fallen in love with Joe, I was actually able to make a crack about my dreadful, ruined wedding. I suddenly felt like a veteran of some futile, distant war.

'Have you got the mobile phone?' Amber enquired as we walked along the thickly carpeted corridor towards the restaurant. I nodded. A tiny cellphone was provided by the Four Seasons as an extension to the phone in our room. I looked at it and just prayed that Joe would get one of my many messages and call.

We sat outside on the terrace, where crisp white cloths flapped stiffly in the dry Californian breeze, and pink bougainvillaea trailed delicately along whitewashed walls like a feather boa on pale shoulders. Beautifully dressed women kissed the air and clutched little bags proclaiming 'Tiffany' and 'Giorgio'. Jewels winked slyly at wrist and throat and sparkled on perfectly manicured hands.

'Wonderful World,' I said, dreamily.

'Yes. But I think it would probably pall after a while.'

'No, the pianist. He's playing "Wonderful World".'

'Is he? Oh yes. So he is. This is where all the movie-execs power lunch,' Amber explained as she put on her shades. 'Imagine all those multi-million dollar deals being sealed over eggs Benedict.'

But I was simply trying to imagine whether or not I'd ever get to speak to Joe again. And what would it be like, when I did? Would we be ecstatically reunited like Jimmy Stewart and Deanna Carroll in *It's a Wonderful Life*!? Or would we bid each other farewell forever, on some misty airstrip, like Bogart and Bergman in *Casablanca*? After the way I'd shouted at him, it was more likely that he'd take one look at me and say, 'Frankly, my dear . . .'

'You must find him quickly,' said Amber, as she snapped a breadstick in half. 'Otherwise some other woman will snaffle him. Straight men are at a premium here,' she announced confidently, 'because, of course, most of the men are gay.'

'*Are* they?'

'Or ambisextrous.'

'I think you're thinking of San Francisco. I say, hasn't Melanie Griffiths lost weight?'

Amber glanced casually at the blonde woman three tables to our left. 'Mmm – suits her. Though I don't think she should lose any more.'

'I agree. Should we tell her?'

'I leave it to you.'

Suddenly my handbag began to warble. I grabbed the mobile phone and flipped it open.

'*Yes*?' I said, my heart pounding.

'Is that Minnie?'

'Yes.'

'This is Cathy from CAA – we spoke yesterday. I'm just calling to say that I have a contact for Joe Bridges.'

'You *do*? That's fantastic!' I exclaimed. My heart was pounding as I groped in my bag for a pen.

'He's staying at the Chateau Marmont Hotel. Let me give you the number, it's 213 626 1010.'

'Oh, *thank* you,' I said again. Then I went into the corridor and dialled the hotel.

'Please can I speak to Joe Bridges?' I said. My pulse was racing. My palms felt slightly damp. There were butterflies tap-dancing on my heart. I was about to speak to Joe! He'd be so surprised. In fact, he'd be *astonished*, but hopefully he'd be quite happy too and he'd –

'I'm sorry, ma'am, but Mr Bridges checked out six days ago.'

'Oh.' My heart sagged, like a sinking soufflé. 'Did he leave a forwarding address?' I asked.

'No, ma'am. He stayed here ten days, and then he left. I'm sorry, ma'am, but that's all the information I have.'

'Oh. Well, thanks.' I snapped the phone shut, then returned to the terrace.

'He was staying at the Chateau Marmont,' I said as I sat down. 'But now he's checked out, without leaving a forwarding address.'

'He's probably found a flat,' Amber said.

'If only I knew where.'

'The Chateau Marmont has a bar. We could go there tonight and ask. He might have got talking to someone and told them where he was going.'

'Maybe,' I said.

'I mean, we don't know where he is right now,' she said as our *hors d'oeuvres* arrived. 'But at least we know where he's been. It's a kind of start, Minty.'

This was true. So at six o'clock we pulled up in the parking lot opposite the Hollywood Hounds Poodle Parlour – 'The Ultimate in Canine Coiffure' – and entered the Chateau Marmont Hotel. It was like something out of the *Munsters*. The Gothic interior was dim to the point of darkness. The walls were a deep, oxblood red. Heavily fringed lampshades hung from the ceiling. I half expected to find a seance in progress. But the atmosphere was lively despite the Stygian gloom.

'Gloria Swanson used to stay here,' said Amber, reading from the guide book as we sat at the long mirrored bar. 'And Errol Flynn. And Boris Karloff. Apparently, it's haunted.'

For me, it was haunted only by Joe. He'd probably sat at this very bar, on the very stool I was sitting on right now. But where on earth *was* he?

'Excuse me,' I said to one of the cocktail waitresses, 'I'm looking for a friend of mine. He was staying here, but he checked out six days ago. He's English and his name's Joe.'

'Joe . . .' she said. 'Joe from London?'

'Yes,' I said. 'Joe from London. And he's a scriptwriter and he's written a film set in Poland about a boy and a dog.'

'I do remember him,' she said, as she mixed me a Martini with a lightning flick of the wrist. 'He was in here a few times. Mid thirties. Kinda cute.'

'Yes,' I said. 'Do you know where he's gone?'

'No. I've been off mosta the past week. Auditions,' she confided. 'Hyundai. But Leo might know.'

'Leo?'

'Yeah. I think I saw him talking to Leo.'

'Leo who?'

She gave me a puzzled look. 'DiCaprio, of course.'

'Oh.'

'Leo comes here quite a bit. He'll probably be in later tonight. Shall I ask him for you?'

'It's OK,' I said, 'I'll ask him myself.'

And so we sat there sipping our drinks for another hour, and then the waitress gave us the nod.

'He's just arrived,' she said. I looked, and there was Leonardo DiCaprio. And now he was coming up to the bar. So I quickly introduced myself, offered him a drink – which he politely declined – then asked him if he'd met Joe.

'Joe Bridges,' he said thoughtfully. 'Well, I was talking to an English guy called Joe a few nights ago. He'd written a film set in Eastern Europe or somewhere like that . . .'

'Yes, that's him. The film's set in Poland.'

'Snowy.'

'Yes, very. And doggy. It's about an autistic boy and a stray dog. Imagine *Rain Man* and *Hope and Glory* meets *Snow Falling on Cedars* and *Lassie*.'

'Hey, that sounds pretty neat,' he said.

'Oh, it is, it's *brilliant*. You see, I'm a friend of Joe's and I'm trying to track him down.'

'Well, I think I heard him say he was having talks with Ron Pollack,' said Leo.

'Who's Ron Pollack?'

'He's a big producer. His production company fields projects to Columbia.'

'Where does he work?'

'On the Sony lot. He's in the phone book, it's called Lone Star,' he said helpfully.

'Thanks,' I said, thrilled with this new lead. 'I'll call him tomorrow.'

'He won't be there,' he said. 'It's Saturday.' Oh. Of course. I'd forgotten. But then my jet-lagged mind didn't know *what* day of the week it was. I wouldn't be able to do anything until Monday. I'd effectively have to waste two days out of my precious five.

I was just feeling a bit low about this the following morning, and wondering what to do, when something wonderful happened. I got an unexpected phone call.

'Mindy?'

'Yes.'

'This is Jed from Insomnia. I think I've got a contact for your friend Joe.'

'You have?'

'I saw a girlfriend of mine last night at a party, and she says she met him at a scriptwriters' seminar. And they swapped addresses.' Oh, they *did*, did they? My delight at being given a new lead for Joe was dampened by a fierce stab of jealousy.

'He's living in Venice Beach.'

'Is there a phone number?'

'No, the phone had been disconnected because the last guys hadn't paid the bill. But I have the address. She wrote it down for me. Gotta pen? It's seventy-nine Harbor Street. You'll find it close to the ocean front.'

Ten minutes later, Amber and I were speeding down Robertson Boulevard towards the coast. I was feeling elated – I was so close now to Joe.

'Venice Beach was built by a tobacco magnate called Abbot Kinney,' said Amber as we sped along.

'Amber, please don't read the guide book and drive at the same time. I'll read it to you, OK? Right. Kinney wanted to create a Venice of America, complete with a system of canals and bridges, meandering streets and even gondolas. It says here that most of the canals fell into disuse and were condemned in the fifties, but a few survive and have been gentrified. It says that it's a Bohemian, arty sort of place.'

Half an hour later we drove into Venice, and found Harbor Street. Amber parked the car next to a yellow sign saying Dead End, and then we walked along looking at the numbers on the white clapboard houses.

'Seventy-five, seventy-seven . . . here it is: seventy-nine.'

It was a corner house, two stories high. I breathed deeply, then rang the bell.

'Joe is going to get such a shock when he sees me,' I said,

smiling into the strong sunshine. 'Do I look OK, by the way?'

'You look fine. Ring the bell again.' And I did.

'You sure I look OK?'

'You look great. Ring it again.' And so I rang it again. Because Joe was taking a long time to answer. We waited another minute or two and then Amber knocked on the door.

'Come out!' she exclaimed with a giggle. 'We know you're in there!' But still there was no reply. And then I rang the bell a third time. But answer came there none.

'Well, he's obviously out. Probably gone to Tesco's or somewhere,' she said. 'Let's leave him a message, go off and explore, and then we can come back later.'

She found a piece of paper in the car, and I wrote, *'Dear Joe, Amber and I are here! Please don't go away – we're coming back. Minty.'*

I had just bent down to stick it under his door when Amber grabbed my arm.

'Hold it!' she said.

'Why?'

'Don't you remember what happened in *Tess of the d'Urbervilles*?'

'Er, no, can't say that I do.'

'Well,' she began, 'Tess was just about to marry Angel Clare, who she loved, but she decided, two nights before their wedding, to confess to him about her past. So she wrote him a letter and pushed it under his door, BUT,' Amber went on melodramatically, and suddenly I was absolutely gripped, 'the letter went under the *carpet*, by mistake, and Angel never got it. Result? *Disaster*. So I suggest you put that note in Joe's mailbox instead.'

So that's what I did. And I put it right inside so that it couldn't possibly be whipped out again by the wind, and then we went down to the ocean front. The Pacific roared in the background, and shone like beaten silver as we strolled along the boardwalk in the breeze. An atmosphere of cheerful tawdriness prevailed. Ageing hippies played didgeridoos and offered tarot readings and psychic healing. There were stalls selling junk food and garish ethnic clothes. Teenagers sailed by on roller blades in a whir of tiny wheels, while seagulls wheeled high overhead, or scavenged and squabbled on the grass. We strolled about a mile, my eyes scanning the crowds like radar in case we should spot Joe. Then we turned round and tried his house again. And still there was no response. So now we went and walked along the short stretches of canal which still remained.

'Wasn't that canal holiday we had *fun,*' said Amber, as we wandered along the towpath.

'Oh yes,' I said, as someone paddled by in a canoe.

'And wasn't it hilarious when Mungo fell in!'

'Very funny, yeah.'

'And you jumped into that disgusting, *filthy* water, not realising that Mungo could swim – duh!'

'Mmm, that *was* funny.'

'You can't buy memories like that, Minty.' I just nodded. 'We must go on another canal holiday sometime, don't you think?'

'Oh yes, we must,' I said. Not. Ever. Never. Never, *ever* again.

'OK, let's see if Joe's back.'

But he wasn't. And by now disappointment was seeping into my soul like drizzle. I was so near to him. And still so far. But he had to come back soon. He *had* to. So to pass the time we walked the other way up the boardwalk, up to Muscle Beach, where gleaming body-builders pumped iron in an open-air gym. Here, the atmosphere was carnivalesque. There were jugglers and faith-healers and fire-eaters spewing flames. A saffron-robed monk whizzed by on roller blades, playing a guitar.

'Good material for your novel,' I said.

'Oh yes,' Amber agreed, as we strolled back to Harbor Street. But still there was no sign of Joe, and by now it was half past four. We'd been waiting for him since eleven. So we drove to Santa Monica, three miles up the coast. Here, we parked at the sea-front under some feathery eucalyptus trees. And by now the sun was sinking with my hopes and the sea had turned pewtery grey, and the lights from the pier were beginning to glint under the dusky, darkening sky. And we walked down the main drag, browsing in the bookshops, and my eyes anxiously raked the milling crowds just in case Joe was here. But we didn't see him. And now it was dark. So we decided to go back to his house one last time. Yet again, there was no reply. So I left Joe another note, with the number of the hotel, and our room number, and my number in London, just in case he'd thrown it away. I also wrote down my number at work, and even my parents' number – just to make quite sure he could get in touch. Then we went back to the Beverly Hills.

'He's probably away for the weekend,' I said, as we sat in the hotel bar later. I had another sip of my Martini. I was feeling morose. There was no sign of Joe, and we'd been sitting drinking for a couple of hours, watching all these chic, affluential people and eavesdropping on the Hollywood gabfest.

'– Tom and Nicole.'

'– indie feature.'

'– Nick Cage got twenty million.'

'– set in Poland.'

'– ratings were great.'

'Joe's got to go back to his house sometime,' Amber observed, as she speared another olive. 'I think he'll ring you tomorrow.'

'But what *if*?' I said with a slightly inebriated sigh, because by this time I'd had three glasses of rather good Merlot and, as you know, it goes to my head. 'What *if*,' I tried again, 'he was there all the time, *hiding*, because he doesn't want to talk to me?'

'Minty,' said Amber. 'I have one thing to say to you: No.'

'But I was *not* nice to him. Very.'

'This is true,' she said. 'But if he knew you'd come all the way to LA to make it up with him, there is no way he wouldn't see you.'

'But what *if*,' I said again, with another large sip of wine, 'what *if*, right, he's got someone *else*?' By now I was on my fourth glass and was bordering on the lachrymose.

'Don't be silly, Minty. He hasn't been here long enough.'

'Yes, but maybe *loads* of women are crazy about him,' I said. 'What *if* – Oh God, look, Cameron Diaz has just come in.' By this time we'd seen so many stars I wouldn't have been surprised if the Lion King had walked in with Mickey Mouse.

'Cameron's bldy 'tractive,' I said as the actress walked past our table.

'Is she?' said Amber. 'I suppose so. I'm a bit celebbed out to be honest.'

'Oh, she's ver 'tractive,' I said. And I looked at her long slim limbs and shining blonde bob and was felled by a jealous pang.

'Amber, look . . . wha-*if*,' I said, aware now that I was whirring my slurds, 'wha-*if*, right, Cameron Diaz . . . salready *met* Joe . . . sfallen madly in love withm?'

'Don't be ridiculous, Minty!' said Amber with another sip of water. 'Cameron Diaz wouldn't look twice at Joe!'

'Oh yes *shwould*,' I said indignantly, as I raised my glass to my lips again. 'Course shwould – Joe's ver 'tractive.'

'Look,' said Amber wearily, 'Cameron Diaz can take her pick in Hollywood, so why would she want to go out with a two-bit writer from London?'

Two-bit writer? Bloody cheek!

'Srude of you Amber,' I said. 'Joe's not two-bit, he's ver lovely and . . . lovely.'

'Look, I'm just trying to cheer you up,' she said. 'I'm trying to reassure you about Joe. Believe me, Cameron Diaz is not going to be interested in him, and that goes for Sharon Stone too.'

'No need to be 'sulting abt Joe,' I said, resentfully. 'Joe's 'tastic.'

'Oh, all right then,' she said crossly as she nibbled on an almond. 'Cameron Diaz *would* definitely be interested in Joe. And that goes for Meg Ryan, Sharon Stone, Gwyneth Paltrow and Cate Blanchett. Happy?' Oh God. *No*! 'They'd all be going mad for him,' she said.

'Do you really think so?' I said, distraught.

'Yes,' said Amber. And she had her mean face on. 'But *especially* Cameron Diaz. I think she'd *really* go for Joe. He's *just* her type.'

I felt sick. What was the point of flying to LA to find Joe if Cameron Diaz was trying to get off with him behind my back? This would not do at all. I could not tolerate competition from leggy, blonde film stars. I stood up.

'I'm just gonna have a word with her,' I said.

'Minty, don't – I'm only joking!'

'No. I'm gonna sort this out. Once f'rall.'

So I went up to Cameron Diaz, who was sitting on a sofa by the piano, talking to Batman.

'Look, Cameron,' I said to her, 'my name's Minty . . .'

'Who?' she said. She didn't look that friendly, to be frank.

'Minty,' I repeated.

'What kinda name is *that*?'

'Well, what kind of name's "Cameron"?' I shot back. 'Unless you're a Scottish bloke.'

'Hey, get outta here,' she said.

'Look,' I sighed. 'I jus' wanna ask you a favour, OK?' I grabbed the edge of the table to steady myself.

'Pardon me?'

'I jus' wanna say, please lay off Joe Bridges, OK?'

'*Who?*'

'Joe Bridges. He's man I love, y'see, an' I've come to LA to find him but I haven't found 'm yet but I'm gonna keep on looking and you can 'ave your pick really, so I'd be *ver* gra'ful if you'd keep your hands off him, OK?'

'Hey, what *is* this?'

'Even if you get . . . work with'm, which you might, 'cause he's a *f'tastic* writer and his screenplay's the dogs bollocks . . . Thanks ver much. Thass all I wanna say. Thought you were *brilliant* in *LA Confidential*, by the way.'

I don't remember what else Cameron Diaz said. She didn't look very pleased. Anyway, my legs were about to give way, so I went and sat down again.

'Come on, Minty,' said Amber, grabbing me by the elbow.

'Why? I'm having a ver *nice* time.'

'Come on.'

'Where we going?'

'Back to the room,' she said firmly. 'I've just landed you a starring role in *The Big Sleep*.'

I woke with a raging thirst, an appalling headache, and a chronic attack of post-alcoholic panic. A swim in the pool went some way to sobering me up, but I felt like shit. Still, I was relieved to learn that I hadn't actually assaulted Cameron Diaz.

'I only got drunk because I was so depressed at not finding Joe,' I said as I took another aspirin and put on my shades. 'To be honest, it's beginning to get to me.'

'Yes, but if what if Joe had walked in, Minty? That could easily have happened.' God. Yes. I hadn't thought of that. 'Imagine,' said Amber. 'Joe walks in to the hotel bar, and what does he see? You, drunk as a skunk, being obnoxious to Cameron Diaz!' What an appalling thought. I was filled with remorse.

'I'll never drink again,' I said. 'Not another drop will pass my lips. This has been a warning to me. God, I hope he rings,' I went on miserably. 'He must have read my note by now.'

But he didn't ring. He didn't ring in the morning as we strolled down the Walk of Fame. And he didn't ring at lunchtime as we drove up to Hollywood Hills. He didn't ring in the afternoon as we walked round the Museum of Contemporary Art. Nor did he ring in the evening as we sat outside, in the Sky Bar, having supper. And I had the mobile phone on me all the time, and I'd made sure it was properly charged up, so that if Joe had phoned me, there's no way he wouldn't have got through.

'You'll definitely get to speak to him tomorrow,' said Amber, as we sat outside, looking at the lights from the city winking like stars. 'Joe's obviously been away for the weekend,' she went on. 'But tomorrow morning he'll be back, because he's got a film to sell. And he'll open his mailbox and read your note and he'll ring you straight away. And as a back-up, we have Ron Pollack. And Ron Pollack will probably have a number for Joe. So we'll ring Lone Star tomorrow. And tomorrow it will all be sorted out.'

But the next morning there was still no answer from Joe. And I was feeling pretty low by now, and thinking that the trip, though enjoyable, had basically been a waste of time. At ten we phoned Lone Star. But Ron Pollack wasn't there. He was on location all day. His assistant said she'd ring him and ask him to contact us, but two hours went by and still we hadn't heard. So I phoned Lone Star again.

'All I need is a contact number for Joe Bridges,' I said. 'Does Ron know Joe?'

'Well, that name does sound familiar,' said the assistant, 'but I can't be sure. I really think it's best you speak to Ron.'

'Well, could you ask him to ring me again.'

'This is a very busy day for him,' she said. 'He's shooting with Steven Spielberg. And, with respect, Millie, your enquiry could wait until tomorrow.'

'No, it can't,' I said, 'because I'm leaving LA tonight. Couldn't you just look in his address book and see if there's a number for Joe?'

'I'm sorry, but Ron has his contacts book with him. In any case, I couldn't give out someone's home number over the phone. I'm afraid you'll just have to wait, and if Ron has time to ring you today, he will.'

Still he didn't ring. So I phoned again, and the assistant said she was sorry, but I couldn't have chosen a worse day and that Ron was incredibly busy. And the hours ticked by and Joe didn't ring either. And I really didn't understand that, because *surely* he'd have looked in his mailbox by now? By this time it was five thirty and we were packing for our flight. And we couldn't really go anywhere because we'd returned the car. I was just collecting my things together, and checking under the beds, when at last, at last, the phone rang. I pounced on the receiver with a pounding heart.

'*Hello*?' I said.

'Mindy, this is Jed again.'

'Oh, Jed, hi,' I said. 'We went to Venice Beach, and we left a note in Joe's mailbox. We were there all day, actually; we kept going back and ringing on his bell, but he never answered and we still haven't heard from him, so I guess he must be away for a few days. We seem to have drawn a blank.'

There was an awkward silence for a second, and then Jed said. 'I'm sorry, but I have a confession to make.'

'What?'

'I gave you the wrong address.'

'Oh!'

'I'm afraid I mis-read my friend's handwriting. Joe isn't staying at seventy-nine Harbor Street.'

'He isn't?'

'No. He's at number nineteen. I'm real sorry. I feel such a dork. But this morning I looked at the note and realised I'd mistaken the one for a seven.'

'Oh,' I said again. And I felt my throat constrict.

'I'm *real* sorry,' he said.

'Oh, not to worry,' I said cheerfully. 'Easy mistake to make.' I looked at my watch. It was six. We were leaving in half an hour. And though I managed to keep a stiff upper lip, my lower one had started to wobble. 'At least I'll be able to write to him now,' I said. 'So thanks for letting me know, and . . . well, good luck with your film,' I added brightly. Then I sat down on the bed and wept.

'Never mind, Minty,' said Amber, as we pulled away from the Four Seasons in a yellow cab. 'It was a long shot. We didn't have enough time. And you very nearly found him.'

'That's what makes it *worse*,' I said dismally. 'Being so *close* . . . And now we've got to go home. I could have met him,' I added bleakly. 'Now I don't know when I'll see him again. And by the time I *do* see him again, it'll probably be too *late*.'

'Well, you'll have to write to him,' she said.

And I thought yes, I will write to him. I'll write to him the minute I get back. The letter would take, what, three or four days to reach him? And then perhaps he'd ring. And so at least we'd get to speak on the phone.

As we drove down Wilshire Boulevard I mentally composed my letter. 'Dear Joe,' I would write. 'You won't believe this, but I came to Los Angeles this week and tried to find you. And I nearly did find you. I was even in the right street. Only I discovered afterwards that I'd been knocking on the wrong door. I think you'd say there was a metaphor in that. The truth is, I was mis-guided. Anyway, why did I decide to come to LA? Well, because, I just wanted to see you again, and tell you how sorry I am about what happened in London that night, and to tell you that you were right: Dominic was an own goal. And I'd also like to tell you . . .' But I had to stop writing, because I couldn't see the paper any more. I wiped my eyes and looked out of the window where darkness was beginning to descend. The sky hung in soft folds of pink and grey and the neon signs had started to flash. The entertainment capital of the world was about to stage its nightly floorshow.

'Oh, look!' said Amber, as we passed a large, square building, framed by an avenue of tall fountains like aquatic poplars. 'That's the Dorothy Chandler Pavilion,' she explained, as the car idled at the lights. 'That's where they have the Oscars. I wonder what's going on there tonight?' For indeed, there was some sort of event in progress. Expensive cars had pulled up, and out of them stepped men in dinner jackets and women in evening dresses. And there were TV crews, and arc lights, and the phosphorescent flash of the paparazzi.

'There's a big premiere,' said our driver. 'I think it's the new Bruce Willis. Wouldja look at this traffic!' he complained. Indeed, the road was now clogged, bumper to bumper, with Mercedes, Porsches and Ferraris. But Amber and I didn't mind. We weren't late. And the sight of so many elegantly dressed people had somehow cheered me up a little. So I wound the window down to get a better view. And there were all these immensely glamorous people, smiling and laughing as they walked into the theatre, occasionally waving at the waiting crowd.

'Oh, look – there's Meryl Streep,' said Amber. 'What a great dress.'

'And that one, there,' I said, as a pretty girl of about twenty-five stepped out of a sleek, treacly, stretch limo. Her silvery sheath spangled and sparkled in the blinding television lights. She was laughing. She looked radiant. And now her escort was taking her arm, and gently tucking it under his own. Then I heard someone shout, 'Over here!' and they both turned and smiled as the cameras flashed.

And as they turned, I gasped. And I gasped because it was Joe.

'Joe,' I breathed. He was standing thirty feet from me, no more. There he was. Right there. And I was about to open the car door and get out, when I felt Amber's restraining hand on my arm.

'Don't, Minty,' she said. 'Don't.'

And she said it for a good reason. For suddenly the girl's arms were round Joe's neck and he was kissing her as though he'd never stop.

'Money well spent,' I reiterated bleakly, as our cab drove towards Primrose Hill. 'Money. Well. Spent.' I emitted a hollow laugh. It sounded like a cross between a cough and a bark. 'It wasn't even *my* money,' I added, guiltily. 'It was yours.'

'I don't mind about that,' said Amber. 'I just wish it had . . . worked.'

'It didn't work,' I said dismally. 'It was a mistake. I feel so . . . terrible.'

'Yes, but at least now, you know,' she said philosophically as we turned into Princess Road. This was true. How did Emily Dickinson put it? Oh yes: 'To know the worst leaves no dread more.' And that image of Joe was the worst. It was seared into my memory as if stamped there by a flaming brand. I pressed my mental rewind and masochistically played the scene through again. Frame 1: Joe stands there, with Unknown Girl. Frame 2: He takes UG's arm. Frame 3: UG smiles up at him. Frame 4: They pose for the waiting cameras. Frame 5: God, I *hate* this frame – Joe and UG exchange a long, lingering kiss. Frame 6: They walk into the theatre, arm in arm. And cut. I had flown six thousand miles to look for Joe, and that was how I'd found him.

'Mummy's home!' Amber called out as she turned the key in the lock. 'My God!' she said, as Perdita came swaying towards her. 'She's doubled in size!'

This was true. Perdita's pregnancy had progressed apace. She looked as though she'd swallowed a large rabbit.

'Mummy's home now,' said Amber again as she bent down to stroke the cat. But where was *my* Mummy? This was odd.

'Mum?' I called as we took off our coats. There was no reply. The sitting room was empty. I went into the kitchen. And there she was, outside, hunched over the garden table.

'Mum, what's the matter?'

'Oh, hello, darling.' Her face shone with false brightness though I saw her surreptitiously mop her eyes. 'I didn't hear you come in,' she said in a voice she was struggling to control. The cat's fine,' she said. 'Pedro's fine. Everything's just . . . fine.' She made as if to blow her nose, but burst into fresh tears instead.

'Mum, what is it??'

'I'm afraid something awful's happened,' she said with a teary gasp.

'What?'

'Something terrible.' She tucked a lock of silvery hair behind her ear.

'Tell me.'

'Things are never going to be the same again.'

'Why? What's *happened?*' And then I knew. It was Dad. Dad had left her. He'd been warning her for months, and she'd ignored him. And now he'd finally gone off. He'd gone off with another woman.

'It's Dad, isn't it?'

'What?'

'This is about Dad, isn't it?'

'No! No, it's not about him. It's . . . this!' Another sob escaped her as she pointed to the front page of the *Evening Standard.*

'RADIO STAR'S MUM IN CHARITY SCANDAL!' trumpeted the headline. 'PROBE INTO MISSING FUNDS!' I looked, aghast, at Mum, and then I rapidly scanned the first two paragraphs:

> *Dympna Malone, mother of London FM's star presenter, Minty Malone, is being investigated following allegations that she embezzled thousands of pounds from the international relief organisation, Camfam. Mrs Malone, a familiar figure on the London fund-raising circuit, has been dismissed as a fund-raiser, pending an enquiry by the Charity Commissioners. Criminal charges may be preferred . . .*

'*Mum,*' I breathed, 'were you stealing?' I was shocked to my core. I was also shocked at finding myself described as a 'star presenter'. 'Did you steal this money?' I asked again.

'Of *course* I didn't,' she said indignantly.

'Thank God for that.'

'It was a grey area.'

'A grey area?' Hadn't I heard that somewhere before? 'Mummy, theft is theft.'

'It wasn't *really* theft,' she said carefully. 'It was . . . redistribution, that's all.'

'What do you mean?'

'Well, Camfam's got *so* much money – millions and millions. People are always giving to Camfam. But three months ago I got involved with the Canine Prosthetics Association.'

'The *what*?'

'The CPA,' she explained. 'They make artificial limbs for dogs. And they've hardly got any money at all. So I decided to give what I'd raised for Camfam to them instead.'

'*Ah*. How much?'

'Only five thousand pounds.'

'How did you raise it?'

'Bring-and-buys, car boot sales – the usual. But instead of sending the money to Camfam I put it in my own account instead. I didn't *keep* it though,' she went on emphatically. 'I paid it straight out again to the CPA.'

'Oh God.'

'But, Minty, these poor little dogs on three legs, it's heart-breaking to see them. I just felt *so* sorry for them. And I've never done anything like this before, and I didn't think any-body would mind. But now they're making this *awful* fuss!'

'I'm not surprised.'

'Camfam have banned me, and I might . . . I might . . .' she put her hand to her eyes. 'I might end up going to *jail*!' This was terrible. Terrible.

'Does Dad know?'

'*Everyone* knows,' she said dismally.

I was surprised by how sanguine about it Dad was when I phoned him later. He sounded quite calm and he said he doubted that she'd get a prison sentence.

'It'll probably be a big fine,' he said, 'as she didn't keep the money herself. She still can't quite see that she did anything wrong.'

On my first day back to work, everyone was very tactful. They all asked me if I'd enjoyed LA, but no one mentioned Mum. And this despite the fact that it had been picked up by all the papers. Eventually, I brought up the subject myself at the morning meeting, so that I could tell them the truth. Because I'd hate anyone to think that my mother had taken the money for herself.

'Still, I suppose it's all publicity for the station,' I concluded with a mirthless laugh.

But the whole thing was dreadful. It was really worrying. And on top of the shock of seeing Joe with his new woman, and chronic jet-lag – I was having trouble sleeping at night. So at three o'clock this morning I turned on my bedside radio and heard a familiar voice:

'That weally is cwap!' I heard Melinda say to one of her late-night nutters. 'I mean, people go on and on about dolphins,' she said. 'But what about the *tuna*?'

'What about the tuna?' said the caller in a puzzled tone.

'Well, they get eaten, just because they're not cute-looking with smiley faces and big foreheads. But who wowwies about *that*?' she exclaimed. I groaned and buried my face in my pillow. A few minutes later she had taken a call about wheelchair access on London's buses.

'I think it's *widiculous* that all the buses have got to be fitted with wheelchair-fwiendly doors,' she said.

'Why is it ridiculous?' asked her guest.

'Because disabled people don't *use* buses – evewyone knows that. I mean, when was the last time *you* saw someone in a wheelchair getting on a bus?'

And she was so rude to her guests! It was unbelievable. If they disagreed with her, they just got abuse.

'Oh, why don't you give your tonsils a holiday!' I heard her say to Kevin from Forest Hill. 'Wind your neck in!' she snapped at Bill from Beckenham. Thank God the audience was so small, I thought as I finally drifted off to sleep, just a few thousand insomniacs and eccentrics and spaced-out kids returning from raves.

The next few days were tense, as we waited to see whether Camfam would press charges. Mum's bank account was investigated by all her other charities to make sure that she hadn't 'redistributed' their money too. The whole thing was hideous. Added to which, Perdita now looked fit to explode. Her distended belly swayed from side to side like a bag and she could hardly drag herself around. We'd prepared a birthing suite for her, in the form of a large cardboard box which we'd lined with kitchen paper and placed in a nook on the landing. And two days went by. Then three. And still she showed no sign of parturiting. The tension was terrible. Then, on the fourth day, I came back from work to find Amber in a complete state.

'I think she's going into labour,' she said.

'Miaaaooooow!!!!!' said Perdita. She was making such a din. She wouldn't sit still, she couldn't bear to be left alone, and she just kept mewing and screaming at us.

'MIAOOOWWWWW!!!!' She was almost hysterical. This wasn't quite what we'd expected.

'I thought Laurie said she'd just slope off somewhere and quietly pop the kittens out.'

'No. I've just phoned him,' Amber replied. 'He thinks she might want us to be midwives, because maiden queens are sometimes nervous.'

And so we both sat there, and stroked her, as the long process began.

'MIAOOOWWWWW!' she cried again, louder now.

'I wonder how long it'll take?' said Amber.

'A couple of hours, I guess.'

We watched a portable telly to pass the time while we waited. First we watched *Blue Peter*, then the *Six O'Clock News*. And then we turned over to *Coronation Street* and watched that too. After that we watched *Brookside* and then the *National Lottery Live*. And still there was no sign. So we sat through the *Nine O'Clock News* and *X-Files*, and still nothing had happened. But by the time the credits were rolling on *Newsnight*, Perdita was having major contractions. One minute she would be lying there, perfectly happily, and the next minute her swollen little body had gone into spasm. And in between these alarming convulsions she was purring like a lawnmower, which surprised us.

By midnight her contractions were much closer together. Every time one came she would open her mouth, go rigid with pain, and emit an eerie, silent scream. It was frightening to see the unstoppable forces of nature take hold. And if either Amber or I moved a muscle, Perdita would get in a panic and cry. By two in the morning she was lying, exhausted, on her side, panting, her little pink tongue hanging out.

'She's ready to conk out and she hasn't even given birth yet,' said Amber desperately.

'Perhaps we should play her some music,' I said. So I turned on the radio. And there was Melinda. We listened for a minute or two, transfixed. If incompetence had been her trade mark before, now it was simple abuse.

'– why don't you hang up, you borwing old fart!'

'– give your tongue a west!'

'– get off the line, you sadfuck!'

'– put your teeth in, Gwandpa!'

'Why is she so *rude*?' said Amber, aghast.

'I guess it's because she hates doing the night shift,' I replied. 'She wishes she was still presenting *Capitalise*, so she takes her aggro out on her listeners.'

'She'll be lucky if she's not reported to the Broadcasting Standards people,' Amber said.

'And now a commercial bweak,' we heard Melinda say.

'Landscape gardening is an art. Why not consult Easiplant? We're experts in this field . . .'

I switched the radio off. And by now it was three a.m. and still Perdita hadn't given birth. Then, suddenly, we saw something. A little bubble appeared, and then something white, and a tiny damp furry thing like a drowned mouse slithered out on to the newspaper. Perdita whipped round, bit through its umbilicus and began to lick the new-born kitten with her rasping tongue.

'It *was* the tortoiseshell at number 31,' I said confidently as tigery stripes were revealed.

'Thank God it wasn't that ginger one,' said Amber, with a smile of relief. And suddenly the kitten stretched its front paws, no bigger than paperclips, and groped its way blindly forward.

'Wow!' said Amber, as it found a nipple and began to suck. Perdita was purring, and mewing, and then she contracted again, and within minutes another kitten slipped out in its sac and was vigorously cleaned up as it latched on.

'Twins!' I said. And then we heard this odd, crunching sound.

'Oh look!' said Amber rapturously. 'She's eating her afterbirth! Isn't that *lovely*, Minty!'

'Suppose so,' I said, queasily.

'Clever Mother Nature,' Amber crooned as Perdita chomped on her placenta. 'It's stuffed with vitamins, you know.'

This was amazing: that someone so repulsed by human childbirth could take to feline obstetrics with such aplomb! The kittens squeaked like toy rats as Perdita licked their wobbly little bodies and gently batted them with her front paws to make them feed. And she was purring and purring, and then her body tensed again.

'*Three*!' we said two minutes later.

'Triplets will be hard work for her,' said Amber. 'She'll have to have help.'

That seemed to be it. Twenty minutes went by and she had three damp kittens swarming blindly over her tummy – they looked as though they were doing breast-stroke through her fur. And we were just half-covering the box with a blanket so that it would be nice and dark and calm, when something happened. She contracted again and a fourth kitten slithered out. This one was black, unlike its siblings, and smaller. And it didn't move in a normal way. Its tiny limbs flailed disco-ordinatedly, and it's head lolled wildly about. Perdita sniffed it, but she didn't lick it. In fact, she ignored it completely. So we dabbed off the membrane with cotton wool, and nudged it towards her, but she treated it as though it wasn't there.

'Perdita, will you please look after your fourth baby,' said Amber, slightly crossly. And she pushed the kitten towards her again, but to no avail. By now, half an hour had passed and the little black one still hadn't fed. And despite Amber's efforts to make Perdita attend to it, Perdita didn't want to know. The kitten was just lying, stiffly, on the newspaper, still damp, while its three siblings sucked for all they were worth. It mewed constantly, as though in pain, and its tiny chest heaved fitfully up and down. Every time we placed it on one of Perdita's nipples, it fell off, as though it had no strength.

'It's going to die,' said Amber quietly. 'Minty,' she said, and she was in tears now, 'I think this one's going to die.' It certainly looked very sick. It was just lying still now, panting pathetically. There was clearly something seriously wrong.

'What shall we do?' said Amber as she tried, yet again, to make Perdita feed it.

'I don't know,' I said with a sigh. I flicked quickly through her cat book, but there was nothing on sick new-born kittens.

'I'm going to ring Laurie,' Amber announced. I looked at my watch. It was a quarter to four. 'I'm going to ring him,' she said again. And she went into the hall and dialled. After a few seconds, I heard her speak. She was describing the kitten to him, and its symptoms, and telling him that it was lying very still in a corner of the box. Her voice was breaking and Laurie was obviously telling her to keep calm, and advising her on what to do.

'What did he say?' I asked.

'He's going to come round.'

'But he's got an exam today.' She looked at me. 'Yes – I know. He told me we should rub it very gently as that helps the circulation.'

So that's what we did, in turns, until we heard Laurie's knock on the door. He was wearing jeans and his pyjama shirt. His hair was standing up, from sleep. He examined the kitten, and tried to get Perdita to feed it, but she remained wilfully oblivious to its existence. Its breathing was very quick and shallow now.

Laurie sighed and shook his head. 'I'm sorry,' he said. 'But there's nothing to be done.'

'What do you mean, nothing?' said Amber.

'This is nature's way,' he said with a shrug. 'Animals are ruthless. When they detect something wrong with one of their litter, they just ignore it and let it die.'

'It's going to *die,*' said Amber miserably.

'If I could do anything, I would. But I can't,' said Laurie. 'It's clearly very sick, so I'm afraid you'll just have to let nature take its course.'

Amber was in floods by now, and I was crying too. And you might say, well, it was just a kitten – how could they be so soft? But it was terrible to sit there, unable to help, while its little life ebbed away.

After Laurie let himself out, we sat up for about an hour longer. By now it was six o'clock. The kitten's breathing was ever more shallow, and it no longer made any sound. So we drew the blanket half over the box and wearily went to bed.

'Do you want me to bury it?' I said as we climbed the stairs. Amber just nodded and sniffed.

I awoke three hours later, with a feeling of dread. I had swung my legs out of bed, and was steeling myself to go and look in the box, when I heard Amber cry out.

'IT'S ALIVE!!!' she yelled. I heard her run upstairs and then she threw open my door. 'Minty, the kitten's *alive*! It didn't die!'

I rushed downstairs and there it was, latched on like the others, Perdita blithely feeding it as though nothing had ever been amiss.

'I don't understand it,' I said. I was now crying too. 'It's wonderful, but I just don't understand.'

'It's a *miracle*, Minty,' said Amber ecstatically. 'That's what it is, a miracle!' She was in raptures. She was laughing and crying, and she went straight to the phone, then stopped herself.

'I can't ring Laurie!' she exclaimed. 'He's sitting an exam.'

'Leave him a message then.'

'Laurie,' I heard her say, 'it's Amber. Thank you so much for coming last night. I'm very pleased to say your diagnosis was wrong. The kitten is alive and well! It's feeding! It's a miracle. I don't know how it happened, but it's OK now. It's been resurrected. So we're going to call it JESUS!'

'Are we?' I said, slightly horrified, as she put the phone down.

'Yes. It was raised from the dead.'

'Can't you call it Phoenix, or Lazarus? I think we might offend a few people.'

'No. We're going to call it Jesus,' she said with a mad laugh – she was beside herself with joy. And then she made another call, from which I deduced she was ringing the local paper.

'Hello,' she said, 'is that the newsdesk? This is Amber Dane and I want to tell you the good news about Jesus. Jesus *lives*!' she added, ecstatically. 'Jesus has risen and oh . . . oh, really? Well, I just thought, you know, local interest and all that. A nice little animal story . . . OK. You're full up this week . . . What? Really? . . . Oh, I see . . . Gosh! Well, thanks. Goodbye.' And then she came into the kitchen where I was making tea. 'They said they don't want to know about Jesus.'

'How surprising,' I said wryly.

'No, the editor says they're much more interested in God.'

'God?' I repeated.

'Yes. God.'

'As in God the Father, God the Son, and God the Holy Ghost?'

'No. As in Godfrey Barnes, the famed fertility doctor. Apparently, he's been a rather bad boy!'

I bought the *Camden New Journal* on my way to the Tube. And there it was. Splashed all over the front page: 'CAMDEN IVF DOC IN BABY SHOCK'. And there was a big photo of Professor Barnes on the steps of his clinic. Underneath, it read: '*Famed Fertility Specialist Godfrey Barnes Admits Fathering Hundreds of Babies.*' All the other papers had headlined the story too. 'IVF DOC FOR THE CHOP!' said the *Mail*. 'GOD FATHER' said the *Mirror*. 'PAPA DOC!' said the *Sun*, rather wittily, I couldn't help thinking, though I was astounded by the story. All those babies. They were *his*. Apparently he'd used his own sperm. He'd been doing it for years. The whistle had been blown as a result of the new openness about fertility treatment. As people had begun to admit they'd had it, so they'd talked about their specialists. And it had been observed that a large proportion of the children born the Barnes way had auburn hair and twinkly green eyes. Naturally, a few husbands started to suspect – they'd put two and two together, and come up with four. And four was the right answer. Or rather, four hundred. Because that's how many there were. Naughty,

naughty God. Now he'd been hauled before the General Medical Council and charged with Serious Professional Misconduct. Some of the husbands were threatening to sue, others were threatening to leave. And it was only a matter of time before criminal charges would be pressed. Poor Godfrey. Poor, silly man. I tried to imagine the bill from the Child Support Agency – it would run into millions.

One of the papers claimed it must be an ego thing – that God had become a megalomaniac. But Godfrey was quoted as saying that his sole aim was to help women conceive. 'It's my job to bring babies into the world,' he'd said to me. Well, he'd certainly done that. This was the ultimate in assisted conception. Most had been done *in vitro*, but in some cases pregnancy had apparently been accomplished by natural means: *'Come on in, Deirdre, and let's get cracking!'*

I thought, with a jolt, of Wesley, and wondered what to do. And the answer was of course to do nothing. Or rather, to say nothing. And that's what we all did. Just as everyone had tactfully kept shtoom about Mum, so we all kept quiet about Wesley. Because everyone at London FM knew that Godfrey Barnes had treated Deirdre. But Wesley brought the subject up himself.

'Godfrey Barnes is clearly round the twist,' he said airily at the morning meeting. 'He was Deirdre's specialist, you know.'

'*Was* he?' we all said.

'Yes. But I've talked to her and there's no question of our baby being . . . involved.'

'Oh, no,' we all said in unison, shaking our heads, 'of course not.' And that was it. We covered the story in the programme, and Sophie had booked one of the other top IVF specialists to come into the studio, live. And though the case was clearly sub judice, the man was doing his best to slag off Godfrey now that Godfrey was down.

'I'm afraid some fertility specialists think they're superhuman,' he said. He shook his head sadly, but his face shone with *Schadenfreude*. 'They come to think rather a lot of themselves,' he went on. 'They think of themselves as "personalities",' he enunciated distastefully. 'Appearing on TV makes them feel like stars. But then what happens is they drop right out of the sky.'

'Well, Godfrey Barnes is a very interesting and charismatic man,' I said.

'That's a matter of opinion,' he replied. 'But now we all know how he managed to achieve such an astonishingly high success rate.'

'He's alleged only to have used his own sperm where the partner's sperm was quite useless,' I pointed out. 'In effect, he was just the sperm donor.'

'I suppose so.'

'Well, if it was me,' I said, playing Devil's advocate in God's defence, 'and I was faced with the choice of anonymous sperm donation or Professor Barnes', I know exactly which I'd go for. And I imagine that despite this . . . scandal' – I hated using that word, although that's exactly what it was – 'many of his patients will remain very grateful to Godfrey Barnes.'

I was right. A week later, Godfrey was struck off. And when I switched on the news that night, there was a noisy protest outside the GMC. About fifty women were standing outside with buggies and baby slings and small children. They were chanting, 'STUFF THE GMC!' and holding up banners saying 'WE LOVE GOD!'

June

'Thank God,' said Mum, the following Saturday. We were sitting by Perdita's box, watching the kittens. They had been feeding all morning, and had now conked out, engorged with milk. They hung on to her pink underside, sleepy and sated, like ticks hanging on a dog. Perdita blinked at us benignly, and purred like a propeller. Then she scooped a protective paw round her dozing brood.

'Thank God,' said Mum again.

'I know,' I sighed, 'it's such a relief. Amber and I were convinced he'd die. He was in a terrible way.' But Jesus seemed to have recovered now from his unpromising start. Like his siblings, his eyes were still sealed, but in five days he had doubled in size. His coat was soft as swan's-down, his whiskers like lengths of cobweb. All the kittens were sweet, but this one was special because he'd hung on in there, and come through.

'I'm not sure about the name, though,' I said. 'I don't really think it works – Fluffy, Muffy, Tinky-Winky and *Jesus*? But Amber insists.'

'Thank God,' Mum said a third time.

'It's OK, Mum. Don't worry. He's fine now. He's absolutely *fine*.'

'Fine,' she repeated, wonderingly. 'That's what I mean. Thank God it's only a fine.'

Oh, right. Mum was still clearly shell-shocked by her close shave with the Law. She had been fined two thousand pounds, which Dad had paid. The missing five thousand had been handed over to Camfam, and Dad had very generously donated five thousand to the Canine Prosthetics Association – a cause he does not really support – in order to make good their loss.

'Thank God,' she murmured again.

'It's OK, Mum, it's all over now.' Indeed it was. It was over in more ways than one. She had escaped prosecution, but Camfam had struck her off and, within days, all her other charities had dropped her like a stone. Mum was finished as a fund-raiser. Her charitable 'career' was at an end. She was clearly finding this hard to adjust to, but at least she had avoided jail.

'I'll have to find something else to do,' she said. This was true. 'No more balls.'

'Well, you can still go, as a punter.'

'It wouldn't be the same,' she said. 'It wouldn't be so . . . exciting.'

'There are other things.'

'Like what?'

'Well . . . bridge. And golf – Dad could teach you to play. You could do that together.'

'Yes,' she said, cautiously, 'perhaps I could. Do you know,' she added quietly, 'he never said a thing. He never reproached me in any way. He just paid up, and that was that.'

'That was nice of him.' He was probably feeling guilty about his affair.

'Yes,' said Mum thoughtfully, 'it was very nice of him. Minty,' she went on, as she stroked Perdita's ears, 'didn't you say you'd seen Daddy standing outside Sadlers Wells?'

'*Did* I?' I'd decided this was best forgotten.

'Yes, you did. At least, I think you did.'

'You know, I can't remember that at all.'

'Really, Minty?'

'Really. I have no recollection of that whatsoever.'

'Oh, then, I must have been . . . mistaken.'

'Yes, I think you were.'

'Balls,' she went on dreamily.

'What?'

'Golf balls. You're right. Daddy and I could play together. I mean, we're going to have time now, aren't we?'

'Yes,' I said, 'you'll have all the time in the world.'

And then the kittens woke up, squealing and squirming and began burrowing into Perdita's side like moles. Suddenly we heard the front door creak open, and Amber came in, face flushed. She'd been for a celebratory lunch with Laurie. He'd had his last exam the day before.

'He's exhausted!' she said. 'He's taken ten exams in the space of one week. The culmination of seven years' work. But he thinks they went well,' she added, happily. 'And I've got good news too.'

'Yes?'

'Well, thanks to me getting tough with Hedder Hodline after that Nice Factor course we did, Minty, the publicity department have finally come up trumps.'

'They have?'

'They've got me extensive coverage for *Animal Passion,*' she said with a grin. 'Including,' she added with an air of triumph, 'a review in next week's *Sunday Times*!'

'Have YOU got the Habitat habit?' enquired Joanna Lumley huskily as I entered the building on Monday. *'Make your home more Habitatable,'* she punned in that sexy, marshmallowy voice. *'For fine furniture, soft furnishings and the latest household accessories – be uninhibited. In Habitat – it's where it's at.'*

Mmmm, I thought. Interesting.

'Step into Harvey Nichols,' suggested Mariella Frostrup as I stepped into the lift. *'And step out again in style. Harvey Nichols, not so much a store – more a way of life.'* Very interesting.

'Hi, Minty!' said Peter, our Sales Director, cheerily as we stood at the coffee machine on the third floor. He was smiling broadly and his face was burnished with a golden sheen.

'You look well,' I said, as I put the money in.

'Just back from the Seychelles,' he said airily. 'It was a freebie.'

'So, we're hitting our targets again, then?'

'We're doing more than that!' he exclaimed. 'We're turning advertisers away!'

'The ratings must be up.'

'The ratings are great!' he replied. 'We've added 15 per cent this month alone, according to RAJAR.'

'Well, I try my best,' I said modestly. 'I say, the coffee's improved.'

'Oh, it's not *you*, Minty!' said Peter. 'No disrespect,' he added quickly. 'You're doing a great job, but it's Melinda we all have to thank.'

'*Melinda*?'

'That late-night show of hers.'

'What do you mean?'

'She's the most offensive presenter on the airwaves. It's cult.'

'*Cult*!'

'Yeah. That's what she calls them sometimes. People love it. We're hoping they'll move her show to a daytime slot.'

'Well . . .' I murmured. I was lost for words. Clearly things were beginning to look up at London FM. I sat in the production office and flicked through the weekend's papers while I sipped my cappuccino. I opened the *Weekly Star* and had a quick look at Sheryl von Strumpfhosen: 'A Sun–Neptune alliance will enable you to forget recent unhappiness,' she wrote. 'Don't be afraid to reveal aspects of yourself kept hidden until now.' Then I glanced through the *Sunday Semaphore*, where Citronella Pratt was fulminating against God. 'Godfrey Barnes got his just desserts,' she declared. 'This mountebank has caused women untold agony and pain.' Not as much agony and pain as *she*'d caused them, I thought. 'This scandal only goes to show that fertility treatment is fundamentally flawed,' she went on. 'Only God the Father can bestow the gift of life, not false "Gods" like Professor Barnes.' I was distracted from this dreadful drivel by a knock on the office door. A delivery man was standing there with a trolley piled high with huge cardboard boxes.

'This *Capitalise*?' he enquired.

'Yes,' I said.

'Sign here, luv,' he said. 'I've got a load more round the back.' So I scribbled my name on the sheet, then idly inspected the cartons. Digiform Systems was emblazoned across them in large, emphatic black lettering.

'Great!' said Sophie, as she swept into the office in a cloud of Joy. 'It's the new Sadie's.'

'Sadie's?'

'Studio Audio Digital Editing equipment.'

'Oh, I know what it means. I thought we couldn't afford them.'

'Well, the station's enjoying a bit of an upturn,' she said. 'In addition to which, we got them at a knock-down price.'

'We did?'

'Yes,' she said, as she removed her Jean-Paul Gaultier mac. 'Thanks to my excellent connections.'

'Connections?'

Sophie removed a pair of gold-plated nail scissors from her Chanel 2005 bag and began to snip off the masking tape.

'I have a . . . well, *friend,*' she began coyly. 'She's my special friend, actually,' she added with a little laugh. 'Anyway, Lavinia is the Chairwoman of Digiform, the digital broadcasting equipment company.'

'I see.'

'I like older women,' she confided. 'And Lavinia's my . . .'

'Sugar Mummy?' I just stopped myself from saying. Now I knew why Sophie was wearing wall-to-wall designer wear.

'. . . lover,' she went on. 'And she offered us a 40 per cent discount if we bought in bulk.'

'Gosh.'

'And so London FM is about to embrace the brave new digital age. Don't you think it's fantastic, Minty, that we're changing at last!'

Oh yes, I thought, we're changing. We're undergoing radical change. But Jack clearly believed there was still room for growth.

'We need to rethink the schedules,' he said at the meeting

a little later. He'd let Sophie take us through the forward planning for *Capitalise*, and then he'd stood up to talk about the sound of the output overall.

'We need more arts coverage,' he announced. 'A film review programme possibly; maybe a slot for painters to discuss their work; more items about books.'

We all nodded. That sounded good.

'Now, this is all up for grabs,' he went on, 'so I'd like you to give it some thought. Other stations may be dumbing down,' he concluded, 'but at London FM we're wising up.'

Spread out on the boardroom table was the usual odd assortment of magazines from which we culled ideas for the show. There was *OK*! and *Celebrity Bulletin*, as well as *National Geographic, Newsweek*, and *Time*. There was also last week's copy of the *National Enquirer*. As the meeting came to an end I was just idly turning the pages when my eye caught a showbiz section called 'Behind the Screens'. There was Gwyneth Paltrow with Ben Affleck; Jennifer Aniston with Brad Pitt; Liz Taylor stepping out with Rod Steiger . . . And suddenly I felt sick. For there, at the bottom of the page, was Joe. With Unknown Girl. Standing outside the Dorothy Chandler Pavilion. And the caption read, 'Introducing British scriptwriter Joe Bridges. Bridges – no relation to Jeff – is new in town, but his star is rising fast. The studios have been quick to spot his potential, as has actress Kelly-Ann Jones. The pair were snapped together at a gala premiere Tuesday last.'

One short paragraph and my day – no, my week – had been ruined. Once again Sheryl von Strumpfhosen had got it completely and utterly wrong. How could I possibly 'forget past unhappiness' when forced to confront photos of Joe with twinkling starlets. *The pair*, I thought bitterly. That's what it had said: 'Pair'.

'She's pretty,' said Sophie. She was reading over my shoulder. 'Don't you think so, Minty?'

'What? Oh, yes. Yes, I suppose she is.'

'How's your love life these days?' Sophie enquired as we walked slowly back to the office. I found this line of enquiry a little intrusive, but on the other hand, she'd confided in me. 'Don't you have anyone special?'

'No,' I said, bleakly. 'I don't. I did,' I added, 'but it all went pear-shaped.' But not pair-shaped. Our relationship had been *im*-paired.

'Do you mean your . . . wedding?' Sophie asked with a delicacy and tact which she had failed to evince a year before.

'My wedding?' I said. 'Oh no, I wasn't thinking of *that*. I was thinking . . .' I sighed '. . . of someone else.'

'What happened?' she asked quietly.

'Nothing happened,' I said, aware of a tightness in my chest. 'I missed the bus, that's all.'

'Well, there are other buses aren't there, Minty?'

'They're not as good.'

'I'm sure you'll meet someone else,' she said as we went into her office.

'I suppose so. I don't know. How did you meet Lavinia?'

'At the Candy Bar. She stuffed a twenty-pound note into my bra.'

'How romantic.'

'It was, actually,' she said with a giggle as we sat down to discuss the day's script. 'Everyone's got their "how we met" stories, haven't they? In fact . . .' she looked very thoughtful, 'we could do something about this in the programme.'

'Could we?'

'Yes, it's the wedding season, isn't it? June Swoon and all that. I think we should do a *Capitalise* special on how to find love and romance.'

'Romance?' I said with a grim smile. 'It's not exactly my forte.'

'Yes,' said Sophie animatedly, 'romance. We'll do it next Tuesday,' she added as she looked at the rota. 'I think it'll be a *big* hit.'

'I will SMITE them!!' yelled Amber early the following Sunday morning. She had just come back with all the papers and had spread them out on the kitchen table.

'I will SMITE them!' she shouted again.

'Who?' I said, coming in from the garden. 'And with what? The jawbone of an ass?'

'Those BASTARDS!' she said. 'That's who I'm going to smite.'

'Why?' I asked. Then I looked at the papers, and knew.

'NOT SO GREAT DANE!' said the headline to the review of her book in the *Mail*. 'BARKING UP THE WRONG TREE,' said the *Independent on Sunday*. But worst of all, by far, was the one in the *Sunday Times*. 'THIS DANE'S A DOG'S BREAKFAST!' it screamed.

'Dog's breakfast!' she spat. 'Dog's breakfast? I'll give them dog's breakfast! I'll feed them *to* the dogs at Battersea *for* breakfast. That *bitch*!' she shouted. 'That *bitch*, Lottie Botty!'

I scanned through Lottie Botty's review, wincing at every other line: '. . . wooden dialogue . . . bizarre plot . . . breathtaking incompetence . . . lamentable style.' Oh God. The one in the *Semaphore* was no better. 'This Dane's not so much the dog's bollocks as a pig's ear,' it concluded. And as for the *Observer* – I'm afraid this is their kindest comment: 'Amber Dane is a fully paid-up member of the lumpen prosetariat.'

Amber's erupting fury had now melted into a lava flow of tears. She was sitting, hunched over the table, soaking the newsprint, when we heard a creak on the stairs. It was Laurie, in his boxer shorts. And I'm not going to explain why Laurie appeared in his boxer shorts on a Sunday morning, because you're all grown-ups and you know.

'Bad news?' he enquired, scratching his unshaven jaw with a sandpapery rasp. He glanced at the reviews. 'Ah. Yes. Bad news,' he confirmed. 'Never mind, Amber.' He put his arm round her. 'I still think you're lovely and clever.' This did nothing to cheer her up.

'I've been a novelist for ten years,' she sobbed. 'Ten years. And look how far I've got. Books are my *life*,' she croaked. 'They mean *everything* to me. And I really felt that, with this one, I was finally going to break through.'

'Maybe you should write them a bit . . . slower,' I suggested.

'You do tend to bang them out. Perhaps six months isn't really long enough to write a g– . . . um, a novel.'

'Or maybe . . .' Laurie began, and then stopped.

'Maybe what?' said Amber.

'Well, maybe it's time to reconsider,' he said softly as he sat down.

'Sorry?' said Amber. He was holding her hand, across the table.

'Maybe it's time to do something else,' he went on. 'Just as I did.' She was staring at him as though he'd just said, 'Maybe it's time for a little vivisection.'

I went up to Pedro, who was perched on top of his open cage, and offered him a sunflower seed. He took it in his beak, flipped it over with his tongue, then cracked it open.

'Maybe it's time for a new direction, Amber,' I heard Laurie say. And as he said that, Pedro suddenly laughed, then spread his wings wide, revealing a rare splash of crimson plumage.

'A new direction?' wailed Amber. 'A new direction? Doing *what*?'

I didn't say anything right then, but I thought I knew.

'*Tired of tittle-tattle? Then turn to* Tatler.'

'Are you happy Minty?' said Wesley.

'Am I happy?' I repeated. 'No, not really.'

'*Tatler. Top-notch gossip with nobs on.*'

Wesley put down his copy of *Mother and Baby Care* and gave me an encouraging smile. 'I mean, are you happy with today's programme?'

'Oh. Sorry. Yes. Yes, the programme will be fine.'

'Running order OK?'

'The running order's fine. First, it's Monica's report on the Wedding Show. Then I interview the romantic novelist, and at two fifteen we open up the lines to the listeners for the phone-in.'

'That's it,' said Wesley as he resumed his reading.

'I just hope we get some good punters,' said Sophie anxiously. 'Listen, everyone,' she announced, clapping her hands, 'have we all got pals lined up with romantic anecdotes in case we start to run short?'

'Yes!' we all said reassuringly. Suddenly Jack came in, went up to Wesley's desk and put down a copy of *Your Baby and Child* by Penelope Leach. He's being so nice about Iolanthe's gymslip pregnancy. Obviously, I haven't mentioned it again; it's a very delicate matter. But, well, I think his attitude to what's happened is absolutely great.

'Thanks for this, Wesley,' he said. 'Can I borrow the Miriam Stoppard when you've finished?'

I mean, it's going to be a pretty major disruption to his life, but he's determined to be supportive.

'Sure,' said Wesley. 'Have you covered diaphragmatic breathing yet?'

'No, she's just started doing her pelvic-floor exercises – very important.'

He really is being so generous and mature about it all.

'What's your view on the TENS machine?' Jack asked. 'Do you think it helps?'

'Oh yeah. We're definitely going to hire one.'

'Jack,' I said, 'could I have a word? There's something I wanted to ask you.'

'Sure,' he said, 'but can it wait till we come off air? I've got to go to the hospital with Jane this morning for her first scan.'

'Jane?' I said.

'Yes.'

'Jane?' I repeated.

'Yes, Jane. My wife. She's having a baby. We told you that.'

'Ah,' I said. '*She's* having a baby.'

'Yes, Minty, she's having a baby. I thought you knew that. Iolanthe said she'd told you. The girls are really thrilled about it, you know.'

'Really?'

'Yes. They're utterly delighted at the prospect of a little sibling.'

'That's good.'

'It's wonderful, because they're being *even* nicer to me now!'

Beep. Beep. Beep. 'It's two o'clock,' said Barry as the slender red second hand juddered on to the twelve, 'and it's time for today's edition of *Capitalise* with Minty Malone.' I felt the usual rush of adrenaline as the studio light flashed green for go.

'Hello,' I said. 'And with the wedding season upon us we're in a romantic mood. In fact, today's programme is devoted to one subject: love. How to find it, how to look after it, and why life can be so damn hard without it. Above all, we'd like to hear from *you*. How did you find love? By a stroke of fate? Or by design? Was love there from day one? Or did it grow as slowly as a tree? We want to hear *your* stories, so call us now on 0200 200 200 and tell us how you met your match. In a moment, I'll be talking to the romantic novelist, Belinda Dougal. But first, our reporter Monica James has been up the aisles – at the London Wedding Show.'

I took my headphones off while we listened to Monica's report in which she'd interviewed five prospective brides on their progress to the altar.

'– he got down on one knee.'

'– he was completely pissed. But so was I.'

'– I think I had a gun.'

'– I took a deep breath and asked him!'

'– I told him I was three months pregnant!'

Monica had mixed the piece with music and atmosphere, interviews with the dress designers, as well as providing some interesting insights into marital traditions. She explained that confetti symbolises fertility; that the veil is meant to ward off evil spirits. That 'something old, something new' refers to the brides' passage from her old life to her new one. It was a good, lively piece, about five minutes long. I back-announced Monica, then Belinda Dougal and I began discussing romantic fiction. She claimed it had never been more popular.

'Why do you think that is?' I asked.

'Perhaps because as people become more cynical about marriage, they need the fantasy of romantic writing more,' she replied. 'In romantic fiction the central relationship is severely tested, but by the end it's been resolved. As we find relationships harder to sustain in real life, perhaps we have a greater need to see love triumphing in books.'

'But it's just escapism, isn't it?'

'No. I feel people do believe in the possibility of finding love. Despite the rocketing divorce rate, most of us take the plunge again. We may be marrying less, and cohabiting more, but we're still looking for relationships that work. In romantic fiction, that's what we finally get.'

'Not always,' I pointed out. 'Not all romantic novels have happy endings, do they?'

'That's true,' she said, judiciously. 'In *Anna Karenina* – a great romantic novel – Anna commits suicide. Tess of the d'Urbervilles is led off to her execution just as she's been reunited with Angel Clare. But even if we don't hear the peal of wedding bells, and even if the lovers die, what romantic fiction does confirm for us is the human capacity for love.'

'Don't you think hi-technology militates against romance these days?'

'Oh no,' she said emphatically. 'I believe it makes it *more* romantic, because people just adapt. Look at all the flirting that goes on over the Internet. And all the website weddings. Technology is simply another string to cupid's bow.'

By now the computer screen was flashing with names and Wesley was whispering in my ear to start the phone-in.

'Thank you, Belinda Dougal,' I said. 'Please stay with us while we hear from our callers. And we're joined first by Geraldine from Blackheath. Geraldine, are you a romantic?'

'Well, I'm not really,' she began. 'In fact, I'm quite cynical. I never thought I'd re-marry, but I've just got engaged.'

'Congratulations! What made you change your mind?'

'It was the irresistible way my fiancé chatted me up. He came straight up to me at a party, introduced himself, and said, "Which end of the bath do you prefer sitting in?" And I thought, what an interesting man.'

'Thanks, Geraldine, and now on Line 4 we have Dee Brophy, who married a tree. Dee, tell us why you did that.'

'Well, I felt a tree would be a lot more romantic and affectionate than some of the guys I've dated,' she said. 'It's a silver birch,' she went on. 'It's absolutely gorgeous.'

'Tall?'

'Yes.'

'Well-built?'

'Very. I fell in love with it at first sight.'

'And were you lawfully, er, wooded, as it were?'

'Oh yes. I found a vicar to conduct the ceremony, I wore a lovely white dress and we had a champagne reception in the field.'

'Now, this brings us on to the subject of alternative weddings,' I said as Dee Brophy was faded out. 'What do we all think of the "Civil Service" now that the church no longer has a monopoly? On Line 3 is Julie, who thinks that wacky weddings aren't necessarily a good thing. Why do you say that, Julie?'

'Well, it detracts from the solemnity of it all. I mean, the law states that premises must be "seemly and dignified". But marrying in a theme park or getting hitched on a football pitch seems to trivialise the whole thing.'

'I agree,' said Lisa on a slightly crackly Line 4. 'I went to a wedding recently, and the couple – who are both scuba divers – got married in flippers and masks. It wasn't exactly a solemn occasion,' she said, 'so I wonder whether or not it will prove binding.'

'On the other hand,' cut in Belinda, 'I think the availability of these non-church weddings makes marriage seem more attractive to people who might not otherwise take the plunge.'

'It's good,' Wesley whispered into my cans. 'Move on to how to meet new people.'

'But before commitment, we have the search,' I said. 'And these days more and more people seem to be giving fate a helping hand. Rachel, for example, from Bounds Green. Hello, Rachel – you're on air.'

'Hello, Minty. Well, I'm a freelance graphic designer,' she began, 'and I work at home. So I found it hard to meet anyone and I was feeling a bit depressed, until a friend persuaded me to join this introduction agency and, well . . .'

'What happened?' I said, agog.

'WAAAAAAAAAAAH!!!' we heard in the background.

'Oh Lord,' she said anxiously. 'That's the baby – I'd better go. But as you can hear,' she added with a laugh, 'it worked. I met five really nice men, and then I met my husband. He was the sixth. And he's gorgeous, and we're just incredibly happy.'

'That's fantastic.'

'Well, *I* joined one of these marriage bureaux things,' said Ruth from Acton indignantly, 'but all the men were old and hideous!'

'You joined the wrong one then,' said Rachel.

'And now on Line 6 we have . . . Tiffany Trott.' That name sounded vaguely familiar. Tiffany Trott . . . Tiffany Trott . . . oh, yes, she was a friend of Helen's sister, Kate.

'Hello, Tiffany,' I said. 'And what's your story?'

'Well, I'd kissed so many frogs, my lips had gone *green*!' she began with a giggle. 'But then I decided to answer a small ad, and that's how I met my bloke.'

'What did his advert say?'

'It said he was an "Adventurous, Seriously Successful, Managing Director, forty-one". So I just call him "Seriously Successful" for short. Anyway, we're brilliantly happy. In fact, we got married two months ago. And the reason I'm calling is to say that it doesn't matter *how* you meet the right person, as long as you meet them in the end.'

'I quite agree,' said Belinda as Tiffany Trott was faded out. I looked at my computer screen again. Ah *ha*.

'And on Line 3 now we have Laurie Wilkes, from Canonbury.'

'I met my girlfriend in a *very* romantic way,' he began.

'Did you?' I said, disingenuously.

'I was her male escort.'

'*Really*?'

'Yes. I was her walker,' he explained. 'She hired me to accompany her to a charity ball.'

'Was that fun?'

'Great fun,' he said. 'And she fell for me *instantly*. Didn't you, Amber?'

There was a guffaw in the background and then Amber grabbed the phone.

'No. It's bollocks – Ooh, sorry, listeners! – I mean, it's *baloney*. We fought like cat and dog until, well, quite recently, actually.'

'What made you change your mind?'

'I can tell you exactly. You see, Laurie's a vet. And one of my cat's new kittens was very sick. I was very upset about it. I thought it was dying, and I didn't know what to do. So at four o'clock in the morning I phoned Laurie, and he offered to come round, despite the fact that he had a big exam the same day. It was then, when he did that, without a murmur, that I realised I'd fallen in love with him.'

I glanced at Belinda. Her eyes had misted over.

'And why did you hire Laurie in the first place?' I said.

'Because I needed a partner.'

'And now you've got one!'

'Yes,' she said happily. 'I have. And what I want to say,' she went on, seriously now, 'is that it's funny how life turns out. You see, the reason why I wanted to go to that ball was because I knew my ex-boyfriend would be there and I was trying to get him back. So I went looking for my past, but instead, I found . . .' she was clearly overcome – she's so emotional – 'Instead, I found . . .'

'Me,' said Laurie.

I could hear Amber sniffing now. And I looked through the glass and everyone was riveted, and Sophie had a tissue to her eyes.

'Laurie was very expensive,' said Amber, laughing now. 'It cost me two hundred pounds to hire him, but I can truly say it was money well spent.'

'Ah, thank you darling.'

'This is *brilliant*,' said Wesley into my 'phones. 'We're getting so many calls.'

It seemed that everyone in London wanted to tell their story.

'– We met hang-gliding.'

'– We met at the Tate.'

'– We met at a funeral.'

'– We met at a singles do.'

'I met my w-w-wife at a p-p-p-p–'

'–arty?' I suggested.

'Yes. At a p-p-p-party,' stuttered Darren from Essex. 'And the amazing thing was . . .'

'Yes?'

'. . . that it was the *same* p-p-p-party!'

'No!' I said. '*Incredible*!'

'– We met on top of a mountain.'

'– We met at primary school.'

'– We met at bingo.'

'– We met at a polo match.'

There must, I thought, be some mathematical paradigm for all this, to do with the random collision of particles. Or perhaps it isn't really so random after all.

'What's your story, Minty?' said Alan on Line 5 suddenly.

'What's *my* story?' I was taken aback.

'Yes. We've told you ours.'

'Well . . .' Oh God. 'It's not very interesting. Anyway, I'm just the presenter here.'

'No, really,' Alan went on. 'What about you? Are you married?'

'Oh no no no,' I said. 'Let's take another call now.'

'No,' he persisted, 'we'd all like to know if *you've* fallen for anyone, and how you met them.'

'Well . . .'

I really didn't like having the tables turned like this. I looked through the glass at Wesley. He shrugged, noncommittally, then whispered into my head-phones: 'It's up to you.'

'What's your story, Minty?' said Alan again.

Oh God, this was embarrassing. But then Sheryl von Strumpfhosen had said, '*Don't be afraid to reveal aspects of yourself kept hidden until now.'* On the other hand, Sheryl was *always* wrong.

'*Do* tell us, Minty,' said Belinda with an encouraging smile.

'Well . . .' I sighed.

'Go on,' she said.

'OK,' I replied grudgingly. 'But it really isn't very interesting.' I nervously cleared my throat. 'Right: last July I was on honeymoon with my bridesmaid,' I began. 'My fiancé had run off, you see, during our wedding, in front of two hundred and eighty people. Bit of a shock. *Anyway,* Helen and I went to Paris and stayed in the Honeymoon Suite of the George V. And on our penultimate day we played table football in a café with this English chap called Joe. I didn't pay him much attention because I was having a nervous breakdown. But then Joe and I met again, by chance, in London. And we began to get on very well – *very* well, actually, for a while – and Joe's . . . what can I tell you about Joe?' I paused for a second. 'Well, Joe's witty, and creative,' I went on. 'He's a brilliant writer, by the way – that's what he does. And he's good-looking but not flash. He's just natural. He's a natural man. And I would have fallen for him earlier, but I didn't, because I was still obsessing about my ex. And just when I'd got over my ex, and realised that I was falling . . .' I paused again. 'That I was falling in love with Joe, something awful happened. I blew it. I lost it with him. I completely lost it. I made a terrible, terrible scene. In public. It was awful. I was vile. I was shouting and swearing at him like a Harpy. And I said I never wanted to see him again.'

'Oh dear,' said Belinda. She looked distraught.

'Yes. Exactly,' I said. 'Oh dear. And I'm not going to tell you why I shouted at Joe, except to say that it was because he'd made me confront something that I'd suppressed for a very long time. And I didn't like it, because I knew he was right. It was as though he'd held up one of those magnifying mirrors. The kind that show you all your defects in unpalatable close-up – all your imperfections, and lines and open pores. There's no escaping them with a mirror like that. And that's what it was like with Joe. And I didn't like the view, so I lost my temper. And if there was one person I shouldn't have lost my temper with, it was him. So I regretted it. In fact, I regretted it very, very much. Anyway,' I went on with a sigh, 'eventually, I phoned him to apologise, but he'd left. He'd gone to LA, to work. And I felt terrible because he'd come to mean so much. I'd assumed we'd be together, because by now I couldn't imagine being apart. I felt just so, so bad. Then a friend of mine suggested that I go and look for him, and so that's what I did.'

'You went to Los Angeles?' said Belinda.

'Yes, I went to Los Angeles and I searched for him. I looked everywhere. I looked in all the bars and cafés, and I phoned loads of agents and film producers. I asked all the actors and scriptwriters I met – anyone who might possibly have a lead. I told them about Joe's film, and how wonderful it is, but they didn't know who he was. I think they do now, though. Eventually I found out where he lived, and I went there. But he wasn't in. I hung around all day, but he didn't come back. And the reason why he didn't come back was because I was standing outside the wrong house. Because I'd been given the wrong address. But I didn't know that until afterwards, by which time it was too late.'

'So you never found him, then?'

'Oh yes, I did find him. On my way to the airport I suddenly saw him, outside a theatre with this woman. And they were being photographed. And they looked very happy together. And then they kissed. And later, I saw their photo in a magazine, and it said they were a "pair". So I did find Joe. But at the same time I missed him. And I miss him now. In fact, I really miss him, because I think he was The One.' I exhaled painfully, paused for a second, then looked up at the computer screen again. 'OK, just time for a few more calls,' I said. 'And on Line 4 we have Ella from Crouch End. Hi, Ella, welcome to the show. What's your story?'

'I don't have a story,' she said quietly. 'I want to talk about *your* story. I think it's very sad and you shouldn't leave it there.'

'I *agree,*' said Belinda roundly.

'I mean, that girl might not mean much to him,' Ella went on.

'I thought of that,' I said. 'But then, Joe isn't shallow. In fact, he's very cautious with women, so I don't think he'd kiss someone like that unless he felt very attached.'

'What sort of kiss was it?'

'Well, you know, a proper one.'

'How long did it go on?'

'Look, I don't *know.* I was driving slowly by in a cab, so I got a pretty good view, but I can only tell you that it was . . .' I heaved another painful sigh '. . . a proper, lingering kiss.'

'Mmm,' she said, thoughtfully, 'but he can't have known her that long.'

'Maybe not, but he's obviously clicked with her very quickly, which means he's keen.'

'Well, I think you should write to him and tell him what happened,' Ella persisted.

'There's no point,' I replied. 'In any case, I'm not sure he'd want to know. He's six thousand miles away. He has a new life now. He's moving on. And so must I.' I picked another caller. 'And now we have Nicola on Line 5, calling from Wandsworth. What's your point, Nicola?'

'Look, Minty,' said Nicola, 'I agree with the previous caller. I think you should try again.'

'Oh, *do* you?'

'Yes, Joe's new relationship may not last very long,' she went on. 'Have you thought of that?'

'Well, yes, I have,' I conceded wearily. 'But I can't hang around for him on spec. I'd be consumed with jealousy and the frustration would probably kill me. So, thanks for the suggestion, but no thanks. And on Line 3, we have Mike. What do you want to talk about, Mike?'

'You!' he said forthrightly, his voice echoing slightly on his mobile phone. 'I want to talk about you and Joe.' Oh God. Not *another* one. 'I'm a cab driver, right,' he explained. 'I listen to you quite a lot, girl, and I feel like I've got to know you a bit. And I agree with the previous callers: you're making a *big* mistake. If I was Joe, I'd be well gutted to know that you'd tried so hard to find me.'

'Well, Joe isn't going to know, because he has a new life now and that's that.'

'That's no bleedin' good,' said Mike. 'I can't believe you're being such a wimp. What, mate? – Sorry, just got to talk to my fare.'

'I agree with Mike,' said Nicola on Line 5. 'You're being a wimp.'

'No I'm not,' I shot back.

'Yes you are,' said Ella on Line 2. 'And you can't be as fond of him as you say you are otherwise you wouldn't give up so easily.'

'Look,' I said – I was getting slightly irritated now – 'not only was I very fond of him, I was in love with him. In fact,' I added, 'I still am, OK? And I didn't just give up "so easily". I went to enormous trouble to find him, and it didn't work. But I did try.'

'Not hard enough, girl,' said Mike on Line 3.

'Look,' I said, 'didn't you hear me say that he's got someone *else*?'

'Yeah, but relationships don't last five minutes in Hollywood, everyone knows that,' he said over the diesel chug of his engine. 'They change partners there like they change their bleedin' shirts.'

'Yes,' said Nicola on Line 5. 'What makes you think Joe's going to stick with this woman?'

'Look, I know all this *logically*,' I conceded. 'But I can only say that it's profoundly discouraging seeing the object of your affection passionately kissing someone else. Though I was at least grateful that it wasn't Cameron Diaz.'

'What have you got against Cameron Diaz?' said Ella.

'Nothing really, I . . .'

'She was great in *There's Something About Mary*.'

'Yes, she was,' I said. 'She was very good in that.'

'No, I preferred her in *My Best Friend's Wedding*,' said Nicola.

'Oh yes,' said Ella, 'that karaoke scene was *hilarious*.'

'*I* think her best performance was in *A Life Less Ordinary*,' said Belinda judiciously.

'Yes. Yes, she was excellent in that,' I agreed wearily.

'Look, can we *stop* talking about Cameron Diaz!' said Mike. 'We're talking about Minty and Joe here.'

'Oh yes,' they all said.

'Now look, Minty,' Mike went on, 'have you got the right address for Joe now?'

'Yes,' I said, 'I have. It's 19 Harbor Street, Venice Beach.'

'Then write to him. Write to him tonight, girl.'

'No, I'm not going to do that.'

'Why not?' Why not? Why not?

'Because a) he lives in Los Angeles, and b) he's got a girlfriend.'

'And c) you're in love with him,' said Ella, 'and d) he's The One.'

'That's right,' said Mike. 'You've got to try to get 'im back because life ain't a bleedin' dress rehearsal! Where to now, mate?'

'That's true,' said Nicola on Line 5. 'We only get one chance.'

'There's nothing worse than futile regrets,' said Belinda. 'Imagine looking back, when you're ninety and saying, "if only".'

'OK, OK,' I said, 'I hear what you all say. But I really would like to change the subject. And on Line 1 now is Lizzie from Hampstead. Hopefully, Lizzie's going to talk about something else.'

'No I'm *not*!' said Lizzie, in a tone of voice which took me aback. 'Now, you listen to me,' she went on, fiercely, audibly drawing on a cigarette. 'You're being bloody ridiculous! Joe's obviously a wonderful man. You clearly had a very *real* connection with him, and you're a complete coward not to go that extra mile.'

'Yes, don't be such a coward, Minty!' said Nicola, crossly. 'I'm disappointed in you.'

'So am I!' said Ella vehemently.

'And me,' said Mike.

My God! This was getting nasty. I glanced through the glass for moral support, but they all seemed to find my discomfiture amusing. I looked at the clock: only two minutes of air-time to go. Thank God for that. I'd had enough of this phone-in. I'd start to wind the programme up, right now, before they wound *me* up any more.

'Do try and put it right,' said Belinda. 'Write to Joe.'

'I *can't,*' I said, simply. 'Life isn't like *A Midsummer's Night Dream,*' I went on. 'Jack doesn't always have Jill. Sometimes Jack opts for someone else. Kelly-Ann, for example. There aren't always happy endings. You admitted as much yourself.'

'But we can make our own happy endings!' said Mike.

'No, we can't. Not if it's just not meant to be. It's destiny,' I added. 'It's Fate.'

'No it isn't!' exclaimed Lizzie. 'The fault, dear Brutus, is not in our stars, but in our *selves,*' she declaimed. '*Julius Caesar,* Act One,' she added crisply.

I'd had enough of this. There was still a minute to go, but I was going to come out early. Tough.

'Well, I'm afraid there we must bring the programme to an end,' I said.

'Just get off your arse, Minty!' said Mike.

'I'd like to thank you all for joining me today . . .'

'Don't be such a sap!' said Ella.

'. . . for this special edition of the programme.'

'You're being a bloody fool!' said Lizzie.

'Do join us again . . .'

'A total *idiot*!' said Nicola.

'tomorrow . . .'

'In fact, Minty,' said a familiar voice, 'you're being a complete MORON!'

'Don't call me a moron, Joe. I've told you that before . . .'

'Well, you are!'

'In the meantime . . .' *Joe*? '. . . from all of us on *Capitalise* . . .' *Joe!* '. . . goodbye.'

'Joe!' I was so shocked I stood up without taking off my headphones and nearly garrotted myself on the lead. 'That was Joe,' I said, as I pushed through the studio doors. 'That was *Joe*!' I said again.

'Yes,' said Wesley, 'it was.'

'Where was he phoning from?'

'That cab.'

'The cab?'

'Yes, the cab.'

'Where is he now?' I said.

'He's in reception,' said Wesley.

'Reception?' I said, as I feverishly groped in my bag for a comb.

'That's what he said. He said he was just being dropped off at reception.'

'Christ, where's my lipstick?' I said.

'By the way,' Jack went on as I found my hand mirror, 'I really liked your cousin's contribution. Isn't she the girl who read at your wedding?'

'Yes. Yes, she is,' I said as I applied mascara with my right hand, and squished on scent with my left.

'Lovely voice,' he said thoughtfully.

'Yes. In fact . . . look, there's something I want to talk to you about, Jack.'

'Tell me later, Minty,' he said with a smile.

I rushed out of the studio towards the lift. Oh Christ – there was an 'Out of Order' notice on it. I flew to the emergency stairs, and began to take them three at a time. Suddenly I saw Monica coming up them towards me.

'Minty!' she called. 'Have you heard what's happened?'

'Yes, I have, I'm just going to meet him.'

'What do you mean, you're going to meet him? He's run off!'

'He's run off?'

'Yes – run off.'

'What are you *talking* about?' I said. This was too much in one day.

'He's run off,' she repeated. 'It's a scandal.'

'But he's only just *got* here.'

'Mr Happy Bot has run off,' she announced.

'*What*?'

'Citronella's husband's run off with someone!'

'Citronella?'

'Yes, Citronella. Her husband's done a bunk! I've just heard.'

'Citronella? Oh. Wow! Well . . .' I said as I resumed my downward flight.

'Can you believe it?' shouted Monica incredulously.

'Yes,' I called up the stairs, 'I can. I mean, she's absolutely frightful and that nanny of theirs is very pretty.'

'Oh, it's not the *nanny*!' I heard Monica shout as I hurtled down the steps and flung my arms round Joe. 'It's not the nanny,' she added gaily. 'It's a *man*!'

July

Pop! Fizzzzzzzz. Chink. *'Everything clicks with Veuve Clicquot,'* intoned Rupert Everett urbanely. *'Veuve Clicquot,'* he went on smoothly, *'Make your clique click with Veuve.'*

'And now a look at London's weather,' said Barry, 'brought to you by Ralph Lauren, the label which looks good in all seasons. It's going to be another warm, sunny day . . .'

I reached out a hand and groped for the 'off' button on my radio alarm. I wanted to concentrate on the papers. 'PRATT FALL!' announced the centre pages of the *Mail on Sunday*. 'Un-nappy Ever After as Happy Bot Gives Chairman the Boot!' Andrew Pratt's predilections were hardly of public concern, but lacking other news, the *Mail on Sunday* had decided to go to town. It described him as a 'pervert', a man whose company extolled the virtues of family life, while his own marriage had been a hollow sham. There was a photo of the Pratts in happier times, smirking outside their country home, and an aerial shot of the copse on Hampstead Heath where Andrew Pratt had been found, *in flagrante*, with 'a friend'. 'We are what we are,' was Mr Pratt's mysterious comment, beneath a shot of him leaving his shuttered house. He had been cautioned by the police, summarily sacked by his board, and thrown out by his wife. He had now gone to France with his lover, who he described, rather grandly, as an 'international hairdresser'. London FM, anxious to avoid adverse publicity, had swiftly found a new sponsor for the weather.

I imagined that this combination of events, not least the loss of her influence with us, would have cast a pall over

Citronella. I turned to the back of the *Sunday Semaphore*, expecting to see that she had not filed. But, greatly to my surprise, there she was. In fact, she seemed in unusually combative form, proudly displaying her emotional distress as though it were a wound sustained in war.

'I will triumph over this,' she thundered defiantly in quasi-Churchillian mode. I could almost visualise her giving herself a victory sign whilst chewing on a cigar. 'I will not be bowed,' she vowed. 'I am suffering, yes, as my sex have always suffered, but I will hold my head high and come through. These experiences are a forge,' she went on melodramatically, 'in which the female heart is tempered like steel. I am determined to prove that women can not only survive, but even flourish, without men.'

'Amazing,' I murmured. 'Absolutely *amazing*.'

'Yes, Minty,' said Joe sleepily. 'It is.' He threw a naked arm across me and pulled me back down into the bed and the papers slithered to the floor in a whisper of newsprint.

'Oh, Minty,' he said.

'Oh, Joe,' I replied.

'Oh, Minty,' he murmured as his lips found mine. 'You're just so . . . repellent.'

'Thanks,' I whispered.

'You're so disgusting to look at,' he added as our limbs entwined.

'Really?'

'Mmmm. I find you so utterly . . . gruesome,' he went on as his hands roamed over my naked back and our breathing increased. 'In fact,' he went on, as his eyes gazed down into mine, so close now that I could count his lashes, 'you're the worst thing that's ever happened to me.

'I hate you,' he added happily.

'I hate you too,' I sighed.

Afterwards, we sat in the garden in the sunshine, in our pyjamas, with a tray of coffee and toast. Amber and Laurie had gone flat-hunting, or perhaps they were tactfully keeping out of our way.

'It really *is* amazing,' said Joe wonderingly. We were side by side on the bench, our arms entwined like the tendrils of my clematis. 'Amazing,' he said again, his head shaking in disbelief.

'And would you have phoned me anyway?' I asked him, for the fourth or fifth time. I needed to be absolutely sure.

'Yes,' he said. 'I would. I was longing to see you again, Minty. I was really sorry about what happened in Café Kick.'

'I was *very* sorry too.'

'I was very, very sorry.'

'I bet you weren't as sorry as me.'

'It's very nice of you to say so, Minty, but I think you'll find I was.'

'No, I believe I was sorrier than you were, because, after all, it was my fault.'

'But I was *particularly* sorry because I'd provoked you, by implying that you were a moron, which, of course, you're not.'

'Oh, thank you.'

'You're welcome.'

'But I was terribly, *terribly* sorry,' I persisted, 'because the torrent of abuse I unleashed on you was, I feel with hindsight, excessive.'

'No, no, no, I fully deserved it, Minty.'

'With respect, Joe, I disagree. It was quite gratuitous, and I'd just like . . .' and here I kissed him '. . . to apologise wholeheartedly and unreservedly again.'

We smiled at each other smugly. It's so nice knowing that you're, well, nice.

'Right, that's enough niceness,' said Joe. 'Let's go out. Let's go . . .'

'Where?'

'To the Tate.'

And why not? So we did. And as we walked to Chalk Farm Tube in the sunshine, Joe was still expressing abundant wonderment at how we'd found each other again.

'I was thinking about you when I got in that cab at the

airport,' he said, as we walked over the railway bridge, 'and the radio was on and suddenly there you were. As if by magic. As if someone had said, "Abracadabra". And hearing you say those things about me, it just –' he squeezed my hand – 'it got to me. As I sat there, listening to you, jet-lagged, and in total shock, everything fell into place. I just *had* to see you – right away. So I asked the driver to take me straight to London FM. It was *you*, Minty,' he said again, wonderingly, as we stood on the southbound platform. (Amber's abuse, you will be glad to know, had long since been erased.) 'It was all because of *you*,' Joe said again. 'I mean, one minute I'm a complete nobody, just another hopeful scriptwriter. The next thing I know, the phone starts to ring and it doesn't stop. And agents are sending stretch limos to collect me, and producers and directors are requesting meetings. But what amazed me was that everyone seemed to know all about my script without having read it. And then ICM sign me up, and they tell me that Nicholas Cage, Kevin Spacey and Leonardo DiCaprio have all been asking to read it. And by now I'm getting invitations to galas and premieres.'

'Which is how you met Kelly-Ann Jones, who you kissed.'

'No,' he said, vehemently, as the train arrived, with a roar, and we stepped on.

'Yes you did.'

'I did not.'

'Joe, you know I hate to disagree with you. But you did.'

'I did not kiss Kelly-Ann Jones.'

'Sorry, that is simply not true.'

'It *is* true.'

'Joe, don't lie to me.'

'I did not kiss Kelly-Ann Jones,' he said emphatically. 'She kissed *me*. I was gobsmacked,' he added. 'Literally. I was so taken aback – I'd only met her once before. But one of the photographers asked for a shot, and before I knew what had happened, her arms were round my neck and her collagen-enhanced lips were pressed to mine! It was all for the cameras, of course. Her star's been waning of late and mine was rising, fast. Anyway,' he went on as we rattled southwards, 'I was getting all these invitations here there and everywhere, and everyone seemed to know who I was. It was as though some *deus ex machina* had suddenly pressed the big green button marked "Go". I couldn't work out how this had happened. Why it was all so effortless when I'd expected to have to sweat and convince and cajole. It was only when I heard you on the radio, explaining what you'd done, that I finally understood. Minty, do you realise, you whipped the Hollywood rumour mill into complete hysteria on my behalf?'

'I had no idea,' I said, again. I laughed and shrugged – it had dumbfounded me as much as it had Joe. 'I wasn't consciously trying to talk you up,' I explained. 'I was just trying to find you. So, in order to identify you, I had to tell everyone about your film, and they all thought it sounded great.'

'You did the most *amazing* PR campaign for me,' he said, shaking his head again, in disbelief. 'It took off like a firestorm. I was the talk of the town.'

'Did you really not know I was there?' I asked as we got out at Embankment.

'Absolutely not,' he replied. 'If I had, of course, I'd have got in touch. I did hear that a British woman had been asking after me,' he added thoughtfully as we walked along the Thames. 'But I was told she was called Emily. And I don't know anyone called Emily. And in any case, there are loads of British women working in LA.'

'Emily?' I said wonderingly. 'How did I become Emily?' And then it clicked. 'Minty . . . Mindy . . . Minnie . . . Millie . . . Em-i-ly. That's what happens with Chinese Whispers.'

'Chinese Whispers,' said Joe. 'That's exactly what it was. And the whispers grew into a whirlwind, and then suddenly there was a bidding war.'

'A bidding war?'

'Columbia were really keen,' he said as we passed the House of Commons and entered Victoria Gardens. 'They bid first. Then Miramax came in, and Warner, and Paramount, and they were all vying for the script. In the end, it went to Paramount.

'Paramount?' I said, as we strolled beneath an avenue of plane trees, then stood for a moment, watching the sun glinting off the silty water.

'Yes,' he said, above the hum of the traffic and the lazy slap of the river against the wall. 'This guy called Michael Kravitz was desperate to get it.'

'Michael Kravitz?'

'Yes, Michael Kravitz.'

'We met him at Barney's,' I explained as we stood up again, and walked on. 'He was terribly nice. We told him all about you. He said he worked for Paramount.'

'He certainly does. He's their Senior Vice-President.'

'And he's the one who bought your film?'

'Yes.' And don't think I'd be so vulgar as to ask Joe what Paramount had paid, but he told me anyway and, look, I'm sorry, I really can't tell you, but believe me, it's a colossal amount. Anyway, that's why Joe's come back to the UK, to sort out his affairs. And, yes, he will be going back to LA again, but I don't want to think about that now.

'So, is Kelly-Ann Jones going to be in your film?' I asked as we strolled towards Lambeth Bridge. I hoped my casual demeanour would mask my hissing jealousy.

'She wants to be,' he replied. 'She's after the role of the boy's teacher – the part I told you about, remember? – but, to be honest, she's too old.'

'She looks about twenty-five.'

'Minty – she's forty-three.'

'Forty-three?' I was astounded. 'Well, she's obviously drinking the right brand of coffee, that's all I can say.'

'No, Minty. This is Hollywood. Her face has been skilfully superannuated – twice.'

'Ah.'

'Close up, she's about as natural as canned laughter. No, I need someone young and fresh-looking for that role,' he added thoughtfully. 'I've got my mental short list.'

'And what about your phone?' I said, as we walked up the steps of the Tate through the milling crowds.

'Phone?'

'I rang you several times on your mobile phone, but you never called me back.'

'Ah – that's because I had it stolen on day one,' he exclaimed. 'My hire car was broken into and it was nicked. That's why you didn't get a reply.' We walked through the echoing marble corridors with their rainbow-shaped arches to the special exhibition at the back. 'ABRACADABRA!' we read in huge black letters.

'Abracadabra!' said Joe, with a smile. Inside, weird and wonderful objects met our eyes. A robotic replica of a Japanese man, a portrait, in chocolate, of Jackson Pollock; red plastic water lilies, ten feet high; and a huge sunburst made of yellow glass. And then we turned a corner and gasped, for ahead of us, on a platform, was a table football like no other. It was over twenty feet long. It had forty rods at least. It was a triple stretch limo version of a pub football game. What was more, it worked.

'*Vous voulez jouer*?' said Joe, and I was suddenly transported back a year, to Paris. He held out his hand.

'Do you want to play?' he said again. I looked at him, and laughed.

'Yes,' I said happily. 'Let's play.'

'It's a wonderful play,' said Mum enthusiastically at supper the following Saturday. She and Dad had come round 'to see the kittens', before they leave with Amber. At least, that was their excuse. Their real reason for coming was because they wanted to check out Joe.

'I love the theatre, don't you, Joe?' said Mum warmly, as she passed him the salad.

'Oh yes,' he said, 'I do.'

'*Super*, darling!' squawked Pedro.

'And the *Winter's Tale* is such a marvellous play.'

'It's a wonderful play,' Joe agreed.

'It's about resurrection, and redemption,' said Amber with a dreamy smile. 'It's about being given a second chance when you thought that all was lost.'

'And what part are you playing, Mrs Malone?' Joe enquired politely as he poured her some wine.

'Oh, I'm not *acting*, dear,' she exclaimed. 'No, I'm just helping out behind the scenes. I'm doing wardrobe. We've hired the costumes from the RSC – they're very elaborate, you know. Some of them have thirty-five loop fastenings!'

'Really?' I said with a wry smile.

'Don't you want to act in any of the plays?' Laurie asked her as I drained the new potatoes. 'I'm sure you'd be very good.'

'Well, I wouldn't mind, actually,' said Mum, blushing slightly. 'In fact, they're holding auditions next week and I might just have a bash. It's Priestley,' she explained: '*When We Are Married*.'

'When are *we* married?' Amber said to Laurie with a smile. She twisted the square emerald on her left hand.

'Whenever you want,' he said. 'Name the day. I'm yours.'

'No! *Really*?' squawked Pedro, shaking his wings.

'Laurie starts full time as a vet on Monday,' said Amber proudly. 'He's going to help all those poor little darling animals.'

'And the first thing I'm going to do,' he said, as Perdita walked in from the garden, followed by her wobbling offspring, 'is to take my scalpel to your cat.'

'Poor Perdita,' said Amber, bending down to stroke her. 'Couldn't she have just one more lot?'

'There are too many unwanted kittens,' he said wearily. 'I feel we should set an example.'

'Any takers for them yet?' Dad asked. He had picked up Tinky-Winky, the fattest, and plonked it, mewing, on to his lap. They were seven weeks old now, and almost weaned. It was time to find them homes.

'Would you like one, Uncle David?' said Amber.

'What?'

'Would you like a kitten?'

'Would I like a kitten?' he repeated.

'Yes. You and Auntie Dympna can have one, if you'd like. You can have Tinky-Winky.'

'Well . . .' Dad looked at Mum uncertainly. 'Yes, I would rather,' he said. 'I like cats, and we've got time to look after one now.'

'And I'd like Minty to have Jesus,' Amber announced, 'as a memento of my year-long stay in Primrose Hill.'

'I'd love to have Jesus,' I said, happily, as I picked him up. 'As long as you don't mind if I change his name. I really don't think it's right.'

'But in Spain, it's a very common name,' she said. 'It's like Felipe or José.'

'I just don't feel comfortable about it,' I said.

'I don't think Jesus feels too great about it either,' said Laurie as he took the kitten from me and held it up with both hands. 'Because the fact is, everyone, that Jesus is a girl.'

'Oh,' said Amber. 'OK, we'll call him Mary instead.'

'Yes, Mary,' said Joe. 'There's something about Mary,' he added with a funny sort of smile.

'Perdita's been such a good mother,' I said. 'She's hardly left her box the whole time. Just dashing out through the cat-flap twice a day, and then rushing straight back to her babies as though the kitchen's on fire. She's taken her responsibilities very seriously.'

'Well, she obviously enjoyed motherhood,' said Amber. 'I do think we ought to let her have just one more lot, now that I know what to do. The birthing process is so fascinating,' she said expansively. 'Both feline and human. I've been reading about it. Do you know that during pregnancy a woman's lower ribs flare out to make room for the growing baby?'

'Really?' I said, glancing at Amber's tub of folic acid by the spice-rack.

'And a baby's brain doubles in volume in the first twelve months, reaching 60 per cent of adult size by the end of its first year.'

'Incredible!'

'Incredible!' Pedro screeched.

'*Incredible*?' said Amber incredulously, staring at him.

'What a *funny* thing!' we all said.

'Anyway, Joe, when do you go back to Los Angeles?' Dad enquired.

'Mid September, but just for a month,' he explained, 'to do some more work on the script. And then shooting starts in February, so I'll go out again for that.'

'And do you think you'll stay out there?' said Dad, asking the question he knew I dared not ask myself.

I started clearing away the plates, aware that my face was on fire.

'I'm not making any plans yet,' I heard Joe say quietly. 'I'm just taking everything as it comes.'

'Quite right too,' said Mum, as I filled the kettle.

'Minty,' whispered Dad later, as we washed up. Everyone else had taken their coffee into the garden. 'Minty,' he said again.

'Yes?'

'There's something I wanted to tell you . . .'

'What?' He was looking uncharacteristically shifty.

'There's something I wanted to explain.'

'Oh?'

'About that time . . .'

'What time?'

'That time you and Joe saw me, outside, er, Sadlers Wells.'

'Look, I don't know what you're talking about,' I lied, glancing into the garden. 'The clematis is lovely this year, isn't it?'

'I feel there's something I should explain,' Dad persevered.

'Sorry, but it's none of my business,' I said as I rinsed a bowl.

'Well, I just wanted to clear it up.'

'Why? I mean, what?'

'I felt it was important,' he went on. 'Because, you see, there was gossip.'

'Gossip?'

'And I didn't want you to hear anything . . . funny about me. Do you understand, Minty?'

'Sorry, Dad,' I said, as I agitated the soapy water, 'but I'm really tired, my brain isn't working at full speed, and even if it was, I don't see how your visit to Sadlers Wells has anything to do with me.'

'People began to talk,' he said, as he wiped another dinner plate.

'Talk?'

'Yes, about me and . . .'

Oh God, I didn't want to hear any confessions. If Dad had had an affair I really didn't want to know. He and Mum seemed perfectly OK now.

'They began to talk,' he tried again. 'They began to talk about me and . . .' I didn't care *what* her name was '. . . Kevin.'

'Kevin?' I repeated.

'Yes, Kevin.'

'Kevin, as in your golf partner?'

'Yes, you see . . .'

'Are you saying there's been gossip about you and *Kevin*?'

'Yes. Because, well, Minty, it's rather embarrassing really, but the fact is Kevin and I both like . . . ballet. And Kevin's wife hates it, and your mother's not very keen, and anyway, she was too involved with her charity work to go. But Kevin and I like it. And we especially like *Coppelia*. So we decided to see it. Together.'

'You were waiting for Kevin that night?'

'Yes. And I'm afraid there've been some very silly remarks about us at the golf club as a result, and I was just anxious that you should know the truth.'

'Ah,' I said. '*That's* why you looked so embarrassed.'

'Yes, it is. Because although Kevin and I felt we had nothing to be *ashamed* of, at the same time we were hoping we wouldn't bump into anyone we knew . . . I was so taken aback when I saw you, and I didn't want to explain it all to you in front of Joe.'

'I see,' I said, and I was laughing now. 'Does Mum know all this?'

'Yes,' he said, 'she does. I know it was a silly deception. But now you can see why I was embarrassed.'

'Well, yes. Or rather, no. Not really. Anyway, it's all all right.'

'Yes,' he said, 'it is. It's all fine. So we're going to *Swan Lake* next week.'

'Thank you for listening,' said Amber, adjusting her headphones in Studio C, 'and do join me for next week's programme, in which I'll be talking to A. S. Byatt about another great Victorian novel, *Vanity Fair*. But until then, from me, and from my guest, William Boyd, goodbye.'

'That was Amber Dane,' said Barry. '*It's a Classic*! was brought to you in association with Borders Bookshop. *Bleak House* is published in paperback by Penguin at the special price of £2.50. And now the travel news, brought to you by Alfa Romeo . . .'

'That was wonderful,' I said to Amber, after she'd shown William Boyd out. 'I was riveted. You're a natural.'

'Do you really think so?'

'Yes, I do. The format's perfect for you.'

'And did I fluff?'

'No, but you popped once or twice, so don't sit too close to the mike. And be careful not to rustle your notes.'

'I really enjoyed it,' she said again as we went up to the third floor in the lift. 'It was so . . . intimate,' she added as she clutched her copy of the book. 'It was so exciting doing it live, and we covered so much ground.' Indeed, they had. The programme was only fifteen minutes long, but in that time she and William Boyd had discussed *Bleak House*, ranging over its themes and characterisation, the world it portrays, as well as bringing in snippets of biographical information about Dickens and the social history of the day. Here and there, they had read short extracts to illustrate their points, and the effect was of a conversation between two people both of them passionately interested in the same book. It was fantastic.

'Fantastic, Amber,' said Jack, with a smile. 'You've got such a good voice, and it was clear you knew what you were talking about. The listeners like to feel they're in safe hands when they turn on the radio, and that's how you made me feel. Oh,' he said, with a laugh, 'sorry, I should have introduced you. These are my two step-daughters, Topaz and Iolanthe.' The girls smiled awkwardly at Amber and me. It was national 'Bring Your Daughter to Work Day', so Jack had brought them in to London FM.

'What did you think, girls?' Jack asked them.

'It was really interesting,' said Iolanthe with a shy smile. She seemed slightly awestruck by Amber.

'I want to read that book now,' said Topaz.

'Good, so you've inflamed at least two hearts today, Amber. Can we go through the line-up again for the rest of the series?' he went on as he tapped into the computer. 'I'm just tweaking the schedules here.'

'Right. Well, next week I'm talking to Antonia Byatt about *Vanity Fair*, then it's Paul Theroux on *Moby Dick;* the following week I've booked John Major to talk about *Barchester Towers . . .'*

'Oh yes, he's a Trollope fan, isn't he,' said Jack. 'That's good.'

'And then there's Victoria Glendinning on *Far From the Madding Crowd*, the German Ambassador on *Buddenbrooks*, and finally, Clare Tomalin on *Great Expectations*.'

'Excellent. We'll see how the reviews come out, and then we might be looking at extending the series. Did you see *Broadcast*, by the way?'

'No.'

He handed his copy to Amber. There, on the inside front page, was a small piece about *It's a Classic*! It said that Amber Dane had been the station's first choice to present the new programme. 'Dane is taking a break from novel-writing,' it said, 'in a bid to bring classic literature to a commercial audience.'

'I'm not taking a break from novel-writing,' she said, with a bitter laugh as we went into the *Capitalise* office. 'I'm giving up. I mean, nine's enough, isn't it? Beethoven wrote nine symphonies for example, and so did Schubert. So did Ralph Vaughan Williams.'

'Oh yes, that's right,' I said, 'nine's . . . plenty.'

I introduced Amber to everyone. Sophie was flirting with her like mad.

'I thought you were *fabulous,*' she said, fiddling with her hair.

'Where's Wesley?' I asked.

'He's gone to get Deirdre and the baby. He's bringing his daughter into work today too.'

'She's a bit young, isn't she?' said Monica. 'She's only three weeks old.'

Suddenly Wesley appeared, the baby strapped to his front, in a sling. Deirdre beamed benignly at us all as Wesley showed her off.

'Here's Freya,' he said proudly.

'That's an unusual name,' I said.

'It was my choice, really,' said Deirdre with an enigmatic smile.

'What lovely hair,' said Topaz, stroking Freya's head. 'It's auburn,' she remarked.

'My great, great, great grandfather on my mother's father's side had auburn hair, apparently,' said Wesley.

'And she's got such lovely blue eyes,' said Topaz.

'That's right,' said Wesley. 'Blue. Just like mine.'

'They're such twinkly eyes!' exclaimed Iolanthe innocently as she peered, entranced, at the infant. 'We're having a baby too,' she said. 'In November. Our Mum's a bit old, really, but we don't mind.'

'We're going to be its godmothers,' said Topaz.

I was going to be a godmother too, I suddenly remembered. Helen had asked me to be godmother to Charlotte Araminta.

'Babies are fun,' said Deirdre gently to the girls.

'Oh yes, babies are *gweat* fun!' said Melinda. She'd suddenly appeared in the office – she was coming in to talk to Jack.

'Wow!' said Topaz, as Melinda put Pocahontas down in her car seat. '*Another* baby!'

'It's nice to see you, Melinda,' I said. I could afford to be generous now. 'How's it going?'

'Actually, Minty, it's going *bwilliantly,*' she said. 'So bwilliantly, in fact, that Carlton TV have offered me a chat show!'

'Really!'

'Yes, I'm going to be the new Jewwy Spwinger. Appawently they like my forthwight style.'

'I bet they do.'

'That's why I want to see Jack – he'll have to up the money a bit if he wants me to stay on here.'

'Well, I hope he agrees,' I said, truthfully. 'You're our golden goose.'

'And how was the birth?' I heard Amber ask Deirdre. 'I bet it was a *wonderful* experience.'

'Well, it wasn't too bad,' Deirdre replied judiciously.

And while everyone babbled about babies and childbirth, I flicked through the day's papers. In the *Independent* was a photo of Godfrey Barnes, whose six-month prison sentence had just begun. According to the article, he was receiving a steady stream of female visitors, and money had been raised for an appeal. Then, just out of habit, I turned to Sheryl von Strumpfhosen. And although she never, ever gets it right – does she? – somehow I can never resist.

'Libra, a delightful cosmic phase beckons,' she predicted. 'For this you may thank activity in Pluto, house of endings and new beginnings. But keep your wits about you this week and don't turn down any invitations.'

'Why don't we go on holiday?' said Joe a couple of days later.

'What?' I said. We were sitting outside on the bench. Joe was working on the script, and I was reading the *Telegraph* arts section, in which the radio critic Gillian Reynolds had given Amber the most brilliant review: 'London FM's new arts programming is a triumph,' she wrote, 'and *It's A Classic*! is set to be the jewel in its crown. Amber Dane has natural authority,' she went on, 'but she is careful not to dominate. Instead she prompts her guests to speak eloquently and passionately about their chosen book. This is radio at its best,' she concluded. 'As for Dane's voice – I could listen all day.'

'That is wonderful,' I said. 'I think it's the first really good review Amber's ever had.' I stroked Mary, who was sitting, purring on my lap. I missed Amber, and Perdita, and Pedro. But I had Mary. And for a few more weeks, I had Joe.

'Why don't we go on holiday?'

'Sorry, what?'

'I said, "Why don't we go on holiday?"'

'Why don't we go on holiday?' I repeated as a tiny ladybird landed on my hand.

'Yes, why don't we?' he said. 'Other couples do.'

Other couples; I liked that.

'I'd love to,' I said. 'But Jack will need at least a week's notice. And where would we go?'

'Well, I know where I'd like to go.'

'Yes?'

'I really hope you like this idea too, Minty.'

'I'm sure I will,' I said as the ladybird flew off.

'It's just something I've always wanted to do,' he said.

'Tell me.'

'So I really hope you go for it as well.'

'Joe, I don't mind *where* we go, as long as you're there.'

'OK,' he said. And he was grinning enthusiastically now. 'Minty, I've always wanted to go on a canal holiday!'

'A canal holiday?'

'Yes, I can't imagine anything more idyllic, can you?'

'Well . . .'

'All that tranquillity.'

'It's quite tranquil here, Joe.'

'That peace.'

'London's very quiet at this time of year.'

'Just the sound of the water lapping against the side of the boat.'

'Yes,' I said quietly. Oh God.

'So much to see along the way.'

'So much.'

'Just you, and me, and the canal. Wouldn't that be great?'

'Mmm,' I said thoughtfully. Joe smiled at me.

'Say yes, Minty,' he said. He looked so happy – how could I say no? Stuff what I'd learnt on the Nice Factor.

'That would be lovely,' I said.

Well, Sheryl von Strumpfhosen did tell me not to turn down any invitations, I reminded myself as I waited for Joe to pick me up a few days later. I didn't need to look at the calendar to know what day it was. It was Sunday, 28th July – exactly a year to the day since my wedding. What had Sheryl predicted then? Suddenly it came back to me. She'd said 'Libra, your love life takes an upward turn this weekend.' And I laughed, because I realised she was right. It *did* take an upward turn. Dominic left me and instead I met Joe. I smiled at that. And then I grinned. Then I began to laugh. And I couldn't stop. I sat there, in the sitting room, quietly rocking with laughter. I sat in the silence of my flat, with my two packed bags, and thought of all that had happened in the intervening year. I reviewed it, spooling it through my mind like the material for a programme, but it was only now that it had any shape. I thought of the George V, and meeting Joe, and Amber's anger with Charlie; I thought of Citronella, and the Nice Factor, and my hair-cut – it's quite long again now. I remembered the ball, and Helen, and Laurie and Perdita and poor Sir Percy and Virginia Park, and I thought of Jack's step-daughters, and Melinda, and of Los Angeles and the Four Seasons. Four seasons. That's what had elapsed. Four seasons in which the wheel had turned for us all.

'And here we are,' I said to Mary. 'We didn't think we'd make it, did we? But we did.' She blinked at me, and purred. I was just filled with happiness. I could afford to be generous about the canal holiday. It probably wouldn't rain – in fact the weather's perfect right now – and the boats are bound to be more comfortable than they were all those years ago. I was unlikely to have to throw myself in the water after someone else's dog, and with just the two of us, it wouldn't be too cramped. Maybe it would even be OK.

I wondered which canal it was. Joe hadn't told me because

he wanted it to be a surprise. I went through them in my mind. Perhaps it would be the Shropshire Union. Or the Trent and Mersey. Or maybe the Kennet & Avon. Yes, that would be nice, I thought to myself – we'd drift through Oxfordshire and the West Country. It would probably be quite relaxing.

There was a sudden honking from outside, the sound of a car door, and then I saw Joe running up the path.

'Right,' he said, as he came in, 'let's get going. Put Mary in the basket, we'll drop her off on the way. And don't forget your passport because the boat yard needs it as ID.'

'*Do* they?'

'Yes, it's a requirement. Those barges are very expensive, Minty. How do they know we won't just nick it?'

'That is extremely unlikely,' I replied.

'Yes, but they don't know that, do they? You've got to see it from their point of view.'

'OK,' I said, 'I'll get it.' Then I locked up the flat, and Joe picked up my bags.

'I say,' he said with a smile, 'your baggage is light! It hardly weighs a thing!'

Then we drove to Amber and Laurie's with the cat. I wanted to stay there a few minutes and get the grand tour of their new place, but Joe was agitating because he'd told the boat yard we'd be there by two. So off we sped again. To be honest, I thought the whole point of canal holidays is that they're meant to be calm affairs, but my stress levels were already climbing fast. Joe was so impatient with the traffic, because it was pretty slow going through the Angel, and then we hit the Euston Road, so I guessed we were going south.

'Which canal are we going on?' I said as we hurtled towards Shepherd's Bush.

'It's a surprise.'

'Go on, tell me.'

'Well, OK,' he said. 'It's the Grand Union and we pick it up at Southall.'

'Southall?' I said.

'Yes, Southall. What's wrong with Southall?'

'Oh, nothing,' I said. 'Nothing. I'm sure Southall's lovely.'

Oh God. This is what happens when you're nice. You agree to go on holiday to Southall.

'Can you read maps?' asked Joe.

'No,' I said truthfully. And he started talking about the A4 and the M4 and Junction this and Junction that and I just kept quiet because, as you know, map-reading is not my forte. But we were driving along on the M4 and I began to notice the signs. And I saw the sign for Junction 3 ahead of us, which announced that Southall was to the right. But Joe didn't turn right. He turned left.

'Joe, the sign said Southall was to the right.'

'It's OK,' he said, as he glanced in the mirror, 'I know what I'm doing.'

'Yes, but . . .'

'And you admit you're a useless navigator.'

'Yes. Hopeless bordering on the moronic but I do know left from right. And we should have gone right there, but we went left, which is not right, it's wrong.'

'This is the alternative route,' he said with what I thought was spurious authority.

'Well, 180 degrees in the wrong direction is certainly alternative,' I said. 'Aren't you bothered, Joe?'

'No.'

'But we're going towards Heathrow now.'

'*Are* we?' he said. 'Oh *no*!'

'Yes, we are. Look – Heathrow, Terminal 4.' Joe kept quiet. 'Terminal 3,' I added, as we passed another sign.

'Oh dear,' said Joe. 'We have gone wrong, haven't we? Look, here's Terminal 2.' Joe swung into the car-park, grabbed a ticket and found a space. Then we got out, and he was smiling, and so was I by now. Then he took our bags and went inside.

'It's OK, I like canals,' I said. 'I would happily have gone on a canal holiday.'

'I love canals too,' he said, as he reached into his jacket and pulled out an airline docket. 'Right, British Airways,' he said, as we headed for the BA counter.

'Joe, where are we going?'

'Well, where would you *like* to go? There's quite a choice, isn't there?' he said surveying the long line of check-in desks. 'There's Lisbon, Madrid, Barcelona, Alicante, Oslo, Gibraltar, or Paris. Do you fancy Paris again, Minty?' And then he handed me the tickets, and I looked, and I smiled as I read: 'Venice, Marco Polo.'

'I told you I love canals,' he said again. 'Though I prefer the Grand Canal to the Grand Union, given the choice.'

'How . . . wonderful,' I said quietly, and I found it hard to say anything else.

'Well,' he said as we headed towards International Departures, hand in hand, 'we both need a break, don't we? I'll be starting work on the film soon, and you've been so busy, so we should spend some time together. Won't it be nice being on our own, Minty,' he said, as we went through the gates. 'Whenever you look up, there I shall be. Whenever I look up, there will be you. Won't that be lovely, Minty?'

'Lovely,' I murmured.

'And we need time together – before I go back to LA. But I hope you'll be coming out there, Minty. The filming's going to be such fun. Now, did I tell you about the casting?'

'No.'

'Well, I think we've got Kevin Spacey on board, and lots of A-list women are interested in the female lead – Sandra Bullock, Julia Roberts, Winona Ryder and Helen Hunt.'

'Wow!' I said.

'But do you know who I really want?'

'No.'

'The one I really want.'

'Tell me,' I said with a smile.

'Cameron Diaz!'

'Cameron Diaz?'

'Yes,' he said, squeezing my hand. 'Apparently, she's dead keen, and I think she'd be perfect for the part. You could come on set and meet her. And do you know, Minty, I've got this funny feeling that you'd both get on *terribly* well!'

'Well . . .'

'Wouldn't that be *fun,* Minty?' he said as the plane took off.

'That would be *super,* darling!' I said.

The Trials of Tiffany Trott

Isabel Wolff

'Very funny, charming, upbeat and unputdownable'

MARIAN KEYES

Tiffany Trott is attractive, eligible and sparky – so why is she (as her bossy best friend Lizzie puts it) 'a complete failure with men'? Stung into indignant action, she decides she'll hunt down Mr Right herself – or even Mr All Right, who's got to be better than the Mr Catastrophics who litter her recent past.

So begins Tiffany's eventful odyssey through the Love Jungle, armed only with her soon-to-be-over-taxed sense of humour, her kind heart and a plentiful supply of optimism. From blindingly bland dates to introduction agencies, via Eat'n'Greet, small ads and Club Med, Tiffany tries the lot in her quest for that tennis-loving, golf-hating Adonis she hopes will be her mate.

But as she ponders her puzzling lack of a life partner, Tiffany watches her friends face problems of their own – and begins to wonder whether marriage and motherhood is quite what she wants after all . . .

'The irrepressible Tiffany Trott – a woman who does not think optimism is an eye disease' KATHY LETTE

'A very, very funny book' NANCY ROBERTS, Talk Radio

'Tiffany stands out. The story of her attempts to land a man really sparkle . . . Wolff makes her quest into a happy romp that slips down as agreeably as ice-cream' *Independent on Sunday*

'Tiffany is an engaging creation with a knack in witty one-liners' *Sunday Express*

Tell Me No Secrets

Maggie Hudson

A fast-moving, hair-raising novel about a notorious criminal gang, and the women who run it

The Sweeting family are well known in south-east London, and not for their honesty. Jock is a professional armed robber and proud of it, and Kelly, his daughter, takes after him. By the time she's 20, she is running with the family gang.

Her sister Jackie, yearning for a life of respectability, marries high-flying policeman Raymond. But his middle-class background has its own kind of hypocritical dishonesty.

And Rosamund, Raymond's unsuspecting sister, meets via the Sweetings the devious and irresistible Kevin Rice – but how long will she last as the wife of a criminal on the run?

When the men in their lives lie, cheat and betray them, Kelly, Jackie and Ros decide that it will be for the last time. Their revenge is both outrageous and apt as they plan the biggest heist of the decade. And after the adventure of a lifetime is over, there will be no more secrets, and no more lies . . .

0 00 651153 8

Olivia Goldsmith

Fashionably Late

'A bittersweet tale brimming with excitement'
Company

Wherever she goes, forty-year-old Karen Kahn is fashionably late. She can afford to be: the star of the New York fashion scene, with her own company, a handsome husband and a deal that could make her millions, she is the apple – and the envy - of everyone's eye.

But she is too late for the ultimate in creation: a baby. Motherhood is proving to be elusive – as elusive as her own parentage, and as difficult as the cut-throat business of couture. Yet Karen is not one to take no for an answer, and late is better than never . . .

'Full of wisecracks, and gossip . . . this is a book for the beach. Olivia Goldsmith can keep you reading' *Cosmopolitan*

0 00 647972 3

£4.99 net

Bestseller

Olivia Goldsmith

'Told with such brio . . . there is plenty to savour'

Mail on Sunday

It's autumn in New York, and in the anything but gentlemanly world of books the knives are out as the new season's list is launched. Stars and wannabees, hustlers and has-beens all scramble for the prizes, the profits and the prestige – not least at big-time publishing house Davis & Dash where success depends on a handful of authors:

Susann Baker Edmonds: the face-lifted megastar whose blockbusters have topped the charts for longer than anyone can remember.

Gerald Ochs Davis: novelist and publishing supremeo – known to his minions as G.O.D. Is his latest offering worth the million dollars he paid himself?

Camilla Clapfish: a demure English rose. A chance romantic encounter brought her elegant little novel to Davis & Dash.

Behind the books and the writers, and the people who make and break them, is a whole world of passion, politics and intrigue. Who will survive in the race to the top?

0 00 649673 3

The Last Place You Look

Norma Curtis

'Sharp, funny and observant' KATE ATKINSON

Faye Reading has given second place to her career as a lighting designer in order to be a good wife and mother – to her husband Nick, their adopted son Samuel and their daughter Isobel. If her lifestyle has been on the reckless side, Nick's conscience, sense and good nature have always compensated, giving her the security she has craved since childhood. At least until now.

For a message on the answerphone, a visit to the doctor and the return of Samuel's natural mother – Nick's wayward young sister – are about to upset the balance of their lives, casting shadows where there was light, and doubt where there was certainty. As they each confront their own personal demons, Faye and Nick must find a way forward, but first they must learn where to look . . .

Theirs is a story of courage, tenderness, fear and faith, which Norma Curtis deftly recounts with her unique blend of dry humour, warmth, wisdom and originality.

0 00 651021 3